Highlander Lord of Fire

By

Donna Fletcher

Cover art
Kim Killion Group

Visit Donna's Web site
www.donnafletcher.com
http://www.facebook.com/donna.fletcher.author

Chapter One

13th century, Scotland

"Don't be afraid, lassie, we're not that far from home. There'll be a nice fire in the hearth and a hot cider to warm you."

"I look forward to it, Finn," Snow said, trying not to let fear creep into her voice as she spoke loudly to be heard over the swirling snow and wind.

"I'm going to tie this rope from my horse to yours so we don't lose each other. With a blinding snowstorm like this one, it's easy to get separated and we wouldn't want that to happen."

"No, Finn, I wouldn't want that," she said, keeping her voice raised just as he did.

"Worry not, lassie, I'll get you home," Finn shouted and patted her arm to reassure her.

Thaw's head poked out from Snow's fur-lined cloak to give a quick bark.

"Right you are, Thaw. You keep Snow safe," Finn called out.

Snow hugged Thaw against her, the pup having sprouted a good bit in the last month, but she still didn't want him wandering on his own in a snowstorm.

"We're all set, next stop… home," Finn said cheerfully, giving his left arm a good rub. "Old wounds can pain in the cold. Can't wait for that warm fire myself and a tankard of ale." He laughed as he walked to his horse.

3

Snow listened, his laughter caught by the swirling snow to drift away as he disappeared in the wildly falling snow. She recalled what Finn looked like, a big, thick, strong man and a fine warrior. She remembered how he had scooped her up with one arm when she was a wee bairn and how his whole body would shake with laughter. She felt safe with Finn and she knew he would see her home safely.

When she and Finn had left her sister Willow's home the snow had been falling lightly, a dusting on the ground. They hadn't been on the road long when the snow began to pour down around them.

She couldn't see anything in front of her. Not that she could see anyway, having lost her sight in a fire about a year ago now. She had been so happy when some of her sight had begun to return, leaving her to see gray shadows. It took time to grow accustomed to it, since she had felt as if ghosts constantly surrounded her, never able to see anyone or anything clearly. She would recall what they looked like, as she had done with Finn, but anyone unfamiliar to her left her feeling uncomfortable and vulnerable.

Her two sisters, Willow and Sorrell, had helped tremendously, but they both had wed and had their own homes now, Sorrell living a distance away and Willow living not that far, a walk that would take less than an hour, but not in the dead of winter and certainly not in a snowstorm.

Willow and her husband, Slatter, had suggested she stay when light snow had begun to fall. But she had already stayed a week to help her sister settle into a new home. It was time she returned home and allowed the couple time to themselves.

Her visit also had allowed her half-brother James time with Eleanor, who had helped look after her when Willow had gone to visit Sorrell. She was a lovely young woman who James had taken to on first sight. Eleanor had equally been taken with him and love had blossomed quickly. A wedding was being talked about and she couldn't be happier for James and Eleanor.

There would never be a wedding for her. No man would want a blind wife. It saddened her at times, especially since she had always dreamed of having lots of children to fill a home with laughter and love. Now she would spend her days going from her sisters' homes to her home with James and Eleanor and enjoying the nieces and nephews that would come along.

Willow was already with child and would deliver in the summer and she would be there to help whatever way she could. Not that Willow would need much help, since she was a skilled healer growing even more skilled with time.

Snow tucked her hood down to keep the snow from whipping at her face. The snowstorm seemed to grow worse by the minute. She worried that Finn was having a difficult time maneuvering his way through the blinding snow that had to be accumulating rapidly on the ground, his pace having begun to slow to almost a crawl.

When her horse came to a stop, she grew even more concerned. Had Finn decided the snowstorm was far too dangerous to continue on? Would they need to seek shelter? She waited anxiously to see what he would say.

Thaw suddenly popped his head out of her cloak and gave a bark.

"It's all right, Thaw," she said, trying to calm him. "We've stopped for a moment."

But Thaw wouldn't settle, he barked again and wiggled to get out of her arms.

"Stay!" she ordered, but Thaw would have none of her command. He wiggled himself free and jumped from her arms.

"Thaw! Thaw!" she yelled, worried she'd lose him in the snow, though his continued barks let her know he was close. "Finn!" she shouted, concerned he wouldn't hear her through the relentless wind.

Thaw continued to bark and with the horses stopped and no sound from Finn, she began to grow uneasy. She couldn't just sit there with the snow whipping viciously around, she had to do something.

"Please, Mum, help me," she pleaded as she slid off the horse.

Her mum had died from complications from the fire that had blinded Snow. Though, not before she had tended Snow's eyes, bathing them day after day in some solution she had brewed. She had told her to keep hope strong in her heart and mind, that her vision would return.

"Never give up hope, my daughter. I named you appropriately. Snow can blind, but it leaves everything fresh and sparkling clear after settling on the land. One day you will see again," her mum had said.

Snow held hope that her mum had been right and that was why she reached out to her when frightened or in need.

Snow kept her hand on the horse's side, following along it until she found the rope Finn had tied from her horse to his. Her hand followed along the rope to Finn's horse, Thaw's barking growing louder.

"Finn," she called out and Thaw stopped barking for a moment then started again. "What is it, Thaw? Did something happen to Finn?" Thaw barked twice, stopped, and barked again.

Snow's stomach roiled. Something was wrong, horribly wrong.

"Where's Finn, Thaw?" she asked and she suddenly felt the pup tugging at the hem of her tunic. He wanted her to follow him. Finn could very well be hurt. But did she chance leaving the horses? Would she find her way back to them?

Thaw's tugs grew more frantic. She tried to untie the rope on Finn's horse to keep hold of it, but the snow, cold, and strength of the knot made it impossible. She had little choice but to step away from the horse, letting Thaw know she'd follow. He didn't let go of her hem, he used it to guide her steps. She counted each one so she knew the distance.

Thaw stopped and so did she.

He barked once and she knew he had delivered her to Finn. She moved her booted-foot forward and touched something.

"Finn!" she cried out, but got no answer.

With trepidation, she slowly lowered herself down, the swirling snow making it difficult to see even gray shadows. She reached out and her hand touched snow, but it was what she felt beneath that frightened her. After brushing the snow away, she removed her glove to touch Finn's chest. There was no rise and fall to it. She moved her hand up to his face, brushing off the snow that had accumulated there and pressed her fingers to his cold lips.

No breath came from his mouth.

He was dead.

She felt around his face and top and sides of his head for a wound and ran her hand over his chest again. There were no signs of blood. His heart must have stopped as her mum would say when someone suddenly died without any apparent reason.

Tears threatened her eyes and she brushed them away. It would do no good to mourn Finn now or spend time senselessly crying when a snowstorm raged around her. But what did she do? Without her sight, how did she determine the direction that would take her home? Thaw would be of no help, since he had yet to learn the path between Macardle keep and Willow and Slatter's keep, though Slatter had promised he'd teach the pup soon.

"The horses," she whispered and slipped her glove back on.

She needed to make sure she stayed with the horses. She would turn and backtrack her steps the best she could. She was bound to bump into them.

"The horses, Thaw. We need to get to the horses," she said, hoping he understood her.

He barked and raced around her and she turned and began to walk, Thaw running ahead of her. She counted her steps and when she reached the spot where the horses should be, she reached out but nothing was there. She took a few steps in one direction, then another, still nothing.

Now what did she do?

Thaw's bark drew her attention and she wondered if he had found the horses.

"Where are you, Thaw?" she called out and he continued to bark.

She followed the sound of his barks, and she realized with every step she took that the snow had reached her ankles. The snow was accumulating fast. Thaw's barks stopped and so did she and she was relieved when she felt him at the hem of her tunic, tugging at it once again.

She followed and Thaw barked a warning too late. She bumped into something. She let her hands explore and found it was a tree trunk. Thaw had brought her to shelter under a tree.

The pup slipped under her cloak to rest against her leg as he always did when he felt she was in need of protection.

Snow reached down and scooped him up, tucking him in the crook of her arm beneath her fur-lined cloak to keep him warm.

"We have a problem, Thaw," she said, turning and lowering her head to keep the wind from hitting her face.

They couldn't find the horses and with no idea where she was in relationship to home, and the snowstorm growing worse, and with no sufficient shelter, their fate was sealed. They would freeze to death.

She had felt helpless many times since turning blind, but never as helpless as she felt now. It wasn't a far distance between Macardle keep and McHenry keep, the clan that Slatter was now chieftain of and Willow and he called home. But she had no idea of direction and to strike out blindly would be foolish.

"I don't know what to do, Thaw," she said, and the pup reached up and licked her face. She kissed the top of his snout. "I love you so much, Thaw." He licked her cheek again, showing her he felt the same.

Snow thought of her sister Sorrell. She would have been on the move already, battling through the snow. but then she had her sight. No matter what she thought others would do, it didn't matter since she had her blindness to contend with.

Think, Snow, think, she challenged herself.

She got a sudden thought. The horses. They knew the way home, hopefully they would instinctively take her there. If she could find them, she could get home.

"We need to find the horses, Thaw. They're our only hope," she said, silently praying they would find them.

Thaw barked and wiggled in her arms.

"You can't go too far from me," she warned and hope he understood.

He barked again and she placed him on the ground. "Find the horses, Thaw."

Snow took careful steps, keeping her arms stretched out in front of her and following Thaw's barks. Every now and again, he'd return and grab the hem of her tunic and take her in a different direction.

After what seemed like a senseless hunt, Thaw started barking non-stop and hope soared in Snow that he'd found the horses. She headed in the direction of his bark, though it was difficult to tell the true direction with the wind swirling the snow furiously around her.

She was relieved to feel him at her hem again, though this time he scurried in front of her and began to growl.

Her heart felt as if it stopped beating for a moment. He was warning whatever stood not far from her to stay away from her. She couldn't see anything. Was it an animal? A person? Whatever it was Thaw had sensed it was dangerous, and she stood blind before it.

Thaw's growl deepened in warning and that's when Snow saw it. A large, shadowy blur nearly on top of her. It had to be a person, but who could it be? A traveler caught unaware in the snowstorm like her and Finn? And would he help her or be of danger to her?

The blur drew closer and Thaw's growls increased, though he didn't attack. He kept a protective stance in front of her.

Thaw's growl didn't seem to bother the blur, he kept approaching and Snow reacted instinctively. Her hand shot out to stop whatever it was from getting any closer.

Her hand met a snout and sharp teeth, and she yanked her hand back.

Her heart felt as if it would beat right out of her chest. And it wasn't the freezing cold that sent shivers rushing through her, it was fear. She forced herself to remain calm. It couldn't be an animal. It would have attacked by now. But why had she felt what she was sure was the head of an animal?

Thaw kept up his steady, threatening growl.

It came to her then… who would wear the head of an animal?

Barbarians.

Chapter Two

Snow almost lashed out at the shadowy creature when he grabbed her arm, but stopped when he let out a growling shout.

"Shelter."

He intended to help her, at least she prayed that was his intention.

She hurried to reach down and scoop Thaw up, but his strong yank prevented her from doing so.

"My pup," she protested and was propelled forward with the strength of his grip. She was grateful to hear Thaw bark and keep pace alongside her as she was hurried through the snow.

Shadows and blurs rushed around her and his firm hold tugged her now and again, preventing her from hitting anything. From his confident pace, he seemed to know where he was going, though how he could see through the raging snow was beyond her.

He stopped suddenly and before letting go of her arm, ordered, "Stay."

She did as he said, fearful of this stranger who wore an animal head, yet fearful of being left alone in the snowstorm. She was relieved to feel Thaw slip between her legs and lean against her protectively. That he didn't bark or growl made her think that the pup had realized the stranger would help them.

13

The man was suddenly in front of her again, his hands at her shoulders as he guided her a few steps and gave her a slight shove. No snow fell around her and the space was tight. She felt Thaw slip in between her leg and her fur-lined cloak to huddle there against her.

The strong scent of old wood filled the space and her guess would be he had placed her in the hollow of a dead tree. And he would no doubt join her, which he did not a moment later.

His one arm slipped past her cloak to settle around her waist as he pressed tight against her, his back blocking the opening. She had no choice but to rest her face against his fur-covered chest and it didn't take long for the closeness of their bodies and his furs to provide some heat.

The warmth felt so good that she found herself wrapping her arms around his waist, beneath his furs, to stay as close to him as she could.

Her arm felt the hilt of his knife resting at his one side. She didn't want to think how dangerous that could prove, but he was being kind to her right now and that was all that mattered.

Besides, she had asked her mum for help and her mum had sent someone. She would have never sent someone that would mean her harm, even if it was a barbarian.

The warmth they shared, the strength of his arm around her all served to relax her, and she found her eyes growing heavy with sleep.

A not so gentle shake woke her.

"We go."

She shook her head, trying to clear the sleep from it. She didn't know how long she'd slept, though she still felt heavy with sleep.

She shook her head again and asked, "Where do we go?"

He backed out of the hollow tree, no answer coming from him.

Fear raced through her. She had no idea where this stranger was taking her and she had no recourse but to blindly follow him. She almost laughed, thinking she was doubly blind at the moment.

Snow and wind snapped at her when she stepped out of the shelter, Thaw following closely, though the wind didn't hit her as harshly as before. There was a lull in the snowstorm and the man was taking advantage of it.

It was when she realized the snow now went well past her ankle that she realized she must have slept several hours. She reached down and scooped Thaw up, fearing the deeper snow would be too difficult for him to maneuver.

To Snow's shock and fear, the man grabbed the pup from her arms and dropped him in the snow.

"He walks."

She barely heard him through Thaw's barks.

"The snow will swallow him," she argued, her head turning to look for his shadow, difficult to find through her shadowy sight.

She jumped when his hand gripped her arm.

"We go."

He yanked her along with him and she had little choice but to keep up with him. She called out to Thaw to make sure he was close by and was relieved each time she heard his nearby bark.

It seemed like hours they walked without stopping, her limbs burning from trudging through the deepening snow.

Finally, she just couldn't take another step and yanked her arm, calling out, "I need to stop."

The next thing she knew she was lifted off the ground and thrown over the man's shoulder.

Thaw protested for her, barking furiously and she was sure the small blur that followed under her dangling head was him.

"I'm all right, Thaw. I'm all right," she said to calm him, fearful he would tire himself out and not be able to keep up. Gratefully, his barking stopped and he kept pace.

There was no point in voicing her anger and besides, she truly couldn't take another step. She, however, wondered over the unrelenting strength of the man and how he could continue his strong pace with her added weight. But most of all she wondered where he was taking her and how he could even see where he was going, the wind having picked up once again and no doubt the snow with it.

How long he walked carrying her, she couldn't tell? Whether it was day or night, she couldn't tell? Where they were, she had no idea. She was completely dependent on this man.

It wasn't long before she grew uncomfortable and called out, "I can walk."

He either didn't hear her or he paid her no heed. He kept walking.

She tapped hard on this back to get his attention. "Put me down."

He ignored her.

Annoyed, she pounded at his back. "Put me down."

He kept walking, but Thaw started barking.

She realized then that Thaw sensed her distress and was fighting for her to be heard. Fearful the man might hurt him, she ceased her demands and assured Thaw she was fine.

It wasn't long after that she was dropped to her feet and Thaw was suddenly between her legs growling.

"Stay," the man ordered.

Where did he think she'd go? And where was he going? He wouldn't leave her, not after carrying her the way he had. Would he?

She heard a noise mingling with the wind, but couldn't make out the sound. She didn't jump this time when his hand gripped her arm and hurried her forward. She felt Thaw keeping pace between her legs.

The wind stopped suddenly.

"Shelter. Stay," he snapped and she heard what she thought was a door close.

She looked around but saw no gray blur that she usually saw when a person was near and no growl came from Thaw. She heard him sniffing around. He was exploring and she should do the same.

She stretched her hands out in front of her and took short, careful steps, feeling her way around. She bumped into something and she explored it with her gloved hands. It was a small table and two chairs sat with it. More careful steps took her to a wall and as she made her way around the room, she felt a door. She

17

came upon a cold, stone hearth next and after that her leg bumped into what she discovered was a bed, a narrow one from what she could feel.

From what she could tell, it was a small cottage the man had left her in. Was it his? But what would a barbarian be doing with a cottage on Scottish land? And whose land was this?

"Thaw," she called out and the pup jumped up to press his paws against her leg. She scooped him up and hugged him tight. "The man has helped us so far. I don't think he means us harm."

Thaw didn't agree, he growled.

"I suppose that animal head he's wearing doesn't help you trust him," she said, rubbing behind his ear, his favorite spot.

He growled again.

"I'll pay heed to your warning, but at the moment we're stuck with him." She held him up in front of her face, wishing she could see more than a gray blur. "And you will do nothing to bring harm to yourself." She smiled when he licked her nose and she kissed his snout before placing him on the ground.

She returned to exploring the small space, hoping to find some type of kindling to start a fire in the hearth. She hadn't gone far when she heard the door open and felt a rush of wind enter along with the man.

Thaw immediately was at her side, letting loose with a growl.

She scrunched her eyes in the direction of the shadowy blur as if somehow that would help her see more clearly. Of course, it didn't. She still couldn't see any better and she wondered if she ever would.

Self-pity will do you no good, she silently reminded herself. *Especially now.*

She managed to make out that he had dropped down by the hearth. Had he gotten wood for a fire? But it would be wet. It would not burn. So it surprised her that not long after she caught a whiff of smoke and felt a touch of warmth. He had got a fire burning.

The heat grew, flaring stronger and stronger throughout the small room.

The man stood and his shadow seemed to overpower the small space. Thaw even backed away to sit closer in front of her, his growl not as strong.

She watched and from his blurred movements she thought he reached up and removed the animal head to place on the table. How she wished she had her sight at that moment. But surprisingly she found it unnecessary.

"What in God's name were you doing out in that snowstorm alone?"

Snow recognized that voice and her eyes scrunched in an angry scowl as she said, "Tarass!"

Chapter Three

"Aye, it's me and how foolish are you to be out in a snowstorm like this on your own," he reprimanded, still shocked from finding her wandering around on her own in the raging snow.

"What are you doing wearing the garments of a barbarian?" she demanded.

"You don't want to know."

He warned in such a menacing way that she held her tongue.

"Explain," he ordered, "and silence your pup's growls or I will."

"Thaw wouldn't growl if you weren't so belligerent," she said with a wag of her finger at him.

"Don't wag that finger at me, woman," he ordered.

"Then don't order me about. You have no right. You're not my husband and thank God you never will be," she said and gave one last shake of her finger.

He was suddenly right in her face, his hand swallowing her fingers in a tight grasp while Thaw growled threateningly at him,

"You would learn obedience soon enough if you were my wife," he said, his face so near that the tip of his nose touched hers. "Now silence that pup of yours." He stepped away from her.

"Quiet, Thaw," Snow ordered three times before the pup settled into a low growl.

It was getting hot in the small space and Snow slipped her cloak off and felt for the back of one of the two chairs to drape it across.

"Tell me what happened, since there is no way your family would let you go off on your own and while you're often more foolish than not, I don't believe you'd be that foolish."

"Your compliments always overwhelm me," Snow said.

"Sarcasm will not help your situation."

"You're right," she agreed with a nod, thinking it would do no good to antagonize him in her current dilemma. She needed his help in getting home.

"Finally, you speak words that make sense."

Snow bit her tongue so hard she thought she'd make it bleed.

"I'm waiting," he said impatiently.

She caught his movements and she surmised he was shedding his furs as she had done with her cloak.

"Light flurries were falling when I left Willow's home with Finn," she began. "The snowstorm seemed to come from out of nowhere. He stopped and tied a rope from my horse to his so he wouldn't lose me,"

"That was wise of him. So what happened?"

"After a while his horse stopped and so did mine. I called out but got no answer. Thaw jumped out of my arms and I went after him. He led me to Finn." Sorrow had her pausing a moment. "He was on the ground dead. I felt no wounds on his chest and head. I assumed his heart simply stopped as my mum would say."

"Finn was a good man."

Snow was surprised he knew Finn and that he offered even a small bit of condolence. Did the Lord of Fire possibly have a heart?

"Of course, you foolishly didn't think to keep hold of the horses when you went in search of Finn."

Nope, he had no heart, she thought and bit her tongue again.

"I tried to find them—"

"In a blinding snowstorm and being blind yourself. Now there's a wise decision."

Snow's anger flared. "What was I to do? My one chance of getting home was to find the horses and hope they would take me there."

"And deliver you frozen to your brother. You should have sought shelter," he argued.

"What does it matter?" she said, throwing her hands up in the air. "You came along and rescued me."

"You could have died," he snapped.

"And I still might," she snapped back.

"You don't think I can see you safely home?"

"I fear that I irritate you so much that you might kill me before you have a chance to do so." She sighed, exhausted. "All I want is to go home. I promise I will hold my tongue while here with you, if you would please just get me home safely."

She startled when he suddenly stood in front of her again.

"I will not harm you. You have my word on that and you have my word that I will see you get home safely."

"I appreciate that, my lord," she said, addressing him properly.

"You think to address me properly when you have failed to do so endless times?"

She bit her tongue again, thinking she might very well lose it by the end of their time together.

"No response?" he asked.

"I promised I would hold my tongue," she said.

"Good," he said and turned away.

"More like biting it," she murmured for her ears alone.

"What was that you said?" he asked, turning back around.

"Just warning Thaw not to bite you," she said and Thaw gave a growl as if protesting her command. "Do you know where we are? Close to my home? My sister's?"

"We're closer to my home. As soon as the snow allows we'll head there and when the weather permits I'll see you get home safely."

The thought of having to stay in unfamiliar surroundings with not a familiar person to help her terrified her. This small space she could quickly become familiar with and easily maneuver on her own, but a village and keep she had little memory of, not having been there since she was young, was another matter. And how in heaven's name had they wound up closer to his home than hers? Had Finn misjudged direction? He knew the area far too well along with the land markers. Had a snowstorm driven him that far off course?

She felt for the chair where she had draped her cloak and sat lost in her worrisome thoughts.

Tarass watched her and he saw how Thaw kept watch on him. The pup's dark eyes followed his every move as he remained firmly planted against Snow's leg. The pup never left her side and though he had grown some he hadn't yet gained the strength and size to protect her adequately. However, that did not stop him from trying and for that he had to admire the pup's confidence and tenacity.

He was much like Snow... stubborn, willful, her tongue snappish, foolishly standing up to those much stronger and more powerful than herself. She was blind in more ways than one.

James, her half-brother, needed a firmer hand when dealing with her. He was much too lenient, letting her wander on her own. Strict watch should be kept over her at all times. Maybe after this unfortunate incident James would see that and do what was necessary. If not, harm was bound to find Snow.

It was difficult to deny her beauty and none did. Many agreed that out of all three Macardle sisters, she was the most beautiful. The three shared red hair and green eyes, though the red color was different for each. Snow's hair shined with a red brilliance that caught the eye as it fell well past her shoulders. Her green eyes had a shine to them as well, not bright or bold, but pleasant as if they greeted you along with the smile she often wore. At least that was what others said about her, since she seldom bestowed a smile on him.

Looking at her now she appeared upset and he could easily guess why. She wanted to go home to what was familiar to her, not be stuck in a place she didn't know. He would have to assign one of the women to attend her since she wouldn't be able to get around on her own.

"I'm going to need to get more wood to keep the fire going," he said.

She turned her head in his direction. "The wood is wet. How do you get it to burn?"

"It needs to be stripped down to where it's not wet, then it burns, but I think a saw a wood pile under a lean-to. There might be some dry wood there."

"What if the people who live here return?" she asked.

"In this snowstorm that would be doubtful, but from the looks of the place I'd say it's been deserted for some time," Tarass said and saw a sadness wash over her, then she shook her head slowly.

"Of course, this must be Janick's place."

"The name isn't familiar to me."

"It wouldn't be. Janick and his wife settled into this cottage after you and your family left. He and Sybil were old then, looking for a place where they wouldn't be bothered and could live their lives in peace. My sisters and I took turns visiting them to make sure they were well and if they needed anything. They were content with each other and a more caring couple than I had ever met."

She smiled and Tarass was struck by the way her whole face seemed to light with the smile and how her green eyes even turned brighter.

"I remember how they looked at each other with such love. How proud he was to admit that his heart belonged to her and always would. How they could always be found holding hands." She wiped at her eyes

25

to stop tears from falling. "That's how they were found, holding hands. Willow found them. Sybil had gotten sick and Willow feared she would not make it. One day she arrived here and found Sybil in bed, Janick sitting in a chair next to the bed, his body slumped over hers and their hands joined. From what Willow could tell they didn't die long after each other. That's a strong love to follow each other into death."

"Love is nothing but pain and sorrow and best avoided," Tarass said.

"How sad for you to believe that."

"Not at all. It frees me to live and—"

"Feel nothing and that's living in fear," she finished.

"I fear nothing!" he snapped.

"We all fear something," she said with a shrug, "and in some ways it makes us stronger." She rested her hand on the table and almost pulled it back, having touched the animal head, but stopped and began to explore it. "Why do you wear this—" She paused, her fingers trying to determine what she touched.

"Wolf's head," he said and while her hand paused, it never left the animal's head.

"Why?" she asked again.

"The fire dwindles," he said, ignoring her question. "I'm going to get more wood."

She stood and slipped on her cloak.

"Where do you think you're going?"

"I must see to my needs and so does Thaw," she said and felt heat stain her cheeks.

"You will not take long," he ordered.

26

His hand clamped around her arm before she had a chance to respond and he led her to the door, Thaw staying close to her side.

The wind howled and whipped as if angry and Tarass walked her to a tree near the cottage.

He took her hand and rested it on the tree. "You will remain here until I come for you."

"As you say," Snow said, having no desire to be caught in the storm alone again.

"Stay with her," Tarass ordered, looking down at the pup and Thaw gave a bark and plopped on his rump beside her.

"I'm going to see if that was a wood pile I saw, then I'll be right back. It's only a few steps away. Call out if you need me."

"I will," she said, though saw no reason she would need him. She waited a few moments to make certain he was gone and when she felt Thaw leave her side to see to his duty, she knew it was safe for her to do the same.

She was quick about it, the furious wind and biting cold forcing her to hurry. She was finished adjusting her garments when Thaw began to bark and wouldn't stop. He remained in front of her like a shield and continued his nonstop barking.

Snow jumped when she felt a hand at her arm.

"It's me. What's wrong?" Tarass asked, leaning close to her face so he didn't have to shout above the wind.

She turned her face, her cold cheek brushing his. "Something or someone must be out there. He only barks like this when he thinks I'm in danger."

27

Thaw gave a loud bark followed by a vicious growl, then he lunged forward into the snow.

"Stay here, and keep your hand on that tree," Tarass ordered. "I'm going after him."

She didn't argue, didn't respond, didn't want to waste time with either. She wanted Tarass to make sure Thaw was safe. She planted herself against the tree, straining to hear Thaw's barks and when they faded her worry grew.

After a moment, she thought she heard someone approach or did it sound like something was being dragged? She couldn't tell and without word from Tarass or a bark from Thaw, it couldn't be them.

She stayed where she was, not knowing what to do. Tarass told her to stay by the tree, but what if something had happened to him? And what if she walked away from the tree, wandered aimlessly, not knowing in what direction to go, since she had turned several times after Tarass had deposited her there. She had no idea of the direction of the cottage.

She strained to listen again when suddenly a hand fell on her shoulder squeezing it tight and saying not a word and began to drag her away from the tree. Her instincts flared and she fought to free herself. The unknown person was strong and fear rose up in her. If he got a good grip on her, she might not be able to break free of him.

Snow kicked, swung, and did whatever she could to yank herself free, but it was a sharp swing of her head that caught him under the chin that did it and once his arm fell away, she hurried off in the snow as best as she could. She didn't know what direction she went in,

28

couldn't see anything but shadows that she quickly avoided.

Were they trees or were there more men like the one who had grabbed her?

The wind made it impossible to determine how much snow had fallen, swirling it around and depositing it deeper in some places than others. She kept her hands out in front of her as she stumbled her way in the snowstorm. She thought to scream out for Tarass, but if there were other men, they would hear her as well.

She continued to stumble around and then like a light in the darkness, she heard Tarass scream her name. She turned, not knowing what direction it came from and took a step as she went to answer him.

Her foot found no solid ground and just before she fell, she screamed out to him, "*Tarass!*"

Chapter Four

Snow tumbled over and over and over, her hands reaching out frantically trying to grasp something to stop her rapid descent. Something jabbed at her side, struck her leg, scratched her face, but she fought through it all as she tried desperately to grab something, anything that would stop her. Finally, she rammed into a tree, more a sapling since it bent with her weight, and she quickly grabbed hold of it and brought herself to an abrupt stop, smacking hard against the snow-covered hill. She didn't know what awaited her at the bottom, though she recalled Sorrell not allowing her to walk too far on her own in the area, having warned her of a steep glen that wasn't far from the cottage, a rushing stream at the bottom. She berated herself for not recalling that sooner.

It took a few minutes for her to gather her wits and not let fear overwhelm her. Her heart pounded furiously in her chest and her breathing came rapidly. She had to calm herself and think what to do. Her breath caught when she recalled that Tarass had called out to her just before she had fallen and she had been able to yell out to him.

She tried calling out to him again, but she barely had a breath to whisper his name. She had to calm herself. She had to let Tarass know where she was.

Her head shot up, thinking she had heard something, but wasn't sure. She needed to get her breath back. She needed to be able to let Tarass know she needed help.

***

Tarass's heart rammed against his chest when he got no answer. Even the wind couldn't hide the fright he had heard in the way Snow had screamed his name. Blind and alone in a snowstorm. He should have never left her. He should have led her back to the cottage and made sure she was safe before he took off. But the pup had sensed something and so had he and he hadn't wanted to lose the trail. He kept alert to the sounds around him, knowing that something lurked in the storm. He'd seen signs of it and so had Thaw.

He called out to her again and was once again met with silence. How would he ever find her in this raging snowstorm? He didn't even know which direction to go in.

"Tarass!"

Thaw didn't wait, he took off at the sound of Snow's frightened scream, barking as he went, and Tarass followed.

The pup hopped and bolted through the snow, not letting anything stop him, his anxiousness apparent in his speed. Tarass kept pace, feeling the same apprehension as Snow called out both their names continually to let them know where she was.

Thaw stopped suddenly and so did Tarass, and he realized why. They were at the top of the glen that ran near the cottage all the way to his land.

Snow had fallen down it.

"Snow!" he shouted.

"I'm here, down here," she called out with effort.

From the sound of her voice, she hadn't fallen to the bottom and into the icy water that waited there. That meant she had somehow managed to stop her fall.

"I can't hold on much longer," she yelled.

Cupping his hands around his mouth so that his voice would carry with more volume, Tarass called out to her. "I'm coming to get you."

Thaw had turned silent while Tarass and Snow talked, now he was barking and inching closer to the edge as if getting ready to jump.

"Stay, Thaw," Tarass ordered firmly.

He paid Tarass no heed. He was worried about Snow and if he didn't do something the pup would dive over the side after her.

Tarass bent down and ordered sharply, "Quiet! I'm going to get Snow and bring her back to you."

The pup sat and gave him a growl as if warning him to keep his word.

Tarass was accustomed to challenges in the cold and the snow. His mother's people had taught him well and he didn't hesitate to go over the side of the glen, axe in hand, to make his descent to Snow.

"Snow!" he shouted as he dug his axe into the snow-covered glen wall to skillfully make his way down.

"Tarass," she called out eager for him to reach her, to be there with her, something she never thought she would ever feel for the insufferable man.

"Call out often so I can make out where you are," he yelled over the howling wind.

Her side hurt and her breathing was a challenge, the swirling snow and wind quickly robbing her of breath when she spoke. But she fought back against the storm, remembering why her mum had named her Snow. She had told her the delicate snow was also a force that could conquer the strongest of men.

"Tarass!" she called out again and did so again and again until it echoed in her head like a litany. She was about to call out his name again when she realized he'd been silent and fear soared in her and had her yelling out, "Tarass, are you there? Tarass?"

"I'm here," he called out, sounding closer to her.

"Don't leave me," she said, for only herself to hear and feeling foolish for sounding so cowardly. But with the terrifying fall and her precarious hold on the sapling, and not able to see anything, she silently admitted that she needed Tarass. Without him, she wouldn't survive.

"Never would I leave you," came the strong voice and a solid arm coiled tightly around her waist. "Put your arms around my neck."

His warm breath fanned her neck and a tingle of relief washed through her. She didn't hesitate, didn't think to argue, didn't think it might be unwise to do as he said. She did something unexpected… she trusted him.

33

She let go of the sapling and wrapped her arms around his neck.

He pressed his cheek to hers, his lips near her ear. "Keep hold of me. Even if we should slip, keep hold of me."

"Aye," she said with a nod and held on, praying all would go well for them.

It was a slow ascent with only one slight slip. It made her realize the immense strength he possessed, holding her firm with one arm while using his axe in his other hand to dig into the snow-covered earth after his feet found firm footing. And so it went slow and steady until they reached the top, a barking Thaw greeting her as Tarass hoisted her up and over the edge to collapse in the snow.

Thaw didn't waste any time showering her face with sloppy licks.

Tarass followed soon after, though didn't collapse in the snow. He was on his feet and he reached down, his hands slipping under Snow's arms, and lifted her to her feet.

"We need to get to the safety of the cottage," he said, pulling her hood up over her head.

She needed to alert him to possible danger, her words rushing out of her mouth. "Someone grabbed me." He stood so close that she felt him tense.

"The cottage," he said and went to take a step.

"Thaw," she said and bent to scoop up the pup. Pain struck her in the side and she let out a gasp as she lifted Thaw.

"What's wrong?" Tarass asked, the swirling wind having carried the distressed sound up to his ears.

"My side," was all she managed to say.

Tarass grabbed Thaw out of her arms, the pup snapping and growling at him, and dropped him to the ground, then got her moving.

Thaw followed them, and snapped and growled all the way.

Once inside the cottage, Tarass placed Snow in front of the hearth. He was completely taken by surprise when she threw her arms around his neck and hugged him tight. His natural response was to wrap his arms around her and hold her tight.

"I cannot thank you enough for climbing down the ravine and rescuing me," she said, choking on the tears that threatened her.

"You are a brave soul for hanging on as you did."

"I didn't feel brave. I was terrified," she admitted, the horror of it all rushing over her.

"Whether you were or not, you didn't let it stop you from doing what you needed to do to survive. You are braver than you think," he said, and realized the truth of his words. She was a courageous, though stubborn woman.

She let go of him suddenly as if she had just realized she was hugging him and stepped away.

He slipped off her cloak and Thaw hurried to her side, jumping up against her leg.

She stopped the grimace that rushed up before it could slip out. It wasn't only her side that pained her but her leg as well.

"You did wonderful, Thaw," she praised the pup, patting his head and rubbing behind his ear. "You helped Tarass save me."

35

He gave a bark and parked himself next to her leg, letting her know she wasn't going anywhere without him.

"You need to let me have a look at your side," Tarass said, having removed his fur wrappings to be left in his warm, soft wool shirt that fell to the middle of his thigh.

"That would not be proper," she said without turning, it being pointless to look at him since she couldn't see him. His hand suddenly on her arm had her instinctively turning.

He winced silently when he saw the red scratches on her face, some swollen, and a bruise forming near the corner of one eye.

"You tensed when Thaw jumped up against your leg, which makes me think you have an injury there as well. You need tending and since I'm the only one here, the task falls to me. And don't bother to tell me you can see to it, since you can't even see if you do have an injury."

"I will not allow you access to what is for a husband's eyes alone," she said with a stubborn lift of her chin.

"With your affliction, the likelihood of you marrying is slim, so there is no need for you to be concerned about that."

Snow felt the sting of his words, a sting she had felt often lately with both her sister's marriages. His words only worsened the pain of that sting. She would never know the touch of a husband's lips on hers or the intimacy shared between husband and wife or the joy of giving birth to the bairns of such a union. That had been

36

denied her and all because of her father's mind illness that had him causing the fire in the keep that had robbed her of her sight and had eventually caused her mum's death. A moment in time that had taken everything from her.

He may have spoken the truth but he needn't have caused her the hurt, and she couldn't keep the sarcasm from her response. "Your compliments truly overwhelm me."

"I do my best to please you."

Laughter accompanied her sarcasm this time. "You do know how to please a woman."

"Believe me, *àst*, I definitely know how to please a woman… many times over."

A pleasing sensation wiggled its way through her slowly almost as if his words caressed her, and she wondered what he had called her since the word was unfamiliar to her.

"You're not looking at my wounds," she said, sounding as though she delivered an edict.

She wasn't sure if it was him or Thaw that growled low.

"Let me at least tend the scratches on your face and look at the wound on your leg," he offered more reasonably. "Some are quite red and swollen and a bruise forms by your one eye." He touched the spot lightly and she grimaced. "I did not mean to cause you pain, and while you can be foolish more often than not this is one time I believe you'd be wise enough to listen to reason." He stepped away from her. "Think on it while I add logs to the fire."

"You found logs?" she asked.

"There is a stock pile of them on the side of the house, plenty to keep us warm. I brought in quite a few before I heard Thaw bark," he said, bending to see to the chore.

Snow felt a bit contrite. He had saved her life more than once today, had provided shelter and warmth for them, and he wanted to tend her wounds. He had kept her safe since finding her and continued to do so. She had no reason to complain.

Still, she could only let him do so much. She might never marry, but that didn't leave her cause to act improperly.

"You may tend my face and leg," she said.

"A wise choice," Tarass said.

"Are you saying I am a wise woman?" she asked.

Her smile told him she was teasing and it brought a smile to his face. "In this situation you are."

"A true compliment, I'll gladly accept," she said and thought the Lord of Fire wasn't as insufferable as she had thought.

That thought came back to haunt her when she felt him lift the hem of her shift and tunic too high and roll up her wool hose to expose the wound on her leg, and she warned him. "You'll not take advantage of me and go any further."

"Rest easy, Snow, I have no desire to poke a bli—" He clamped his mouth shut, realizing how his words would sound.

She, however, finished his words for him. "A blind woman. You have no desire to poke a blind woman. Isn't that what you meant to say?" She shoved his hand

38

away from her leg. "And I have no desire to be poked by an insufferable arse."

Tarass learned not to feel. It did little good to feel. It only brought pain and sorrow. So he often spoke in the same manner, not giving thought or caring about others' feelings. This time, however, his own words had disturbed him. Not that he would apologize. He never apologized. That was another thing he learned not to do.

"The wound on your leg needs cleaning," he said, thinking she would respond to sound reasoning.

"Give me the cloth and I will see to it myself," Snow ordered.

"No!" he said sharply. "I will see to it and you will rest afterwards and I will hear no more about it."

"You cannot dictate to me," Snow argued.

"I just did," Tarass said firmly, his hand going to rest at her ankle. "And do not fight me on this, Snow. You will not win."

Thaw growled from where he sat beside her.

"You'd be wise to teach the pup to let someone tend you when necessary," Tarass said.

His words had echoed Willow's when someone the pup didn't know had attempted to help Snow when she had stumbled and Thaw had snarled and snapped at him. She didn't want to admit Tarass was right and she wouldn't, though she would let Thaw know Tarass could tend her.

"It's all right, Thaw, Tarass helps me," she said, reaching out to touch the pup.

Thaw quickly stood to receive the pat and rub and know that all was well.

"I'll see to your face first and then your leg and you should seriously consider letting me look at your side," he said as he stood.

"I feel no blood there, so it's probably nothing more than a bruise."

"Can I at least have a look at your side to make sure no blood has seeped through your garments?"

That he asked instead of demanded had her nodding consent, since it would be wise to make sure her injury wasn't worse than she thought. She went to move off the chair when she felt Tarass's hand at her arm helping her and she was grateful since she felt a jab to her side.

He caught the wince in her eyes that she tried to hide, making him anxious to have a look. He turned her so that her wounded side faced the hearth, the flames casting sufficient light on her. He noticed right away a tear in her garment below her right breast, to her side, and he pressed his fingers lightly against it. She winced and pulled away, but not before he thought he felt something there.

Then he looked at his fingers. There was blood on them.

"I need to see to your side. There's blood there," he said.

"I will not expose myself to you," she said, the thought unnerving that she should even be partially naked in front of him.

"You don't have to," he said. "I can cut the cloth around the wound to expose it enough for me to tend it."

Her shoulders slumped in relief. "That would work."

"It would be easier if you laid down on the bed," he said and was glad she didn't object when he led her there. "I'll see to your face and leg after seeing to your side."

"I am grateful for your help and will make sure James knows how honorably you treated me," she said.

"For a half-brother he worries much about you and your sisters," Tarass said as he went to the hearth to get the bucket of snow that was now warm water and place it at the side of the bed.

"My sisters and I are lucky that he is a good and honorable half-brother who continues to keep his word to our father to look after us and see us kept safe."

Tarass moved one of the chairs to the side of the bed, sat, then took his knife and cut a piece of cloth from the blanket and draped it over the side of the bucket.

"I'm going to cut away at your garment now," he said.

"All right," she said, her stomach growing unsettled, not only with worry for her wound, but with having Tarass touch her in too much of a familiar way. It wasn't right, but there was no alternative. Of course, her blindness made it all the more difficult since she couldn't see how he looked upon her. She was completely dependent on him not only to tend her but to be truthful to her.

Tarass was as gentle as he could be and thankfully Snow didn't wince once, but he did when he finally exposed her wound.

"You grow silent and your hands grow still. What's wrong?" she asked, unable to keep the worry from her voice.

He didn't hesitate to tell her the truth. "A stick has managed to embed itself in your side. How long the stick and how deep it goes, I don't know."

"The only way to find out is to remove it," she said, trying to be practical like her sister Willow, but fearful nonetheless.

"True enough," Tarass agreed, but he had seen men with similar wounds and once the object was removed some bled to death.

"How deep it is, is what matters," Snow said. "So let's be done with it and, Tarass," —she paused briefly— "if anything should happen to me, please let my family know I love them."

"Nothing is going to happen to you... you're too obstinate," he said, the thought that she would die sending a sudden anger through him.

"Then we have something in common," she said and was surprised when he laughed.

Thaw seemed to understand what was happening and jumped up on the bed to curl against her other side and stare at Tarass.

"He's watching you, isn't he?" Snow asked.

"Like a hawk ready to attack his prey," Tarass said, the pup's eyes intent on him.

Snow caressed the pup. "It's all right, Thaw. Tarass helps me."

Thaw looked at her and whimpered.

"All is well, worry not," she assured him softly.

He turned his attention back to Tarass to keep watch.

"I'm not going to lie to you, this is going to hurt," Tarass said.

"Then be done with it quickly," she advised, her one hand gripping the blanket beneath her.

He carefully used his knife to probe at the top of the embedded stick and he wanted to curse seeing Snow cringe in pain, but not saying a word.

It took a couple of more pokes and prods, and winces and a grasp or two from Snow, with the knife to get the stick high enough for him to grab it and pull it out.

Tarass smiled as he announced, "It's a little one."

"It didn't break off in there, did it?" Snow asked anxiously, and Thaw whined.

"Not that I can see," he said, taking a closer look at the wound that thankfully bled little. "I'll clean it and wrap it. As soon as you possibly can, have Willow look at it."

"My thought as well," she said, relieved.

After he got the wound cleaned and tore a strip of cloth from the blanket, he helped her to sit up, Thaw sticking close to her.

"It will make it easier to wrap the wound," he said, and she didn't argue.

He slipped his hand inside the ripped portion of her garment to slip the cloth around to her back when he hit a spot that caused her to gasp and gave him pause. The spot was badly swollen.

43

"That's it," he said. "You're disrobing and I'm going to look over every part of you to make certain there are no more potentially dangerous wounds."

Chapter Five

"I most certainly will not disrobe," Snow said emphatically.

"You would die for the sake of propriety?" he asked and gave her no chance to answer. "Another stick, stone, who knows what could be embedded in you. If it's not removed quickly it will fester and you will fever and die. That's what your stubbornness will do for you."

She could hear her sisters in her head warning her to do what she must to survive, especially Willow. She would have had Snow's garments off by now and searching every part of her body. But it was far different standing in front of her sister naked than Tarass.

It needed to be done, but there had to be a way that it could be done without her being completely naked in front of him.

A thought came to her, making her feel hopeful. "What if I disrobe and keep a blanket around me and you glance at the areas causing me pain or discomfort?"

He shook his head, though answered the opposite. "Fine, we'll do it that way." Anything that would allow him to make sure she was all right. He would do whatever it took to see her returned safely and unharmed to her family.

Tarass moved the chair away from the bed and helped her to stand, then he gathered up the blanket on the bed and directed her hand to it. "Here's the blanket. I'm going to stand by the hearth with my back to you until you tell me you're ready."

"Your word on that?" she asked.

"You have my word," he said, annoyed that she felt the need to ask and walked over to the hearth. "My back is to you."

Snow had to take his word that he spoke the truth, no other options left to her.

She hoped to hurry out of her garments, but they were damp, actually more than damp and it was difficult getting them off. The pains that struck her didn't help either and while she fought with the stubborn garments she kept telling herself that she was wise to do this.

She pulled and tugged and gasped a few times as she struggled to shed her tunic and shift after finally shedding her wool hose.

Tarass warned himself to let her be. This was the way she wanted it. She'd get out of her garments eventually. But every gasp and wince was like the tip of a dagger poking him. Until finally she gasped one too many times.

"That's it," he said, turning and walking over to her.

"You gave your word," she said as she heard him approach and hurried to push her shift down where it was entangled at her shoulders just above her breasts.

"What good does my word do when you need help?" he said and grabbed hold of the bunched shift and lifted it up over her shoulders, only to have it get stuck around her neck and head.

"Let me be. I'll do it myself," she argued, her voice muffled by the garments and her hands fighting his.

Thaw sprung up from where he sat on the bed, protesting along with Snow, his snarls aimed at Tarass.

He paid her no mind as she continued to struggle, until his arm caught her around her naked waist and held her firm. "Stay still or I will take my dagger and rip your garments off you."

The threat had the desired effect. She froze against him.

A low warning growl emanated from Thaw and he poised himself for attack.

"Calm your pup now," he ordered Snow.

She didn't hesitate, the snarl warning her that he was about to attack. "Enough, Thaw, I'm not in danger. Tarass helps me."

The pup sat but kept up a low growl, letting Tarass know he was watching him.

It took only a couple of moments to free her of the strangling garments and leave her standing naked in front of him.

She didn't know why she closed her eyes, since he was nothing more than a gray shadow to her. Perhaps it served as a covering, a blanket of sorts that left her feeling less vulnerable. By not seeing his shadow, he couldn't see her.

"I'll be quick," he said softly.

That he was now trying to be courteous only made it more difficult.

47

He had no intimate interest in Snow. He wanted only to see what wounds she had suffered and tend them. But as he began to examine her, thoughts of what a lovely body she had kept interrupting. He'd never seen a woman so perfectly proportioned. She had just the right roundness and curves that blended beautifully and flawlessly, cream-colored skin with the exception of the bruises and scratches that had him shaking his head.

He needed to stay focused and it didn't help that he had to lift one of her breasts, that fit nicely in his hand, to look at a bruise that had formed there.

Snow stiffened and wished she could crawl under the blanket and never come out. "Is that necessary?"

"There is a bruise beneath your breast. I want to make sure nothing is embedded there," he explained as her chilled breast rested in his warm hand and he watched as her nipple puckered even more than it had.

"Please hurry," she said, annoyed that the warmth of his hand at her breast felt pleasing.

She was right, he needed to hurry and be done with it, since he felt his loins begin to stir. Something he had never expected.

He ran his hand over several bruises and winced when he saw the numerous scratches. "I need to clean these scratches. Some are quite red and swollen."

"Hurry," she said again and squeezed her eyes closed tighter.

"There's also a large bruise on your back and some smaller ones in various places. And a sizeable scratch on your thigh. But I don't see anything embedded

48

anywhere. I'll hurry and see to these, then get the blanket around you."

"I would be most grateful," she said, trying desperately to keep control, not cry, not rail against the indignity of her situation.

He isn't attracted to you. He has no desire to poke you. He does not look upon you with any intimate interest. You hold no appeal to him, not even naked.

She continued her silent chant to help her get through this humiliating ordeal. And what disturbed her even more was that he proved what she had thought. No man would be interested in a blind woman.

All her hopes and dreams of having a loving husband and family of her own came crashing down around her.

Tarass went down on his haunches, wet cloth in hand, after having cut another piece from the blanket and soaking and rinsing it in the bucket, to tend the scratch on her thigh.

He could be mannerly when he wanted to be, though that wasn't often, but damned if her thatch of red hair between her legs didn't beckon his eyes and entice. Or that her slim thighs didn't invite him to spread them apart and—that did it. He stood and grabbed the blanket, Thaw giving him an evil look and a low growl as if he knew what he'd been thinking.

With deft hands, he quickly wrapped the blanket around her. "I can see to the rest with you covered up."

With such a sudden change of mind, she wondered if he found her so unappealing that he could no longer look upon her. She should be grateful, since it brought the humiliating ordeal to a rapid end. She took hold of the two ends, he shoved in her hands, and closed the blanket tight around her, shielding herself.

Tarass silently cursed himself. Snow had been a thorn in his side from the day he had met her. He wondered if she remembered that day so long ago, when young, they had met for the first time. It had stuck in his memory. She had stuck in his memory.

He shook his head. That was a long time ago. He wasn't a young, carefree lad anymore. He was a fierce warrior who had returned home to claim his birthright and make all those responsible pay for what had happened to his mother and father.

Now was not the time to think on this. He needed to see to her wounds and see her returned home safely. There was one other thing he needed to make sure of.

"No one can find out about you being naked in front of me or we will be forced to wed," he said.

"You need not worry about that. I have no wont to wed you," she said, and she didn't. So why had his words hurt her? "I will tell my sister I tended the areas that pained me and that I could reach. Everyone is aware we have no like for each other so they will easily accept my word." She kept her chin up and her shoulders back as she spoke, though the weight of the endless day lay heavily upon them. "I don't believe anyone will question it. Once you return me home we'll never have to bother with each other again."

"I imagine you're right," he said and wondered why he felt as if he'd just been stabbed in the gut. "I'll see to your face and—"

"No," she said, shaking her head. "I can do the rest myself. At least that way part of what I say will be the truth."

Tarass was about to argue, but realized she was right. It was much better for them both. He should have never broken his word to her. He should have waited until she had shed her garments and wrapped the blanket around her. So why hadn't he?

It had upset him to hear her struggle with her garments, and in pain, and stand there and do nothing. Why he had let it disturb him, he didn't know. But it was done. He'd get her home and make sure they're paths crossed as little as possible. She'd been right about people accepting the explanation, it having been obvious he and Snow didn't care for each other.

"I'll keep my back to you. Do what you must and let me know when you're done," he said.

She was blunt. "I do not trust your word."

"There's nothing I can do about that. My back remains to you. Do what you will." He turned his back on her and went and sat on a chair. "The bucket of water and cloth are not far from your right foot." He intended to say no more after that, but a thought had him deciding otherwise. "Is there anything you can recall about this man who grabbed you?"

Snow was relieved for the change in conversation. "His grip on my shoulder was strong. He didn't speak. When he went to drag me away, I fought him."

"You fought him?" Tarass asked, not sure he had heard her correctly.

"I did." Fear had her recalling it clearly. "I kicked at him, swung at him." She shook her head. "But to no

51

avail. Finally, I swung my head and caught him under the chin, sending him stumbling enough for his hand to fall off me, then I rushed off in the snow, hoping it would swallow me up enough that he wouldn't be able to find me. I didn't know in what direction I went and I was frightened he might not be alone. That was why I didn't call out to you at first, for fear someone else might find me."

Tarass's stomach twisted tighter and tighter with each word she spoke. It took courage to fight, to defend yourself. But it took tremendous courage for a blind woman to fight and run off in a snowstorm.

"You're a brave woman, Snow."

"Is it bravery or the instinct to survive that forces courage upon us?" she asked.

"Not all have courage. And instinct to survive comes in many ways. Some surrender easily. Some beg for mercy. Some are fearless and some are fools."

"It takes a fool to be fearless," she said with a light laugh.

He chuckled as he said, "So you think yourself a fool."

"Aren't we all fools one time or another?"

"I'd like to argue that, but I can't, since there have been times, when thought upon, that I was a fool," he admitted.

"And I as well," she said, surprised that he would admit such a thing. "I am done. You can turn now."

She had wrapped the blanket around her from under her arms down and was sitting on the bed with her back braced against the wall, her feet tucked up nearly under her. She had braided her hair, though loosely, letting red strands fall free around her face. The scratches were more prominent there after being tended, and still, she was beautiful.

"Tell me of a time you were a fool," he encouraged, needing to stop finding her so appealing. He'd only recently been with a willing woman, but then his appetite to couple never seemed satisfied.

"That would be the first time we met," she said with a smile and rubbed her bare arms, feeling chilled. "I believe I was eight years and you were ten and three years."

"You remember that?" He stood, grabbing her cloak from the chair to take it to her. "I have your cloak, let me drape it around your shoulders."

Snow leaned forward, eager for the warmth of the fur-lining. The warm fur ran another shiver through her, followed by another one when Tarass tucked the cloak around her and over her chilled feet.

He sat beside her on the bed, the side of his arm resting against hers. "So do you remember?" he asked again.

She was glad for the cloak's warmth and for his added warmth, the cold sneaking in through the walls.

"I remember it quite clearly. Father brought me and Sorrell with him when he came to your keep to speak with your father. You dared Sorrell to climb a tree with you and got mad when she climbed higher than you. You went and told your father and mine that Sorrell had climbed high in the tree when you warned her not to climb the tree. Your father gave her quite a tongue lashing."

"Which you interrupted by shouting '*liar, liar*' and punching me where a young lass's fist should never touch and sending me to the ground."

Snow chuckled. "I was short. It was the only spot I could reach."

He laughed himself and shook his head. "Did I ever suffer for that one. First with the punch from you and second for lying to my da."

"You deserved both, though I didn't think you remembered it."

Tarass laughed again. "That's a memory you don't forget. Your punch might not have had much strength to it, but where it hit, it didn't have to."

"My da yelled at me and Sorrell praised me."

They both grew quiet.

Then Tarass asked, "Do you remember my features?"

"I remember your eyes. They were such a bold blue they frightened me. They reminded me of the sky when a storm was drawing near. And you were so tall."

"You were petite then and still are. My father actually admired your courage, for one so small, to strike out at me."

"That was the only time I saw your da and I was terrified of him. He was so big, a giant in my young eyes, and I feared he would devour me for hitting you and my sister for climbing the tree, and I worried my da would not be able to stop him."

"Yet you defended your sister anyway."

She smiled. "I was a fearless fool that day."

"No," he contested, "you were brave, though I don't blame your da for not bringing you with him after that when he visited again."

"I didn't want to go with him, though Sorrell did, but my da wouldn't let her go." She laughed softly. "He had heard her plotting revenge against you."

"Well after all these years she finally got her revenge by marrying Ruddock and the Clan Macardle claiming fealty to him instead of me."

"You can blame that on fate and love. Fate brought Ruddock and Sorrell together and love did the rest."

"Love does nothing but get in the way of things," he argued.

"You don't wish to marry for love?"

"A marriage's sole purpose is for gain, whether to strengthen ties, expand holdings, or grow more powerful. That's what a marriage will bring me."

"I wish to love, wed, and have a bushel of bairns, but due to my blindness I never will. How sad that you have the chance to have it all, and yet you don't want it," she said, turning to look at him though she could only see a gray shadow.

"I don't need love to have a wife and bairns. As I said, love gets in the way of things and I refuse to let it get in my way."

"How would love get in your way?" she asked but didn't wait for a response. "Love doesn't hinder, it helps. You're not alone. There's someone there to share your smiles, your laughter, your tears, your sadness."

"I need no such help," Tarass said as if affronted that she thought he did.

She reached out, her hand touching his arm and traveling down it to take hold of his hand, her fingers wrapping around his to give a light squeeze. "Everyone needs help one time or another, whether if it's just to hold someone's hand or give a hug or a kiss. Or remind them that you love them."

At that Thaw moved from where he laid curled by her side to her lap, placed his paws on her chest and licked her cheek.

Snow smiled and laughed softly as her hands went to capture his face and give his snout a kiss. "I love you too."

Tarass watched the pair with annoyance. Or was he annoyed that she had let go of his hand? He grew even more annoyed at himself for thinking it. But he had enjoyed the way her small hand felt wrapped around his and how she had given it a squeeze as if saying, *I'm here with you, you're not alone.*

It was an intimacy that was foreign to him, since it hadn't stirred his loins… it had stirred his heart.

Thaw settled himself in her lap, curling himself in a ball and closing his eyes, completely content.

Snow yawned and turned once again to Tarass. "I never asked and I'm curious. What brought you out in a snowstorm and dressed in barbarian garments?"

"I was returning from meeting with some of my mum's people. I honor her name and tribe by dressing their way when I visit with them."

She scrunched her brow when another thought came to mind. "The blinding snowstorm must have confused us all. It threw Finn off course and yourself as well, the direction all wrong for all of us being in the area we were in."

"I was to meet someone. That was what brought me to that area."

"Someone you knew?" She gasped. "Could it have been the man who grabbed me?"

"No, I am familiar with this man. He had information I was looking for."

Curious, she asked, "What information?"

"Information about the man who killed my parents. I intend to find him and kill him."

Chapter Six

Tarass sat in a chair by the hearth staring at Snow sleeping, Thaw curled at her feet and his eyes opening now and again to look at him. The pup was keeping a cautious eye on him and he had to admire him for it.

He had been surprised at her response when he had told her he intended to kill the person who had killed his parents. She had told him she would do the same if it were her parents. She hadn't asked anything more about it after that, and he hadn't wanted to offer any more.

She had fallen asleep as they discussed the weather and what it would take to make it home, her head lolling to the side until it had finally settled on his shoulder. He had sat there with her resting comfortably against him and a slight snore coming from Thaw curled in her lap. He had listened to the wind whipping around the small cottage and the crackle of the fire in the hearth. He had felt more content than he had in years, and it had surprised him.

It hadn't been until the fire had died down considerably that he reluctantly left the bed, lying Snow down on the lumpy mattress, while Thaw moved to curl at her feet, of course, after giving him a growl.

The fire was once again blazing and he felt sleep poking at him, but his thoughts weren't ready to rest. There was far too much on his mind. It hadn't been long after they'd first met that his da had left and not long after that his mum and he had taken their leave. His mum had told him they were going to join his da. He asked about their home and who would protect it and she had told him not to worry it rested in good hands until their return. He had wondered over his da's departure and theirs as well. He had worried that it had something to do with his mum's people. But each time he had asked her, he had gotten the same response. Everything was fine. He was not to worry.

He had been shocked when his da met up with them on their journey and even more surprised at where their journey had ended... his mum's tribe. He had missed Scotland, and he had promised himself that someday he would return. He had thought it would be with his mum and da. He had sworn to himself and his mum's tribe that he would revenge their death. And he would let nothing, absolutely nothing, stop him from doing just that.

His thoughts began to settle as sleep began to poke at him. He added more logs to the fire so the heat would stay strong until morning, then he snatched his furs off the table where he had laid them to dry and went and placed them over the cloak that covered Snow.

With no other choice, the ground too cold to sleep on, he stretched out on his side beside her.

Thaw lifted his head and went to growl.

"Quiet," he ordered in a harsh whisper, "I keep her and you safe."

Thaw gave a low growl, stretched himself to his feet with a yawn, and moved up to settle himself against Snow's stomach.

59

Tarass thought that Thaw was lucky Snow would never marry, since no man would allow the dog in bed with him and his wife. The strange thought troubled him, recalling Snow's words about wanting to fall in love and have a family. It was a shame, since he had no doubt Snow would make a wonderful mum.

***

Snow woke buried in warmth that she didn't want to emerge from, and she didn't. She remained snuggled under her fur-lined cloak. A noise close to the bed had her opening her eyes to see a shadow standing over her. She was ready to scream when she recalled where she was and who was with her.

"The snow stopped sometime last night, though the sky remains ominous. I'm going to have a look. We may be able to make it to my keep before the snow starts again. Get dressed while I'm gone. Your garments are dry and on the table and your hose are in your boots by the bed. Is there anything you need help with before I leave?"

"No," she said, sitting up, "though if you could take Thaw with you, I would appreciate it. He probably needs to go out."

"I can do that. I'll be out front the whole time."

"I also appreciate that," she said, worried that he would wander off leaving her completely alone and vulnerable.

"Come on, Thaw, you're coming with me," he said with a wave to the pup.

60

Thaw didn't move from Snow's side. He actually leaned against her arm as if letting Tarass know he wasn't going anywhere.

Snow looked down at the gray blob that was Thaw to her. "It's all right, Thaw. You go with Tarass. I'll be right here waiting for you." She scooped him up, kissed him on the top of his head, and placed him on the earth floor. "Go with Tarass, I'll be right here."

Thaw looked to Snow than to Tarass.

"We'll be right outside," he said and wondered why he was even bothering to talk to the pup.

"Go now, Thaw," Snow urged in a more commanding tone and the pup trotted over to Thaw growling all the way.

"I'll knock before I enter," Tarass said, then opened the door, a burst of cold air rushing in and the pup and he hurried out quickly.

With little time before he returned, Snow hurried out of bed with a wince, her side still painful, and into her dry hose, then her boots, surprised both were warm. She made her way carefully to the table, found her garments folded on top, though she didn't rush to slip into them for fear of getting herself tangled up. She tempered her movements and got the garments on much easier than she had gotten them off.

A sigh fell from her lips when she finished, relieved she was no longer naked, no longer exposed to Tarass. It had been unnerving and humiliating, and she didn't want anyone to ever know of it.

A bark came before the knock at the door and she turned to face it with a smile. Thaw came running in and sped right to her. She went to snatch him up.

"He's wet from the snow and you're dry and warm," Tarass said.

Snow leaned down and patted Thaw. "Sit by the fire, Thaw, then I will give you a hug."

Tarass shook his head as he watched the pup do as Snow told him. It was as if the pup understood her every word.

"The sky hints of more snow, but my keep is not far from here. The snow on the ground will slow us down some, but it shouldn't take us long to reach it if we can keep a steady pace. How does your wound feel today?"

"It's sore but not as bad as yesterday," she said. "I'm ready to leave when you are."

"As soon as I see to dousing the fire, we'll go," he said and hurried to see it done.

Snow slipped on her cloak and gloves and made her way to the door, Thaw following close by.

"Can you see me enough to follow behind me?" Tarass asked, watching her take cautious steps and stretching her hands in front of her as if making sure nothing blocked her way.

"You're a gray shadow to me, but it is enough for me to follow as long as you remain in front of me," she said with confidence, eager to do anything that would help get her home sooner.

"Stay close to Snow, Thaw," he said after they stepped outside, then shook his head. Now he was talking to the pup as if he could understand his every word.

Snow realized soon enough why he wanted her trailing behind him. He made sure to clear somewhat of a path for her to follow. There was far too much snow for him to clear it enough to set a quick pace. It took time and effort to go only a short distance. At least it felt like a short distance. At the laborious rate they traveled, she thought it might have been wiser for them to remain at the cottage.

She didn't give up, though, she kept going, her legs growing heavy with fatigue as she trudged through the snow. She didn't dare take her eyes off the gray shadow that was Tarass. She feared being abandoned again. She stayed on his tail, taking step after endless step, while silently praying they would reach their destination soon.

A worry took hold when she noticed Tarass's shadow had faded some. How had he gotten farther away from her? She rushed her step to catch up and felt her boot catch on something. She went flying forward so fast, she had no time to stop herself from toppling head first into the snow.

Tarass turned at the sound of the barking, shocked to see Snow's face planted in the snow. He rushed to her. She was already struggling to stand when he reached her. With a firm grip on her arm, he got her to her feet and kept hold until she found firm footing.

"What happened?" he asked, wiping away the snow on her face.

She coughed and shook her head. "I'm not sure. I think I tripped over something."

Thaw was still barking and digging furiously in the snow.

"Quiet, Thaw, all is well," she ordered, but the pup didn't listen.

63

The pup was not only disobeying Snow, he had stopped digging to look up at Tarass, then to the spot on the ground.

"I believe Thaw is angry at whatever it was you tripped over. I'll assure him all is well. You stay right here. Don't move."

"He can be stubborn at times," Snow said, dusting the snow off herself.

"I wonder where he gets that from?" Tarass said with a chuckle that quickly faded when he spotted what Thaw had revealed… an arm.

"What's wrong?" Snow demanded. "Your laughter ended suddenly. Something is wrong."

She might be blind but Tarass had learned quickly that she was astute to her surroundings. He didn't for once think to keep it from her, not after the ordeal she'd been through.

He returned to her side and rested his hand on her arm. "It's a dead body."

Shock turned her silent. Though only briefly. "Who?" she asked.

"I don't know. I don't want to remove the snow to reveal anymore of him and leave him vulnerable to the animals until I can get some men out here to dig him out."

She nodded. "That would be wise."

Though, she couldn't help but wonder if it was the man who had grabbed her. If so, that would mean he had not waited around to make another attempt to grab her. Why then had he tried in the first place? Had she misunderstood his actions? Had he been trying to help her? She'd never know if it was him, since she couldn't identify the man.

"Give me a moment to leave a marker so he can be found when I return for him," Tarass said and with a command in his voice, shouted, "Thaw, stay by Snow."

The pup hurried to her side to sit and lean against her leg.

After a bit of a search, Tarass uncovered a substantial rock. It took some effort to lift and place in front of the dead man's exposed arm, then he covered the arm with a good amount of snow. He had noticed that Snow tried to follow his movements, not always successfully.

He couldn't imagine living with such a debilitating affliction. He couldn't live constantly dependent on someone for the simplest need. It would make him insane. How she managed to remain strong was remarkable.

"All done," he said as he approached her.

"How far are we from your home?" she asked.

"Not far. There's a small rise up ahead—"

"And your home sits just beyond," Snow said excited to discover they were close.

"You remember from your only visit there?"

"I accompanied Sorrell when she visited with Twilla, the old woman who occupied your keep in your absence. Sorrell made sure to stir my memory of different places so I wouldn't forget what the surrounding area looked like. Though, she did mention that your keep had fallen into disrepair after being abandoned for several years."

"It has seen much improvement since my return. You'll see for yourself—" He caught his words to late.

"Hopefully, one day I will," she said. "We should go. I look forward to food and a warm bed tonight."

"I will make certain you get both. Stay close," he said as he walked around her.

Snow turned around and settled what sight she had on the gray shadow in front of her.

"Ready?" Tarass asked.

"Ready and eager," she said with a light laugh.

"We go," he said and started walking, marveling at her light humor in a difficult situation.

It wasn't long before they reached the rise. The slog up it wasn't easy and Tarass made sure to keep hold of Snow's arm. He stopped at the top, giving her time for her labored breathing to calm.

"Not far now and it's a good thing since it's starting to snow again," he said. "It's a light snow but it was a light snow that started this all."

"We should go," she said, her breath still labored, and Thaw agreed with a bark.

The distance wasn't far but the snow on the ground made the trek seem endless.

After a while Snow began to make out other gray shadows and the bigger they grew the more difficult it became to see Tarass.

When he was about to meld with the other shadows, she called out to him, "Tarass!"

His hand was on her arm instantly. "What's wrong?"

"You're beginning to blend with gray shadows that draw near."

"We are almost at the village and the keep is not far away," he said and his hand moved down along her arm to take her hand. "Hold tight to my hand."

She closed her hand around his and Thaw gave a bark.

"Keep up, Thaw," Tarass ordered and the pup grumbled and growled as he followed along.

Snow was surprised when they were met with an endless round of greetings as they entered the village. She thought most of the villagers would be inside, out of the cold.

"Tell me this is your bride and not just a woman to warm your bed for the winter?" a man called out with robust laughter.

Thaw planted himself in front of Snow as soon as Tarass stopped and let out a warning growl as the thick-chested man approached.

"This wisp of an animal will not make much of a meal," the man said.

Snow gasped, her hand falling away from Tarass to reach down and snatch Thaw up in her arms. "You will not dare touch my pup," she threatened.

Tarass shook his head. "Rannock, meet Snow of the Clan Macardle."

"The blind Macardle sister?" Rannock asked with a scrunch of his nose. "What is she doing with you?"

"I came across her in the snowstorm," Tarass said and continued before his friend could ask more questions. "I'll explain later. Right now, we need food and shelter from the cold that has burrowed into our bones. She'll be staying with us until I can return her home safely. I also need Runa. Snow was injured in a fall."

"I'll bring Runa to the keep," Rannock said and he took the wolf's headdress that Tarass handed him.

Snow turned her head toward Tarass. "You will command him not to harm Thaw."

"Rannock jests. He will not harm Thaw."

"I would never harm a creature who carries the name of our great god Thor," Rannock said.

Snow didn't correct him. It was better that Rannock thought Thaw was named after a god. The barbarians here would then surely leave the pup alone. Though, she did wonder if Tarass thought the same of Thaw.

She didn't take a chance, though, she held onto the pup.

The warmth of the Great Hall was most welcoming as was the bench Tarass set her on.

"Lord Tarass, welcome home," a woman's voice called out.

Snow couldn't help but hear in her voice how pleased the woman was over his arrival.

Tarass returned the greeting. "It is good to be home, Fasta. I need food and a hot drink to warm us and a room made ready for our guest. This is Snow of the Clan Macardle and she will be staying here until I can return her home."

"The blind Macardle sister?" Fasta asked.

"Aye and I will also need someone to assist her while she is our guest, since it will be impossible for her to maneuver her way around the keep on her own," Tarass said.

Snow wondered how they were familiar with her name when she hadn't been here since Tarass's return home. Though, perhaps, he had voiced his annoyance with her to his clan. A thought she disliked, but she also disliked when things were decided for her and in front of her as if she wasn't there or she had no say in the matter. But she wasn't home with family. She was at the mercy of the man she had verbally battled with on more than one occasion. And he was right about her making her way around his keep. She would hold her tongue unless, of course, there came a time she couldn't.

"I will see to everything, my lord, and will you want a bath prepared for you later?" Fasta asked.

Snow thought her question sounded more like an invitation and she couldn't help but think that Fasta and Tarass were more than lord and servant. Though, his direct and abrupt response squashed the thought.

"I'll let you know later, Fasta," Tarass said.

Snow had placed Thaw on the floor after she had sat and she looked around for the gray blur as she shed her cloak. It was quickly snatched off her and out of her hands.

"I'll see that you get clean, dry garments, and have your cloak taken to your room," Tarass said. "Thaw sleeps by the hearth." He took her hand and pointed it in the direction where the pup was curled up. "You are both safe. Do not worry."

"I appreciate your generosity, Lord Tarass," she said, relieved to see Thaw content.

He much preferred when she called him Tarass, but it was better she addressed him properly in front of others, so tongues wouldn't wag.

"I will get you home as soon as possible," he said and stepped aside as servants appeared with food and drink.

Snow's stomach grumbled at the delicious scents and Thaw gave a bark.

"I need food for Thaw," Snow was quick to say.

"He does not fend for himself?"

Snow recognized Fasta's voice. "No, I give him food from the kitchen in the morning and the evening."

"Dogs find their own food," Fasta said, though sounded as if she admonished.

"You will see that the pup eats as Snow says. He is our guest as well," Tarass ordered.

Snow caught the reprimand in Tarass's tone and she worried the woman might hurt Thaw. "I can share my portion with Thaw."

"Thaw will have his own food," Tarass commanded with such authority that he had Fasta apologizing.

"Forgive me, my lord, I am unaccustomed to the ways of this land."

Snow spoke up. "I would feel more comfortable giving Thaw some of my food."

"Do you suggest I would harm your dog?" Fasta accused.

"I don't know you or your ways and I will not take a chance with anyone harming my pup," Snow said defensively.

"Enough!" Tarass commanded. "No one will harm Thaw. He will be fed according to Snow's directions."

"As you say, my lord," Fasta said. obedience in her voice.

Snow remained silent, since Tarass's orders were clear.

"Bring food and drink now," Tarass demanded sharply.

Snow heard the woman scurry off.

"I will return shortly. You're safe here," Tarass said.

Snow listened as his footfalls faded away and she sat alone, or at least she believed herself alone. She had never been inside the keep when she had had her sight so she had no memory of it. Her one visit here when she was young had been in the summer and she and her sister had been left outside to occupy themselves.

Fear welled up inside her with such unfamiliar surroundings and not being around family or friends. There was no one here to rely on and Fasta was not someone she would trust. A shiver ran through her even though the fire's warmth surrounded her. She turned to the one who never failed to bring her comfort.

Before she could call Thaw to her, his nose was nudging its way under her hand on her lap. She scooped him up and hugged him tight, placing her face next to his.

"I need you now more than ever," she whispered and the pup licked her face and cuddled against her, letting her know he would not leave her side.

His closeness helped, but it didn't alleviate her fears. How could it when she was stuck here with the

Lord of Fire? A man who had made it clear that
obedience was expected above all else.

Fear ran a shiver through her and she jumped when
a wool shawl fell around her shoulders.

Chapter Seven

"You're still cold?"

"Tarass," she said, wondering why she hadn't heard him approach and worried that she hadn't. How would she detect when he was near if she couldn't hear his footfalls? Or had she simply been too deep in thought to have heard him?

"You shiver," he said, trying to ignore the way his name slipped in a whispery softness from her lips. A sudden thought narrowed his brow. "Does something trouble you, Snow?"

She went to make an excuse, any excuse than to tell him the truth, but she decided otherwise. "All is unfamiliar to me here." She was surprised when he sat beside her on the bench, feeling his leg press against hers, though she was not surprised to hear Thaw send him a warning growl.

"You know *me* and that's all that matters," he said softly and wanted to tuck the stray red strand of hair falling on her cheek behind her ear, but he didn't want to startle her. And it was far too familiar of a gesture if anyone should see it. "I give you my word you are safe here and you will have all the help you need in maneuvering the keep. My healer, Runa, will be here shortly and will see to making sure your wound is healing along with your many scratches. You will be returned safely and well-healed to your family."

73

Donna Fletcher

It can't be soon enough, Snow thought, but said, "I appreciate your help."

Snow was caught off guard when he moved away from her and she found herself missing his warmth. His leg hadn't been the only part of him to rest against her. As he had talked, his shoulder had pressed against her and his face had been so close she had felt his breath whisper across her cheek. And strange as it was to admit, she had felt safe with him there beside her.

A mixture of voices sounded and Tarass was quick to say, "Food and drink are here. Enjoy. I will return soon."

With chatter, the shuffling of feet across the floor, and the food being set on the table, Snow had difficulty distinguishing anything and Thaw must have sensed her distress, since he had remained on her lap staring and growling at anyone who got close to her.

"A dog at the table and we're called barbarians."

Thaw snarled and Snow calmed him done with a soothing stroke. She recognized Fasta's snappish voice and chose not to acknowledge it. She had no wont to argue. She wanted her time here done and be on her way home, never to return here again.

"Please extend your hand so I may introduce you to Nettle, and make sure that dog doesn't bite her," Fasta said with an annoyance that was obvious. "She has been assigned the chore of looking after you."

Snow no soon as raised her hand then she felt a hand grab it, give a shake, then heard Thaw's snarl stop and felt his head stretch up for what she assumed was for a rub.

"Nice dog. What's your name?"

74

"His name is Thaw," Snow said and he barked as though confirming his name.

"Named after the powerful god Thor. You have a lot to live up to."

Snow didn't bother to correct her.

"I'm pleased to meet you, Thor. You're a handsome one with that chestnut colored hair and those black paws."

Thaw gave a bark as if appreciating the compliment.

"It's so nice to meet you, Snow," Nettle continued. "I'll take good care of you. You are so beautiful and—"

"That's enough, Nettle," Fasta scolded. "Keep hold of your tongue and serve Snow well. I imagine she requires help feeding herself so see to feeding her."

Snow stared after the shadow that retreated.

"She's off to torment some other poor soul," Nettle whispered as she sat across from Snow at the trestle table. "There's a bowl in front of you and food on platters. Shall I help you?"

"Thank you, Nettle, but I can feed myself," Snow said and wondered over the woman. Curiosity always had her wondering what people, she'd only met since blind, looked like.

"Let me know what you need help with and I'll see to it," Nettle said.

With this stranger given the chore of helping her, Snow felt the need to know more about her. "You have a Scottish tongue while other tongues I hear are unfamiliar to my ear."

"Lord Tarass found me along the way home, starving and grubby I was. My mum threw me out after my da died. Told me she never wanted me and named me Nettle, after the stinging Nettle plant, because I stung her so badly when she birthed me. She was a mean one, never wanted bairns. My da did, though, and he was a good da." She laughed softly. "We often talked about running away but my da was too honorable a man to do such a thing. Not so my mum. She had a man in her bed a week after she buried my da and put me out a couple days after that. Though, not before she told me that I was like my da too ugly for anyone to ever love me."

"That's terrible," Snow said, appalled that any mum could do or say such horrible things to their child.

"I'm lucky Lord Tarass offered me a home and barbarian or not, I accepted it."

"Lord Tarass is a Scot as well," Snow clarified.

"Aye, but he mostly has barbarians with him," Nettle said softly as if she didn't want anyone to hear her.

"Are you telling tales again, lass?"

Snow smiled, recognizing the voice. "Twilla."

"It's wonderful to see you again, Snow," Twilla said and gave her a hug. "How are you doing? And who is this fine looking pup?" She reached down and gave Thaw a rub behind his ear.

Thaw gave the old woman a quick look and accepted her attention graciously, then plopped his head down and closed his eyes, deciding the woman posed no threat.

Snow had met Twilla before she had lost her sight and from what Sorrell had told her, the old woman hadn't changed much since then. She was old but saucy with long sliver hair she kept in a braid, rail thin, though not for a lack of a hardy appetite, and dark blue eyes with the keen sight of a hawk.

"I'm doing well, Twilla, and this pup is Thaw," Snow said. "And how do you fare?"

"At my age, as long as I wake each morning, I'm good," Twilla said with a laugh. "I heard Lord Tarass found you in the snowstorm and brought you straight here."

"And how lucky was I that he did," Snow said, going along with Tarass's explanation so that no one knew they spent time alone together in the cottage. It would make for a difficult situation, neither of them wanting to be forced to wed.

"No doubt you'll be with us a few days with this endless snow," Twilla said.

"It was a light snowfall when we arrived. Has the snow grown worse?" Snow asked, having hoped it hadn't since she wanted to return home as soon as possible.

"It's raging out there again," Twilla informed her, "but you're safe here now so no need to worry. Eat, you must be hungry." She leaned past Snow and grabbed foods, from different bowls and boards, to place in Snow's bowl. "There's some salted hake and cod, tasty bread, and stewed kale. What's this ale doing here? Go fetch a pitcher of the freshly made cider, Nettle."

Nettle was up and off in a flash.

"If you're wondering about Nettle, she's a good lass, though pokes her nose where it doesn't belong at times. She's ten and seven years and by all rights should be wed with bairns of her own by now, but she's a plain one and not built too sturdy so the men Tarass brought home with him don't favor her much and there aren't many Highland men that visit here. She'll probably spend her days serving here in the keep, but at least she has shelter and a clan to look after her."

Snow felt a kindred spirit in Nettle, like her, she was destined to be alone.

"Now eat and tell me about Sorrell and Willow and their new husbands," Twilla urged as she took a seat across from Snow.

Nettle returned with the cider and the three women talked and laughed and for a while Snow felt herself at home.

"What are you doing here, Nettle?"

The lass jumped and almost fell off the bench at Tarass's demanding question. "Fasta gave me the chore of helping Snow, my lord."

"Go get Fasta and return here with her," Tarass ordered.

"You need to eat and get some rest," Twilla said.

"I need no coddling, Twilla," Tarass snapped.

Twilla snapped right back at him. "Need it or not, I give it."

Snow ignored the two, placing Thaw on the ground along with her bowl that Twilla had filled again for her.

"Do not feed that pup until you have eaten," Tarass ordered.

"I have already eaten and I will feed my pup as I please," Snow said more calmly than she felt. "Has something happened? You snap and snarl as badly as Thaw."

"Nothing that concerns you," Tarass grumbled.

"I would hope you would tell me if it concerned me," Snow said.

"You need not concern yourself about anything."

"I am not your wife. I am a guest, though if I were your wife I still would demand the same. I will not be treated like a child. If there is an issue that pertains to me, I expect to be informed about it," she said, determined not to be ignored.

"If you were my wife, you would learn fast enough not to demand," Tarass said tersely.

Snow's response was just as curt. "Thank the heavens that's not now an issue nor will it ever be."

Twilla watched the play of words between the two and a smile crept over her face.

"You summoned me, my lord," Fasta asked, preventing anymore exchange between the pair.

"You assigned Nettle to Snow?" he asked his authoritative tone demanding an explanation.

"Everyone is busy with this snowstorm. She was the only one available," Fasta explained.

"I like Nettle, she will do fine," Snow said, upset the two spoke in front of the lass as if she wasn't capable of helping Snow. It reminded her of how people spoke in front of her with no regard to how their words would affect her.

"I will speak to you later, Fasta," Tarass said, dismissing her, then turned to Nettle. "You, Nettle, will hold your tongue while helping Snow."

"Why? Is there something you don't want her to tell me?" Snow asked.

"You, *Snow*, will not interfere when I speak to my servants," Tarass scolded.

Snow stood and Thaw hurried to her side, having gobbled down his meal. "I most certainly will when it concerns me." Thaw punctuated her words with a snarl. "Now if you will excuse me, I am in need of a wash and rest. Nettle, please help me to my room."

Nettle didn't wait, she hurried around the table and took hold of Snow's arm. "This way."

Tarass's hand swung out to grab hold of Snow's arm as she walked past him.

Snow turned her head to face him, at least she hoped she looked directly at him. "Don't bother to tell me about obedience. Need I remind you again I'm not your wife? I am a guest and I expect to be treated accordingly."

"It's a good thing you aren't my wife."

"Why? Would you punish me?"

Tarass leaned in close, his cheek brushing hers as he whispered, "I would take you to our bedchamber and teach you what it means to obey your husband."

Snow swallowed her gasp and where her response came from she couldn't say. "Or perhaps I would teach you what a wife not only needs but wants from her husband." She pulled her arm free. "Let's go, Nettle."

She walked away glad Nettle had hold of her arm, afraid her trembling legs would fail her.

"I'm assuming your anger has something to do with the body you came across in the woods?" Twilla asked after Snow was gone from the room.

Tarass swerved around to glare at the old woman. "How do you know about the body?" He shook his head while answering his own question. "Rannock."

Twilla ignored him and continued with questions. "Has the body been retrieved? Do you know the identity of the person? Friend or foe?"

"Enough, Twilla," Tarass ordered.

"No, it's not enough," Twilla snapped. "Year after year I stayed here, alone, and guarded your home so it would not fall to another clan. As long as a MacFiere occupied the keep, the surrounding clans had to protect it, so I stayed and kept my promise to your da. I thought all of you; your da, mum, and you would return. It broke my heart to learn of your parents' death, and I want revenge for their murders as much as you do. So for my loyalty alone, I ask that you tell me what goes on. I am sure your da told you that I know many of the MacFiere secrets and will take them to my grave, meaning you can trust me with anything... *my lord*."

Tarass remembered Twilla from his time here and she was right. His dad had told him to trust Twilla above all else. That she knew things about the MacFiere clan, things she had given her word would remain unspoken. And she had kept her word to Tarass's annoyance.

"The snowstorm is too dangerous to send the men out to retrieve the body," Tarass said.

"If it is too dangerous for your men, then it is even more dangerous for others. The body will be left undisturbed and buried even deeper than it already is."

"I want to think that, but I can't be sure. What if he wasn't alone? What if others search for him?"

"Unlikely in this snowstorm," Twilla assured him. "Where had you gone and why wear the garments of your mum's people?"

81

"I had trading talks with a tribe and with the weather turning bad, I didn't stop to change my garments," he explained, something he didn't do often, feeling he owed no one an explanation for anything. But Twilla had sacrificed for the clan and his da had talked about rewarding her upon their return home.

"An excuse," she said with a dismissive wave of her hand. "You prefer those garments over Highland garments. You do your da a dishonor by not wearing his plaid."

"I had forgotten how outspoken you are," Tarass said with a slight shake of his head.

"At my age, what difference does it make?" she said with a grin, sending her wrinkles folding into each other.

"How do you get Rannock to tell you things he shouldn't," Tarass asked curious she had gotten his friend to talk.

"I told him I'd find him a wife within a moon circle."

Tarass nodded. "Another thing I had forgotten… how you match people."

"It's a gift the heavens gave me. I know when I see people who are meant to be together." A sadness filled her face. "And I know when people are not meant to be together. It's a shame when two people, who are wrong for each other, are forced to wed. Unfortunately, it happens more often than not."

"So who is meant for Rannock?" Tarass asked.

Twilla smiled. "When the time is right, I'll let you know." Her smile grew. "I knew as soon as I saw your mum and da together that they were perfect for one another."

"They did love each other," Tarass said, recalling memories of them. "They were always holding hands, smiling, laughing, whispering to each other. They had something special."

"Love. They were deeply in love. I'm sorry you lost them both, but one would have never wanted to live without the other," Twilla said.

"I know. I thought the same when I found them. The attack had been brutal. I don't know how my mum and da found the strength to crawl to each other and grasp hands, but they did."

"Love. Love gave them strength." Twilla sniffed back a tear as she stood and walked around the table. She placed her hand on Tarass's arm. "Eat and rest, tomorrow is another day and hopefully the heavens will let me wake tomorrow."

Tarass laughed. "You've been saying that for as long as I can remember."

Twilla chuckled. "And I'm grateful the heavens have listened and continues to grant my request."

Tarass watched the old woman amble off, her gait not as slow as one would think for her eighty years.

"Tarass," she called out as she continued to the door. "So you are aware… you've already met your future wife. It's a perfect match you'll make, just like your mum and da."

Tarass stared after her, too stunned by her words to respond. His marriage would be a beneficial one, nothing like his mum and da's loving marriage. He wanted power and wealth. It was key to surviving in this harsh world.

Love had done little for his mum and da, though he had to admit he envied what they had shared. He had never seen anyone love with the strength and honor as his parents had. And he sometimes had wished he could find a love with the courage and conviction like theirs. But love such as theirs was rare and did not come along that often.

You've already met your future wife.

Twilla's prediction had him glancing in the direction Snow had gone, and he shook his head. "Impossible. We'd kill each other."

He walked off, continuing to shake his head.

Chapter Eight

"The wound does well as do your other less harmful wounds," Runa said.

"I appreciate you tending them." Snow closed the soft wool robe, that had been left on the bed for her, more tightly around her.

"I have heard what a talented healer your sister Willow is, I would love to meet and talk with her."

"I am sure she would enjoy visiting and learning from you."

Runa laughed softly. "I would be the one who learned from her. When Lord Winton, Tarass's father, announced that he and his family would be returning to Scotland, he invited anyone interested in joining him to become part of Clan MacFiere. Tarass had made strong friendships and many young warriors chose to go because of him. while I had no thought to leave my home. The old healer who taught me urged me to go and learn the healing ways of this land, and return with new knowledge. I arrived with the second group who came here. Already I miss home."

Runa laughed again, a little tinkling laughter and it made Snow wonder over her appearance. From what she could judge, Runa was taller than her, but not by much, and she had a gentle touch and a soft voice. She sounded young and for some reason Snow thought, more sensed, she was pretty.

"I have yet to speak with another healer, which is why I would very much enjoy meeting your sister."

"Willow will enjoy meeting you as well," Snow said and was unable to stop a sudden yawn.

"You need to rest and I need to return and see how the new bairn and exhausted mum is doing, the reason for my delay in seeing to you sooner. But you need not fret, as I said your wounds do well."

Nettle went to Snow as soon as the woman left. "Runa is a pretty one with long blonde hair and a gentle way about her. All the men chase after her."

Snow wondered if Nettle described Runa for her, since she was blind and couldn't see the healer. Or if it was just her way about her. She did appreciate a description, it helped to picture the person in her mind when she spoke with them, instead of staring at a blurry shadow.

"Runa says to rest, let me get you settled in bed."

"Not yet, Nettle, I need to dress and take Thaw out before I settle for the night," Snow said and got a bark from Thaw. "He's been patient but needs to see to his duty."

Thaw barked again as if in agreement.

"I can take him out right after I settle you," Nettle suggested.

"I appreciate the offer, but he won't leave me, not here in unfamiliar surroundings."

"He'll come with me, he's a good boy. Right, Thaw?" Nettle asked, casting the dog a smile. "Come on, Thaw," she encouraged with a summoning pat to her side as she walked to the door. "Come on, we'll go outside."

Thaw stared at her after parking himself between Snow's legs.

Nettle opened the bedchamber door. "Come on, Thaw, let's go. We'll be right back. Snow is safe here."

The dog didn't budge.

"What's going on here?" Tarass demanded, causing both women to jump at his unexpected appearance.

"Thaw has to see to his needs before settling for the night and he won't go out without Snow, my lord," Nettle was quick to explain.

Tarass shook his head and walked toward Snow. "I saw Runa. She tells me you need rest, but otherwise you do well."

"Aye, and I will rest as soon as I see to Thaw," Snow said and heard Thaw growl. "He'll bite you if you reach for him," Snow warned, knowing Tarass drew close by how loud Thaw's growl was growing.

"He can try," Tarass challenged.

Snow scooped Thaw up in her arms. "I need no help from you to see to my dog's care."

"I wasn't seeking permission," Tarass said, trying not to glance down at the robe she wore. It was obvious she was naked beneath and he couldn't stop the memories of her enticingly naked body from springing up in his mind.

He stood close, his blurry image consuming the space in front of her, and she suddenly felt vulnerable as she had when she stood naked in front of him.

"You are exhausted from your ordeal. I will take him outside and return him to you quickly. Tell him to go with me."

Snow realized Tarass was reminding her of the cottage when Thaw had gone with him after she had commanded the dog to go. Thaw had to go out and she needed Tarass to leave. She kissed the dog's snout and in a firm voice, ordered, "Go with Tarass, Thaw. He will take you out and bring you back to me. I am safe here. Now go with Tarass while I wait for you to return." She kissed him again, then placed him on the floor.

"Come with me, Thaw," Tarass commanded and the dog looked to Snow. "He looks to you."

"Go now, Thaw, and hurry back to me," Snow ordered.

Thaw gave a bark, walked in front of Tarass, then looked back as if letting him know he was ready to go.

"I'll have him back shortly," Tarass said, letting her know they were leaving. "Nettle, get her settled in bed, then bring her a hot brew."

"Aye, my lord," Nettle said and closed the door behind him and Thaw.

"Lord Tarass is such a handsome man. All the unwed women want him, but he has made it clear that he will wed to benefit the clan. A few don't care and warm his bed anyway. Tongues wag that there is no one woman that can please him, his appetite for coupling too great for a single woman to satisfy."

Snow realized now why Nettle was told to hold her tongue, she had a wagging tongue and could keep nothing she heard to herself. She had to smile, since at the moment that suited Snow just fine. Not that she needed to know about Tarass's thirst for coupling. She cared not who he coupled with, though she did feel sorry for his future wife unless of course the woman wouldn't care. She, on the other hand, would not want a husband who wasn't faithful. It would mean he did not love or respect her enough to be an honorable husband.

She had no worries, though. She and Tarass would never be husband and wife.

***

Tarass stood wrapped in his fur-lined cloak. The wind was strong and the snow fell heavily and surprisingly, Thaw was taking his time seeing to his needs.

"He prowls to learn the lay of the land," Rannock said as he approached Tarass. "He's got good instincts about him for a runt."

Thaw's head snapped to the right and he let loose with such an angry growl that it had both men's brows shooting up.

"I don't think he cares for you calling him a runt," Tarass said with a chuckle.

"I apologize," Rannock said with a bob of his head at the pup. "Anyone named after the god Thor should be treated with respect."

Tarass held back the laughter that rumbled up in him. If his clan wanted to believe the pup was named after Thor, so be it. Though, why they believed a Highland woman would name her dog after a Norse god he'd never understand.

"The men are ready to go as soon as the snow slows," Rannock said, turning his attention to Tarass.

"With night fallen, tomorrow will be soon enough. Unless it worsens overnight. If so, the retrieval of the body will have to wait for another time."

"At least the snow will keep it hidden."

"While the men are out there, widen your search some and see if you come upon two horses and another body," Tarass ordered.

"Another body? Horses? What goes on, Tarass?"

"Snow was on her way home when the snowstorm hit. From what she could tell, the man escorting her suffered a sudden death and the horses got away from her."

"So you found her wandering aimlessly around in the snowstorm?" Rannock asked.

"I did."

Rannock rubbed at his chin and his eyes narrowed. "You brought her straight here?"

"No questions, Rannock," he ordered.

Rannock's brow shot up. "I understand."

"So Twilla is finding you a wife," Tarass said and watched Rannock's cheeks burn bright red. The man was thick-chested, with arm muscles that his shirt had difficulty containing, good features, long, flaxen colored hair, and a scar that ran along the one side of his jaw, not to mention the various scars on other parts of his body, proof of what a ferocious warrior he was. But when it came to women, he was a complete failure.

Rannock's head hung low as he spoke as if he was about to admit to a horrendous crime. "I have no choice. You know better than anyone how difficult it is for me to speak to a woman."

"You mean to speak to a woman you think might make a good wife, since I know firsthand you have no trouble speaking to a woman otherwise."

Rannock rubbed at his chin, this time more roughly. "My tongue gets tied in knots. It's a curse. That's what it is a curse."

"Did you tell Twilla that you like Runa?" Tarass asked, casting a glance at Thaw, still taking his time.

"She'd have no interest in me," Rannock said, shaking his head to confirm his words to himself.

"You don't know if you don't try."

"And what of you, Tarass? Don't you want someone in your bed who wants to be there?" Rannock asked.

"I want what's best for this clan."

"What's best for this clan is to have a leader who has a wife who gives him lots of bairns and lots of love."

"I don't need advice from you," Tarass warned.

"I give it whether you want it or not. I always have and I always will, and you know that." Rannock reminded.

Tempering his annoyance, Tarass said, "And I count on it, my friend."

Thaw barked as he ran toward Tarass.

"All done?" he asked the pup without thinking.

Thaw barked and looked toward the keep, then barked again.

"We'll speak in the morning, Rannock," Tarass said and turned toward the keep.

91

Thaw bolted up the stairs and was in the room and on the bed curled beside a sleeping Snow before Tarass entered the room.

Nettle jumped out of the chair by the fire as soon as Tarass entered the room.

"She was already asleep when I brought the hot brew to her," Nettle said, casting an eye at the tankard that sat on the chest beside the bed. "I didn't want to disturb her so I left it there in case she woke. Snow told me earlier that it wasn't necessary for me to stay the night with her. She said she preferred to be alone. What do you wish me to do, my lord?"

Tarass didn't question the lass's words, since it would be just like Snow to say that. "You can leave, but return at first light."

"Aye, my lord," Nettle said, but didn't make a move to leave.

And she wouldn't until Tarass did and that thought annoyed him. It wasn't that Nettle didn't trust him, she was doing what was proper, not leaving a female guest unattended with a male. And if he dictated otherwise, tongues would wag and Snow's reputation could be ruined.

"Add another long to the fire, then you may take your leave," Tarass ordered and turned and left the room, taking the stairs to his bedchamber on the above floor.

With the night cold and the wind howling outside, Nettle added three more logs. One would burn fast, but three would take more time and keep the room warm. She walked quietly to the bed and adjusted the blanket over Snow's shoulder and smiled when she saw that

Thaw was cuddled against her sound asleep. She tiptoed out of the room, leaving the door slightly ajar so when she returned in the morning she could enter without disturbing Snow, if she still slept.

***

Snow struggled to make her way through the snowstorm. She couldn't see anything in front of her, but she heard Thaw barking and she had to get to him. She kept her hands stretched out in front of her and stopped abruptly when she heard a growl. Her hand went to her cheek, having thought she felt something wet at her face. Or was it the snowflakes hitting her cheek?

She saw it then, the dark shadow beside her, not a blurry gray shadow, but one as dark as night and she screamed, "Tarass!"

***

Tarass woke with a start, sitting up and glancing around his bedchamber. All was quiet, the fire low, which meant he had been asleep for some time. He couldn't understand what woke him, then he heard it.

A bark that drew closer until it was outside his door.

Snow!

He rushed out of bed and wrapped his plaid around him as he hurried to the door. Thaw continued barking and when he opened the door, the pup ran to the stairs, stopped, and looked back at him.

"I'm coming, Thaw," he said and rushed down the stairs behind the pup.

"Tarass!"

Fear like he hadn't felt, since the day he had learned of the attack on the village where his parents had been visiting and not knowing if they had survived, ran through him when he heard Snow scream his name in terror. He jumped over the pup and ran for her room.

He snarled as he flew into the room, ready to rip apart the person who dared to attack Snow and in his home where he'd told her she'd be safe. He was relieved to find no one there and hurried to the bed, seeing Snow was caught in a nightmare, battling the blanket caught up around her.

Thaw jumped on the bed, this time whimpering, worried over Snow.

Tarass yanked the blanket from around her and wanted to grab her and hold her tight, but he didn't, fearful it would continue to make her feel confined.

"Wake up, Snow, it's Tarass, you're safe. Wake up," he said and shook her gently by the shoulders.

Snow's eyes opened wide and she was ready to scream, seeing the shadow hovering over her.

"It's me, Snow. Tarass. I'm here. You're safe," he said quickly, seeing the fear that consumed her face.

Snow jolted up, her hands stretching out, connecting with his bare chest and hurrying to wrap her arms around his neck and hug him tight.

Tarass's arms instinctively went around her, hugging her to him just as tight. "A nightmare. You had a nightmare."

"I was caught in the snowstorm again. Someone touched me. It wasn't a gray shadow I usually see. This one was a dark blur, as dark as the night, and I knew it was evil."

"You're safe. You have nothing to fear here," Tarass assured her, though he didn't like that she had dreamt of a dark evil shape. Dreams could sometimes warn of things to come.

Snow's breathing began to calm, though her heart continued to thunder in her chest and her arms remained firm around Tarass.

Tarass kept tight hold of her. She wore a soft pale yellow nightdress that was a thin barrier between her breasts and his bare chest. Fear had puckered her nipples hard and they poked at him through the soft wool. And he silently cursed himself for even letting himself think about it.

Thaw crawled over, from where he waited at the foot of the bed, to nudge his head under Snow's arm. She let one arm fall away to rest on the pup's head and let him know all was well, then she hurried it back around Tarass's neck.

"You are safe with me. I'll let know one harm you," he assured her again.

Safe. How long had it been since she felt safe? When she had her sight. She hadn't felt safe since losing it, not knowing who was in a room with her, who approached her or how to simply maneuver through a room. She certainly hadn't felt safe in the snowstorm and if it hadn't been for Tarass, she would have never survived.

At the moment, with his arms tight around her and her body pressed firmly against his, she felt safer than she had ever felt since going blind, and she couldn't imagine letting go of feeling that secure, at least not yet.

Tarass gave no thought to releasing her, not until she was ready. He could feel her body still quivering with fear and he would keep hold of her until it dissipated even if it took all night.

He did think, however, talking to her might help calm her. "Thaw came and got me. I imagine he tried to wake you and when he couldn't, he ran for help." When she didn't say anything he continued, "You know my whole clan believes the pup is named after the mighty god Thor and will treat him with respect even though he snarls at most of them."

He felt a small chuckle run through her. "He is named after a winter thaw and not the god Thor, right? A winter thaw fits well with Snow."

"Thaw and I fit perfectly together," she said as she plucked her face out of the crook of his neck and turned it up toward his face and didn't realize the distance between their lips.

Her lips brushed his with a delicate faintness that could barely be felt, yet it sent a sharp jolt to her senses, sending a rush of tingles through her. Instinct had her hurrying back away from him, while passion-filled pokes urged her to return to his arms and his lips.

Thaw hurried into her lap as she moved away and she quickly snatched him up in her arms to hug him to her.

Tarass stood with haste and stepped away from the bed. The way her lips had brushed his could barely be called a kiss, and yet he had never felt as much intensity from a kiss than he had from the faint touch of her lips on his. If a faint touch could produce such a bolt of pleasure, what would a full kiss feel like?

He had to restrain himself from finding out, a good reason to leave, and yet he didn't want to. He wanted to linger in that shot of pleasure that aroused him enough to turn him hard. Another reason to take his leave quickly. And still...

"I will go. You need more sleep," he forced himself to say as he backed away from the bed and turned toward the door.

"Tarass," she called out.

"Aye," he said, not turning around.

"Thank you."

"Sleep," he snapped and left the room, closing the door behind him.

He went straight to his bedchamber and dropped back against the door after closing it. He couldn't get the faint touch of her lips on his off his mind. It had followed him all the way up the stairs and into his room and had turned him hard, rock hard.

He would get no sleep if he didn't ease his ache. He thought of the various women always available no matter when, day or night, but the thought of burying himself deep inside any of them brought him no satisfaction. Nor did the thought of poking anyone else.

Damn, he didn't want to poke anyone but Snow.

He shook his head. That wouldn't happen. That meant marriage and she was not what he wanted in a wife. Marriage to her brought no benefit with it and with her being blind she would be more of a hindrance than anything.

Snow was not for him, not for one night, not ever. He would do something he had never done. He would deny himself for tonight and tomorrow enjoy a good poke with some woman.

But as he slipped beneath the blanket in bed, the insane thought came again.

Nobody but Snow will satisfy you.

Chapter Nine

Snow had been surprised and relieved when Nettle told her that the snow had stopped and with the accumulation minimal, it had to have been sometime in the middle of the night. The villagers were now busy clearing paths. She'd also been surprised to hear that Tarass had taken Thaw out for his morning walk and the pup had actually gone with him without protest. But then Thaw had gone to Tarass for help last night, a sign that he trusted him.

She nibbled on her lips as she thought about last night and how her lips had brushed against Tarass's lips. Such a faint brush, yet such a jolt to her body. She shivered slightly at the memory. It had been the first time her lips had ever touched a man's lips and though it hadn't been a kiss, it had felt like one. At least she thought it did, but perhaps that was because she had never been kissed.

Thaw's growl caught her attention. He had sat by her side since entering the Great Hall, growling now and again, which meant someone passed by too close to her to his liking. She and Thaw had finished the morning meal hours ago and was told by Fasta she and the pup were to stay put and not get in anyone's way, since Nettle was needed for a chore in the kitchen.

Nettle had assured her she wouldn't be long, but it had been a while now and Snow was growing restless.

However, she didn't dare take a chance and try to maneuver without help in unfamiliar surroundings.

She tried to listen to what was going on around her, but there was too much noise and she couldn't distinguish all the sounds or shadows.

"I've brought you a hot brew," Nettle called out to let her know she approached.

Snow liked Nettle. While her penchant to detail everything might annoy others, it helped Snow greatly. It was like Nettle painted a picture for her and she could see it clearly. She had detailed the various foods on the table this morning and where each sat, making it easier for Snow to help herself.

"I've placed a tankard in front of you," Nettle said when she reached the table.

"Thank you, Nettle. You have been most kind and helpful and I do appreciate it."

"I enjoy assisting you and I'm grateful you don't mind my chatter. I sometimes think it's because I spend so much time alone that I talk endlessly when around others. I do try to mind my tongue, but I fear it's a helpless cause."

"It's the way you detail things that helps me see through your eyes. Like now, can you tell me what goes on? It almost feels like everyone is running about and I think I hear whispers but I'm not sure."

Nettle sat and slid close to Snow, keeping her voice low. "Everyone wonders about the two dead men Lord Tarass's warriors brought to the village."

"Two dead men? Are you sure?" Snow asked anxiously. She and Tarass had come across one body.

Where had the other body come from or had Tarass sent his men to search for Finn's body?

"Aye, many saw the bodies being carried into the village not long ago. It couldn't possibly be anyone in the clan since all are accounted for, so that's why tongues are wagging. That and Lord Tarass wears a scowl and Rannock wears a scowl as well, and it's never good when they both wear scowls."

Snow recalled meeting Rannock when she first arrived, his comment about Thaw not making much of a meal still on her mind.

"Do the people worry that they are in danger with the discovery of two dead men?" Snow asked.

Nettle chuckled. "Not with Lord Tarass leading them." She lowered her voice, her chuckle gone. "From the tales I've heard, Lord Tarass is not only a skilled warrior but a vicious one as well. There are not many who would challenge him and those who do have rarely lived to tell the tale."

"Is your tongue wagging again, Nettle?" Fasta scolded loud enough for all to hear.

Nettle hurried to her feet, but Snow responded before the lass could.

"We share a conversation, which I very much enjoy," Snow said with an air of authority her sister Sorrell would surely compliment.

"Nettle is needed in the kitchen. She can take you to your room before she goes, since she will be gone for some time," Fasta said.

Snow heard the annoyance in Fasta's voice and also the satisfaction it brought her that she was sending Snow to her room.

"That won't be necessary," Snow said. "I will wait here for Nettle."

"It will be quite a while before she is free," Fasta argued.

"It doesn't matter. I'm content here," Snow said and to make it clear she would hear no more, she turned away from Fasta to where she knew Nettle stood. "I will see you later, Nettle."

"Do not get in anyone's way," Fasta snapped. "Nettle, the kitchen… now."

It didn't take long for Snow to grow bored. At home she would be busy, walking through the village with Thaw, visiting with the new mums and the elderly, or spending time in her mum's solar secretly trying to teach herself to stitch while blind. She had loved to stitch when she had her sight. She would make garments for the new bairns born to the clan and make repairs on the garments of those in the keep, and she missed doing it.

Eleanor had come upon her one day and had offered to help guide her stitching with a row of loose stitches she could follow by touch, and it had helped greatly. It was still difficult to accept how dependent she was on others, but Sorrell had often scolded her when Snow had made mention of it.

"You're no more or less dependent than any of us," Sorrell would say. "We're family and each of us depends on one another for something."

But Sorrell and Willow had their own families now with others depending on them. While she should feel grateful she had James and Eleanor and the clan, there were times she felt more in the way of things than being helpful to anyone. No one certainly made her feel that way, but with her sisters marrying and James and Eleanor close to marrying, she had begun to feel more alone than ever.

Feeling tears well inside her, she stood. Feeling sorry for herself, especially in a strange place, would do her no good.

"Come, Thaw, you will guide me while we walk," Snow said, grabbing her cloak that lay beside her on the bench. She had brought it with her, hoping to get outside for a bit.

Thaw barked, then took hold of the hem of her tunic in his mouth and gave a tug.

She had realized when they had taken their morning walks that Thaw actually guided her. He'd bark and push against her leg to let her know something was in her path and, on several occasions, he had taken the hem of her tunic in his mouth and tugged her in a particular direction, keeping her on course. Pleased by his innate ability to help her, she had begun to teach him with commands.

Snow was pleased when Thaw got her through the Great Hall and outside with bumping into only one table. She wasn't surprised that none of the shadows around her offered any help since, Thaw still managed to snarl and grumble, with her hem in his mouth, if anyone approached them. For a little fellow, he presented the air of a mighty beast.

"Let's see if we can find Tarass," Snow said, curious to find out about the two dead men.

Thaw dropped the hem of her tunic, barked, then leaned against the front of her legs, preventing her from taking another step.

It was an action he took when warning her not to take another step, which meant he warned her of the stairs. They had practiced going up and down the stairs at home and Thaw had learned quickly. She had wondered if it was familiarity with his surroundings that had made it easy for him. She would find out now.

"Guide me down the stairs, Thaw," she ordered as she had done at home when teaching him about the stairs.

Thaw stepped down and barked once and Snow followed. With each bark he alerted Snow to another step until they had reached the bottom and Thaw barked several times, letting her know there were no more steps.

Snow smiled with glee as she reached down, rubbing and praising the pup. "You did wonderful, Thaw. I'm so proud of you. Now to find Tarass."

Though she had Thaw to help maneuver her, she couldn't help but feel apprehensive. When she had first arrived at Willow's new home, her sister had taken her around and detailed the village and keep to her and Thaw. It had helped greatly and it had taken only a couple of days for her to feel comfortable in walking around on her own. Of course, there were some mishaps along the way, but she had expected that.

Here, however, she had no idea where she was venturing. She had to rely completely on Thaw. No one offered assistance, but then again Thaw's snarls kept people at bay.

The snow scrunched beneath her feet as Thaw kept her on a cleared path that wound its way through the village. She was just rounding what she assumed was a cottage when something hit her cheek. Thaw snarled and snapped, but didn't leave her side, and Snow quickly raised her hand to her face.

Snow.

"My lady, I'm so sorry. We didn't see you. Our Apologizes. Please, I beg of you don't tell Lord Tarass."

The voice of a young lad continued begging for mercy.

"Was it meant for you?" Snow asked.

"Aye, there is only me—Roy—and Todd against three," he explained.

"That's not fair. You need another to help you. I can help," Snow offered, since she was already being reckless by taking a chance on walking through the unfamiliar village with only Thaw to guide her. Why not be even more reckless, or was she being impulsive, by taking a moment to have some fun?

There was a moment of silence before Roy finally spoke. "Excuse me, m'lady, but you're blind."

"I'm not addressed as my lady, my name is Snow, and if you tell me where to throw the snowball I just might hit someone or at least distract them so you can hit your mark."

A moment of silence followed again.

"There's also my pup, Thaw. He will force them from their hiding places," Snow said.

Hesitation proceeded the response. "What of Lord Tarass?"

"Is he here? He can join in the fun if he wants," Snow said with a chuckle and heard the young lad laugh.

"Lord Tarass is not about, but the three are watching us now," the lad said, keeping his voice low.

"Then have Todd fetch me a snowball or two and a few for you and him as well and tell me where to throw them and as soon as they retaliate, hit them with all your might," Snow said. "But don't let them see what you have planned. It needs to be a surprise attack."

"Aye, my… Snow," Roy corrected himself. "Todd is making the snowballs now. We should be ready soon to attack."

"And don't worry if I get hit with snowballs. They'll be expecting you to protect me. Go after them, and victory," she encouraged.

"Aye, Snow," he said with joyous enthusiasm.

"Listen, Thaw, I have a chore for you," Snow said.

The pup sat, leaning against her leg to let her know he was listening, and fixed his eyes on her.

"Follow the snowballs when I throw them and chase our foe from their hiding spot," she explained, though didn't know if the pup understood.

"All here say the pup is like the god Thor, mighty and fearless," Roy said.

Snow smiled. "That he is."

"We're ready," Roy whispered and slipped two snowballs to Snow. "Todd has a pile of snowballs a short distance to your right. Todd and I will walk away as if our talk is done. Standing where you are, if you throw straight ahead of you, you'll hit their hiding spot."

"Perfect. Now I'll wag my finger at you as if scolding you, then you and Todd can shake your heads and walk away."

"Aye," Roy said.

"Now be on your way," Snow ordered with a wagging finger and as soon as she heard Roy and Todd walk off, she threw the snowballs and smiled when she heard someone yell out.

"I'm hit. It's a ruse."

Snowballs started pelting her.

"Get them, Thaw," Snow ordered and dropped down to reach for the pile of snowballs and started throwing them.

Thaw charged toward the group, barking and snarling as if he was ready to tear someone apart. Snow was proud of him as she continued her assault and smiled when she heard one lad yell.

"Thor's coming for us... run!"

"Turn to your left and throw," Roy called out.

Snow did as the lad said, snowballs continuing to rain down on her as she enjoyed the fun of a good snowball fight just as she had done with her sisters throughout the years, even though Sorrell always won.

Snowballs flew, Thaw barked, laughter and yells were heard, then suddenly like a snap of the fingers all turned silent.

"What goes on here?" Tarass demanded.

Snow couldn't resist, she just couldn't. She turned until she caught sight of the large gray blur and let loose a snowball.

The sharp, loud gasps let her know she had hit her mark and she wasn't surprised when the gray blur moved to stand in front of her.

"Did you just hit me with a snowball?" Tarass demanded.

"Since I'm blind and can't see, you would need to be the one to answer that," she said with a chuckle and wasn't surprised to feel Thaw lean against her leg.

Tarass couldn't stop himself from smiling, though chased it away when he saw the shocked look on the young lads' faces.

"Be gone or be punished," Tarass snapped at the lads and they scattered, disappearing in a heartbeat.

"They've done nothing wrong," Snow said, coming to their defense, "except have some fun in the snow. Something I've missed myself and was pleased to enjoy with them."

"You could have been hurt," Tarass argued.

Snow laughed. "Snowballs bring laughter not tears."

"What are you doing walking out here alone?" he demanded, noticing how her flushed cheeks brightened the green of her eyes and how her lips appeared rosier in color from the cold. She didn't only look beautiful, she looked happy, and for a sheer moment he felt a spark of happiness himself and it startled him, not having felt it for some time.

"I was looking for you," she said.

"Where is Nettle? Why isn't she with you?" he asked, annoyed.

"Fasta ordered her to the kitchen," Snow said and thought she heard him swear.

"So you ventured out of the keep on your own?"

"Not on my own. Thaw is with me," she said, looking down to the pup still leaning against her leg.

Thaw barked.

Tarass shook his head, trying to comprehend how she put so much faith in the pup. "Why were you looking for me?"

"I heard about the two dead men that your warriors brought here and was wondering about them," she said.

"That doesn't concern you."

"It most certainly does," she argued. "Do you know who they are? Is one Finn? Do you know who the other one is? Did your men find my horses?"

"Leave the matter to me," he ordered.

"No!" she said, shaking her head. "If you did find Finn, I wish to express my gratitude and take him home for burial. And I would like to know about the other dead man. The one I tripped over. Or are both men unknown to you? And are they unknown to me?"

"I will discuss it all with James," Tarass said.

Snow was ready to argue, then thought better of it. She reached out to touch him and her hand landed on his shoulder. She trailed it down until her hand rested on his chest. "Please, Tarass, don't leave me in the dark and ignorant of this situation. I want to know what goes on. I will worry less knowing, rather than left to wonder."

Tarass couldn't believe his own words and that he smiled. "Only if you promise me no more snowball fights."

"A compromise," she said with a laugh. "Only snowball fights that you participate in."

"Agreed," he said without hesitation and was shocked that he did, but then she had looked to be having so much fun with the lads that he had envied her.

"I'll win you know," she whispered, leaning her head toward him,

He bent his head down. "You can try."

"A challenge I cannot refuse," she said with a soft laugh.

He chuckled himself. "A challenge I look forward to."

"We're ready," Rannock called out.

Tarass made the decision quickly. "The two dead men were taken to a hut. I'm going there now to see if they can be identified. You may come if you wish."

"Thank you, I do wish to see for myself." Snow sighed. "Though, I will need your eyes to help me see."

"My eyes are your eyes," he said, again his words surprising him. When had it become so easy to talk with this woman? They had fought and disagreed often. How had he come to enjoy her company? And why had he gotten the feeling that he missed seeing her this morning?

He took her arm to hook around his as they walked through the village together, Thaw keeping pace with them. He saw the curious stares and he knew they wondered about him and Snow. But he and Snow would never be, and it surprised him to feel a twinge of regret at the thought.

Rannock and Runa were waiting for him when he and Snow entered the hut.

Tarass acknowledged them both, letting Snow know they were there. He also acknowledged the one dead man.

"Finn is one of the men, Snow," Tarass said.

Sorrow filled her face. "At least you found him and he can have a proper burial. I hope his death was quick and he did not suffer when his heart suddenly stopped."

"It wasn't a stopped heart that took his life," Runa said. "It was a severe blow to the back of his head that killed him."

Chapter Ten

Fear wasn't a foreign feeling to Snow, but this time when it crawled over her it was slow and prickly as if hundreds of bugs were feasting on her. Had Finn's assailant not seen her in the snowstorm? Had the blinding snowstorm protected her from meeting Finn's fate? Or dare she believe that Finn had been the target? But why? Why would someone want to kill Finn? He was a good man and had been a good husband for twenty years before his wife took ill and died two years ago. They had no children, but the clan was his family and the young bairns loved him. He often whittled animals for them to enjoy.

"I don't understand," Snow said, shaking her head. "Why would anyone want to hurt Finn?"

"You told me that you weren't alerted to any problem until the horses stopped and you got no response when you called out to Finn," Tarass reminded. "You or Thaw heard nothing before that? And what of Thaw? Didn't he alert you to something being amiss?"

"The wind was howling around us and the snowfall so heavy that Finn attached a rope to the horses so we wouldn't get separated. I kept Thaw on my lap, tucked inside my cloak, worried I'd lose him in the storm and—" She paused, her finger going to her lips as she thought a moment. "Thaw did grow restless at one point, anxious now that I think about it, but I assumed it was the storm. Do you know the other dead man? Could he have been the one to attack Finn? What caused his death?"

"He'd been stabbed, though I don't believe that's what killed him. He had wrapped a strip of cloth around the wound and stopped the bleeding," Tarass explained. "He probably continued walking, perhaps searching for shelter and, weak from his wound, probably collapsed and froze to death."

"Is he known to anyone?" Snow asked.

"I don't believe so," Tarass said.

"I've never seen him," Runa said.

Rannock agreed. "I haven't either."

Snow found herself shaking her head again. "This is all so puzzling."

"If I have any further need of you, Runa, I'll send for you," Tarass said, dismissing the healer and with a bob of her head at him took her leave.

"Perhaps you should see if any of your clan knows this man," Snow suggested. Once again she was reminded that it was moments like these, not being able to see faces of those with her, that troubled her the most. Tones of voices compensated some, but not as much as seeing the expression on a person's face or in their eyes.

"A wise point," Rannock said and looked to Tarass, "though the painted markings on his arm does tell us he's not from around here."

"Permanent painted markings?" Snow questioned.

She was met with a moment of silence before Rannock responded.

"I could be wrong about them being markings."

"I'll take you back to the keep," Tarass said and took hold of her arm once again.

When they stepped outside, Snow stopped and asked, "Why did you have Rannock lie to me?"

"What are you talking about?"

"I'm blind, not ignorant," Snow snapped. "That pause before Rannock answered was obviously due to a silent exchange between you two. What is it you don't want me to know?"

"You are perceptive," Tarass said with a bit of annoyance. "Perceptive enough to realize if I didn't want you to know that I'm not about to tell you, since it doesn't concern you?"

"If it has anything to do with Finn's death, I should know," she argued.

"No, not you, your brother, and I will relay all to him when I return you home."

"As you say," Snow said and began walking.

After a moment of hesitation, Tarass fell in step surprised by her agreeable response. Not that he trusted it, nor her silence. Both warned him something was afoot.

"Leave this be, Snow," he ordered.

"As you say, Lord Tarass," Snow said.

Her obedience in this matter did not set well with him. "You're not going to obey me, are you?"

"I will do as you say as a guest in your home," she said with a pleasant smile.

"And once you leave here?" he asked, but knew what her reply would be.

"That doesn't concern you," she said.

His annoyance flared sparking his temper. "If you were my wife—"

"Thankfully, I'm not."

Thaw agreed with a bark.

They didn't speak again until they were in the Great Hall and Snow was seated at a table.

Tarass leaned down near her. "You will—"

"Stay put," she finished.

"I wish I could trust you to do that, but since I can't, you will have Nettle with you at all times until your departure." He called out to a servant, cutting off her response. "Bring Fasta and Nettle to me."

"When will you return me home?" she asked.

"Hopefully tomorrow."

"I look forward to it," she said with a generous smile.

He couldn't wait for her to leave. She was nothing but a problem, needing looking after all the time, getting into things she shouldn't, questioning him, and disobeying his every word. She was a nuisance and disruptive, and courageous, though blind. He shook his head. what was he thinking? He had to get her home. Get her out of his life.

"You summoned me and Nettle, my lord," Fasta called out.

Tarass stood, his tone stern. "Nettle is to remain with Snow at all times while she remains a guest here. She is to do nothing else but tend to Snow. Is that clear, Fasta?"

"Aye, my lord," Fasta said with a bow of her head.

With the unwavering obedience Snow heard in Fasta's quick response, she could tell that something

115

had caused the woman to obey without comment. More than likely the anger in Tarass's voice matched the angry scowl on his face.

"When will our guest be leaving, my lord?" Fasta asked.

"That doesn't concern you, Fasta, and I'm sure it's no problem with Nettle helping her since you constantly request she be placed elsewhere."

"She is a trying soul," Fasta said, defending herself.

Snow's heart ached for the young woman that she was made to feel unwanted and in front of others. She hated when others talked about her as if she wasn't there and to hear it done to another was too much for her to take.

"You're both extremely cruel people talking about Nettle that way while she stands here in front of you. You both should be ashamed of yourself," Snow scolded, her tongue sharp, and Thaw added a snarling bark as if agreeing.

Complete silence followed. Not a word or sound was heard.

Tarass leaned so close to Snow that their noses almost touched.

A rumbling growl started low in Thaw and began to grow in warning. Snow wisely ordered the pup to be quiet.

"Don't ever dare reprimand me," he ordered and when she went to speak, he pressed his finger to her lips. "Not a single word from you. You will obey me while you are here or I will see you confined to your room."

It took a strong willpower to hold her tongue, but the thought of such confinement and the dire warning in his voice, did much to stop her from responding.

"Rannock, my solar," Tarass ordered and walked off.

Snow wondered when Rannock had entered the Great Hall. She knew others were around, having heard footfalls scurrying about.

"Don't let her get into any more trouble or you'll be the one to suffer, Nettle," Fasta said.

"Aye," Nettle said, and held her tongue until Fasta was out of sight. "They're all gone."

Snow offered an apology. "I'm sorry if I've caused you trouble."

"You haven't. Actually, it was quite nice to have someone defend me."

"Sit and have hot cider with me," Snow offered.

Nettle sat and added more cider to Snow's tankard and filled a tankard for herself.

"This is a treat. I never get to sit and enjoy a hot cider," Nettle said. "So tell me, did you see the two dead men? Do you know either one?"

There was no pretense to Nettle, she was who she was and Snow liked that about her.

"One man was a friend and belonged to my clan," Snow said.

"I'm so sorry. I will offer a prayer for him," Nettle said.

Snow heard the genuine sympathy in her voice and it was comforting. "I appreciate that, Nettle."

"You didn't know the other man?" Nettle asked.

Snow shook her head, then stopped. "I don't believe so, but then no one detailed his features to me. Although Rannock made mention of a painted image on one of the man's arms."

"One like Lord Tarass's?"

"Lord Tarass's arm holds a painted image?"

"A crude blue arrow runs on the inside of his forearm, from the fold to the wrist. It can be seen clearly when his sleeve is rolled up or when he's bare-chested. Naturally, I asked someone about it and was told that the arrow depicts one of the sacred ruin symbols of the heathen barbarians. It's often worn on their shields when they go into battle. It supposedly represents victory. Maybe that's why Lord Tarass is so victorious."

The image Nettle had painted of the arrow made Snow realize just how strongly Tarass had embraced his mother's heritage. It made her wonder if the dead man had been the one Tarass was supposed to meet with and he didn't want it known or perhaps he didn't know the identity of the man.

"Did Rannock detail the painted image for you?" Nettle asked.

Snow thought it best she didn't tell Nettle that Tarass forbid it.

"No, he didn't."

"I could detail it for you and describe the man," Nettle offered.

Her offer was far too tempting. "I don't want to get you in trouble."

Nettle laughed. "I'm always in trouble no matter what I do." She lowered her voice. "We can be quick.

We'll be there and back before anyone knows we're gone. And I'll make sure to tell one or two of the servants here that we go to Runa since your wound pains you. We can stop there after seeing the bodies."

Snow couldn't help but smile. "You remind me of my sister Sorrell. That would be just the thing she would do."

"And would you go with her?"

"Absolutely," Snow said and stood.

Thaw roused himself from where he lay sleeping at Snow's feet.

"We go on an adventure, Thaw," Snow said and the pup barked.

***

Nettle was true to her word, letting a couple of the servants know they were going to see Runa should anyone ask. And she kept a quick pace as she kept hold of Snow's arm and hurried her through the village, Thaw keeping close to Snow.

When the pace slowed, Snow understood they neared the hut.

"A body is being carried out," Nettle whispered.

"I think that would be Finn. He's probably being prepared for the journey home."

"Bless his soul," Nettle said with a bob of her head. "It's the perfect time to sneak in. No one guards the hut."

"Then let's hurry," Snow said and looked down where a blur of gray sat against her leg. "You wait outside, Thaw, and let us know if anyone comes this way." She had to tell him again when he went to enter the hut with them. "Guard, I won't be long."

Nettle began detailing the dead man as soon as they entered. "He has height to him and is thick in size, long brown hair, fair features, nothing that distinguishes except for his nose. It's crooked, probably broken a time or two. His garments are like those Lord Tarass wears when he dons his mother's peoples' dress."

"Is there a headdress of an animal laying nearby?"

"No," Nettle said after looking around.

"The painted image," Snow reminded.

"Oh my goodness," Nettle said. "The markings are all over his arm and up the side of his neck. I've never seen anything like it. I thought the markings would be crude, but they're quite beautiful. A skillful hand certainly had to have done such an intricate design, though I have no idea what it all represents."

"We better go," Snow said and Nettle agreed, taking her arm and leading her out of the hut.

"Good Lord," Nettle whispered as she directed Snow around something.

"What's wrong?"

"Lord Tarass is in the distance and he stopped when he saw you. He now heads this way."

"Are we close to Runa's cottage?"

"Not at all," Nettle said.

Fear trembled the young woman's voice and Snow felt bad that she was the cause of it.

"He's looking straight at us," Nettle warned.

"Then we stay where we are and I will do the talking."

"What are you doing here in this area when I was told you were in pain and needed to see Runa?" Tarass demanded.

"My fault."

Snow recognized the voice. It was Twilla.

"I told them Runa was busy tending someone and offered them a hot brew in my cottage while they waited. Besides, Snow appeared too pale to continue walking. I figured after she rested a bit, I'd see that she got safely to Runa."

Tarass looked to Snow. She did look pale. "Your wound pains you?"

She didn't like to lie. Lies had a way of growing and suddenly erupting and he did sound concerned. So she went for the truth in a roundabout way. "The pain has eased." And the pain had eased... since yesterday.

"I'll take you to Runa," Tarass said.

"Let me give her a hug first, she's such a sweet thing," Twilla said. "Nettle, bring her to me. These old bones ache too much for me to take another step."

Nettle took Snow's arm and walked her the few steps to Twilla, then stepped away.

Twilla hugged Snow and whispered in her ear. "Be careful, don't provoke the Lord of Fire or you may release the devil himself."

Snow forced a smile, the old woman's warning words frightening and alarming her, but she didn't want anyone to see that. James had warned her time and again about making the Lord of Fire angry.

"You don't know what he's capable of, Snow," James would say.

121

Tarass had shown her some kindness so was he truly as formidable as so many warned? And did she want to take the chance and find out?

Tomorrow.

She would go home tomorrow and this all would be over.

***

Snow laid in bed unable to sleep, the day's events churning in her mind. She felt a twinge of guilt when she had seen how concerned Tarass had been when he had taken her to Runa.

Runa had even commented when they had been alone for her to examine Snow's wound that Lord Tarass had seemed so anxious she had worried that he would remain in her cottage to see the wound himself. Not a proper thing for him to do at all. Still tender to the touch, Runa assured her that the wound showed no signs of turning putrid. She had been glad to hear that since she couldn't see the wound herself.

Thaw laid sound asleep at the bottom of the bed, having moved there when Snow had disturbed him with her twisting and turning. She wished sleep would capture her and hug her tight, ridding her of endless, frustrating thoughts.

It seemed like forever before her eyes finally grew heavy and sleep drifted over her, and she was plunged once again into a nightmare.

The snowfall blinded, Snow couldn't see anything. She called out for Thaw, but he didn't answer her. She took a step and heard the snow crunch beneath her boots. She kept taking cautious steps one after the other, yet felt as if she remained in the same place since nothing changed around her.

One more step, one more, then another and another, she silently encouraged herself and thought she saw the snow clearing up ahead. She took an eager step and suddenly felt herself tumbling to the ground. She hurried to get herself up out of the snow, but plopped down on her bottom when she realized her foot was stuck on something. She stretched her hands expecting to find her foot stuck beneath a tree branch. She was shocked to feel cold flesh and even more shocked when she suddenly was able to see what trapped her. It was an arm and painted on the inner forearm from fold to wrist was a drawing of an arrow.

She started screaming. "Tarass! Tarass! Tarass!"

Thaw flew off the bed and out the door, making a mad dash for Tarass's bedchamber, barking all the way up the curving staircase.

Tarass was at the door by the time the pup reached it, and Thaw hastily turned and headed back down the stairs, Tarass nearly on top of him.

He rushed to the bed and yanked Snow up in his arms, wrapping her tight against him. "I've got you. You're safe, Snow. You're safe."

She flung her arms around his neck and she had no intention of letting go of him. He was alive and there with her and that was what mattered. The thought jolted her. She had been terrified to think Tarass was dead. What did that mean? Did she care for this man?

Impossible.

123

They did nothing but argue and disagree, and yet when frightened she looked to him for comfort and safety. When in his arms, she felt the safest she had in years. Like now. There was no other place she wanted to be but here warm and snug in his arms, and protected.

"It was a nightmare, nothing more. I'm here and you're safe," he assured her again.

His words soothed and his arms comforted, and she snuggled her face in the crook of his neck.

The way she settled herself against him, he knew she didn't plan on going anywhere and either did he. He would stay with her and comfort her for as long as she needed him to.

He situated them comfortably on the bed and pulled the two soft blankets over them. He would wait until she was in a peaceful slumber before he left her.

He settled himself around her, forgetting one thing… he had run naked from his bedchamber.

Chapter Eleven

Tarass woke with a start, jolting Snow awake since she was wrapped in his arms. He hadn't known what startled him until he looked at the bottom of the bed to see Thaw standing there, wagging his tail at Nettle.

Tarass saw the shock in the young woman's wide eyes and the way her mouth hung open. "You will say nothing about this, Nettle," he ordered sharply.

Snow hurried away from Tarass, her hand rushing to push at his naked chest, but as she did, he moved and her hand fell low on his stomach. She realized then that he was completely naked and she hurried her hand off him, yanking the blanket up around her as she scrambled to move away.

He grabbed her before she fell off the side, and she stiffened. "Any further and you'll fall out of bed."

He let her go, not expecting a response, not wanting one. What he wanted and needed was for Nettle to keep what she saw here a secret and that might be impossible for her to do.

Tarass left the bed, not caring about his nakedness. He walked to the door and shut it and saw Nettle pale.

"I'm going to warn you again, Nettle. You are to say nothing about what you saw here, since nothing happened between Snow and me. If you allow your tongue to wag, I will be forced to wed Snow, and you will lose your tongue. Do you understand, Nettle?"

"Aye, my lord. I will say nothing," Nettle said a quiver in her voice.

"I'll have your word on that."

"You have my word, my lord," she rushed to say.

"Make sure you keep it or you'll have no tongue to wag," he threatened again and walked out of the room without saying another word.

Snow hurried to speak when she heard the door close with force. "I had a nightmare and Thaw went and got Tarass. He comforted me and we must have fallen asleep. Nothing happened between us. He doesn't wish to wed me and I don't wish to wed him."

"I don't want to lose my tongue and I don't want you forced into marriage. I saw nothing, so there is nothing for me to say."

"Thank you, Nettle. I owe you much," Snow said with relief and a touch of sorrow, wondering how one moment Tarass could be so kind to her and the next so cruel.

"It is I who owe you. It has been such a pleasure serving you and I will miss you when you go. You spoke up for me when no one else did, and this morning, on my way here, two women who never said a word to me, approached and talked with me. Of course, the talk was about you and the snowball fight you engaged in yesterday and how much the young lads enjoyed it, but at least they talked with me and actually seemed to enjoy it. It felt so good to be included in chatter with others."

"How nice for you, Nettle, and I will miss you as well," Snow said and eased herself out of bed, hoping today she would be able to go home. "It isn't snowing again, is it?"

"No, and hopefully we're spared any more snow, giving you a chance to get home."

"Time to dress and get Thaw outside," Snow said, guiding herself along the side of the bed to the end and reaching for her garments that Nettle had left on the chest in front of the foot of the bed.

The door suddenly burst open and Tarass stood there. "Come, Thaw, outside with you."

"I will see to him," Snow said, feeling the need to keep Thaw with her.

"See to yourself. When you're done meet us in the Great Hall," Tarass ordered. "Now tell Thaw to go with me."

His snappish tongue warned her she was better off not arguing. "Thaw, go with Tarass. He will take you outside."

Thaw trotted over to Tarass and right out the door.

"Will I be able to go home today?" Snow asked.

"I'll make sure of it," Tarass said and hurried the door closed behind him to follow Thaw down the stairs.

He was angry with himself for having foolishly fallen asleep in her bed last night and for being naked. He was also angry that he had slept so comfortably beside her that he hadn't woken during the night, something that had become a habit of his, though not with Snow. He had slept soundly and felt more rested than he had in some time.

Never had he slept through the night when he had shared a bed with a woman. And he had always made sure to take his leave of a woman before sunrise. It was an action that he felt made it clear that he wasn't interested in any more than what they had shared that night.

The pup rushed through the Great Hall and he had no problem keeping up with him. He was glad for the cold air that stung his face when he stepped outside.

"Angry so early in the morning?" Rannock asked as Tarass descended the stairs.

Tarass didn't like when he allowed how he felt to show, but Rannock was a friend and often saw what others didn't.

"Women can annoy," Tarass said.

"You're only finding that out?" Rannock asked with a laugh. "Though I've heard many a man say, if you're annoyed with a woman watch out, it might be you're annoyed with yourself for falling in love with her."

"Are you saying that I'm falling in love with Snow?" Tarass snapped with an angry snarl.

"That set a burr in you." Rannock laughed again. "What happened?"

"Nothing. She goes home today. I want six warriors to ride with us. Have them ready. We leave after the morning meal," he ordered and turned away from Rannock, calling out for Thaw who was already a distance ahead.

Tarass walked with a strong gait and a deep scowl through the village. Everyone left him alone, not even calling out a greeting to him. All knew it was best to leave him be when he got angry. Otherwise his tongue would unleash a lashing that left far worse scars than any weapon.

His own foolishness had nearly cost him all his well laid plans. He intended to make a beneficial marriage, not be forced into one, and he certainly had no use for a blind wife. He needed Snow gone so she could no longer distract him. He needed to keep his attention focused. It troubled and worried him that someone had killed Finn and while with Snow.

"Thaw!" he snapped, ready to return to the keep and when he heard no bark, he looked around and didn't see the pup. "Thaw!" he called out and still the pup didn't answer. Had he run back to the keep without Tarass seeing him? "Thaw!" he shouted again.

Tarass headed back to the keep, asking some of the villagers if they had seen the pup, but none had. He hurried up the stairs and called out for the pup as soon as he entered the Great Hall.

"Thaw!"

Snow shot to her feet with such force she sent the bench rocking. "You've lost Thaw?" she cried out and hurried around the table, stretching out her arms. "Nettle, get me outside."

"Aye," Nettle said.

"Get her a cloak," Tarass ordered sternly. "I'll take her out."

"How could you lose him?" Snow asked, panic rising in her.

"He's not lost. He has to be somewhere in the village. I thought he might have returned without me," Tarass found himself explaining, something he never did.

"You weren't keeping watch on him," she accused, fear causing her voice to rise.

Tarass took hold of her arm and kept his voice tempered, seeing and hearing how worried she was that the pup could be lost. "He's never wandered off far before. Something must have caught his interest."

"And if you had been watching him, you would not have lost him."

"He's not lost. He's somewhere in the village and I will find him," Tarass said as if it was already done.

"*We* will find him," she corrected.

Nettle returned with her cloak and one for herself.

"You need not help, Nettle," Tarass said.

"She comes with us," Snow ordered, slipping on the cloak Nettle had handed her.

Tarass bent his head, his lips near to her cheek. "Command me again and you will wait in your bedchamber while I search for Thaw."

Snow turned her head enough that she hoped she looked him in the eye. "Try keeping me from finding Thaw and you will regret it."

"You dare threaten me?"

"It's not a threat. It's a promise."

"I'm a lucky man not to have to wed you," he whispered.

"Pray that your luck continues and we find Thaw or—"

"Or what?" Tarass challenged before she could finish.

Her sister Sorrell popped into her head and words she would use shot out of her mouth. "Or I'll cut your balls off.

Loud gasps echoed around the room, though Snow thought she also heard a chuckle in there somewhere.

"Be careful, Snow, you don't want to know why they call me Lord of Fire."

His harsh whispered threat sent a shiver through her.

"We will find, Thaw, you will eat, then I will take you home."

"I have no appetite, I'd rather go home after we find Thaw," she said, keeping as calm as she could.

"You'll eat first or you won't go home until tomorrow," he ordered.

If she could see, she would walk home, but that wasn't possible, and she wisely kept quiet.

Tarass couldn't believe that she had spoken to him the way she did, but then he hadn't dared thought that she would tell his da that he lied when they had been young. Snow had surprised him then as she did now and all the times when he had stopped at the Macardle keep and Thaw would growl and bark endlessly at him. She would defend the pup regardless of what he had threatened.

Giving it thought, he realized when those Snow loved were threatened, she spoke up without thought to any consequences, and that took courage. And in that sense, she would make an excellent wife, since a husband could count on her, defending him and their bairns.

Tarass kept a firm hand on her arm as they descended the stairs so she wouldn't fall in her haste, some spots slippery from the snow. He wasn't surprised when Snow started shouting for Thaw as soon as they reached the bottom.

"Thaw! Thaw! Come here at once!" she yelled, worry ringing out with her command. "Now, Thaw!"

They took only a few steps when they heard a bark.

"Thaw!" Snow called out again, her heart pounding in her chest that the bark came from him.

The bark grew stronger and closer and Snow continued calling to him.

"There he is," Tarass said as soon as the pup came into view.

Snow let out a heavy sigh as if she'd been holding her breath far too long and she gripped Tarass's arm, her legs growing weak with relief.

Thaw barked continuously as he ran toward Snow, and she smiled. She truly believed the pup understood that she couldn't see and did what he could to help compensate for it.

Snow reached down to scoop him up as soon as he jumped against her leg. "Where were you? You had me so frightened."

Thaw licked her face, his tail wagging furiously as happy to see her as she was to see him.

"You can't wander off like that," she scolded much too softly and with a smile.

"His curiosity grows along with him just like with a young bairn. Though, I don't think Thaw would have wandered off if he was with you," Tarass said. "He's far too protective of you."

Snow hugged Thaw tightly and lavished his head and snout with kisses before he wiggled in her arms to be released. When she placed him on the ground and he started barking, she understood.

"Your little adventure made you hungry," she said with a laugh. "You want to eat?"

Thaw barked several times in response, then grabbed the hem of Snow's shift and tugged to help her up the stairs.

"Nettle, take the hungry pup and feed him while I help Snow up the stairs," Tarass ordered.

"Go with Nettle, Thaw. She will see that you eat," Snow said, not wanting to keep the pup waiting while she made her way up the stairs.

Thaw barked and darted up the steps.

"He really is hungry. He's already at the top," Nettle said and hurried her way up the stairs, though with more caution than Thaw.

Snow was grateful that Nettle let her know what went on. It allowed her to see instead of wonder what went on around her.

Tarass took her arm again. "Hold tight. The steps are slippery in spots and I don't want you to slip and fall."

Snow reached out and rested her hand over his. "Before we go, I want to apologize to you. I was so frightened that Thaw might be hurt somewhere or that I'd never see him again that I behaved badly and in your own home." She shook her head. "I should have never done that and I am truly sorry."

Tarass was shocked not only by her genuine apology but by the fact that she felt she behaved badly and sought to correct it. He would never apologize or even admit there was reason he should. He recalled what she had said to him one time when he was at the

133

Macardle keep and he demanded she apologize for calling him pigheaded.

I apologize for calling you pigheaded. And I apologize for the next name I call you and the one after that, since I'm bound to insult you again.

"You once extended apologies for future names you'd call me, so I believe you're well covered when it comes to that," he said.

Snow cringed. "Names are one thing, threatening to—"

"Cut off my balls," he said with a smile he was glad she couldn't see.

She cringed again. "My sister Sorrell popped into my head."

"That explains it," Tarass said and couldn't stop from laughing. "Though, I don't believe you need your sister to be as courageous as you are."

She tilted her head to look at what she hoped was his face. "Or as foolish."

"You are no fool, Snow. You protect those you love no matter the consequences and that takes courage. A husband and bairns would be well-protected with a wife like you."

"No man wants a blind woman for a wife," she said but kept the thought that followed to herself. *Especially you.*

She was grateful her stomach chose to grumble loudly.

"You're hungry. You need to eat and it's cold out here," he said and placed his hand to the small of her back while he kept firm hold of her arm as he guided her up the stairs.

They were a couple of steps away from the top when Rannock called out to him.

"Lord Tarass, a troop approaches."

Tarass turned and instinctively Snow turned with him, her boot catching on a patch of ice.

Her foot went out from under her and she felt herself tumble backward, then she felt a wrench to her arm. The next thing she knew… she was wrapped in his arms as they went tumbling down the stairs together.

Chapter Twelve

"Tarass?" Snow called out, her sight blurrier than usual.

"I'm right here." Tarass gave her a squeeze, his arms still tight around her.

Snow realized then she was lying on top of him and her fright drifted away.

"Easy with her. I don't know if she's hurt," Tarass said.

Snow felt herself lifted off Tarass and her fright returned.

"That is so nice of you, Rannock, to help Snow."

Snow was relieved to hear Nettle's voice letting her know what was happening.

"Are you hurt?" Tarass asked, getting to his feet and placing a hand on Snow's shoulder.

Snow winced from the unexpected pain.

"I knew I wrenched your shoulder keeping as tight a hold on you that I did." He had felt the abrupt pull when she had fallen backward,

"It's a good thing you did or my fall might have been far worse."

"She's right," Rannock said. "Keeping hold of her and wrapping yourself around her softened her fall."

"Are you hurt?" Snow asked, anxiously. Worried he had hurt himself protecting her.

Her hand rushed up to touch him and find out for herself. It landed on his cheek and she ran her fingers slowly and methodically over his face, feeling along his cheeks, forehead, and jawline, then up the back of his neck.

Tarass stopped her there, grabbing her hand. "I'm good."

He should have stopped her sooner, her soft touch leaving a titillating tingle on his face and causing his loins to tighten.

"The troop will be here soon," Rannock reminded as he watched the intimate exchange between the couple.

"Someone looks for shelter after the storm?" Tarass asked.

"Someone looks for something, but it's not shelter. James Macardle arrives shortly," Rannock said.

"My brother is here?" Snow asked, turning to where she heard Rannock's voice and settling her eyes on the large, gray blur.

Tarass looked down at Snow's hand that had gripped his arm at the news. It was almost as if she were anchoring herself to him, not wanting to be separated from him. And it frustrated him that he liked the thought.

The door to the keep opened and Thaw came rushing out and down the steps barking furiously.

"He would not cease his incessant barking," Fasta said and, glad to be rid of the pup, hurried to shut the door.

Thaw jumped up against her leg and Snow reached down to pat him, wincing as she did, the pain catching at her shoulder.

"You will see Runa," Tarass said, giving her no choice in the matter.

"After I see my brother," Snow said, knowing that arguing with him would do little good.

"The relief on your brother's face at seeing you as he approaches, shows how much he has worried about you," Nettle whispered at her side.

Snow was glad to hear Nettle detail the scene for her. It was so difficult not being able to see what was going on. She was learning to adapt as best she could, but there were times she was simply impatient. This was one of those times. She would love to have seen the look on James's face herself. She didn't think of James as her half-brother. He was her brother and he cared and protected her as a brother should.

"He is getting off his horse in haste and it appears he is headed straight for you," Nettle said.

"Enough talk, Nettle," Tarass snapped.

Snow wanted to tell Tarass to let Nettle be that she helped her, but she was suddenly grabbed in a tight hug. If Nettle hadn't alerted her to James's approach, she would have startled in fright.

An unexpected pain stabbed at her side and she assumed her previous wound had suffered in the fall.

"Thank God, you're safe," James said. "When the horses returned without you and Finn, I was beside myself with worry. The raging snowstorm didn't allow for a search. It wasn't until this morning we were able to start searching. I was losing hope when our tracker picked up a trail beneath the snow that led here. Where is Finn?" He looked around searching for him and met with Tarass's stern face. "Forgive me, Lord Tarass, I was so relieved to see my sister safe that I failed to greet you properly, though I must say I am in your debt for giving my sister shelter."

"Lord Tarass rescued me, James," Snow explained. "I was alone and got lost after Finn died—"

"Finn is dead? What happened to him?" James asked, shaking his head, shocked, and trying to comprehend what he'd been told.

"This shouldn't be discussed out here," Tarass said and pointed up the stairs to the keep. "And I'm sure you and your men could do with a hardy drink or two and some food."

"That's generous of you, Lord Tarass," James said.

James went to take Snow's arm, but Tarass reached out, getting hold of her first.

"Your sister just took a tumble down the steps. I want to make certain she gets up the stairs safely," Tarass said.

"Are you all right?" James asked, resting his hand on her arm.

"Aye, I am, worry not," Snow said.

"I've done nothing but worry about you since the horses returned." James kept pace with Snow and Tarass as they climbed the stairs. "We've all been worried sick about you. Eleanor had wanted to come with me on the search, but I advised her to remain home in case you arrived while I was gone."

They entered the Great Hall, James's small troop following him in, the tables already being set with pitchers of ale and hot cider and bowls of food.

Tarass slipped Snow's cloak off and went to hand it to Nettle when he saw the young woman pale.

Nettle pointed to Snow's side. "She's bleeding,"

Snow went to touch her side, but Tarass grabbed her hand.

"Leave it," he said. "Nettle, go fetch Runa."

James got upset seeing the patch of blood. "Something must have stabbed you when you fell."

"It's from a previous wound," Tarass said.

"A previous wound?" James asked. "When? How?"

"While my healer tends her wound, I'll explain everything to you, James," Tarass said.

Snow didn't like that she wouldn't be present when the men talked. But what did she have to worry about? Tarass didn't want to wed her so he would make sure to omit many things.

Runa came rushing in and hurried straight to Snow.

"Nettle, take Snow and Runa to Snow's bedchamber and help her with whatever she needs," Tarass ordered.

"Aye, my lord." Nettle reached out and took Snow's hand, and whispered, "There are many about, it is best I guide you."

Snow nodded and went with Nettle, Thaw following close by.

They weren't far away when Snow heard James say, "Tell me all of it."

***

"With your wound tearing open and the bump on your head from the fall, you shouldn't travel home today," Runa said after examining her.

"Willow's place is close, I'll have James take me there, then she can tend me," Snow said.

"Still, the journey will not be easy with the amount of snow that has fallen. It would be wiser to remain here," Runa advised again.

"Thank you for your advice, Runa, but I prefer to go home, or at least to my sister's keep," Snow said.

"I understand and I look forward to meeting Willow one day," Runa said. "I'll secure your wound with a thicker and tighter bandage. Hopefully, it will make your ride easier."

Snow had nothing to gather, the few possessions she had having been strapped to the horse she had ridden when she had left her sister's home. Yet, strangely enough, she felt as if she was leaving something behind.

Nettle led her down the stairs, Runa following behind her.

"You do well?" James asked anxiously? "Tarass told me how he happened upon you, rescued you from your dreadful fall, and brought you directly here to be looked after until he could contact me."

"Aye, I wouldn't have survived if it hadn't been for him. I am most grateful to him," Snow said and she truly was, even though he could prove maddening at times. But that mattered little, since she'd probably never see him again. "I am doing well, James."

141

Donna Fletcher

"Is this so, Runa?" Tarass asked.

Snow wasn't surprised he asked his healer to confirm it and she was quite sure Runa would speak the truth to him and even more sure of his response.

"With her wound tearing open and the bump on her head, I advised Snow that it would be wiser she remain here at least one more day," Runa said.

"That settles it then, Snow will remain here until Runa claims her fit to travel," Tarass commanded.

Snow had been right about his response and she was prepared for it. "That's not your decision to make."

"I'm sure James would agree with me, right James," Tarass said, turning to him.

"It's not James's decision either, it's mine," Snow said and before Tarass could say more she continued, "James, I think it would be wise to take me to Willow. Not that Runa hasn't been a great help, but I'd prefer my sister to tend me."

"Are you sure you can ride? Willow's home is close but the snow-covered ground makes the journey a bit more difficult," James said.

"I could send men to bring Willow here to you," Tarass said, annoyed she was not only being foolish but stubborn as well.

"That won't be necessary," Snow said.

"You're being pigheaded," Tarass snapped.

"That right is reserved for you and you alone," she said with a smile.

"Snow!" James scolded. "Lord Tarass only considers what is best for you."

"I am capable of considering what is best for me and it is best you take me to Willow."

"Does she ever listen to reason, James?" Tarass asked, his tongue sharp.

"Far too often," Snow said and reached out her hand. "Lord Tarass."

Tarass took her hand, closing his large one firmly around her small one and feeling now that he had hold of her, he wouldn't let her go. He would make her stay until she was well enough to travel whether she liked it or not.

This would be the last time she would feel his hand wrapped around hers. Why did that thought disturb her? And when had she grown to favor the simple gesture? She pushed the disconcerting thoughts away.

"I appreciate all you have done for me, Lord Tarass. You have been most kind and hospitable, and I am ever so grateful. However, it is time for me to take my leave. My heartfelt thanks for all you've done for me." Tears were close to filling her eyes and she slipped her hand out of his, having to give a little tug since he didn't easily let go. She quickly turned her head. "James, we should leave now."

"A good idea, since it will take us longer than usual to reach Willow's home," James said.

Snow was grateful her brother agreed, since she needed to leave before the sadness that was rapidly growing in her caused her to spill tears. She didn't understand it and she needed to be away from here to make sense of it.

"I'll send a troop of my warriors with you," Tarass said.

Tarass's commanding tone left no room for James to object.

143

"That is generous of you, Lord Tarass," James said.

Tarass took Snow's arm to walk down the stairs and she didn't resist. She didn't want to. She wanted to feel his protective touch once more before they said good-bye. His hand remained on her arm when they reached the bottom of the steps and she wondered... did he not want to let her go?

His hand drifted off her and she silently admonished herself for such a foolish thought.

"Nettle," she said, reaching out her hand in search of the young woman.

"Right here," Nettle said, taking her hand.

Snow pulled her into a hug and whispered, "I will miss you so much."

Nettle sniffed back tears. "And I you. Life was so good with you here."

They hugged and Nettle stepped away.

"I've come to say good-bye."

"Twilla," Snow said, recognizing her voice.

Twilla wrapped Snow in a hug and whispered, "You'll be back."

Her words stunned Snow. There would be no reason for her to return here.

"Take care," Twilla said for everyone to hear.

Snow felt a large presence in front of her and she knew instinctively who it was.

"I would tell you to be good, but I don't think that's possible," Tarass said, keeping his voice low. "Take care and stay well."

His hands were suddenly at her waist and he lifted her onto a horse, and then he was gone.

Snow held onto her tears until she was sure she was well away from the village. Thaw sat on her lap and licked the tears as soon as they began to fall.

"Snow, what is it? Are you in pain? Shall we turn back?" James asked, his voice frantic with worry.

"No, I'm just glad I'm going to see my sister," Snow said, using Willow as an excuse, since she wasn't certain why sadness gripped her heart so strongly.

"If you don't feel well, you'll let me know and we'll stop and rest," James said.

Snow smiled, though tears ran down her cheeks. "I'm blessed to have you as a brother, James."

"I am glad you feel that way, since I'm beyond happy to have three wonderful sisters," he said.

They rode in silence for a bit when Snow suddenly asked. "What of Finn?"

"Worry not, Lord Tarass said he'd keep him until the weather permitted a proper burial."

"I cannot understand why anyone would want to hurt him," Snow said.

"Don't worry about that. Lord Tarass and I talked and we'll get to the bottom of Finn's unfortunate demise."

Snow was silent the remainder of the trip, James having asked her repeatedly if she needed to rest. Though, she could have done with a rest, Snow wanted to get to her sister. She needed Willow and it wasn't her wound she needed her for.

They arrived mid-morning and Snow fought to keep her tears contained, but as soon as she was taken off the horse and she heard Willow's voice, she burst into tears and stretched her arms out.

She was instantly wrapped in Willow's arms and quickly guided up the steps, Thaw keeping close to her side, and hurried into the keep. She was relieved when Willow took her to the bedchamber she had left only two or was it three days ago.

"It's all right," Willow soothed. "You're here with me now. You have nothing to fear."

Snow couldn't stop her tears. She remained in her sister's arms and let them fall. She was grateful Willow didn't question her. She simply held onto her and let her cry. She hadn't cried like that since her parents died, and she wondered what was wrong with her.

Finally, Snow's tears slowed and she eased out of her sister's arms.

"Are you in pain, Snow?" Willow asked.

It was a pain she couldn't explain and didn't understand. "I don't know."

Willow took her hand. "James sent word ahead that you were coming here and what had happened, including Finn's death. We can talk about all that over a hot brew, but first I should see to your wound.?"

"That would be good," Snow said, feeling tears creeping up on her again.

It didn't take long for Willow to let her know that her wound did well and would heal if she rested and didn't do anything too strenuous.

It wasn't long after that Willow had Snow in a nightdress and tucked in bed, Thaw curled up asleep beside her. "You will stay with me and Slatter until I deem you fit enough to return home. Unless, of course, you wish to reconsider my offer and remain here with

Slatter and me. We both would love to have you live with us."

Snow reached for her sister's hand, Willow having sat beside her on the bed. "I appreciate it, but I think it best I stay at Macardle keep."

"If you change your mind, you are welcome here any time," Willow assured her. "Now tell me what brings so many tears to your eyes."

Snow shook her head. "I don't know. I suppose it's everything. The ordeal of getting lost in the snowstorm, Finn being killed, having to stay with Tarass."

It wasn't lost on Willow that her sister didn't address Lord Tarass accordingly.

"Was he insufferable as usual?" Willow asked.

"He rescued me. He put his own life in danger to rescue me and he saw me kept safe," Snow said, not realizing she was shaking her head as if she was just comprehending what he had done. "Thaw even made some peace with him."

Snow was thinking of how Thaw went to Tarass for help when she suffered a nightmare and she wondered what she would do if her nightmare returned, not having Tarass there to soothe her. But she didn't say any of that to her sister.

"So he treated you well?" Willow asked.

"He did," Snow said without hesitation and rubbed at the bump in the back of her head. "He even wrapped himself around me as I fell down the keep steps, saving me from suffering far worse than a bump to my head."

"Who would have thought the Lord of Fire could be chivalrous," Willow said.

"Maddening as well," Snow said, but with a laugh and recalled the times he had ordered her about. Her smile was wiped away by a yawn.

"Your body tells you it is time to rest and heal," Willow said and stood to help her sister stretch out beneath the blankets. "Nap and we will talk again later. You are safe now."

Snow whispered as she snuggled under the blanket. "I was safe with Tarass."

Willow closed the door quietly behind her and went in search of her husband. She almost bumped into him when she turned a curve on the staircase.

"I was just coming to see how your sister was," Slatter said, taking his wife in his arms and planting more than a light kiss on her.

"You tempt me," she accused with a laugh.

"As often as possible," he said and went to tease her neck with kisses when he saw a disturbed look in her green eyes. "What troubles you?"

Willow was glad her husband knew her so well that he could tell when something troubled her and that he never hesitated to ask her about it.

"Is it your sister?"

Willow sighed. "I never thought it could happen and I feel terrible for her, since it's impossible. It will never go anywhere."

"What are you talking about?" Slatter asked, her words making no sense.

Willow couldn't believe what she was about to say. "I think Snow has fallen in love with the Lord of Fire."

Chapter Thirteen

Snow sat in her mum's small solar, snug in the warmth of a shawl, wool hose kept her legs from feeling chilled, and her feet were kept toasty warm from the heat of the flames in the hearth.

It had been two weeks since she had left Tarass's home and ten days since she had left Willow's home. She didn't understand why it had felt different being at Willow's this time, but it had. As much as she had always found solace being with Willow, this time she hadn't. More so when Willow had suggested that perhaps she had found herself unwittingly caring, or more bluntly, losing her heart to Lord Tarass.

Snow had laughed and claimed it impossible. She had stopped laughing when Willow pointed out that Snow wept as if she had lost a deep love as she had done when their parents had died. Willow had set the idea in her mind and Snow had wondered if it had been on purpose. Had Willow thought it was something Snow should consider so that in the end she would realize it was something that would never be? Only then would she heal from it?

Leave it to her practical sister to force her to give it thought and that was what she had been doing since her return home. James had been worried that she was spending too much time alone brooding and had assumed it had been the ordeal that had caused it. Then

149

he worried that preparations for his and Eleanor's wedding, a few months away, contributed to her melancholy.

She had assured him she did well and there was no need for concern. She could tell by the tone of his voice that he hadn't believed her. But what did it matter, since she was finding it impossible to believe that it was love that was causing such a heavy sadness in her. Had she truly been foolish enough to have fallen in love with a pigheaded man like Tarass? If so, how had it happened? Was that why her heart ached every time she thought about him? And was it why she couldn't stop thinking about him?

She sighed heavily, as if in doing so it would release the sadness that overwhelmed her. She smiled when she felt Thaw uncurl from the ball he had wrapped himself in near her feet and jump into her lap to lick her face, as if he sensed her melancholy and was offering comfort.

Her arms instinctively went around him and she hugged him tight. She was surprised how much he had grown in the last two weeks, but happy he still fit in her lap, though she feared not for long.

"I am foolish, Thaw," she said, a tear trickling down her cheek. "We have each other and that is all that matters."

Thaw licked her cheek, catching her tear and snuggled against her, letting her know he felt the same.

They settled comfortably together in the chair.

"Maybe I should accept Willow's offer and have us go live with her and Slatter. I may not have bairns of

150

my own to love and enjoy, but I would have Willow and Slatter's bairns to love and enjoy."

Thaw barked and Snow assumed he liked the idea.

A knock sounded at the door, Snow had been keeping it closed after entering, making it clear she preferred to be alone.

"It's Eleanor, Snow. I have a message from your brother."

Snow bid her to enter.

"Sorry to disturb you when you look so warm and comfortable, but James requests your presence in his solar on an important matter," Eleanor said.

There was something in Eleanor's tone that had Snow questioning, "Is there something wrong, Eleanor?"

"I don't believe so."

"Yet, you sound doubtful."

"He is not alone."

For some reason, hope sprang in Snow. Was it Tarass?

"Who is with him?" Snow asked calmly, though felt anything but calm.

"Lord Polwarth," Eleanor said.

Snow's stomach plummeted and she thought herself a fool ten times over for thinking Tarass might miss her.

She forced a smile. "Lord Farrell Polwarth is an old friend of my father's. He's probably asked to see me."

"That must be it," Eleanor said, joy returning to her tone. "I only caught a snatch of their conversation and my thoughts went wild when an arranged marriage was mentioned, then a short time later I was asked to fetch you. I wrongly assumed that perhaps the marriage had something to do with you. A foolish thought since your brother would never see you sent away."

"I'll be there as soon as I refresh myself," Snow said.

"I can help," Eleanor offered.

"Not necessary, I'll do fine."

Arranged marriage.

The words wouldn't leave her head as she went to her bedchamber. James would never do that to her... marry her off to a man the age her da would be if he were still alive. He would not marry her off at all since Ruddock, Sorrell's husband, had granted her and Willow the right to choose their husbands once James had pledged the clan's loyalty to him.

She had met Lord Polwarth on several occasions throughout the years. He was a man of wealth and prestige. He had married twice and buried both wives, neither having given him any children. She remembered him as a man with fine features, good height and solid build. He lived a good three hour ride from here, and the last she had seen him was at her da's funeral. So what brought him here now?

Thaw guided her down the stairs and though she hadn't needed his help, having easily mastered the stairs she had traveled up and down since she was a bairn, she followed his lead. It was good practice for him.

Eleanor was waiting for her in the Great Hall.

"Cook has something for Thaw and I thought I'd take him outside while you talk with James and the guest," Eleanor said.

Thaw barked when he heard Cook mentioned and he eagerly went with Eleanor after permission from Snow. She paused at the solar door, her stomach suddenly growing unsettled.

James is well aware that you are to marry a man of your own choosing.

Why then this unease?

Snow knocked, hurried to be done with it.

"Snow, how wonderful to see you again."

Snow was glad Eleanor had informed her that Lord Polwarth was in the solar with James, since she didn't recognize his voice and certainly would have startled when he greeted her so robustly and took her hand to lead her to a chair.

"You remember Lord Polwarth, Snow?" James asked.

"I do," she said after sitting. "He was a good friend of our father's."

"And I miss him to this day," Lord Polwarth said.

"What brings you here, Lord Polwarth?" Snow asked, unable to contain her trepidation.

James responded. "Lord Polwarth has an offer for you, Snow, which he insisted I present to you."

"It is not of James's doing. It is my thought and my thought alone," Lord Polwarth said, taking full responsibility.

"And you are under no obligation to accept it," James added quickly.

153

Donna Fletcher

Snow's stomach churned more and more with every word spoken, sending an awful unease to run through her, even though James said she was under no obligation to agree to the offer. It also sounded obvious that James hadn't wanted to present the offer to her, that he already knew her answer. So why bother her with it?

She silently admonished herself. She was under no obligation to accept whatever proposal Lord Polwarth offered, but James, on the other hand, could not deny granting such a powerful man his request.

"I will hear your offer," Snow said, her worry beginning to ease. James was leaving this up to her. Unlike before with Sorrell when he'd been forced to arrange a marriage for her that would benefit the Clan Macardle. Luckily, Lord Ruddock had saved Sorrell from that. And who had been the person to force James into arranging the marriage?

Tarass.

Her heart fluttered in her chest at the thought of him and she rested her hand against it.

"Are you unwell?" James asked, worried.

"No, I am good. It's the suspense that patters my heart," Snow said with a smile, though it was the thought of Tarass and how he had been a menacing savior to the Clan Macardle before Lord Ruddock had stepped in. How could she even think she loved a man who had irritated her far too many times and had demanded from her clan far too much.

But then life demanded far too much of far too many. Why should she or her clan be any different?

154

"I am an old man, something I cannot deny," Lord Polwarth began. "But I still have much vigor left in me. I have loved two women and buried both with heavy sadness. Unfortunately, neither gave me any children. I have wealth and respect."

Snow didn't reject his hand when he took hold of hers.

"I ask that you consider becoming my wife. I will treat you well and see that you want for nothing, and—"

Snow didn't let him finish. "Why me, Lord Polwarth? I am blind and would be a burden to you. There must be many a young woman who would make a more suitable wife."

"Perhaps, but on my last visit here your father spoke to me about how worried he was that you would never wed, never find a husband who would treat you well, never know the joy of having bairns of your own, and that it was his fault. He told me his last wish would be for you to find a husband who would be good to you and keep you safe."

His words brought tears to her eyes. She never blamed her da for the accident that blinded her. It had been the illness that did it, not her da.

"Your father and I were longtime friends. We fought side by side in battle from when we were young. I would like to grant your father his last wish and at the same time, gain a beautiful and kind wife who hopefully will give me a child to carry on my clan name and inherit my land and wealth. I ask that you give it thought. You have much to gain with this union, most

155

of all a home of your own and a man who would be the kind of husband your da wanted for you."

James responded as she thought on the offer.

"It is very generous of you, Lord Polwarth, but my sister is quite content with her life here."

She had been content when her sisters were with her and promises made that they would never part. They would always remain close and that hadn't changed even though Sorrell now lived a distance away. Snow, herself, had encouraged Sorrell to go and be happy with Ruddock. And while she might not have been able to see how much Willow loved Slatter, she had heard in her voice when she spoke about him. Now it was James and Eleanor's time and while this was still her home, it no longer felt like it was.

Then there was Tarass and her foolish thoughts about him that would get her nowhere and only bring her more sadness.

She made her decision quickly before she could change her mind.

"I accept your offer of marriage, Lord Polwarth," she said and didn't need to see the shock on James's face. She heard in his gasp.

"I am overjoyed," Lord Polwarth said. "We shall wed posthaste."

"Within the week," Snow said. "I want time to tell my sister Willow and send a missive to Sorrell."

"Of course, whatever will make you happy, my dear," he agreed. "I can't tell you how thrilled I am that you have accepted my offer."

After more talk, that Snow remembered little of, Lord Polwarth took his leave, eager to return home and arrange for the arrival of his bride.

"Do you truly want this, Snow?" James asked after Polwarth left.

Snow spoke honestly with her brother. "I don't know, James. I only know that all is different now and I don't know where I belong."

"Then I urge you not to rush into this marriage. Tell him you prefer to wait until spring and give yourself time to see if this is what you truly want."

Snow shook her head. "It is better I do this now and be done with it."

"I think it is a mistake."

"Perhaps it is," Snow agreed with trepidation of her own. "But it gives me a chance to have something I thought I'd never have... a husband and my own family. And he is a trusted friend of our da and he will keep me safe."

"There is that," James said, "and he did seem genuinely happy not only to see you but appeared thrilled when you accepted his offer."

"Then it is settled and there is much to be done before this wedding can take place."

"What can I do to help make this easy for you?" James offered.

Snow didn't stop to think. "There is something that would help greatly."

"Tell me and I will see it done."

"Lord Tarass has a servant named Nettle. She was of great help to me when I was there and I would like it if you could ask him if he would release Nettle so she could serve me in my new home. A wedding gift of sorts."

"I will do my best to see it done."

***

"You can't do this."

Snow wasn't surprised when Willow and Slatter arrived only hours after her missive had reached her sister the next day.

"I know it seems sudden and perhaps foolish," Snow said, having thought of nothing but her hasty decision all night. Had she made a wise choice or a foolish one she would regret? No answer ever came to her.

"Sudden? Foolish?" Willow threw her hands up in the air. "It's preposterous. You will tell Lord Polwarth you changed your mind."

"Did Snow say that to you when you told her you wed me?" Slatter asked, slipping his arm around his wife's back at her waist.

"That's different?" Willow argued.

"How? She supported whatever you wanted. Shouldn't you do the same for her?" Slatter asked.

"She doesn't love him," Willow said, shaking her head. "Snow knew I loved you without me saying that I loved you. This will be a loveless marriage and that is no marriage at all."

"But at least it is a marriage," Snow said, "something I thought I would never have."

Willow moved away from her husband to take both her sister's hands in hers and gave them a gentle squeeze as she whispered, "You love another."

"I don't know that for sure."

"I do," Willow said. "I see it in your eyes when you talk about him, hear it in your voice, just as you did with me and Slatter."

"Love was there between you and Slatter," Snow reminded. "There is only me in this love you speak about and a one-sided love is no love at all, if it is even love." A tear tickled at her eye and heaviness filled her heart.

"At least give it time," Willow urged. "James told me that he suggested you wait until spring to be sure this is what you want. I agree with him. Please wait."

"And if Lord Polwarth changes his mind, what then? Do I lose the only chance of having what I want most, a good husband and a family of my own? Right or wrong, Willow, I need to take this chance."

"Sorrell will have a fit and try to stop this when she learns of it," Willow said.

"Why do you think I wed so quickly?" Snow said with a laugh.

Willow laughed as well, though she didn't think for a minute it was the reason for the hasty wedding. She knew the truth. She had seen it that day Snow had cried in her arms. Snow loved the Lord of Fire whether she wanted to admit it or not and perhaps, in the end, this was best for her. Lord Tarass would not make Snow a good husband. He would not love her as she was deserved to be loved.

Willow hugged Snow tightly. "It's time to plan your wedding."

***

Tarass had traveled all night to get home, not that he was looking forward to returning home. And then again he was. He shook his head at his mixed thoughts and sank back in the chair before the fire in his solar.

He had found himself restless when at home, an unusual occurrence and the reason he had left a few days after Snow had gone to her sister. He told himself it had nothing to do with Snow, and yet there was an ache in him when he thought about her, which was endless and refused to go away. It had been the driving force that had returned him home. He wanted to see her, needed to see her so that he could put this nonsense to rest, clear her out of his mind once and for all.

A knock sounded at the door and it opened before he could tell the person to go away. He wanted to be alone.

Rannock entered and came to stand in front of him. "Nettle has a request that cannot wait."

"If I say it can wait, it will wait," Tarass snapped, tired and irritable.

"Not this request?" Rannock persisted.

Tarass's scowl deepened as he unfurled out of his slouch, his shoulders going back, his chest out, his chin up as he sat straight and in a commanding manner. "Tell me what is so important that it cannot wait."

Rannock waved toward the door and Nettle suddenly appeared in front of Tarass.

Nettle bobbed her head respectfully. "I'm sorry to disturb you, my lord, but I haven't much time. Snow asked if you would release me to serve her in her new home."

"What new home?" Tarass demanded a sense of urgency rushing over him.

Nettle smiled. "The new home she leaves for today with the man she weds at noon."

Chapter Fourteen

"It's Slatter."

Snow smiled as her brother-in-law took her arm. "You needn't escort me. I can maneuver the Great Hall well now."

"I know. It is but an excuse for me to have a few moments alone with you." He kept his voice low as they walked slowly through the hall. "This decision is yours, Snow, but I wanted to make it clear that if at the last minute you change your mind, I will gladly see Lord Polwarth escorted out of the keep and sent on his way."

"Do you not like him?" Snow asked anxiously. "And, please, your honest opinion, Slatter."

"My honest opinion would be, I don't know. He seems a pleasant man and while I know him only by name, I've heard no bad words said about him."

"Still, you seem hesitant."

"One truly never knows someone until they've spent time with them. A pleasant manner could hide a devious man. So, if you are unsure, speak up and reject this marriage. Then you will come live with Willow and me and our many future bairns and be well-loved."

"You are a good man, Slatter," Snow said.

"Shhh, you'll ruin my reputation," he warned with a laugh.

Snow laughed along with him, though her heart felt heavy, so heavy she feared it would break in two. She had not slept all night, her thoughts on this day, this marriage. Was it the right thing to do? Had she rushed foolishly into it and would she regret it? Should she change her mind?

Lord Polwarth had been nothing but kind to her even letting her know that he would not hold her to her word if she should decide differently, since this was a sudden decision for her. He had visited throughout the week, had sat and talked with her, held her hand or took her arm and had been more than kind and mannerly to her.

Thaw was pleasant to Lord Polwarth except when he placed a hand on her, then he growled and snapped. Lord Polwarth had assured Thaw that he meant her no harm and had assured Snow that the pup would grow accustomed to him.

"What do you whisper to my sister?" Willow asked when they reached her.

"A last minute escape," Slatter said in a conspiratorial whisper.

"When? How?" Willow asked in hushed excitement. "I knew you'd come to your senses."

"Slatter teases," Snow said and could all but picture the disappoint on her sister's face.

Willow went to punch her husband in the arm for getting her hopes up, but he grabbed it, wrapped her in a hug, and pressed a kiss to her cheek.

"I told her if she changes her mind we are here for her," Slatter whispered near her ear.

Willow hugged her husband. "Bless you."

163

"I am sorry for the delay, Lord Polwarth. The cleric should be here soon," James said as he and Polwarth entered the Great Hall, having finished in the solar.

"There is time enough," Lord Polwarth said, then laughed, "though, with my fifty years, you never know. Snow, you stun the eye." He took her hand as soon as he reached her side. "You are beautiful, my dear." He kissed her hand to the annoyance of Thaw, who growled at him.

Eleanor had said something similar to her earlier when she had finished helping her get ready for the ceremony. Snow thought it kind of her to say, since she believed she looked little different than usual. A gold-colored tunic covered a deep green shift and Eleanor had swept her hair up in some fashion, though some strands were left free to partially fall along her neck.

"How kind of you, Lord Polwarth," Snow said and eased her hand out of his upset that she felt a great unease at his unobtrusive kiss.

That was another thing she had given thought to, intimacy with Lord Polwarth. He seemed kind enough, and yet the thought of coupling with him left her feeling unsettled. And now that his kiss to her hand left her feeling uneasy, she worried how she would react to a more intimate kiss.

Did she follow through with this marriage or did she heed Slatter's words and go live with them and be well-loved?

The door opened and a short, rumpled cleric entered, servants rushing to help him close it, the wind that rushed in with him too powerful for his frail demeanor.

"Gray clouds and wind, another storm brews," he said, shaking his partially bald head.

Snow placed her hand on her stomach, wishing she could stop the churning from growing worse. Or was her upset stomach an omen she should pay attention to? What was it her mum had often said?

If a decision causes discomfort or doubt, pause and give thought.

In her sadness and self-pity, had she unwisely committed to something that wasn't right for her?

"It is good we see the ceremony done with haste so that my new bride and I may be on our way home before the weather keeps us here," Lord Polwarth said.

"But there is the small celebration that's been prepared," Willow argued, not ready to let go of her sister.

"I fear the weather prohibits us from lingering. We'll celebrate another time," Lord Polwarth said and once again took Snow's hand. "It is time, my dear."

Snow let herself be directed where to stand, her mind churning as much as her stomach. Did she want this? Should she stop it?

Did she love Tarass?

A pain so sharp struck her that she thought she'd been stabbed in the heart. There was no denying it, no matter how much she tried. She had fallen in love with Tarass. How that had happened, she had no idea, but she could no longer allow herself to deny it. And finally realizing that made her also realize that this marriage she had agreed to was a mistake.

She was jolted out of her thoughts when the cleric began the ceremony.

She had to stop this, but how? How did she tell Lord Polwarth she didn't want to wed him?

The door flew open, banging violently against the wall, causing everyone to turn and see a gust of swirling wind and snow sweep in along with a man, the hood of his fur-lined cloak covering half of his face. He didn't hesitate to toss the hood back.

Tarass stood there a moment, still as a statue, his eyes aglow with fire and his stance one of a warrior ready to attack. His eyes latched onto Snow and strong strides brought him further into the Great Hall. Twelve of his warriors suddenly filed in and followed behind him, dividing into two groups of six that flanked him as he strode forward.

"Snow belongs to me," Tarass shouted, his voice echoing off the high ceiling.

Shock to hear Tarass's voice and hear him claim she belonged to him stunned Snow silent. She couldn't believe he was there. Couldn't believe he demanded that she belonged to him. And yet, her heart swelled with a sense of joy. She was relieved when she felt Willow take her hand and squeeze it, letting her know she was there beside her.

Polwarth spoke up. "Snow does not belong to you, Lord Tarass, she is about to become my wife."

To the shock of everyone, Thaw went running to Tarass, yapping all the way, then stopped in front of him, and turned to bark at Lord Polwarth.

"Wise choice, Thaw," Tarass praised the pup, then called out, "You're wrong, Polwarth. Snow will not wed you, she *belongs* to me. She became mine not only on the night we spent together in the cottage in the woods when I rescued her, but the night we slept together in my guest bedchamber," Tarass said to the astounding shock of all around him.

"You never mentioned that," James said, when he found his voice.

"You lie," Polwarth accused.

"Watch who you call a liar, Polwarth," Tarass warned, his hand going to the hilt of his sword at his waist.

"You never mentioned this before and you expect to be believed now?" Polwarth demanded. "And don't think to have Snow confirm or deny this. It is inconceivable that you would tarnish her reputation this way."

"I tarnish nothing. I keep what is mine and Snow is mine," Tarass said, challenging the man.

"Prove it," Polwarth said, returning the challenge.

"Fetch her," Tarass ordered sharply and the warrior to his right hurried out of the keep.

Snow gripped her sister's hand, shock and that twinge of joy turning to dismay and apprehension. Why was he doing this? Why was he claiming she belonged to him? Why reveal secrets that would force James to demand he marry her? Something he had made clear he had no wont to do.

Silence reigned while after a few moments a young lass entered the Great Hall and came to a stop beside Tarass.

"Tell them, Nettle. Tell them what you saw when you entered Snow's bedchamber that morning."

Nettle didn't hesitate to obey. "I saw Lord Tarass naked in bed with Snow."

167

Gasps circled the hall and once again Snow squeezed her sister's hand.

"Is this true?" Willow whispered in Snow's ear.

Snow nodded, though didn't explain that it was all innocent and nothing happened between Tarass and her, since it would make no difference. He had been in bed naked with her and that was all that mattered.

"It matters not to me that you soiled her," Lord Polwarth said. "I will wed Snow and keep her safe from the likes of a barbarian."

"Even with my seed planted firmly in her belly?" Tarass asked, taking several steps toward the man.

Snow was shocked at his words, since there was no chance of that.

"You are a crude man," Polwarth accused.

"I am a man who keeps what is mine and I will repeat it until you finally grasp it. *Snow belongs to me*," Tarass said, claiming it so once again.

"Then step forward, wed her, and keep her from ruin," the cleric challenged with a firm voice.

"That is madness. You cannot mean to give this kind and beautiful woman to the devil himself," Polwarth protested.

"There is a witness who saw that Snow gave herself to the devil and now she belongs to him," the cleric said, pointing to Tarass.

"The lass lies for the Lord of Fire," Polwarth accused.

"I do not lie," Nettle said, affronted. "I speak what I saw. I speak the truth."

"Do you swear by all that is holy and your heavenly soul that you speak the truth?" the cleric asked.

"I would not lie and condemn my soul to hell," Nettle responded.

"There you have it," the cleric said. "The lass protects her soul and speaks the truth. No more proof is needed. Give yourself pause, Lord Polwarth. What would your friends think of you marrying a woman who gave her body and soul to the devil?"

Snow clung tightly to her sister's hand, listening as her reputation was shredded with nothing more than a few words and with only parts of it being the truth. While she thought of speaking up, of defending herself, it wouldn't matter. That Tarass had been in bed with her was wrong in itself. That he'd been naked only made it worse.

She jumped when she felt a hand grab her arm and powerful fingers close tightly around her soft flesh.

"You will be my wife?" Tarass asked.

Why... was on her lips, but never slipped past them.

"I will not be a witness to this travesty," Lord Polwarth exclaimed and stormed out of the keep.

Snow stood beside Tarass, his grip firm on her arm as if he never intended to let go of her, and it wasn't long before she heard the cleric begin the ceremony. She was surprised when Tarass spoke the vows without hesitation and even more surprised when she did the same.

When the cleric pronounced them husband and wife, Snow thought herself dreaming. She had woken today prepared to exchange vows with Lord Polwarth and here she was wife to Tarass, the Lord of Fire. She was still wondering how it had happened.

"We leave for home now," Tarass announced.

Willow protested. "You cannot wed my sister and leave without any further words of explanation."

"I can and I will, and I owe no explanation," Tarass said. "This is done. Snow is mine now and she will obey me."

Slatter laughed. "Good luck with that. There isn't a Macardle sister that obeys her husband and I for one would have it no other way."

Willow turned a smile on her husband.

"The marriage document must be changed, signed, and sealed," the cleric reminded. "And I wouldn't mind a drink while seeing it done."

"Nettle, help my wife with whatever she needs and see that the men secure her belongings," Tarass commanded.

"Aye, my lord," Nettle said.

"Snow," he said, his hand releasing the grip he had on her arm to drift down and take hold of her hand. "Take time with your sister. We leave after the documents are signed."

"Why?" she asked softly.

"Because I am your husband and you now have no recourse but to obey me," he said, authority ringing in his every word.

Snow shook her head. "No, that's not what I ask. Why did you marry me?"

"There'll be time for us to talk later," he snapped. "Go with your sister."

Snow felt his hand fall away from hers.

"There is only one reason he would come here, stop the wedding, and claim you as he did," Willow said, stepping around her and hooking her arm around Snow's to lead her to a table. "The Lord of Fire loves you."

Chapter Fifteen

Snow sat silently in her husband's arms on his horse.

Her husband.

It wasn't that it was difficult to accept she was married. After all, she was to wed today. It was who she had married she found so difficult to grasp. Also, the reason why he married her, which Willow had insisted was because he loved her. That was simply impossible. She didn't want to think on the many times he had told her he would never take her as a wife. So why had he?

He had not spoken up about being in your bed until he discovered you were to wed. There would be no other plausible reason for him to marry you unless he couldn't stand the thought of another man having you.

Her sister had repeated that again and again and coming from Willow, a person who saw reason in most everything, it would make sense. But Willow hadn't been privy to the various times Tarass had pointed out that he would not wed a blind woman. And there was that time in the cottage when he stopped himself from saying, though she had finished it for him, he wouldn't poke a blind woman.

Did that mean he had no intention of sealing their vows? If that was so, then again she had to ask, "Why did you wed me?"

She hadn't planned on speaking her thought aloud, but she was glad she did. She raised her head, hoping she looked him in the eye as she waited for his response.

"Why did you agree to wed Lord Polwarth?" he asked, failing to keep a biting anger out of his voice.

She thought to tell him that it didn't concern him, but then she hoped if she answered him, he would in turn answer her.

"He was a friend of my da's and offered me a chance of having what I've always wanted… a caring husband and family."

Tarass was glad she couldn't see him cringe with anger at the thought of Polwarth coupling with her. It sent a rage through him that made him want to beat the man.

"What about love? I thought you wanted a husband who loved you."

Her soft laughter was filled with sorrow. "Who would love or even wed a blind woman? You certainly made it known you wouldn't, so why did you wed me?"

"Did you even give your decision to marry Polwarth thought?"

She was wise to the way he ignored answering her question and she wondered why.

"Not at first," she admitted honestly. "With my sisters wed and James and Eleanor planning their wedding, I suppose I felt a burden to them all. Lord Polwarth's offer lifted that burden."

Anger continued to stir in Tarass. She was far from a burden and he hated that she felt that way and that Polwarth had taken advantage of it. Or was he angry because if he had not arrived when he had, he would have lost Snow to Polwarth? And that thought made him feel like a knife had been thrust through his heart.

"Slatter reminded me just before the ceremony that if I changed my mind he would escort Lord Polwarth out and I could go live with them and be well-loved. That got me thinking."

Tarass owed Slatter for that.

"I wasn't sure if marrying Lord Polwarth was the right thing to do, until…"

"Until what?" Tarass asked.

Snow wasn't about to tell him that it was finally admitting to herself she was in love with him that made her decide she couldn't marry Polwarth."

"Until it struck me that it wasn't what I wanted," she said, which was the truth.

"Why didn't you speak up when I arrived."

"Your arrival shocked me and by the time I could gather my senses, you sealed our fate. I either wed you or faced disgrace. Not that gossiping tongues won't see me shamed."

"I hear one person say anything against you and when I get done with him or her not another hurtful word will be spoken about you—*ever*."

His threat sounded more like a promise.

Silence followed for several minutes.

"Why did you let Lord Polwarth think I could be carrying your bairn when you know that isn't possible?"

"It will be soon enough."

His response struck her silent. He did intend to seal their vows. The thought thrilled and frightened her.

"Lord Tarass," came a shout as one of his warriors rode toward them. "Something you need to see."

Tarass directed his horse to follow the warrior and after bringing the animal to a stop, he dismounted and lifted Snow off the horse.

"What goes on?" she asked, curious as he took her arm and she walked with him.

"I don't know," he said and stopped and lifted her hand to rest it against a tree. "You will stay here until I come for you."

"I'll go with you," she said and reached out for him.

"No." Tarass took her glove-covered hand and placed it back on the tree. "You'll do as I say and stay here, and I won't hear another word about it," he warned when he saw her ready to argue. "You forget you are my wife now and that means you obey my every word." He looked at the pup and ordered, "Thaw, guard Snow."

Thaw barked and sat himself against Snow's leg.

"There is nothing to fear, my warriors keep watch over you. I will return soon," he said and went to walk off.

"Where is Nettle?" Snow asked, the young woman would at least detail what was going on around her.

"She was sent ahead with your belongings to ready everything for you," Tarass said. "I won't be long, and don't dare move away from that tree."

Snow wasn't fearful, not with the swarm of warriors around her and Tarass himself. She was more curious of what was happening. What was it that Tarass needed to see for himself? After a few minutes, her impatience got the best of her. Thaw's did too, since he'd moved away from her leg to sniff around, which meant he was bored with sitting.

"Shall we go find Tarass, Thaw?" she asked in a playful tone she often used when asking if he wanted to go for a walk.

Thaw barked in agreement.

"Find Tarass," she said and Thaw barked, then took the hem of her shift in his mouth and led the way.

***

Tarass stared at the pool of blood in the snow, the light snowflakes vanishing as soon they touched the blood.

"It's odd, my lord," the young warrior said, his eyes also fixed on the blood.

"Aye, Dolan, it is," Tarass agreed.

"That much blood in one spot and not a trace of it anywhere else. No drag marks. Nothing. It makes one wonder if the blood rose up through the soil, but that would make no sense." Dolan shook his head. "Not a good omen, my lord."

"What's not a good omen?" Snow asked as she approached Tarass.

"What are you doing here?" he demanded, turning around. "I told you to stay by the tree."

"I got curious," she admitted.

"So you disobeyed me."

"Forgive me, my lord, but we've been married only a couple of hours, so I'm not used to being a dutiful wife yet," she said with a soft smile and dramatically

176

pressed her hand to her chest as if it was a heartfelt apology.

Tarass leaned his face down near hers. "I'd watch that flippant tongue of yours, wife."

"My tongue often has a mind of its own."

"Then control it or else." He hurried his finger to her lips to stop her from speaking. "And don't ask me or else what. You don't want to know." His cheek brushed hers as he lifted his head and though he didn't show it, the touch of her smooth cold cheek sent a warm shiver through him that stirred his loins. Damn, but he had missed her.

"The omen?" she asked and though she couldn't see Tarass, she sensed he shook his head.

"Nothing for you to worry about," Tarass said and caught Thaw inching closer to the pool of blood. "Get away from that, Thaw!"

"Away from what?" Snow asked about to step forward.

Tarass turned once again to keep her from moving and his eyes shot wide. He barely had enough time to shove her out of the way of the arrow sailing directly at her.

"Attack!" Dolan shouted and the warriors rushed to draw their weapons ready to fight.

Tarass stood with his weapon drawn as well, his back to his wife, ready to keep her safe.

The warriors stood perplexed when no other arrows rained down on them or warriors charged them.

A frantic bark from Thaw had Tarass turning to see that his wife had landed face first in the pool of blood and was struggling to get out of it. He rushed to her side and slipped his hands under her arms to lift her out and plant her feet on a clean patch of snow.

Snow spit and wiped at her face with her glove-covered hands. "What did I fall in?"

"Blood," Dolan said, his eyes so wide they looked as if they'd burst from his head.

"Blood?" Snow asked, though she had heard him clearly. "Whose blood?" She went to wipe at her mouth again, the thought of being soaked in blood turning her stomach.

Tarass grabbed her wrist. "Don't. You'll only spread it around your face. I'll see to it." He turned to Dolan. "Bring me a cloth and a blanket."

"Thaw? He isn't covered with blood, is he?" she asked worried for the pup.

"His paws. They'll clean off fast enough in the snow when he follows us," Tarass said and kept hold of her wrist as he guided her to a cropping of stones and helped her to sit on one.

He was annoyed with himself for not thinking of the pool of blood when he had shoved her out of the way of the arrow. But there had been such little time and his worry had been that more arrows would follow.

"What happened?" she asked.

Tarass scooped up a handful of snow. "I'm going to clean your face with snow."

"Aye, that would work good, though I fear my garments are ruined. Blood is never easily removed from clothing," she said, fighting to keep the quiver out of her voice.

She wanted to remain calm but the image of herself, in her mind, covered in blood wasn't helping.

178

And whose blood was it? A slaughtered animal? A murdered human? Not knowing made things worse.

"You'll not wear these garments again," he ordered and began to scrub her face with the snow.

His touch was gentle, but she had known it would be since he had been gentle with her when he had tended her wounds in the cottage. She was glad he took extra care cleaning around her mouth and her eyes, though she wondered if the bitter taste would linger in her mouth. He was thorough, cleaning her face with handful after handful of snow.

"There is nothing I can do with your garments except cover them. I'll wrap you in a blanket when I'm done and you'll wear my cloak the rest of the way," he ordered.

"You'll be cold," she said, thinking of the snow falling on him.

"We're not far from home," he said as if somehow that made a difference.

"Tuck me close against you once we're on the horse and wrap your cloak around us both, then we'll both stay warm," she suggested.

"Lift your chin," he snapped, annoyed that she thought of his well-being when he had completely forgotten about the pool of blood when he had shoved her out of the way of the arrow.

He scrubbed her neck, pushing the snow high up along the nape of her neck into her hair. He wanted to rid her of every speck of blood, but only a soak in the tub would do that.

"Please tell me what happened," Snow said. "Unable to see and not know what goes on around me can leave me fearful at times, something I don't like to admit."

That he had ignored her when she had first asked him what happened and not considered how it must feel to be left in the dark to your surroundings made him realize just how brave she had to be to live as she did, seeing nothing but shadows.

Tarass took hold of her hands and began slipping off the blood-soaked gloves. "I shoved you out of the way to avoid the arrow that was coming straight at you."

She shivered at the image it painted for her and at the cold snow he rubbed over her hands.

"We were attacked?" she asked, trying to make sense of it.

"That's the strange part. Only one arrow flew at us, then nothing," Tarass said.

"That's not the only strange part. There is the unexplained pool of blood and while I by no means enjoyed landing in it, it was a better alternative to what an arrow would have done to me. I would not want to die on my wedding day."

The thought of her dying filled him with a dread that turned to rage.

"You will not die!" he said as if commanding it so.

Snow chuckled and took hold of his hand as he cleaned hers. "Someday I will, but not today thanks to you."

How could this petite woman arouse him with a simple touch and thoughtful words?

"Don't make me regret it," he snapped, annoyed at himself, and she laughed, her whole face lighting with glee and his arousal grew. And he grew more annoyed.

"I fear you just might," she teased with a smiling laugh.

He smiled in spite of his frustration and knew a day would never come that he would regret marrying her.

A sudden shiver trembled her whole body.

"I need to get you home," he said, having lingered too long in the cold instead of rushing to clean her up and be on their way.

He snatched the cloth, Dolan had brought him, off his knee and hurried to dry the areas he had washed with snow. When he was done, he helped her to her feet, discarding her bloody cloak and wrapped the blanket around her, covering as much of her bloody garments that he could.

"Thaw?" she asked and the pup jumped up, his paws at her leg.

"He's been busy sniffing and rolling around in the snow. He's all cleaned off," Tarass said. "He will sit on your lap and keep you warm for the rest of the way home."

They were soon on their way, Thaw snuggled in her lap, another blanket wrapped around her and Tarass sharing his fur-lined cloak with them as Snow had suggested. They were snug and warm all three of them.

Snow smiled, her head resting against her husband's chest, thinking how Tarass and Thaw were her family now and soon...

A flutter caught at her heart. How could she be joyful and at the same time anxious of coupling with her husband?

She told herself not to worry. Sorrell and Willow had no difficulty with it, but then their husbands loved them. Then there was her blindness. Would either make a difference? She didn't know, but she would find out tonight.

Chapter Sixteen

Snow sat in the cloth lined tub, the water beginning to lose its warmth, though she cared not that it did. Nettle had assured her that she had scrubbed her body clean, that there was not a spot of blood on her.

Tarass had ordered a bath prepared for her in his bedchamber as soon as they had entered the Great Hall. She might not have been able to see the faces of those in the hall when Tarass yanked the blanket from around her revealing her blood-soaked garments, but Nettle had expressed what many must of thought.

"Good Lord, so much blood and you're still standing?"

"Silence, Nettle!" Tarass had commanded. "Lady Snow is unharmed."

Once they had reached his bedchamber, he had ordered Nettle to wash Snow down before she got in the tub. He made it abundantly clear that not an ounce of blood was to touch her bath water. Then he was gone and Snow hadn't seen him since.

That was perfectly fine with her, since she would have never been able to relax and enjoy the warm bath if he was present.

"A pool of blood," Nettle said, shaking her head as she busily gathered the soiled cloths she had used to wash Snow. "I still cannot believe it. No one can. And where did the blood come from?" She continued to shake her head perplexed.

Thanks to Nettle's propensity for chatter and detail, she found out more about the incident with the pool of blood than Snow had known. Snow had been amazed to learn that the pool of blood had appeared to sit there like a tiny lake in the middle of the pristine snow, not a sign of anyone or thing being dragged off. All wondered how that could be, and worried it was an evil omen, indeed. And where had the single arrow come from? No one had been caught thus far and with the snowfall growing heavy it was unlikely clear tracks could be found.

It was a mystery, one that made no sense.

Nettle added a bucket of hot water to Snow's bath and kept her voice low as she spoke. "Whispers circulate, not that I believe them, that death stalks you. The man Finn, the other body found in the snow, unknown to everyone, and now a single arrow that many believe…"

"What do they believe, Nettle?" Snow asked when the young woman's words had drifted off, a strange occurrence for Nettle. When no answer was forthcoming, Snow urged, "Please, Nettle, I need to know."

Nettle kept her voice to a whisper. "They believe you bring death with you and that the arrow was meant for Lord Tarass."

A bad omen indeed.

Is that what Tarass's clan thought of her… a bad omen?

"I count on you to not only be my eyes but my ears as well, Nettle. Please keep me informed about all you see and hear," Snow said, suddenly feeling vulnerable in her new home.

"Aye, my lady, I'll keep close watch of all that goes on," Nettle promised.

Snow rested her head back on the rim of the round tub, the heated water soaking into her, soothing and relaxing her limbs. She wasn't surprised when her eyes grew heavy, having gotten no sleep at all last night.

"My lady," Nettle said softly.

Snow's eyes fluttered open.

"The bed would be much better for a nap than the tub."

Snow nodded and let Nettle help her out of the tub and dry her off.

"Oh, I forgot your nightdress and robe," Nettle said, flustered she had forgotten it. "Wait under the bedcovers so you stay warm while I run and fetch it."

Snow sunk into the warmth of the bed, the soft wool blankets adding more warmth. Her eyes closed and sleep claimed her as soon as her head touched the pillow.

When the door shut behind Nettle, Thaw stretched himself out of the ball he had curled in before the hearth and went to the bed and jumped up on it to curl against Snow's side and fell asleep once again.

***

Nettle stood by the side of the bed, nightdress in hand, staring at Snow sleeping peacefully. It was her task to look after Lady Snow and that meant making sure she was dressed properly. She was not dressed properly for a nap or bedtime. She needed her nightdress, but she looked so peaceful Nettle hated to disturb her.

"Something wrong, Nettle, that you stand there staring at my wife," Tarass asked from the open door.

Nettle jumped and turned, not having heard the door open. "Forgive me, my lord. I forgot Lady Snow's nightdress and went to fetch it only to find her asleep when I returned. My lady was so tired she was falling asleep in the tub and she looks so content now, I hate to wake her."

"Don't," Tarass ordered, "leave the nightdress and see that a bath is prepared for me in the guest bedchamber."

"Aye, my lord," Nettle said and hurried from the room to see it done.

Tarass went to the bed and looked down at his sleeping wife. A soft blush stained her cheeks and her lips were parted ever so slightly as she breathed softly. Her red hair was still damp, a strand clinging to the side of her face. He reached down to move it and Thaw's head popped up and he gave a small growl

"Quiet, you'll wake her," Tarass ordered in a commanding whisper. "And don't think you'll be sleeping in bed with us. It's the floor for you."

A low grumbling growl came from Thaw, then he laid his head down and closed his eyes, staying right where he was.

Tarass didn't chase him off the bed, not this time since he was keeping Snow warm. It had been a difficult day for her and it was good she rested. And good that she was naked in his bed.

He continued to experience bouts of dread when he thought about how close he had come to losing her today, not once but twice. First in marriage to another man, then by an arrow. Though now, some of his warriors were speculating that the arrow could have been meant for him. He would think that himself if he was getting closer to finding out who had his parents killed. But he hadn't. It was as if a door had suddenly been slammed shut in his face when it came to finding out anything more about the attack on the Sandrik village where his parents had been brutally killed.

He had hoped to find out something about the dead man, that Snow had accidentally found when she tripped over him, while on his visit to his mum's people. But her people hadn't told him anything he hadn't already known. The one thing he had discovered, to his frustration, on the unplanned trip was that he had missed Snow.

It had made no sense to him and he had denied it for as long as he could, until he admitted that something was amiss when it came to her. He decided he had to return home and see Snow again, if only to put this aching unease and foolishness to rest.

The rage that had ripped through him upon discovering Snow was to wed that day made him want to beat someone senseless. Actually, he had wanted to beat the man who had the audacity to lay claim to her when she belonged to him.

Looking at her now in his bed, safe and sleeping peacefully, filled him with overwhelming relief. She was his wife. No one could take her from him, not now, not ever.

***

Snow woke slowly, content in the warmth that she was wrapped in. She lay there in the quiet enjoying it. When she finally opened her eyes, it was dark, no shadows danced around her and when she went to move she realized something—no, not something—someone was wrapped around her.

Panic took hold and she couldn't think straight. How had someone gotten into her room? In her bed? And where was Thaw? Fear sent her into flight.

"Thaw!" she screamed and scrambled out of bed almost falling to the floor, but righting herself and hurrying away, then bumping into something, turning, and trying to feel her way in the dark.

Something was wrong. She knew her way around her room. She hit something again and realized Thaw was barking furiously.

"Snow! It's Tarass. You're safe here in our bedchamber," he said and rested his hand gently on her shoulder. She slumped against him in relief, recalling where she was and that she was his wife.

"I forgot," she said with a sigh and his arms wrapped around her and he eased her against him. She jumped out of his arms with a slight shove. "Good Lord, we're both naked."

Tarass couldn't keep the chuckle out of his voice. "That we are and we're allowed to be since we're husband and wife." He thought reminding her again might temper her concern.

"I need my nightdress," she said, trying to cover what she could of herself with her arms.

"I prefer you naked," Tarass said, gently brushing her arms off her breasts and stomach. "You have the most beautiful body and I enjoy looking at it. And if you recall, this isn't the first time I have seen you naked."

That reminded Snow of something, and she had to ask, "Why did you marry me?"

"You'll catch a chill. Come to bed and I'll keep you warm," he said and slipped his arm around her.

Snow stepped away, his arm falling off her, and asked again, "Why did you marry me?"

"We'll talk while in the warmth of the bed," he urged.

Snow had no intention of being denied an answer. "My sister said you wed me because you love me. I told her that wasn't possible. You made it clear you couldn't love a blind woman."

Tarass was glad she couldn't see him cringe at the words he'd once said to her.

"So since you don't love me, why did you marry me? Nettle was the only one who knew about that night you fell asleep naked in my bed and she'd be too fearful of you to say a word. And no one but you and I know that you saw me naked in the cottage. There was no reason for you to do what you did… stop the wedding and marry me."

"What difference does it make. We are wed and we will stay wed," he said.

"We have not sealed our vows yet, the marriage can be undone."

"Never! You are my wife and you will stay my wife," he said with a command that sounded as if he claimed it law.

His word was law here in his clan, but that didn't answer her question that he continued to ignore.

"Tell me why you wed me or else," she said, tossing out her threat with a lift of her chin.

Tarass grabbed her chin in his hand. "Or else what, wife?"

Snow didn't need to see his face to tell he was annoyed with her. She placed her hand on his hand that had hold of her chin. "Or else I will wonder forever why a man who intended to marry a woman who would benefit his clan wed a blind woman who brought burden rather than benefit to him or his clan."

"You are no burden, *ást*."

His tone had softened and she wondered as she had the last time what the foreign word meant that he called her.

"I am no benefit either, so I will ask you until you answer me. Why did you marry me?"

"You aren't going to let this go, are you?"

"No, I need to know. I feel vulnerable enough standing in front of you naked. I feel even more vulnerable not knowing why you married me."

His hand went slowly around her waist to give the opposite side a gentle squeeze and draw her closer to him. Then he scooped her up in his arms and carried her to the edge of the bed to sit, and settled her in his lap.

She rested her hand gently on his cheek, the warmth there sending a slight tingle through her. "You will tell me?"

"You may not believe me."

"Will it be the truth?" she asked.

"Aye, on that you have my word," he promised.

"Then I will believe you. Now tell me why you wed me."

"Willow was right... I married you because I love you."

Chapter Seventeen

"I don't understand," Snow said, shaking her head.

"I don't understand it either, but there it is. I've fallen in love with you and not a simple fall, a hard one, if not harder than that tumble you took down that hill. It tumbled and stabbed at me until I was too battered to fight it." It was Tarass's turn to shake his head. "I told you that you wouldn't believe it. I barely believe it myself. But how do I deny something that refuses to let go, that drives me mad with endless thoughts, that—" He shook his head again. "It's done. I love you and that's all there is to it." He took a quick breath. "I hope someday, somehow, you might grow to love me, or at least grow fond of me."

Snow smiled. "Strange, you had told me time and again that you would never marry let alone love a blind woman. I thought for sure my sister was wrong, and yet she had been right not only about you but about me as well."

"What about you?"

"Willow told me before I would admit it to myself that I love you and though I fought it, like you, it wouldn't leave me alone. The realization of just how much I love you hit me when standing before the cleric with Lord Polwarth. I couldn't marry him when I knew I was in love with you." When no response came, Snow smiled. "Did I strike you speechless?"

"Aye, you did," Tarass said, his wits returning to him. "I feared you hated me too much to ever love me even a little." He chuckled. "Not that I deserved your hatred, of course."

Snow laughed with him. "There were many times I felt I did hate you, deserving of course." Her voice turned soft. "Until I found something in you that I didn't think existed... kindness. Though I daresay, you would not want anyone to know that of you."

"You'll keep my secret then?" he asked with another chuckle.

"I don't think it's much of a secret to those who truly know you," she whispered close to his lips.

Her faint breath teased his lips and he didn't hesitate to kiss her gently.

It was a tender, lovely kiss, but it wasn't enough for her. She ached for much more, but she needed to remind him of something. "You once said you'd never poke a blind woman."

He brushed his lips over hers and felt the light shiver that ran through her naked body before responding. "Aye, I did, and I meant it."

Snow snapped her head back as if he had slapped her in the face, so great was her surprise. If he didn't want to seal their vows, why claim he loved her?

Tarass took hold of her chin, keeping her eyes set on him, though she couldn't truly see him, but he wanted her to know that he saw her.

"I won't poke you," he said sharply before he softened his tone. "I intend to make love to you. Actually, I've ached to make love to you. I've thought almost about nothing else but making love to you. And

I fear you will grow quite tired of how much I intend to make love to you."

She brushed his hand away. "What if it is I who demands more?"

He laughed. "Then I have surely died and gone to heaven."

"Not without me," she scolded lightly. "I could not bear to live without you."

His heart felt as if it faltered. He had hoped one day she would love him, if only a little. To hear her say she wouldn't want to live without him filled him with joy and made him realize she loved him as much as he loved her, since he wouldn't want to live without her either.

He ran the back of his fingers over her cheek and down along her jaw. "I feel the same. I could not imagine life without you." He took hold of her jaw and brought his lips to hers to brush them lightly, teasingly.

"I am so glad you came and rescued me just in time," she whispered.

"I am too or else I would have had to make you a widow."

Snow yanked her head back again. "You wouldn't have."

"When I said you belonged to me, I meant it. No one will ever take you from me."

His hand went to the back of her neck to hold it firm as his lips came down on hers in a kiss that tingled every inch of Snow's naked body. It was a strong kiss that demanded and gave at the same time and Snow didn't hesitate to respond.

Tarass kept a firm arm around her waist as he dropped them back on the bed together, never breaking the kiss. But then Snow wouldn't let him. Her arms had hurried around his neck and her lips had opened eagerly for him. He thought she'd startle when his tongue slipped into her mouth, but her tongue had quickly joined his and they both were soon lost in the heated kiss.

He moved his hand off the back of her neck down along her body to grip her backside in a firm squeeze and she moaned with pleasure. Her moan grew when his hand drifted up, lightly caressing her soft skin before he reached her breast and cupped it in his hand, his thumb grazing her nipple.

A vicious bark sounded before Thaw hurled himself onto the bed and stood, teeth bared and growling, over Tarass.

"I'm not hurting her," Tarass said a bit too forcefully, annoyed at being disturbed.

Thaw wasn't at all appeased. His snarl deepened.

"Tarass does not hurt me, Thaw. I am good. I am not hurt," Snow said calmly and stretched her hand above her head searching for the pup.

Thaw's growling eased, though it didn't stop as he slipped the top of his head under her hand.

Snow rubbed behind his ears and under his chin, his favorite spots. "Tarass loves me, Thaw. He keeps me safe like you do."

Tarass remained silent. Though he wanted to throw the pup out of the room and lock the door, he knew that wouldn't be a good idea. Snow loved Thaw and, while he'd never admit he was a bit jealous of the pup—a crazy thought—he'd never do anything to come between their special bond. But he damn well wouldn't let the protective pup stop him from making love to his wife.

"I would never hurt, Snow, Thaw," Tarass said and gave the pup a rub behind his ear.

"I don't want to put him out of the room and have him think he did something wrong, especially with our return here. He needs to learn this is his new home now, but this situation isn't helping the matter," she said, not sure of what to do.

Tarass agreed, though not verbally. He wanted the pup to protect her and if he was put out of the room it would confuse him. In time he would learn, but that didn't help him tonight.

"Tell him to go sleep by the hearth as he'd been doing. We'll get beneath the blankets and we'll have to be quiet," Tarass said, "for tonight at least."

Snow reached out to touch his face, resting her hand on his cheek. "You do love me."

"I told you I did."

"Aye, you did, but not to get angry at Thaw for disturbing us and not putting him out of the room tells me just how very much you love me and makes me love you even more," she said and kissed him.

Tarass slipped his hand around to the back of her neck and deepened the kiss.

Thaw growled.

Tarass dropped his head back on the mattress to look up at the growling pup. "I am not hurting her. I love Snow."

196

Snow chuckled, reached out to find her husband's face, her hands landing on his chest that she followed up to his face to cup and plant kisses all over it. Then she reached out for Thaw, took hold of his face and rained kisses over him.

"See, Thaw, I love you both," she said and repeated the process. "Now you show him, Tarass, that you love us both."

"You want me to kiss the pup?" he asked, thinking her crazy.

"It will help him understand and hopefully let us make love tonight, uninterrupted."

The idea of kissing the pup was not appealing, but far less appealing was not finishing what he had started with his wife. Tarass grabbed his wife's face and rained lots of kisses over it and she began to moan softly. Before Thaw could growl, he took hold of the pup's face and kissed him a few times, and cringed when the pup licked his face.

"I think he understands," Tarass said, wiping his cheek with his arm.

"Go sleep now, Thaw," Snow ordered gently.

The pup jumped off the bed and curled up by the hearth.

Tarass helped his wife slip under the blankets. "This is a far different wedding night than I had planned."

Snow cuddled against him and loved when his arms wrapped around her to tuck her close. "Aye, far different than what I expected as well."

"What did you expect?" he asked, curious. "You intended to stop the wedding to Lord Polwarth, so there would have been no wedding night to expect with him. So it is a wedding night with me you had thought on. So again, what did you expect?"

"I expected to be anxious and fearful, but I'm not."

"Fearful of what? Not me, I hope. I would never hurt you, *ást*," he said, caressing her back.

"What is that name you call me?"

"It means love in my mum's native tongue."

"You've called me that twice before," she said, remembering the cottage where she had first heard it.

"I suppose I knew I loved you before I knew I loved you," he said and kissed her softly. "Now tell me what was there to be fearful of tonight?" He kissed her again.

"I'm not sure, but the fear disappeared as soon as you told me you loved me," she said and returned the kiss.

"I'm glad. I don't want you to fear me, at least not in bed," Tarass said with a slight laugh. "Ouch, did you just poke me?"

"You deserved it. besides, someone has to start poking."

"We don't poke, wife, we make love," he whispered and kissed her as his hand roamed over her intimately and she sighed with pleasure, though it quickly turned into a moan. "Quiet or you'll wake Thaw and end this before it can start."

Snow did her best to keep quiet, but it was difficult with his hands teasing her senses awake with his every touch. And when he took one of her taut and sensitive nipples into his mouth for his tongue to tease, she thought she'd scream with pleasure. She kept her

198

moans low, fearful Thaw would disturb them again, an unbearable thought.

Her body moved against his as if it had a mind of its own, a need of its own. When his hand slipped between her legs and stroked her, she almost vaulted off the bed if it weren't for him throwing his legs over hers to stop her.

"Tarass," she whispered and heard the aching need in her voice.

"Good God, wife, you feel as beautiful as you are," he said and buried his face in her neck to nibble along it.

His hand continued to tease between her legs and she thought she'd go mad. She bit her tongue to keep the moans locked away, but feared she'd fail in keeping them from escaping. She thought to reach out and explore him as he did her, but he had taken such command of her body that the only thing she could do was respond to his touch. And she did, her body writhing against his as if begging him for more, begging him not to stop, begging him to appease her ache.

She felt his manhood, thick and hard, against her leg and for a moment she wondered how he'd fit inside her, then she didn't care. She wanted him inside her, not only to bring her pleasure but to seal their vows, their love, their life together from this day on.

Thaw's growl and bark had Tarass ready to leap off the bed and throw the pup out of the room until he realized Thaw wasn't barking in their direction. He was barking at the door.

"Someone approaches," he said and hurried off his wife and out of bed to grab his sword. "Stay where you are."

Snow wrapped the blanket around her, fear chilling her skin and turning it to gooseflesh. Who dared to come to their bedchamber so late? An intruder? Or someone bearing bad news? Either way did not bode well.

Tarass went to stand near the door, sword in hand, taking no chance. Everyone knew it was his wedding night and he was not to be disturbed, he had made it clear. And as much as he didn't want to believe that someone had gotten passed his sentinels, he had to consider it. Especially now with a wife to protect.

A knock sounded at the door, but still Tarass stood ready.

"It's me, Rannock."

"This better be life or death," Tarass called out and laid aside his sword, then reached for his plaid and wrapped it quickly around him and before opening the door he turned to his wife. "I'm opening the door for Rannock to enter."

Snow was pleased that he let her know and tightened the blanket around her.

Tarass remained silent when he opened the door, knowing that the news couldn't be good for his friend to disturb him on his wedding night.

"It took only one person to see it and wake the whole village," Rannock said. "You need to see it yourself and calm the people."

"Send Nettle here, then wait in the Great Hall for me," Tarass ordered.

Rannock nodded and left, Tarass closing the door.

"What is it?" Snow asked anxiously.

"I don't know," he said, as he slipped his plaid off to hurry a shirt on and wrap his plaid around him. "But since Rannock disturbed me on our wedding night, it can't be good. Nettle will stay with you while I'm gone."

"I'll go with you," Snow said, rushing out of bed and bumping into a chair as she searched for her clothes. His hand was on her arm in an instant.

"You'll stay here," he ordered and walked her back to the bed.

"I want to go with you," she insisted.

"Get into bed, wife, and stay there."

His demanding tone spoke louder than his words and Snow held her tongue and got into bed, pulling the covers around her.

Thaw barked again, though wagged his tail this time.

"Nettle is here," Tarass said and opened the door.

"My lord," she said with a bob of her head.

Tarass could tell by her disheveled appearance that she had rushed to dress and he was glad the lass hadn't wasted any time in getting here.

"You'll stay with Lady Snow," he commanded and Nettle bobbed her head again.

"I hope not to be long, wife," he said and was out the door.

Snow was out of bed as soon as she heard the door latch. "Fetch my clothes, Nettle."

"Aye, m'lady," Nettle said and went to the chest against one of the walls and started hunting through it.

201

"Do you know what happened?" Snow asked.

"No, I came straight here. I didn't hear or see anything and Rannock wouldn't tell me anything until my endless questions annoyed him so much that he at least let me know that I was being summoned to stay with you while Lord Tarass tended to an urgent matter."

"I can't wait here. I must know what's going on," Snow said.

"I'm curious myself," Nettle said.

"Help me dress and we'll see what we can find out," Snow urged pleased that Nettle was as curious as her.

Snow ran her hand over the soft wool shift Nettle got her into and an equally soft tunic she placed over it.

"These are lovely," Snow commented, the soft wool warming her chilled body.

"They belonged to Lord Tarass's mum. She was petite, but courageous from what I'm told. She was much like you."

Snow was surprised that Nettle thought her courageous and pleased to learn something about Tarass's mum. But there was no time to linger on those thoughts. She needed to find out what was going on. She was in the dark enough with no sight. She didn't want to be more in the dark and not aware of what went on in her new home.

Thaw followed the two women down the stairs, Nettle guiding Snow's steps.

The crisp, cold air stung Snow's face as soon as she stepped outside and she pulled her hood up over her head to block the wind and snow.

Nettle hooked her arm around Snow's. "Snow covers the stairs, m'lady, go slow."

Thaw followed the pair down the steps, keeping watch on Snow until they reached the bottom.

"Thaw runs ahead," Nettle said, watching the pup rush off. "He heads to the crowd gathered in the middle of the village."

"Hurry and get us there, Nettle," Snow urged.

"Much snow has fallen in a short time," Nettled explained as she kept tight hold of Snow's arm and headed to the crowd as Thaw had done.

"Fear not, this will be dealt with!"

Snow recognized her husband's strong, commanding voice ring out and, though he had warned against it, she couldn't stop a twinge of fear from striking her. What could have driven people from their warm beds in the middle of the night to go outside in the cold and falling snow?

Nettle eased their way through the crowd, though when people saw who she brought with her, they parted leaving a path for Lord Tarass's new wife.

When they got near to the front of the crowd, Nettle caught sight of what had frightened the people. She came to an abrupt halt, shivered, and gasped, "Oh, Lord, have mercy on us."

Chapter Eighteen

"What is it?" Snow asked in a whisper.

"Another pool of blood, that devours the snow," Nettle murmured, tales of the first pool of blood having circulated the clan.

"The dwarfs, Fjalar and Galar, are here. They look for more blood," someone in the crowd called out.

"They search for knowledge like they did with Kvasir," another called out.

Rannock's strong voice rang clear. "Then none of you have anything to worry about since the lot of you lack knowledge."

"Heads are nodding and smiles are breaking out," Nettle whispered to Snow. "They are happy to be ignorant."

Another person spoke up. "Someone here is wise like Kvasir and the dwarfs want his knowledge. What if they choose the wrong person and drain him of his blood by mistake?"

Gasps rushed through the crowd.

"Fear replaces the smiles," Nettle told Snow.

"I will see to this. You have nothing to fear," Tarass commanded.

"This danger arrived with your new wife. It is she who the dwarfs want," someone shouted.

Nettle wrapped her arm around Snow. "We should leave."

"No," Snow said. "Stand me out in front of the crowd and do not argue over it with me."

Nettle did as she was told, then stepped to Snow's side while Thaw wasted no time in running to her and taking a protective stance in front of her.

Snow kept her voice strong and clear. "I've brought no danger to your clan. What knowledge I have is easily obtainable by all, and I will not be maligned for something that doesn't involve me. Look to yourselves, for I have nothing to do with this."

Tarass had been annoyed when he first caught sight of his wife making her way through the crowd. She had disobeyed him and now here she stood in front of his clan having her say, and he couldn't be more proud of her.

"If I hear anyone malign my wife, the consequences will be severe," Tarass warned, his powerful voice carrying out over the crowd. "She had no part in this, and this," —he pointed to the pool of blood in such stark contrast to the pure white snow— "is not the work of dwarfs. It is humans who did this, and I will find them and see them suffer. Now go home, sleep, and know you are safe."

Grumbles and whispers were heard as the crowd dispersed.

Tarass turned to Rannock. "I don't want a drop of this blood left here or seen anywhere in the village by morning."

Rannock kept his voice low. "What if the dwarfs are here?"

"Then it will be their blood that is spilled," Tarass said and walked around the pool of blood, smaller than

205

the one they had come upon in the woods, and went straight to his wife.

"Your husband approaches… hastily," Nettle said and stepped aside.

"You disobeyed me," Tarass scolded sharply.

"Who are these dwarfs and this Kvasir?" Snow asked, ignoring his reprimand.

"That matters not," he chided, taking her arm. "Nettle, you are no longer needed tonight."

"It does matter," she insisted as he forced her into step beside him before she could bid Nettle good-night. "It could be a clue in solving the mystery of the two pools of blood and perhaps they are connected with Finn and the stranger's death."

"Lord Tarass!"

He stopped and turned to see one of his warriors running toward him, the shocked look on his face alerting him to what was bound to be more disturbing news.

The warrior kept his voice low. "The body, my lord… it's gone."

"Which body?" Snow asked.

Tarass sent his wife a scowl, then realized she couldn't see it. His annoyance grew when the warrior turned to her and answered.

"The stranger with the markings."

"How…" Tarass shook his head, knowing the answer as did his wife.

"The pool of blood was used to distract," Snow said.

"Did all the sentinels leave their posts to find out what was happening?" Tarass asked, his temper sparking.

The warrior lowered his head. "Aye, my lord."

"Yet, you're the only one who stands before me."

The warrior bobbed his head, but said nothing.

"Wait for me at the hut," Tarass ordered and turned away from the warrior.

"Please don't have Nettle fetched again. I'll go with you," Snow said, locking her arm more firmly around her husband's, determined to remain with him.

"It is cold and the snow falls heavily. You need to be inside where it's warm and safe," he argued.

Snow rested her hand on her husband's chest. "It is our wedding night and while I'd prefer to be in our bedchamber together, what I want most is for us to be together wherever that might be. So please don't send me away from you."

Married a few hours and his petite wife had already worked her way deeper into his heart.

He took her hand in his and scolded, "Where are your gloves? Your hands feel like ice."

"I was in a rush and forgot them," Snow said.

Tarass caught sight of Nettle at the keep steps and shouted, "Nettle, fetch Lady Snow's gloves."

"Aye, my lord," she said and lifted the hem of her garments to carefully, yet quickly, climb the snow-covered steps.

"We wait here for her," Tarass said.

Snow snuggled against him. "Good, then it gives you a chance to tell me about the dwarfs and who

Kvasir is and why your clan thought of them at the sight of the pool of blood."

Tarass felt more content standing there in the snow and cold, his wife snug against him, then he had in some time. His mum had told him not to settle for anything but love when it came time for him to choose to wed. After his parents' brutal deaths, his only thought had been to do whatever was necessary to find the person responsible and make him pay with his life. He liked to think that somehow his mum had had a hand in bringing Snow to him to make sure he married for love.

"It's a tale told by my mum's people. Kvasir was born of two gods. He possessed great wisdom and he taught and spread his wisdom in his travels. The dwarfs, Fjalar and Galar, were jealous creatures and wanted his wisdom. They captured Kvasir and drained him of all his blood, hoping to gain all his knowledge."

She glanced up at him, seeing only a gray blur and wishing she could see her husband's face clearly. She recalled when she had last seen him, but he had been young, with fine features and an arrogant stride of youthful confidence. She wondered what he looked like now, though she had no doubt that arrogant stride of youthful confidence had become more powerful and confident with age.

"So the pools of blood could be a message of sorts." She scrunched her brow. "Someone searching for knowledge? What knowledge? And why two pools of blood? Or was it simply a distraction to steal the body and put fear in your clan?"

Tarass admired her quick perception, his own thoughts being the same.

Snow gripped his arm. "You search for the person responsible for your parents' death. Could this be a message that if you gain that knowledge you will die? The arrow that almost struck me could have been meant for you, the marksman having missed his target. Someone wants to keep knowledge from you, perhaps the knowledge of your parents' deaths."

"You piece puzzles together quickly, wife," he said, hugging her.

"Not all puzzles," she said, frowning. "I can't understand why we dally out here on our wedding night when we should be in our bedchamber making lo—"

"I have the gloves, my lord," Nettle called out as she approached.

Tarass slipped his hand beneath his wife's cloak to give her backside a hasty squeeze. "I will rectify that soon."

He took the gloves from Nettle and dismissed her for the night once again. He slipped the gloves on his wife's hands, then took her arm.

"We will see this done quickly," he said and took her arm.

Tarass stopped to talk with Rannock briefly, explaining what the warrior had told him and that he was on his way to speak with the warriors who had failed to do their duty. He ordered Rannock to send four other warriors to the hut.

"Do you mind waiting inside the hut?" Tarass asked as they approached the area.

"I don't mind. the dead can't hurt us," Snow said.

209

Tarass escorted her inside the hut. "I won't be long." He turned to Thaw, the pup having followed them in. "Guard Snow, Thaw."

Thaw gave a bark and pressed against Snow's leg.

"I won't be long," he said again and left.

"You all failed tonight!"

Snow cringed at the powerful anger in her husband's voice and felt sorry for his warriors, though they had failed him and needed to face the consequences of their failure. She recalled the last time she was here and moved slowly, bumping into the edge of a table. She reached out and found the table empty. It had been the one her friend had laid upon.

"Rest in peace, Finn," she said and turned, recalling Nettle saying something about the tables the dead men rested on lay close to each other. A few steps and she touched an empty table. Even with the commotion the pool of blood had caused, wouldn't someone have seen the body being removed from the hut.

She heard sniffs and low growls and called out to Thaw. "What is it, Thaw? What have you found?"

She followed his sounds and found him in one of the corners of the hut, digging. She was about to lean down to find out what he was up to when she heard a slight crack. She reached out and touched the crudely built wall, that did little to keep out the cold, and the section moved against her hand. She pushed at it and the section fell away.

Thaw gave a yap and scurried past her leg.

"Thaw," she called and followed after him.

210

She had only taken a few steps when Thaw returned to her and gave her hem a tug. He wanted her to follow him and without thought, she did.

When a branch brushed her cheek, she knew he had taken her into the woods and she stopped, realizing her mistake. "Thaw, we need to go back and get Tarass."

He barked, then tugged at her hem again.

He was desperate to show her something and she was desperate to alert Tarass to her whereabouts.

"You can show me, Thaw, but first..." She cupped her hands together so her voice would carry far, and shouted, "Tarass! Tarass!" She hoped he heard her and she planned to call out to him again, but first she took a cautious step forward to appease Thaw, who was tugging wildly at her hem.

Her foot hit something and she crouched down, her hand reaching out to touch a body.

Thaw started growling low and deep as he made his way around her and climbed up on the body to position himself protectively in front of her.

Something or someone was there with them.

His growling intensified, letting her know that whatever it was... was drawing nearer.

"Snow! Snow!" came her husband's frantic calls.

Thaw barked repeatedly while Snow shouted to her husband, "Tarass! Tarass!"

She was relieved to hear pounding footfalls, but she also heard a scurrying of sorts.

"Snow!" Tarass shouted when he caught sight of her and snatched her up off the ground to hug her tight.

Thaw kept barking.

211

"I'm here, Thaw, Snow is safe," Tarass assured him.

"He's letting you know someone was here and ran off," Snow said.

"Search the woods!" Tarass commanded and his warriors trailing him took off, though two remained behind, aware their lord and lady were not to be left unprotected.

"There's a body," Snow said, pointing to the ground. "I think it's the man with the markings. Thaw discovered the scent and was digging. I leaned on a section of the hut wall and it collapsed, then Thaw led me here."

"Bring the torch closer," Tarass commanded and when the warrior did, Tarass saw that his wife was right. "Dolan, get Rannock and more warriors."

"Aye, my lord," the young warrior said and hurried off.

Snow went to speak.

"Not a word, wife," Tarass ordered. "You have disobeyed me twice tonight and put yourself in unnecessary danger."

"You're right. I followed Thaw without thinking. It was foolish of me and I called out to you as soon as I realized my mistake. I'm truly sorry."

That she admitted her mistake and apologized for it caught him off guard. He expected her to argue and make excuses, but he should have realized that was not what his wife would do. She spoke her mind to him and she spoke the truth.

"We will discuss this later," Tarass said.

212

"Aye, my lord," she said softly, hearing footfalls approach and feeling as he might, that it was not a matter to be discussed in front of others.

While dark and gray shadows remained for Snow, she felt the heat of several torches around her and her husband's hand clutching hers. He squeezed it now and again to either make it clear he had no intention of letting her go or to remind her that he was there with her. Either way, it comforted her.

Snow listened to the conversation between her husband and Rannock, offering no opinions, at least not yet.

"How do you get blood from a dead man who's been frozen for a couple of weeks?" Rannock asked after some discussion.

Just as Snow had thought, someone had taken the dead man's blood. "Your healer might know, if not, my sister would," Snow offered and couldn't stop the yawn that rushed up and out of her mouth.

"You're tired," Tarass said and got annoyed that it took a yawn for him to realize it. It had been a long, exhausting day and his wife needed sleep, which meant…

He silently let loose a string of oaths in his head, frustrated that their union would not be sealed tonight.

"See that the hut is repaired and the body returned there and keep two warriors, front and back of the hut, on guard," Tarass ordered. "We'll discuss more on the morrow."

Snow yawned again as they walked away, Thaw following along with them.

"You need sleep," Tarass said.

213

"I was so concerned over marrying Lord Polwarth that I didn't sleep at all last night, the reason why I am so tired tonight," she admitted and to prove it true, another yawn escaped her.

Tarass scooped her up in his arms and got a snarling bark from Thaw for it.

"You should have told me," he said.

Snow didn't respond, content in her husband's arms. She might be tired, but it was her wedding night and their vows must be sealed. She almost chuckled, since what she truly wanted was to make love with her husband, and being in her husband's arms reminded her how she had felt when naked in his arms, and her passion sparked and ignited.

Once Tarass placed her on her feet in their bedchamber and took her cloak, she was eager to shed her garments, but his strong command stopped her.

"Leave your shift on to sleep. The room has chilled and it will keep you warm." He went to the hearth to add more logs.

"You'll keep me warm," she said.

"You need sleep, if I get in bed with you, you will not sleep," he said with snarl that rivaled Thaw's.

Her eyes went wide and anger bubbled inside her. "You don't intend to sleep with me?"

"Not tonight," he said. "You're exhausted and need sleep."

"You decide when I sleep?" she argued.

Tarass did his best to temper his annoyance, but it wasn't easy. He wanted to say the hell with it and whether she was tired or not, make love to his wife.

"Aye, I'm your husband and know what is best for you, especially when you're too stubborn to realize it."

Her mounting anger chased her exhaustion and she nearly ripped her tunic as she tore it off herself and threw it aside.

"You don't command me when to sleep or what to wear to bed." She grabbed the sides of her shift to tug it off.

"Don't dare take that off!" he ordered sharply.

"Or what?" she challenged.

"You will obey me on this, Snow," he warned. "Leave the shift on and get in bed."

Thaw raised his head from where he was curled asleep by the hearth and started growling.

Snow stuck her chin up defiantly. "You're not officially my husband until our vows are sealed so until then I'll do as I please, and I please to sleep naked." She yanked off her shift and stood naked, her hands on her hips. "Now what are you going to do?"

"Teach you obedience," Tarass said.

Donna Fletcher

Chapter Nineteen

"What are you doing? Why is Thaw snarling so badly?" Snow demanded, worried for Thaw, though she knew Tarass would not harm the pup.

"He's being put out of the room, since he won't tolerate what I'm about to do to you," Tarass said.

Snow heard the latch on the door close and Thaw's barks and scratches against the door, and she hurried forward to rescue the angry pup.

The next thing she knew she was scooped up in her husband's arms and what happened next shocked her. She found herself thrown over his legs, after he sat on the bed, and his bare hand rested on her backside. Her first thought was to warn him that he better dare not take his hand to her bottom in a punishing manner, but then another thought came to her.

"If a paddling entices you, I suppose I can endure it."

"It's not a paddling I had in mind, wife," Tarass said and his hand gave her backside a squeeze before it slipped between her legs and his finger worked its way ever so slowly and firmly inside her.

She gasped. "What are you doing?"

"Giving you what you want, wife."

She gasped again when she felt more than one finger enter her and couldn't hold back another gasp when his other hand slipped underneath her, his finger finding one of her nipples and playing with it until it turned rock hard.

There was no denying that he was bringing her pleasure. Her senses were alive like never before and if he continued, she would certainly experience the satisfaction her sisters had spoken about, and she had never thought she would experience, but…

"I want you inside me. I want our vows sealed."

Tarass yanked her off his legs and onto her feet, his hands gripping her shoulders. "And our vows will be sealed when you obey me and rest, for God help me, wife, my thirst is too great for you to have you only once this night."

His hands fell off her and he walked to the door. "Sleep well and I will see you in the morning."

Snow stood stunned. He had taught her more than he had intended. He might have wanted her to learn to obey him, but she had learned that he would deny himself when he believed her too tired and his passion too demanding. He had put her well-being before her own needs. There was only one problem with his decision.

She was not as delicate as he thought.

"Tarass," she called out softly.

He didn't turn or take his hand off the latch. "What?"

"At least give me a kiss before you leave."

A low growl rumbled in his chest and he warned himself against even responding to her.

"Please, I don't want either of us to take anger to bed. I'll slip on my shift." She followed the bed to the end and searched with her hands to find where she had dropped the garment. Her fingers found the soft wool and hastily snatched it up. "I'm putting it on now." She struggled a bit to slip it over her head, but when she finally got it on, the material fell softly down her body.

He warned himself not to do it, but he had to agree with her. He wanted to take no anger to bed with him this night.

She stretched her arm out in front of her to reach out for him.

Tarass took hold of her arm with reluctance and warned himself not to take her in his arms even though she wore the shift. He'd never be able to let her go if he did. His manhood was hard and throbbing with the want of her and his mind was filled with images of making love to her.

It would be so easy to surrender to his need, to her, but she needed to learn to obey him. Something she had failed to do again and again, and he feared it would one day cost her dearly. She had to learn, even if the lesson hurt him possibly more than her.

"One kiss," he snapped.

"One kiss," Snow repeated and stood on her toes as he brought his head down, and their lips met.

Snow felt his hesitation, the tenseness in him, and she knew he fought his own passion. She kissed him lightly, letting her lips linger on his until her tongue peeked from her mouth to tempt his lips apart.

His lips wouldn't budge. They held tight. He was a stubborn man, but then he claimed she was a stubborn woman.

Snow brushed her lips over his before she moved them off his, then she rested her hand on his cheek and said softly, "Thank you for rescuing me today from my own foolish decision to wed a man I didn't love. It thrills me to be wed to a man I love with all my heart." She let her lips brush over his as she turned her head away.

A growl rose up deep from within his chest. "Damn it, wife."

His hand was at the back of her neck in an instant, holding it firm as his arm coiled around her waist to yank her against him, and his lips came down on hers in a kiss that punished and pleased all at once.

Snow's arms went around her husband's neck when he lifted her with his one arm, leaving her feet to dangle above the floor as he kissed her like a man long starved for the taste of her. He didn't let up. He punished her lips with a passion that raced through her, tingling every inch of her senseless.

He kept hold of her as he walked to the bed and he reluctantly pulled his mouth away from hers when he set her on her feet, and said, "You did that on purpose, wife."

Snow heard more passion than annoyance in his voice, and she smiled. "Aye, I did."

Tarass planted his nose against hers. "Now you pay the price."

She gasped when he ripped her shift off her, sending gooseflesh running over her entire naked body and an endless throb between her legs.

Tarass scooped her up and dropped her on the bed, then yanked his garments off and fell down over her, planting his hands on either side of her head to support his body so that his chest faintly brushed hers.

219

"The whole time you were gone from me I couldn't get you out of my head," he whispered.

His breath fanned her lips in a whisper of a kiss, sending gooseflesh rushing over her.

"I thought of you in my bed and what I would do to you." He faintly touched his lips to hers. "Not just for a few minutes or an hour, but for the whole night. How I would explore your body with my hands and lips, discover your most sensitive spots, responsive spots, familiarize myself with every inch of you... and make you mine." He brushed his lips back and forth slowly over hers. "You belong to me, wife, now and forever."

How was it that this man continued to steal her heart over and over again? He could be maddening, stubborn, demanding, commanding, and still she loved him.

"And you belong to me, husband, now and forever," she whispered and faintly touched her lips to his.

"Our vows and consummation may officially bind us, but the words we just exchanged bind our hearts and souls," he said.

When his lips came down on hers, Snow rushed her arms around his neck and pulled him close. Since going blind, she hadn't thought a man would ever love her, let alone find a man who would want to wed her, and here she was in the arms of a husband who not only had wanted to marry her, but made his love known.

Tarass pulled his mouth away from hers, not that he wanted to. "You make it difficult to go slow."

"Then don't," she said and eased her legs apart. "I am eager to feel you inside me."

"Good Lord, wife, you're going to have me spill my seed before I get inside you," he said, his manhood aching so badly he feared his words would prove true.

Snow grabbed his cheeks with her hands, keeping her eyes focused on the gray blur in front of her. "No, you mustn't do that. Your seed belongs in me where it will flourish and grow a bairn made of our love."

He rested his brow on hers. "You fire my passion with words alone."

"Then slip inside me and love me."

"I want to, but I also want to touch and kiss every inch you."

"We have all night and morning," she whispered with a smile.

He smiled himself, then realized she couldn't see it and gave a soft chuckle. "You are wicked, wife."

"I know nothing about being wicked in bed, but you could teach me."

"I have a feeling you won't need lessons," he said and before she could say anymore he kissed her.

It was no simple kiss. It was a kiss filled with the deepest of passion, of need, of want, of an insatiable hunger and his wife responded in kind.

He wanted to go slow, have her experience the full pleasure of making love, but his passion had simmered too long from when they had first been disturbed. He couldn't wait and he sensed she couldn't either with the way she eagerly arched against him, inviting his manhood to enter her.

Snow was lost in a haze of passion, barely able to focus. She gripped his arms as his lips drifted down along her neck to nibble there and send more

221

gooseflesh rushing over her. She would lose her sanity if she did not feel him inside her soon.

"I've waited long enough, husband, do your duty," she snapped, then moaned from the pleasure his nibbles brought her.

"Or what?" he teased, raising his head to see her eyes heavy with passion.

She looked about to chastise him when tears suddenly glittered in her eyes and he felt as if he'd been punched in the stomach.

"Or you will greatly disappointment me," she said, a soft moan leaving her lips as she arched and rubbed against his manhood.

The idea that he would disappoint his wife angered him. "Never, ást, never will I disappoint you." He kissed her gently. "I love you more than you know."

Snow had no chance to respond, his kiss capturing her words, though it wasn't the reason for her slight gasp, which his kiss also captured. It was feeling his manhood probe between her legs and the tip slip slightly inside her.

"Hold me tight," he ordered, not wanting to hurt her but suddenly realizing how petite she was next to him and, though he felt how wet she was, he worried his sizeable manhood would cause her undue pain.

This was one time she obeyed him without question, her slim hands gripping his arms with all the strength she had.

He pressed his cheek against hers. "You will tell me if I cause you pain."

"You cause me pain," she said hastily.

"I've barely entered you," he said, ready to pull away from her.

"Exactly," she said and released a moan combined with a chuckle as she worked her hips to instinctively urge him further into her.

He brought his lips to her, but didn't kiss her. "I'll give you what you want, wife, and more than once tonight."

"Promise," she whispered against his lips.

"Aye," he said, "now open your mouth and spread your legs farther."

Snow once again didn't hesitate to do as he said and his lips came down on hers. He didn't slip slowly into her, he plunged quickly into her. She let out a small cry that faded into his mouth.

Then he began to move.

His lips left hers, and there were no more words after that only her moans of pleasure.

She tossed her head back with each strong thrust, moans falling liberally from her lips. She could feel the width and length of him and loved that he fit so perfectly inside her. It felt like they were one, never to be parted.

She only wished she could see his face, though his growing groans as he drove in and out of her let her know of his mounting pleasure.

Everything faded around her and all she could feel was his steady thrusts and her passion turning so wild and demanding that her body responded of its own accord.

Their bodies worked in an instinctive rhythm that intensified to the point that Snow thought she'd scream.

223

She did when suddenly her body exploded in such a powerful, mind-shattering sensation that she couldn't help but cry out. The exquisite sensation rippled through her body, her moans flowing along with it.

As soon as his wife cried out in climax, he let himself go and joined her, letting loose a growling groan that intensified as his powerful climax went on to last longer and bring greater satisfaction than he'd ever experienced.

He collapsed on her, stripped of strength, something that had never happened to him before this. Her arms went around him to squeeze tight, though he felt her lack of strength as well.

They were both spent and that made him smile.

He rolled to his side, his wife's arms keeping hold of him, and his arms went around her. They remained locked together in more ways than one. He didn't want to let go and he could tell she didn't either.

At that moment, he fully understood what his mum had told him about love.

When you find true love, you never want to let it go.

"I never want to let you go, *ást*," he whispered.

"I never want you to let me go," Snow responded softly.

They fell asleep like that, until a chill woke Tarass and he pulled a blanket over them, stirring Snow awake to press closely against him. He ran his hand down over her backside to ease her even closer and his manhood instantly sparked to life.

She had to be sore from the pounding he had given her, especially since she had been a virgin, but she

224

hadn't complained, hadn't said a word about it. He needed to leave her alone.

"I want you," she whispered, surprising him.

He was ready to slip into her again, but said, "You must be sore."

Snow kissed and teased his neck with light nibbles. "You deny me pleasure, husband?"

Tarass turned her on her back, spread her legs apart, and knelt between them. "I'll watch you as you climax this time."

He realized his words too late and Snow felt his regret when he tensed.

"Hearing your groans as they grow lets me know what my eyes can't see." She chuckled. "Though you might bring the roof down on top of us."

He went to chuckle himself when her small hand reached down, brushing his leg as she searched for his manhood. And when she found it, he feared she might be right. His groans just might bring the roof down on them.

"You are large and soft yet hard," she said as she stroked him. "I love the feel of your manhood."

"He's yours to touch anytime you want," Tarass said, trying to keep control, her gentle, innocent touch driving him mad.

"I'm pleased he belongs to me."

Her sigh of pleasure was difficult to ignore. His manhood certainly didn't ignore it. It grew in her hand.

"You swell even larger," she said on a soft gasp. "It is amazing that you fit inside me so perfectly. Though, I think it would be wiser for us to make sure you do fit."

Tarass smiled and laughed gently so that she could hear what she couldn't see. "I agree wholeheartedly."

"You feel like you're ready," she said, giving his manhood a tug.

He slipped a finger inside her and he was relieved to hear her gasp and not wince. "You're ready as well."

"For you… always," she said with a wickedly, passion-filled smile.

He eased her hand off him, grabbed her backside and tugged her forward to meet his manhood, and slipped into her, smoothly and slowly, filling her with the length of him.

Snow moaned as he did, taking all of him with ease and pleasure, delighted to have him inside her once again. She knew it wouldn't be long before she climaxed, having grown far more excited when she touched him than she had ever expected. Actually, a few words, a simple touch, was all that was needed to stir her passion for her husband. She found it both exciting and worrisome, since she feared he might grow tired of her demands on him.

She let out a long, slow moan as he began to move inside her and her thoughts turned to the pleasure he brought her with little effort. Lord, but she loved her husband and joining with him made her love him even more.

She feared disappointment showed on her face when she climaxed much too fast to her liking, but it was surprise that replaced the disappointment when her husband teased her to life once again and she joined him in another overwhelming satisfying climax.

Sleep claimed them once again and Snow thought it had to be morning when she woke to her husband's hands roaming her body intimately.

"I can't keep my hands off you," he whispered.

It was a quick joining and when she woke once again it was to find Thaw in bed with them, sleeping between them, Snow having felt past the pup to touch her husband's arm.

"You put Thaw between us on purpose," she said when she felt his hand close around hers.

"The last time I slipped out of you, I heard you wince. I couldn't trust myself or you not to make love again. Thaw was the easiest solution to the problem, though don't think it will become a habit."

Snow laughed gently. "A wise decision, since I am a bit sore, though it was well worth the small discomfort."

"I will have Runa sent to you," Tarass said, feeling guilty that she suffered some discomfort.

"Not necessary. Willow explained what I should do if the problem presented itself."

"Your sister looks out for you. I am grateful for that," he said, bringing her hand to his lips to kiss.

She sighed heavily.

"What's wrong?" he was quick to ask, while Thaw lifted his head to lick her face.

"I fear I will make a terrible wife," she admitted.

"Why would you think that?"

"You kiss my hand and you spark passion in me. I will be far too much of a demanding wife in bed."

Tarass laughed, not a chuckle, but a hefty laugh. "You will never be too demanding for me."

227

Donna Fletcher

"You think it's humorous, but what if I am?" she asked seriously.

He laughed again. "Then you will have worn me out and I will go to my grave a happy man."

Snow felt him move off the bed. "Where are you going?"

"If I remain here with you any longer, Thaw will find himself put out of the room again. Besides, I have duties to see to you."

"I'm one of those duties," Snow said, sitting up in bed, ignoring the blanket that fell to her waist, leaving her breasts exposed.

"Now *you* did that on purpose. Even one night together tells you how much I enjoy your breasts," Tarass accused, turning his head away as he slipped on his shirt.

Thaw jumped off the bed and barked at the closed door.

"Someone approaches," Tarass said.

Snow just finished covering herself when a knock sounded at the door.

"It's Rannock and it's a matter that cannot wait," he called out.

Tarass opened the door.

"James Macardle is here on an urgent matter and must speak to you posthaste," Rannock rushed to say.

"What matter?" Tarass asked as he walked to fetch his boots.

Snow's eyes went from one gray blur to another, though she turned her head away from both when she thought she caught a flash of color from the flicker of a flame. But it was so brief, she couldn't be certain. Her

228

brother's arrival the day after her wedding was more concerning than what had probably been nothing more than her imagination as was Rannock's hesitation to respond. It sparked alarm in Snow.

"Tell me, Rannock," Tarass ordered.

"Lord Polwarth claims that Lady Snow is not legally your wife."

Chapter Twenty

"Fetch Nettle," Tarass ordered Rannock, "and have James wait in my solar."

As soon as Snow heard the door close, she was out of bed. "Don't think you're leaving me out of this conversation."

"This is for me to see to," he said and grabbed her garments that she fumbled around to find and handed them to her.

"It involves me," she insisted, slipping her shift on, her arm getting stuck in the wrong hole.

Tarass shook his head as his hands stilled her arms. "You're too stubborn for your own good."

He eased her arm out of the one hole and into the correct one. He couldn't imagine how difficult it must be for her to depend on others to help her with simple things he took for granted. And he didn't want her worrying about whatever senseless claim Lord Polwarth thought he had. There was no way he'd let anyone take his wife away from him.

"I can be agreeable and pliable—"

His laughter interrupted her. "I have yet to see that side of you, wife, though I admit you are pliable in bed."

Snow jabbed him in the chest. "This matter concerns me and I will not be left out of it."

"I will tell you all that is discussed," he said to appease her.

A knock sounded again and Nettle announced herself, and Tarass bid her to enter.

Snow had asked her mum once how was it that she rarely argued with her husband and yet so often got her way? Or how Sorrell, a handful to say the least when young, had complied so easily to their mum's orders, but not to others?

It's the maneuvers that matter more than the battle, Snow. That's what her mum had told her and that's what had her holding her tongue.

"Help Lady Snow and have her wait in the Great Hall for me," Tarass ordered Nettle, then kissed his wife's cheek. "I will join you there as soon as I can."

As soon as the door closed, Snow said, "Thaw is impatient to go out, Nettle. Take him to see to his duty while I wait here for you."

"Would you not rather enjoy the morning meal in the Great Hall while I see to Thaw?"

"No, I'm not hungry yet, but Thaw is in need, so please hurry and see to him."

Thaw barked as if he agreed.

"I won't be long," Nettle said.

"Take your time. I'm in no hurry. I'm going to sit by the fire and enjoy the peace and quiet, though I would appreciate it if you could hand me my comb and a strip of cloth."

"Aye, m'lady, as you wish," Nettle said and fetched the comb and cloth to give her before turning to Thaw. "Time for a walk, Thaw."

231

Snow got busy on her hair as soon as Nettle left, giving it a good combing, then braiding it and tying the end with the strip of cloth. She returned to the edge of the bed where her husband had helped her into her shift and felt around, happy to find her tunic. It was easy to get on as were her shoes she had left by the side of the bed.

The maneuvers she had planned were going well. She didn't want Nettle to know what she intended for fear she would get the young woman in trouble. This was her own doing and she would be the only one blamed.

Snow made her way carefully down the stairs, keeping her shoulder to the wall and inching her foot out to feel for the edge of each step. Surprisingly, she made it down the stairs more easily than she had thought she would. When she entered the Great Hall, she stopped and waited to spot a gray blur nearby.

She stepped forward as soon as she spotted one and bumped with some force into the edge of a table and winced.

"Are you all right, m'lady," a female voice asked.

"Aye, but I do need help to get to Lord Tarass's solar," Snow said, making it seem imperative.

"I'll take you," the woman said and Snow held out her arm.

"Your name?" Snow asked as she followed along with the woman.

"Maude, m'lady."

"You are most gracious to help, Maude. Thank you," Snow said.

Maude left Snow at the closed door as directed and she waited until she heard the servant leave, then swung open the door and entered.

"Snow!" James said in surprise and hurried to her.

"I suspect my husband told you I wouldn't be joining in this discussion, but I thought it was best I did," she said and smiled after James took her hand.

"Obedience is a difficult lesson for my wife to learn," Tarass said, annoyed that yet again she disobeyed him, though why did he ever think she would? If nothing else, she was consistent in her disobedience.

"And punishments can be quite enlightening," Snow said, her smile spreading and her eyes sparking with a hint of passion as she recalled her husband's hand on her backside when she'd been tossed over his legs.

She was suddenly yanked away from James and felt herself tucked against her husband's side.

"Punishments?" James asked, concerned. "You don't harm my sister, do you, Tarass?"

"Tarass would never harm me, James," Snow said and patted her husband's chest. "He loves me and I love him."

She almost laughed when she felt a growling rumble in his chest.

"He loves you and you love him?" James asked, shaking his head. "I thought you hated each other? How did you two ever fall in love in one night?"

"He's loved me for ages," Snow said with a ring of joy in her voice.

"That's right, Father mentioned visiting here with Tarass's father," James said. "So you met when you were younger."

"And she was just as stubborn then as she is now and still not good at holding her tongue when she should," Tarass said and gave the side of her waist a squeeze.

"I am happy and relieved to hear this. I've so wanted Snow to find love as her two sisters have done and as I have done with Eleanor. But I worry over this claim Lord Polwarth has made."

"What claim?" Snow asked, her stomach roiling with worry, recalling what Rannock had said about her not being Tarass's lawful wife, and she hurried her hand along her husband's arm to reach for his hand.

He took hold of her hand before her hand reached his elbow, and he closed his fingers around hers locking them together, making it clear they wouldn't be separated.

"Explain it, James," Tarass said.

James cleared his throat, a habit Snow had noticed he'd do when he had unfavorable news to deliver.

"Lord Polwarth claims that your marriage is invalid because when the cleric wed you, he didn't know that even though Tarass's father was Christian, Tarass wasn't raised one. He was predominately raised with his mum's barbarian beliefs. Polwarth believes that completely invalidates the marriage, since the vows were meaningless to you."

"Why did he not address this when Tarass claimed I belonged to him? Why wait and say it now?" Snow asked.

"Questions I asked him myself," James said, "He claims he was shocked and upset by it all and didn't realize your marriage would be invalid until this morning. He arrived at the keep shortly after dawn, insisting I amend this dreadful mistake and have you returned home so that he could honor the marriage agreement."

"He's a fool if he thinks that will happen," Tarass said. "Our marriage is lawful, our vows sealed, and no doubt the cleric will agree."

James nodded. "I thought the same myself until I recalled that Lord Polwarth is the largest benefactor of the monastery the cleric belongs to. Without his support, the monastery would not survive."

"The cleric would lie for him?" Snow asked.

"The cleric doesn't matter," James said.

"It's the Abbot who decides," Tarass said.

Snow recalled the tales Eleanor had told her about the abbey she had been a postulant at and the things that Mother Abbess had done. How Ruddock's father's generous support helped the abbey, allowing anyone from his clan to seek shelter there when necessary and without question.

"The monasteries depend on the nobles to support them and in turn, the nobles count on the monastery's support when necessary... no matter what that support may entail," Tarass said.

"So the abbot will agree with Lord Polwarth?" Snow asked, her worry growing.

"There's a good chance of it," Tarass said.

James cleared his throat again.

"There is something else, James?" Snow asked worry creasing her brow.

"I was going to have Eleanor speak to you about it so you could decide for yourself, but now that I know you love each other, that changes everything. It is something you both should know," James said and cleared his throat again. "Polwarth made it known to me that if by chance you were with child, his healer could easily dispose of the problem."

Snow gasped, her hand going to rest protectively against her stomach as if Tarass's child already nested there. She snuggled closer to her husband, his arm growing tighter around her as his body tensed with anger.

"If Polwarth dares to come near my wife, I'll crucify him for all to see," Tarass said, his words fueled with fury.

"Polwarth left me to go directly to the abbot to speak with him. I rushed here as soon as he was gone," James said. "I wouldn't be surprised if you received a message from the abbot later tonight or tomorrow. Polwarth was eager to see this done."

"I appreciate you alerting us to this situation," Tarass said.

"I caution you to be careful. Polwarth is a man on a mission. He was adamant about seeing this done and appalled that he hadn't been wise enough to stop your wedding and protect his friend's daughter from what he claimed would be a horrible fate. I fear he will do anything to see Snow taken from you."

"That will never happen," Tarass snapped. "Snow and I are husband and wife and nothing will change that. Not now. Not ever."

"I am glad to know you feel that way out of love for my sister and that what started as a forced marriage never truly was one," James said. "Now I must take my leave before the heavily gray skies dump more snow on us."

"I'll see you out," Snow said and reached her hand out.

Tarass reluctantly let her go, knowing she probably wanted a few moments alone with her brother.

"I am overjoyed for you, Snow," James said when they entered the Great Hall, then laughed softly. "Though, I never would have expected it to be the Lord of Fire you fell in love with or he you."

"I know. It's strange, and yet it feels so right."

"That's all that matters," James said and patted her arm. "Remember, though, I'm always here if you need me."

Thaw's barking was heard before he was seen and when the pup spotted James he made a mad dash for him, his tailing wagging like crazy.

James leaned down to greet the pup.

"Oh, m'lady, tongues are wagging furiously with that body being drained of blood last night," Nettle said, hurrying into the Great Hall, her cloak dusted with snow.

James stood straight, his eyes wide. "Body? Blood drained? What goes on here?"

Nettle gasped. "I'm sorry, m'lady, I didn't see him there."

"Learn to hold that tongue, woman," Rannock ordered, appearing behind her. "No need upsetting Lady Snow with gossip."

"It's not gossip. It's truth," Nettle argued. "And Lady Snow has the right to know."

"What gossip? What truth? What body? What blood?" James asked, anxious to know what was going on.

"That's not for you to decide, Nettle," Rannock said.

"What isn't for Nettle to decide," Tarass asked, entering the Great Hall.

James hurried to speak up before anyone else could. "What is this about a body and drained blood? This does not bode well with the other problem you face."

"What other problem?" Rannock asked.

"There's another problem, m'lady," Nettle whispered to Snow, having stepped closer to her, though Nettle's whisper wasn't much of a whisper.

"That does not concern you," Rannock said.

"Anything that concerns, Lady Snow, concerns me," Nettle argued.

"Enough! I'll hear no more about it," Tarass snapped. "If I wish you to know, you will be told." He turned to James. "This is best discussed in private." He leaned down and whispered in his wife's ear. "I suppose there's no point in telling you to wait here."

Snow whispered back, "Not if you don't want me to disobey you again."

She caught his muffled oath as he straightened and took her arm, and she smiled.

Snow sat after entering the solar again and Thaw planted himself next to her leg. She reached down to pet him while her husband wasted no time in detailing what had happened last night.

"Good Lord," James said when he was done. "This is terrible and bodes worse than I thought for you both. When Polwarth learns of this, and he will learn of this—wagging tongues spreading news fast—he will claim it some barbaric ritual to prove Tarass practices a heathen belief and have further proof to invalidate your marriage."

Snow's stomach churned with worry. Her brother was right. This did not bode well for them at all.

"Perhaps I should take Finn's body home," James said. "It's obvious someone is out to cause you harm, Tarass, and at least with Finn's body gone, he can't be used to cause more distress."

"You're probably right, James," Tarass agreed. "I'll have a cart prepared that will make it easier for you to transport Finn's body in the snow. While I see to it, why don't you join Snow for some food and drink, since her grumbling stomach tells me she's hungry."

"Be careful, Tarass," James cautioned as he took Snow's arm, "Polwarth is a powerful man with many friends."

"I'll heed your warning, James," Tarass said and kept his eye on the door after James and his wife left. It wasn't long before Rannock entered the solar, closing the door behind him. Still, Tarass kept his voice low, taking no chance anyone would hear him. "I have a matter that needs immediate attention."

239

***

"What are you doing here? You have a bedchamber," Tarass said, finding his wife in the room, sitting by the hearth her bare feet stretched out to the flames, she had occupied when she had been a guest.

"I wanted a quiet place where I wouldn't be disturbed," she explained.

"No one would dare disturb you in our bedchamber."

"Even you?" she asked with a smile and stretched her hand out to him.

"You got me on that one," he said with a brief chuckle and scooped her up in his arms.

He carried her to the small bed and sat, bracing his back against the wood headboard and positioning her comfortably on his lap, making sure to tuck a blanket over her bare feet.

Thaw joined them on the bed to cuddle at her feet and Tarass didn't chase him away.

"Are you troubled over what brought James here that you seek solitude?"

"It's more than that," she admitted. "I feel like I'm suddenly in a giant puzzle with pieces that don't seem to fit, which means there are pieces missing, but where are those pieces? How do I find them?"

"That is how I feel about the murder of my parents. I have some pieces but not near enough to see the clear picture."

"Why did your father leave here suddenly and leave you and your mum behind? I recall people talking about it, and my da shaking his head over it. Then one day you and your mum were suddenly gone. What happened?"

"That's another mystery I'm trying to solve."

Chapter Twenty-one

Snow gazed at him in confusion and for a brief moment, thought she caught sight of the outline of his chin, but it was gone so quickly she believed it her imagination.

"You were never told of the reason for your hasty departure from your home?" Snow asked.

"Or the reason for my da's sudden departure," Tarass said. "I was told he'd been called away on an important matter, but I never learned what that matter entailed, though not for lack of trying. I often asked my parents about it and was told it was nothing to be concerned about." Tarass shook his head. "I knew it wasn't the truth, but I thought one day they would finally tell me. That day never came and I believe it has something to do with why my parents were killed."

"Do you think they were trying to protect you from something?"

"Why not tell me?" He shook his head. "It makes no sense."

"I recall my parents mentioning something about your family leaving because of the way your mum was treated. That many in your clan didn't like that she was of barbarian descent."

"I've heard the same, but the problem with that explanation is that I don't recall anyone in the clan treating my mum poorly. Besides, my da would have never allowed it and my da wasn't one to run from a problem."

"But your family did run, so perhaps the problem was too much for your father to handle," Snow suggested.

"My da was a strong and skillful warrior. I never knew him to run from anything and my mum was the same. I saw her brandish a weapon with skill and ease. It doesn't make sense that they were so fearful they would run."

"I know why parents would run," Snow said, "for I would do it as well."

"Tell me, wife," he said, his eyes falling on her with curiosity, still trying to comprehend how lucky he was that she loved him and she was there snug in his arms.

"If all else failed, I would run to protect my child," Snow said.

It pleased him to know his wife would be courageous enough to do what was necessary to protect a bairn of theirs.

"I've thought of that. But wouldn't you tell our bairn why you ran?" he asked.

Snow tilted her head and scrunched her brow, giving his question thought. "I'm not sure. What if what I knew, a secret of sorts, placed him in even more danger?"

"But if others knew it as well and he didn't, not knowing certainly wouldn't help him."

"True," she agreed, nodding, "and secrets don't always stay secret." She shook her head. "It is puzzling." She rested her hand on his chest. "The dead

man I tripped over. He was here for a reason and not far
from your home. He could have been bringing you a
message."

"Or he could have been here to do harm."

"Have you been able to find out anything about
him?" Snow asked. She felt his body tense slightly.
"You know something. Tell me." His hesitation told her
of his reluctance to respond. "Why wouldn't you want
to share it with me?" She gasped at a sudden thought.
"Is it that you don't trust me? We are only wed a day
and I suppose we really don't know each other well,
though I feel so comfortable with you like I've
somehow known you forever."

He kissed her gently to stop her from saying
anymore. "I've trusted you since that day you told my
da I was lying about Sorrell climbing the tree, seeing
how fiercely you protected your sister. And that trust
deepened when you spoke to me and challenged me—
and definitely frustrated me—like no other ever did or
would attempt to do. You have my trust, my heart, and
my love."

She smiled and kissed him quick, glad her lips
landed on his so perfectly, as if she could actually see
them.

"I will keep them all safe and tucked away inside
me," she said. "Tell me what you found out."

"Not going to let it go, are you?" he asked with a
chuckle.

"To solve the puzzling mystery, we need all the
pieces."

Tarass relented and had a feeling he'd be relenting
often to his wife. "I left shortly after your departure to

visit with my mum's people and see what they could tell me about the dead man with the markings on his body."

He didn't tell her that he'd left because the keep wasn't the same without her there. Or more simply that he missed her, a revelation that had startled him. He left, thinking distance would change that. It had worsened it.

"I found someone, who told me what I'd already known myself, an elder in a tribe known to my mum's people. He told me the man was probably a Pict, also known as the painted people, from northern Scotland, though he said no Pict had been seen for about two hundred or so years now. And it was not like they could be missed with the way they marked their bodies. He said they now mostly lived in the old tales and legends, since their time had come and long gone. I'm familiar with the legend of the Pict and knew they were no more. I still question whether the dead man was a Pict or not. I thought perhaps the dead man could be from one of the tribes far north that keep to themselves and are rarely seen, but I couldn't confirm that."

"I was told you have a marking on your arm? It is unusual to have one. Why do you?" she asked, curious.

"It's a custom of my mum's people, a single marking designating something that pertains to the individual. Mine shows I am a victorious warrior many times over."

"I can attest to that since you've rescued me more than once and thankful I am for it," she said, "which reminds me. That day you found me in the snowstorm.

You mentioned you were meeting someone. Did it have anything to do with your parents?"

"I'm going to be honest with you, wife."

"Is this something that is one time only or something you intend to do often?" she asked with a soft giggle.

He poked her in the side. "Very funny. I will always be honest with you."

"Or say nothing at all?" This time no humor filled her voice.

How had she gotten to know him so well?

"Sometimes it is better you don't know," he said.

Snow took hold of his hand and brought it to rest against her chest. "It is not easy being blind. Sometimes it's actually frightening, but I have no choice in the matter. So when you tell me that you purposely keep me blind to something that goes on, it not only hurts more than I can say, but frightens me as well. Please, don't make me any more blind than I already am."

Tarass rarely regretted anything. The last time was when he hadn't been there to protect his parents. It had hurt worse than any physical wound and he felt that hurt now.

He rested his cheek to hers before his lips tenderly touched hers in a brief kiss. "You have my word, *ást*, from this moment on, I will tell you everything."

"That pleases me more than you know, husband," she said and smiled. "So what is it you haven't been honest with me about that you're about to be honest with me?"

"That day I found you in the snowstorm... I was to meet with Finn."

246

"My Finn?" she asked, surprised.

"Aye, your Finn."

She shook her head. "Why?"

"He provided me with information."

Her brow went up. "What information?"

"Any and all information he came across when James sent him with messages from clan to clan."

"He spied for you?" she asked, shaking her head again, not believing it.

"He kept me apprised of things going on in the area. I had received a message that he had something important that he had discovered and would meet with me on his way home with you."

"That's why he agreed with me about leaving my sister's when everyone else had urged me to stay in case the snow worsened. And why we were closer to your home than to mine. He detoured to meet with you, and, of course, he didn't have to worry about me since I couldn't see."

"I had hoped that he might hear some gossip about my parents that would help open a door to what happened here that caused my da not to return home and my mum to flee with me."

"You think he may have learned something and that's why he was killed?"

"It's possible," Tarass said.

"You think the dead man was the one who killed him?"

"That's something I don't know, but what I do know is that Finn was the one marked for death, whoever killed him had no interest in you or you would be dead now too."

***

A light snow was falling when Snow took Thaw outside later in the day. Nettle walked with her, detailing everything she saw around them.

"The village is quiet, many feeling safer inside than out, though most agree that if the dwarfs wanted to find their prey, nothing would stop them. But I don't know what the dwarfs would want with the likes of this group since they're all claiming ignorance."

Snow chuckled.

"Runa is busy with demands for amulets to keep them safe."

That news brought a worry to Snow. If a cleric or the abbot arrived and saw that, it would not bode well for her and Tarass. But she couldn't nor would she prevent anyone from seeking and using something they believed would protect them.

"Runa is busy enough, having three women near ready to give birth," Nettle went on talking. "Two are first births and the other a third birth. Helga doesn't need much help. All are amazed at how easily she delivers her bairns. But some say her mum or grandmother, maybe both, had been a healer and she knows about birthing better than most."

"Do not keep Lady Snow out long, Nettle, the snow grows heavier," Rannock ordered.

"I know how to look after Lady Snow, you don't have to tell me," Nettle said.

"You're busy talking and not paying attention," Rannock argued. "Do you not see how the snowfall has turned heavier?"

Nettle planted her hands on her hips as she took steps to stand right in front of Rannock. "Do you think I cannot see that for myself?"

"Watch your tongue with me, woman," Rannock said.

"You make demands that are not necessary," Nettle said, standing face to face with Rannock.

An arm hooked around Snow's. "Let the couple argue since it's the only way they'll ever get together, and come join me for a hot brew."

Snow recognized Twilla's raspy voice and followed along with the woman, Thaw keeping pace beside her.

"Nettle and Rannock?" Snow couldn't help but shake her head. "An unlikely pair to me."

"As perfect and unlikely a pair as you and Tarass?" Twilla's chuckle was as raspy as her voice. "The one you're looking for isn't always the one you find."

Snow thought about Sorrell and Willow and their husbands, and how true Twilla's words were.

Twilla led her to a chair at a table after entering her cottage.

Snow pushed her cloak off her shoulders to fall over the back of the chair as she settled into the seat.

"A hot brew to warm you and heat my old bones," Twilla said.

Snow turned her head in the direction of Twilla's voice and saw the flicker of a flame, orange and yellow in color, in the hearth. It swayed and shivered as it ate at the log. It couldn't be her imagination. She watched as it faded slowly, such a glorious sight, and she rubbed at her eyes, hoping to somehow bring the image back into focus, but it was lost.

Keep hope in your heart, my daughter, and you will see again.

She kept hope strong that her mum had been right and her sight would return at least enough for her not to depend on others to help her. But like her sister Willow, there was a practical side to her, which reminded that she also had to be prepared if her sight never returned.

Twilla placed a tankard by Snow's hand. "It's hot be careful."

"What was Tarass's mum like," Snow asked, hoping to gather more pieces to the puzzle. "I recall some about his da, though it was more fear I had of him. I thought his head touched the sky when I looked up at him from a young bairn's small height."

"He was a big man, much like his son, though Tarass is a bit taller. He's as handsome as his da and carries himself with strength just as his da did. His mum was a beautiful woman. It was difficult for men not to glance more than once at her." Twilla laughed. "It was even more difficult for his da to handle. She had a kind yet strong nature and was a good wife and mum."

Snow decided to ask. "Why did his da leave here suddenly only to have Tarass and his mum do the same?"

"You ask what Tarass has asked endlessly, but only his mum and da have the answer."

For some reason Snow didn't believe her. "It must have been difficult for Tarass's mum—"

"Haldana. Her name was Haldana."

"Difficult for Haldana in a new home with no friends to talk with."

"Haldana had Tarass's da. They were inseparable. They needed no one else, though after Tarass's grandda came to adore Haldana, many in the clan came to admire and respect her. And for a good reason. She was a wise woman and offered wise advice."

The rasp in Twilla's voice wasn't enough to hide how much the woman cared for Haldana. And Snow suspected that Twilla and Haldana had come to be good friends and that Twilla knew more about Tarass's parents than she was saying. But why? Why wouldn't she confide to Tarass what she might know about his parents that would help him?

***

"Where is my wife?" Tarass demanded when he came upon Nettle and Rannock arguing.

The two looked around and Nettle paled.

"She was here a moment ago," Nettle said.

"I saw her myself," Rannock agreed.

"She isn't here now and are you sure it was only a moment ago that you saw her? The snow-covered ground shows no signs of footfalls," Tarass said, fear jabbing at him. "She could not have gone off alone unless Thaw led her somewhere." His anger was growing. "How could you let this happen after the problems of last night." He spotted Runa and called to her. "Have you seen my wife, Runa?"

Runa shook her head. "No, my lord, I have been busy tending to a birth and I'm on my way to see how Helga does, since her husband fetched me. But if I see her I will tell her you are looking for her."

Tarass turned to Nettle and Rannock. "Find her. Now! And know this will not go unpunished."

The pair hurried off in opposite directions, Nettle thinking that Snow may have returned to the keep and Rannock thinking her endless curiosity may have taken her to the shed where the one body was being kept.

Tarass stood where he was, fear starting to creep over him. Where had she gone? Wherever she had gone off to, Thaw was with her and while he was still only a pup, he fiercely protected her. If, God forbid, she was hurt, Thaw would go for help. He would run to find him and bring him to her.

"My lord, you search for Lady Snow?"

Tarass turned to see the young lad, Roy, who had participated in the snowball fight the last time Snow had been here.

"You know where she is?" Tarass asked.

"I saw her go with Twilla to her cottage."

"Good for you for keeping a sharp eye, lad. You will make a fine warrior one day. Go to the kitchen and tell Cook I said you were to get a treat, a good-sized treat."

The lad beamed with pride, bobbed his head, and took off running.

Tarass went to Twilla's cottage and didn't bother to knock. He opened the door and walked in anger spewing with his words. "Never do that again."

Snow looked at him bewildered while Twilla grinned.

"What did I do?" Snow asked.

"You went missing and I feared the worse."

"Oh," Snow said and went to stand, tripping on the hem of her cloak as she did.

Tarass's arm caught her at the waist and steadied her, and he never felt so relieved to have her wee body safe in his arms.

"My apologies, husband, I can only guess that Nettle and Rannock were so busy arguing that they never saw me walk off with Twilla. I'll make sure it doesn't happen again."

How was it that his wife could deflate his anger with nothing more than a few choice words and leave him with a heavy dose of guilt when he hadn't done anything wrong.

"I certainly don't want to worry you needlessly," Snow said, placing her hand on his arm.

"You've got yourself a good wife, Lord Tarass," Twilla said.

He caught the grin on the old woman's face. "I should be angry with you, Twilla."

"For heaven's sake, why?" Snow asked.

Twilla laughed. "For not telling him that you were the one I knew would be his wife, and a perfect one at that."

Snow laughed. "He wouldn't have believed you."

"You know him well," Twilla said.

253

"As he does me," Snow said and looked up at her husband and thought she saw the outline of his chin as she had thought she had done earlier, but once again it faded.

"Visit with me again, Lady Snow. I enjoy talking with you," Twilla said.

"I will, for I enjoyed our talk as well," Snow said and sensed the old woman had much to tell her.

Tarass helped his wife on with her cloak, and Thaw rushed out the door as soon as it opened to hurry and roll around in the snow as he followed them through the village.

"Dusk has fallen and the snow has turned heavy," Tarass said, keeping a firm arm around hers as they walked.

"Is it possible to share the evening meal in our bedchamber? I prefer to be alone with you the rest of the night," she said.

"I was thinking the same myself and I will see it done."

"Good. I am hungry for food and my husband," she said with a wicked smile and raise of her brow.

Tarass leaned his head down. "I'll make certain both appetites are well satisfied tonight, wife."

"You found her," Rannock called out as he hurried toward them, Nettle at his side.

"No thanks to either of you," Tarass snapped.

"I take full responsibility as does Nettle, but at the moment there is something you need to know," Rannock said and didn't wait for permission to speak. "A cleric has arrived from the monastery and he demands to see you."

254

Chapter Twenty-two

"I will go with you to hear the message," Snow said, slipping her cloak off after entering the Great Hall and Nettle taking it from her. "Nettle, please see that Thaw is fed while we see to this."

Snow didn't need to see her husband to know he was angry. She had felt it in the muscles of his arms as they grew taut around her. He was the one who made demands not answered to them.

When her husband didn't argue with her, she grew concerned that his anger had mounted and he might react poorly to the messenger. Not a wise choice, since it would only reflect badly on the already difficult situation.

Tarass led her out of the Great Hall and when he stopped shortly afterwards, Snow tugged at his arm before he could open his solar door. "Anger will not benefit this matter."

Tarass took a needed breath, feeling as if he hadn't been able to breathe, his anger choking him.

He leaned down and rested his brow to hers. "I will not lose you, *ást*. I wasted enough time refusing to listen to my heart, I will waste no more."

"You can never lose me, Tarass. I love you far too much, and I am far too stubborn and relentless in my love for you to let anyone take me from you. We are

255

one and will remain one and that is the message this person can take back to the abbot."

Tarass kissed his wife and his tightening loins let him know he should see this meeting end quickly and enjoy the evening alone with her in their bedchamber.

Tarass kept hold of his wife's hand as they entered his solar.

A short man, wearing the dark brown, hooded robe of the monastery clerics, turned from where he stood, holding his hands out to the fire. His plain features were marked with heavy lines from what appeared to be a perpetual scowl.

"I am Cleric Norman and I have a dire message from Abbot Bennett that you must adhere to immediately," the cleric ordered with an air of superiority. "And she," —he pointed to Snow—"must leave. This is a discussion for men alone."

Tarass didn't respond. He walked his wife to a chair near the hearth and after he helped her sit, he turned to the cleric. "You do not enter my home and make demands of me." He approached the cleric in strong strides. "And never, *ever*, think you can dictate to me when it comes to my wife. Now you will deliver your message and I will give you my response in the morning at which time you will take your leave from my home."

Snow heard the well-deserved quiver in the cleric's voice when next he spoke.

"I was given orders to remain here and see that Abbot Bennett's message is adhered to until his arrival."

"What makes you think that I would adhere to anything Abbot Bennett has to say when barbaric blood runs through me?" Tarass asked, turning a glare on the man that was meant to frighten. And it did.

Cleric Norman visibly began to tremble. "Think of Mistress Snow and what it would mean to her reputation if you refused to obey the Abbot."

"Why don't you tell us the message, Cleric Norman, then I can decide whether my reputation is threatened," Snow said.

She didn't see his eyes turn wide, but she certainly heard how her words affronted him.

"That is not for you to decide," Cleric Norman chastised.

"No, it is me, *her husband*, to decide," Tarass snapped sharply.

"You are not her husband, Lord Tarass," Cleric Norman said, taking a step away from him. "Abbot Bennett's message will explain it all and why it is necessary for you to immediately comply with his demand."

"Tell us," Snow said before her husband could explode with fury, since her own ire had mounted his had to be near to exploding.

"Aye, my wife is right, tell us," Tarass ordered curtly.

"The cleric that wed you did not know that Lord Tarass is not a Christian, in which case it invalidates your marriage," Cleric Norman said as if those few words were an explanation in itself. "Abbot Bennett had hoped that perhaps you hadn't consummated the invalid vows, but if you have then he orders you to cease from committing any further sin. Lord Polwarth has graciously agreed to honor his commitment to Snow and wed her so that her reputation remains unsoiled. Abbot Bennett will arrive in a few days to escort Snow to Lord Polwarth's home where they will wed and this unfortunate matter will be laid to rest."

Snow stood so quickly that it startled the cleric.

"I will agree to no such nonsense. I am Lord Tarass's wife, our vows properly exchanged and sealed many times over."

Cleric Norman gasped.

"Not you, Cleric Norman, nor Abbot Bennett, or Lord Polwarth will take that from me," Snow warned. "I remain Lord Tarass's wife not only until the day I die, but beyond that."

"I'll reiterate what my wife said," Tarass said, proud of the way his wife had spoken up and also made it clear she would remain his wife. "We are husband and wife and nothing will ever change that."

"You would live in sin? Ruin this innocent woman?" Cleric Norman asked outraged.

"Abbot Bennett can validate the ceremony that was performed with the blessings of the church or if it's another ceremony that would please you, I will join hands with my wife in the old ways of my mum's people."

Cleric Norman gasped loudly "You would partake in a pagan ceremony?"

"Let me make this simple for you, Cleric Norman," Tarass said, going to his wife and locking fingers with hers to hold up their clenched hands for him to see clearly. "My wife and I are bound together forever and no man, no force, *nothing* will part us." He lowered their hands to rest between them. "Tomorrow you will return to the monastery and deliver that message to Abbot Bennett."

"You mean to openly defy Abbot Bennett's orders?" Cleric Norman asked in disbelief.

"You said it yourself. I'm not Christian so I am not obligated to follow his orders," Tarass said. "Now you will excuse us while we retire to our bedchamber. A servant will see you fed and a bed provided for you."

"Mistress Snow, you are a Christian. You can't mean to defy Abbot Bennett and go sin with this man," Cleric Norman said affronted once more.

Snow couldn't keep the smile from her face. "Loving my husband and making love with him is no sin, Cleric Norman, though enjoying it as much as I do might be."

Tarass stifled his chuckle as he watched Cleric Norman's eyes look about to pop out of his head in shock. There had been times Snow's unruly tongue had frustrated him. This wasn't one of them.

"I will report this to Abbot Bennett," Cleric Norman threatened.

"Do as you please, Cleric Norman," Snow said, "I answer to only one man… my husband."

Tarass went to the door and opened it, calling out for a servant.

Maude entered and bobbed her head.

"See that the cleric is fed and shelter provided for him, but not in the keep," Tarass ordered.

Cleric Norman followed the servant out, though not without complaint and warning that they both would be answering to Abbot Bennett for refusing to comply with church doctrine.

Tarass paid him no heed. He said nothing until he and his wife were climbing the stairs to their bedchamber. "So you answer only to your husband?"

Snow chuckled as Thaw guided her up the stairs by the hem of her tunic.

Tarass followed behind, glad to see the pup continuing to learn how to help Snow.

"When I deem it wise to do so," Snow said with another chuckle.

Tarass said nothing more until they entered their bedchamber and Thaw trotted off, after getting a rub and kiss from Snow, to curl up by the hearth for the night.

"This is not going to go away easily," Tarass said, placing his hands at her waist and turning her to face him.

Snow fell gently against her husband, her arms going around his waist. "I didn't think it would, but our love is worth fighting for, don't you think?"

"I don't think... I know it is," he said, "but what I know more is that I want you naked in our bed so I can make endless love to you."

It wasn't only that he couldn't get enough of making love to his wife, it was that the more he made love to her, the more he buried himself deep inside her, the more he laid claim to her, the more she became his, the more they became one, then no one—not the heavens themselves—could separate them.

Snow's stomach spoke up before she could, grumbling loudly.

Tarass laughed, though disappointment jabbed at him. "It seems there is another part of you that needs feeding first."

"Food can wait. I want you," Snow said, running her hand down along his plaid to hastily slip beneath it and take hold of his engorged manhood to gently squeeze and stroke.

"Snow," he said in a taut warning, knowing he needed to stop her but not wanting to. Her small hand felt so good teasing him with playful tugs and enflaming him even more with her innocent touch, though there was no innocence in her touch.

"I never dreamed I would love the feel of your manhood, but I can't seem to get enough of it," she said in a breathy whisper.

"It's all yours to touch any time you want," he said, thinking it might not have been wise to tell her that since his wife's touch brought him much too close to climax, much too fast.

Her stomach betrayed her and rumbled again.

Tarass snarled beneath his breath, though he was sure his wife heard it. "You need to eat first."

"You were quick once last night in the middle of the night. Can't we do that now and then take our time later?" she asked eagerly.

"You are a dream come true wife," he said and hoisted her off her feet to carry her to the bed and drop her down on it.

She was quick to spread her legs and hoist her garments as was he to push his plaid aside and fall between her legs to enter her easily, being she was so wet and ready for him.

He tried to restrain himself, hold back his climax, after only a few strong thrusts. Damn, but his wife could make him lose control, something he'd never done. Never had he barely entered a woman and climaxed, but his wife's playful manner, whether teasing words or touches, enflamed his passion to the point of no control. And he was there now so close, so ready, so eager to burst with pleasure. But was his wife?

"Snow," he all but growled, fighting to keep control as he felt her clench him tight when he plunged into her again and again and again. He threw back his head and moaned in sweet agony.

That did it for Snow. She couldn't see his face, but hearing him moan, un his need told her what she couldn't see. He was ready and she was relieved since she couldn't hold on another minute.

"Now, Tarass, now!" she cried out in her own sweet groan.

Tarass let out a roar that Snow feared the whole keep heard or perhaps he wanted it heard, particularly by Cleric Norman. And she joined him, not the least bit concerned who heard either of them. Besides, she couldn't help it, her climax was so undeniably pleasurable. And each time she felt him release, his seed spill into her, she prayed a seed would take root and a bairn would grow from their love.

Tarass dropped down on her, spent from a climax that left him completely satiated and more than ever in love with his wife, something he still found surprising and sometimes terrifying. Never had he expected to find love and perhaps the terror that he could lose her was the reason why he thought he'd never love. He didn't want to deal with the God-awful pain of losing someone you loved.

The thought of Lord Polwarth actually taking Snow from him not only infuriated him, but terrified him as well. Not that he would ever let it happen, but then he had not been able to protect his parents from being killed.

He would not lose his wife. He would take her away to his mum's land and people and live there if necessary. He would let no one take her from him.

Snow's gurgling stomach had Tarass rolling off her to lay beside her, his hand reaching out to lace his fingers with hers.

Snow sighed contented and locked her slim fingers with his strong ones, needing to be joined with him one way or another.

"You need to eat, wife," Tarass said, his breath beginning to calm.

"Aye, we'll eat and then be ready to make love again," she said with a soft sigh, the last tingle of climax fading away.

Tarass turned on his side to look at her. Her cheeks were flushed, her bottom lip plump from biting back some of her moans, and passion still lingered in her lovely green eyes. She was a beautiful woman, even more so after making love.

"I please you that much, wife, that you can't get enough of me?" he asked with a slight chuckle.

Snow reached out and rested her hand against his jaw. "You please me so much, husband, that I truly feel you will grow tired of me making demands on you."

Tarass turned his face into her hand, his lips faintly brushing along her palm before he kissed it, sending a brief quiver through her. "I can put your fear to rest, my dear wife, since that shall never happen."

"You say that now, but—"

Tarass kissed her silent. "No buts, wife. If anything, it will be you who grows tired of my demands."

Snow giggled. "Would you care to wager on that?"

He laughed along with her. "I don't think that's wise, since we may kill each other trying to win the wager."

"Or we may have a gaggle of bairns," she said, the thought pleasing her.

Tarass smiled, favoring the thought, though her rumbling stomach had him responding to that. "Time to eat."

Snow grabbed his arm when he let go of her hand and went to move off the bed. "Tarass."

He didn't like the worry he saw on her face that only moments ago was wearing a smile.

"Whatever happens, I want you to know that my love for you grows stronger with every minute and every hour of the day, and no one will ever take my love for you from me."

His heart swelled with joy hearing how much she loved him, but his stomach clenched with worry that she sounded as if she feared she would be taken from him.

He leaned over and kissed her gently. "I'm glad your love for me grows as rapidly and strong as mine for you. And if I must remind you every day for the rest of our days that I will never let anyone take you from me, then I will. You are mine, wife, now and always."

***

Tarass held his wife's hand as he guided her to the dais in the Great Hall the next morning. He and Snow were looking forward to sending Cleric Norman on his way and was disappointed when they found him absent from the hall.

"He hasn't been seen yet," Maude told Tarass when he asked her about the cleric. "He was shown to a cottage, but complained about Ann's screams. Her first birth wasn't an easy one. The cottage he occupied was next to hers."

"Is she and the bairn well?" Snow asked with haste.

Maude smiled. "She and the tiny lad does well, m'lady."

"And the cleric?" Tarass asked, a pang of worry stabbing at him at the thought of Snow screaming in agony to deliver their bairn. He didn't know if he'd be able to abide hearing his wife suffer in so much pain.

"He insisted on being moved as far away from the screams as possible, my lord," Maude said. "He was placed in the only other available cottage."

"Gilbert's cottage," Tarass said, thinking of the seasoned warrior that had passed peacefully in his sleep while he had been away.

Thaw's bark alerted Snow to his return, Nettle having taken the pup outside after Tarass had forbid Snow from rushing out of bed this morning. She had been glad, since he had teased her body, all of it, senseless with kisses that had her exploding in not one but two climaxes.

"The snow turned heavy overnight and hasn't stopped," Nettle said, shaking the snow from her cloak, Thaw doing the same, giving a good shake, before approaching the dais.

Thaw ran around to the back of the dais to hop up and place his front paws on Snow's leg.

She rubbed him and kissed him and told him how much she loved him. Then asked him if he was hungry.

Thaw dropped to his butt and barked.

"I'll see Thaw gets fed, m'lady," Nettle said.

Hearing that, Thaw ran barking to Nettle and followed her to the kitchen.

"If I were a jealous man, I would think you loved that pup more than me," Tarass said.

"But you're not, you're a wise man who knows that while my heart is overflowing with love for you, it still has room to love others."

Tarass brought his face close to hers and nibbled on her ear before saying, "You measure your words well, wife."

Gooseflesh ran over Snow and she scrunched her shoulders as his nibbles continued to tease her.

"I do not care!"

The shout tore Tarass and Snow apart.

"I leave now. This cannot wait. Abbot Bennett must be made aware of this," Cleric Norman said with a raised voice as he entered the Great Hall alongside Rannock.

"What is the problem now, Cleric Norman?" Tarass asked when the man reached the dais.

"The pagan act that has taken place here will not be tolerated," Cleric Norman threatened. "That a man having been drained of blood is unacceptable."

"It was no pagan act and it is none of your concern," Tarass warned harshly.

"It most certainly is," Cleric Norman argued. "A concern that needs to be immediately addressed by the clergy. I do not want this poor woman,"—he nodded at Snow—"to suffer more than she already has at the hands of a barbarian. There is no telling what you may do to her."

"I've already done quite a bit to her, Cleric Norman," Tarass said and heard his wife chuckle.

"You're damning her soul to hell and I will not let that happen," the cleric said, jutting his chin out. "I leave now to let Abbot Bennett know what depraved things go on here."

"It's a bad snowstorm. He shouldn't leave," Rannock said.

"I will not be kept hostage another minute in this heathen place," Cleric Norman said.

"You're free to take your leave whenever you want," Tarass said. "Though, I advise against it with the snowstorm."

"I'd rather take on the perils of a snowstorm than stay among pagans," Cleric Norman spat.

"Rannock, have his horse readied and supply him with food," Tarass ordered.

267

"I want nothing from you," Cleric Norman snapped. "I will reach the abbey in time for prayers and supper."

"Not in this storm," Rannock said.

"I have faith," Cleric Norman said with a raise of his chin and turned to Snow. "Mistress Snow, I pray you will come to your senses and be ready to take your leave with Abbot Bennett when he comes to collect you."

"Waste not your prayers, Cleric Norman. I will not leave my husband," Snow said with a strength that left no debt that she meant it. "I pray you have a safe journey."

Cleric Norman turned and hurried from the keep.

"Should I send anyone with the fool?" Rannock asked.

Tarass shook his head. "No, the fool can take a risk with his own life, but I won't risk the lives of any of my warriors. Send him on his way and hopefully his faith will see him safe."

The day continued quietly, the snow keeping most in their cottages with a few warriors seeking the company of others and drink and food in the keep. Tarass had ordered it left open to all, a safe and warm haven for those who needed it.

It wasn't until the next morning, when the snow had stopped, though the wind and the bitter cold continued, that news reached Tarass and Snow.

Rannock stood at the dais as he did the day before, though this time alone, his brow scrunched heavy with worry. "Another pool of blood has been found, my lord."

Chapter Twenty-three

"Don't bother to argue with me on this, Snow, you're not going," Tarass said, standing. "The snow is too deep and the day too cold. You are staying here where it is warm and safe."

Snow startled when his finger landed on her lips, stopping her from speaking.

"I've spoken. It is done. You will stay here," he said, making it clear he wouldn't tolerate an argument from her. "Nettle will return with Thaw soon. Until then you will not—*will not*—move off this chair."

Snow's hand gently removed her husband's finger from against her mouth. "I feel chilled and would prefer to sit closer to the hearth."

Tarass took her arm and guided her to the table where he knew she preferred to sit. "This is where I better find you, wife, when I return." He kissed her lips quickly to stop any further discussion.

Snow watched the gray blur that was her husband walk away and scrunched her eyes. Was that a shape she saw? It certainly appeared to have form. Her hand went to rest on her stomach as if somehow her touch could calm the excited flutters that flourished there. Was it possible? Was more of her vision returning? Even if it was only shapes she saw, that would be wonderful. It would make it so much easier for her to

269

get around, to navigate unfamiliar places, and allow her to be less dependent on others.

She hoped it was so, but she didn't want to let herself get too excited and she certainly didn't intend to share the spark of hope only to disappoint others. She would wait and see what came of it, and pray.

Snow settled her hands around the warm tankard a servant placed in front of her and waited impatiently to hear something, anything, of what was going on. Gray blurs passed by her, some rushed, others slow, but it was the whisper that wasn't a soft whisper that caught her attention.

"His appetite is great. She will never be enough for him."

"Unlike me, who can please him in ways that would shock her."

Snow didn't recognize the one voice. It was too hushed, though she could tell it was a woman. The other voice she recognized, it was Fasta.

"She will be gone soon," the hushed voice said as if certain.

"Not soon enough."

A slight shiver ran through Snow at Fasta's reply. The unknown woman was quite sure that Snow would soon be gone from here while Fasta wanted Tarass in her bed. Or was it that she wanted him back in her bed? Had Tarass coupled with the servant? In what ways could Fasta please Tarass that Snow couldn't? She certainly didn't have vast experience when it came to coupling, but things seemed to come naturally when making love with her husband. If she lacked some way in making love, she'd want to know about it.

The voices trailed off as the gray blurs walked away.

Snow had no doubt that both women intended her to hear them. They also probably thought that she would say nothing to her husband, too embarrassed or too proper to dare discuss coupling with him. They were wrong.

"It is cold, windy, and deep with snow out there," Nettle said as she approached Snow after entering the Great Hall.

Thaw barked and ran around the table, his front paws landing on Snow's leg and a low whimper coming from him as he looked at her.

"My goodness, he is an intelligent pup. He senses that you're upset and I see that you are. But, of course, you are. How could you not be? Everyone else is. Another pool of blood being found does not bode well for the clan," Nettle said, her voice filled with worry.

Snow was relieved that Nettle surmised her worry was related to the news of the pool of blood. She hadn't planned on telling anyone, but her husband, of the conversation she had heard between the two women.

"What is being said?" Snow asked eager to find out anything she could as she gave Thaw a hug to let him know she was fine.

Nettle sat opposite Snow and kept her voice low. "They fear that until the dwarfs get the knowledge they seek more will die."

"There was a body with the blood?"

"No, only the pool of blood, but most believe a body will be found soon enough."

"Are all accounted for in the clan?" Snow asked, praying everyone was safe.

"Lord Tarass has ordered a count, though no one has reported anyone missing," Nettle said, sounding relieved.

"Let's hope it remains that way."

"If the tale about the dwarfs are true, I hope they've found the knowledge they seek and are well gone by now," Nettle said, a shudder running through her.

That was the ultimate question. The pools of blood meant something, but what? The last time she and Tarass had discussed the pools of blood, she had thought it more a warning for Tarass about his parents' deaths, but she wondered if someone could be seeking knowledge. Could the pools of blood indicate that knowledge had been found? But what knowledge could be learned from a dead man with markings? And no body had been found with the first pool of blood or so far with this third pool of blood. So what could either of them represent?

The noise of the servants busy placing dishes of food on the table intruded on Snow's thoughts.

"If she needs anything else, you'll have to come get it, Nettle. I'm too busy to be doing your chore."

Snow recognized Fasta's snappish voice and this time she spoke up. "Your chore is to serve in the Great Hall and you will do so or I will have you assigned a different chore."

"That's not your decision," Fasta said.

"It is my decision. I am the lady of the keep and you will address me properly and obey my commands

272

or you will no longer serve this keep in any capacity," Snow commanded, anger so strong in her voice that Thaw barked.

"Aye, *my lady*," Fasta said after a moment of hesitation.

"Now apologize to Nettle for being so rude to her," Snow ordered. She didn't need to see Fasta's face to know how angry her command had made her. She heard it in Nettle's small gasp.

"I apologize, Nettle," Fasta said quickly.

"A warning, Fasta," Snow said before the woman could walk away. "If you retaliate against Nettle in any way because of this, you will rue the day."

"Aye, *my lady*," Fasta said and hurried off.

Nettle kept her voice low and an eye on Fasta's retreating back as she spoke. "No one in the keep would miss her."

"Fasta isn't liked?" Snow asked, though wasn't surprised to hear it.

"She thinks herself important, demeans others, and demands as if she's lady of the keep. She believes Lord Tarass favors her bed and has tried to convince others that he's shared it several times, but none believe her tales. They all know Lord Tarass has no interest in her. He pays her no special attention. She is a servant like all the other servants." Nettle smiled. "Except me. Others have told me she's jealous of my new and important position in the keep, and that she can't dictate to me anymore."

Snow was relieved to hear that, though it didn't mean she wouldn't bring it up to her husband. She wanted to hear his thoughts on Fasta.

"She can't dictate to you anymore, Nettle," Snow confirmed. "And if she causes you any grief, you are to tell me immediately."

"I will, m'lady," Nettle assured her.

"Now let's enjoy the morning fare before it turns cold," Snow said and Thaw stopped scoffing down his food, set by the hearth, long enough to bark in agreement.

***

"People are already looking to blame and you know what that means," Rannock said as he stood with Tarass staring at the pool of blood held as if in a goblet of snow.

"Fear will reign and innocent people will suffer," Tarass said, having seen it and the results of something worrisome left too long unexplained to fester and spread fear. "Besides taking count of the people, see if any animals are missing. This blood had to have come from somewhere."

Rannock shook his head. "Why? Why the pools of blood? What do they mean?" He lowered his voice. "Could the tales be true? Are the dwarfs seeking knowledge?"

"Someone is seeking something and, whether dwarfs or human, they will pay for what's been done here. Like the others, this had to have been done when no one was about, which means the person or persons had knowledge of our sentinels."

Rannock's eyes went wide. "You think someone in the clan is responsible?"

274

"It's a possibility to consider."

"But why would anyone in the clan do something like this?"

"I don't know, but we need to keep the thought in mind and keep our eyes and ears alert," Tarass said.

"If you want to know all that goes on in the clan just ask Nettle, she seems to know everything," Rannock said with a disgruntled huff.

"What is it about that woman that annoys you?"

"She never stops talking and she constantly details things. She says who's in the room, who they are, what they're doing, and when she's outside, she talks about the weather and who is around, and what bairn belongs to who, and she even details what the pup is sniffing at. It's endless," Rannock said and was surprised to see Tarass's brow scrunched deep in thought as if he didn't believe him. "It's true, my lord."

Tarass nodded. "It is and I'm annoyed I haven't taken note of it myself."

"What does it matter? The woman will never shut up."

"No, she won't and I don't want her to."

"Why not?" Rannock asked, thinking him crazy.

"That is why my wife favors her. Nettle's details allow my wife to see what everyone else is seeing, and I'm grateful to her for that, since it's something I should have been doing myself."

"Oh, I never thought of that," Rannock admitted. "Nettle helps Lady Snow to see the keep, imagine the people, and get to know them."

"Nettle helps her to be part of the clan, something I have failed to do," Tarass said even more annoyed for not realizing it.

"You've been wed but two days."

"You know I don't tolerate poor excuses," Tarass said, "and neither should you. You should ask yourself why it's so easy for you to speak to Nettle and no other woman. You never search or falter your words when you talk with her."

"Argue is more like it," Rannock grumbled.

"Why? Is it that you both avoid something?"

"I don't avoid anything," Rannock grumbled again.

"I am not blind, but I've learned I can be. I argued endlessly with Snow before I realized I had feelings for her, that I refused to acknowledge. Maybe there is something about Nettle you refuse to acknowledge."

"I like Runa," Rannock argued.

"Do you? What is it you like about her?"

Rannock grinned. "She's beautiful."

"What else?"

Rannock went to speak and nothing came out of his mouth.

"What annoys you about Nettle?"

"What doesn't annoy me about Nettle," Rannock said, shaking his head. "Her endless chatter, her refusal to obey my commands, her constantly pointing out things. That she finds everything curious, smiles all the time, and she's plain to look at."

"Then why do other men look at her?"

Rannock lips turned up in a snarl. "Who's looks at her?"

276

Tarass kept his smile from surfacing. "A few men have given her more than a glance. I wouldn't be surprised if one or more makes their interest known soon."

"It's because she has an important position in the keep now. That's why men have shown interest in her," Rannock argued.

"Or they find her attractive," Tarass said. "Either way, someone's bound to claim her soon."

Rannock grumbled again, then said, "I need to see to the count of the people and animals."

"Check with the cook as well and see if any animals were slaughtered in the last two days and what was done with the blood."

"I never thought of that," Rannock said with a nod. "I'll see to it, and I'll see to having this cleaned away."

"One other thing, Rannock," Tarass said. "Send a few warriors to see if the cleric made it to the monastery."

"You think this could be his blood?"

"I don't know, but if it is I want to know before anyone else does," Tarass said and headed back to the keep.

He spotted Nettle heading toward the hall that connected the kitchen and called out to her.

She turned and hurried over to him. "My lord, Lady Snow asked to wait for you in the room—"

"She's claimed as her solar," Tarass finished.

"I do believe she has claimed it as such, my lord," Nettle agreed with the smile she wore spreading. "The hearth was left to burn out and a chill has set in. I got a fire going, plied her with blankets, and left Thaw snuggling at her feet. Now I'm fetching m'lady a hot brew."

Rannock was right, the woman could detail things. "You take good care of Lady Snow."

Nettle's smile captured her whole face. "Thank you, my lord, though it is no chore in serving Lady Snow. She is a kind and wonderful person, and I am honored to be in her service."

"That is good to know, Nettle. I want to talk with you. Please direct one of the servants to take the hot brew to Lady Snow, then meet me in my solar."

"Have I done something wrong, my lord," Nettle asked nervously.

"There is nothing for you to be worried about, Nettle," Tarass assured her and spotted Fasta. "Have Fasta take Lady Snow the brew."

"No, my lord, that would not be wise," she said in haste to keep him from calling out to the woman.

"Why is that, Nettle?" Tarass asked, concerned he had failed to see something else.

"It's a bit of a tale, I'd prefer to tell after I make sure Lady Snow gets her hot brew."

"Very well," Tarass said with a nod. "Meet me in my solar when you've seen to it."

Tarass went to his solar, wondering if he'd been blind to more things than he'd realized. Had he been so bent on revenging his parents' death that he hadn't paid enough attention to the reason for their deaths. And what of Fasta? Why hadn't Nettle thought it wise for the woman to take a brew to his wife? He was eager to talk with Nettle and was glad he didn't have to wait very long to his relief.

"Lady Snow rests comfortably," Nettle said proudly.

"You do well by Lady Snow, Nettle. Now tell me why you didn't want Fasta to take the brew," he said impatient to find out.

Nettle settled into detailing what had taken place in the Great Hall earlier. She left nothing out and spoke with pride of how Lady Snow had defended her.

Tarass kept his anger contained, recalling Rannock's words how Nettle knew all that went on in the clan. "Is there any reason you would know why Fasta would take such liberties to speak as she did."

"You asked so I shall be truthful and tell you what I told Lady Snow."

"That is what I want, Nettle, the truth."

Nettle bobbed her head. "Fasta believes herself privileged because she implies that you share her bed."

All Tarass could think was that she told Snow this, but he wouldn't ask Nettle his wife's response, he would ask Snow himself.

"Of course, everyone knows you don't," Nettle said and continued as if knowing what he'd ask next. "You would find no interest in her. It was plain to most, maybe a few, or perhaps I saw what others didn't. That you loved Lady Snow long before you brought her here."

"And what made you believe that?" he asked, thinking the young lass more astute than even Rannock believed.

"You complained about her after each visit to the Macardle keep and talked about her often. Only someone in love has a person on their mind that much."

If only he had been so astute, he could have saved himself time and trouble.

"You observe things well. I need you to keep keen eyes and ears on all that goes on in the keep and outside it as well. If anything—anything at all—seems amiss, I want you to tell me and only me."

"Aye, my lord, that will be an easy task for me. I love to watch people. It became a habit when few, mostly none, would talk with me. I watched and listened and saw things that most ignore."

"Like what, Nettle?" he asked.

"I don't want to gossip, my lord," Nettle said.

"Gossip might provide a clue as to the problem we're presently having."

Nettle hesitated a moment, though saw no way out of telling what she saw. "The young warrior Dolan is sneaking into Maude's cottage at night."

"How do you know this?" Tarass demanded, knowing the warrior had sentinel duties at night.

"I sometimes have trouble sleeping so I walk through the village late when everyone is asleep so that I am tired when I return to bed and finally am able to sleep." His nod permitted her to continue. "Fasta seeks endless charms from Runa, and I heard her complain that one brought the wrong man to her. It seemed the charm had Helga's husband seeking out Fasta. She didn't deny him and was now worried he'd gotten her with child, since his seed takes root easily, Helga having three bairns in the four years since wed."

Tarass was stunned at what the woman knew and realized Rannock was right. The woman saw and heard everything.

"And Rannock pines over Runa and hides when he sees her. He can't bring himself to talk to her, though I don't see how she'd be good for him. She barely glances at any man."

Tarass almost smiled. Had he and Snow been that obvious? Had Nettle been the only one to see it? He almost shook his head. Twilla had and said nothing. But then perhaps love needed to find its way in its own good time.

"You will keep watch for me, Nettle, and keep me apprised of all that goes on," Tarass said.

"Aye, my lord," she said with a nod.

Tarass left his solar shortly after Nettle, letting her know that Snow would send for her when needed. Then he climbed the stairs and entered the small room that his wife had claimed as her solar.

"Snow," he said, letting her know it was him when he entered the room, keeping it foremost in his mind that she needed to see through his eyes just as Nettle so generously shared hers.

She turned in the chair to face him, the blankets Nettle had piled around her falling away.

"That's a good fire burning in the hearth," he said as he reached her and took hold of her hand she stretched out in his direction. "And Thaw sleeps soundly there close to the hearth."

"Aye, it kept me warm while I've waited impatiently for you, though Thaw didn't last long at keeping my feet warm since I moved them too much, disturbing his sleep. I apologize for not remaining in the Great Hall as you instructed, but I longed for some quiet."

"You stayed in the keep that's what matters," he said.

"Do not keep me waiting any longer. Tell me about the pool of blood," she said eagerly.

"It was just that, a pool of blood. No tracks around it. Nothing that led anywhere."

"And no body?" Snow asked.

"No body," he confirmed. "I have all in the clan being accounted for and the animals as well. And anything that has been slaughtered for kitchen use in the last two days. I've also sent some warriors to see that Cleric Norman made it safely to the abbey. Other than that there is not much to tell. It still remains a mystery."

"And brings fears to the clan," Snow said.

Tarass scooped her out of the chair to sit and place her in his lap. She curled to rest against him comfortably. He kept his one arm around her waist and draped the other over her backside, his hand giving her cheek a gentle squeeze.

Of course, it was enough to stir her passion, but she had questions for him first.

"A mystery that needs solving just like the mystery of what I overheard earlier. Why Fasta could satisfy you in ways I never could."

"I don't know, shall we find out," he teased and nibbled at her ear.

Gooseflesh rushed over her. It always did when he teased her that way. But she would not be deterred. "So you admit you poked Fasta."

"You know I didn't," he said and kissed her lips softly.

"How would I know that?" she asked, trying to ignore his kisses she enjoyed far too much.

"Because I wouldn't be teasing you about it if I had. If guilty, I'd be lashing out at you, demanding to know why you would ask me such a thing."

"You're right," Snow said with a smug smile. "You lashed out at me when I accused you of lying about Sorrell beating you at climbing that tree." She tapped his chest. "This is a good thing to know about your husband."

He kissed her again and she got lost in its lingering tenderness, then rested her head—content—on his shoulder after his lips left hers.

"I will see that Fasta is removed from the keep," Tarass said.

"I appreciate that, but I am the lady of the keep and this is for me to handle."

"Are you telling me you can fight your own battles?" he asked with a chuckle.

"And why wouldn't I be able to fight my own battles?" she challenged with a smile. "I've battled you the mighty Lord of Fire and won."

He laughed so hard, he shook both of them. "You believe you've won battles with mc when I've had you removed from my presence, had you apologize when you felt you'd done nothing wrong, though you did, and had to rescue you numerous times?"

Snow kissed his cheek. "The only battle that counts is the one where I was victorious, and that was the battle for your heart."

"That wasn't a battle, wife, that was complete surrender," he said and kept her tight in his arms as he stood. "And now I'm going to be victorious and have you surrender completely to me."

Snow chuckled. "We'll see who surrenders first."

Chapter Twenty-four

The snow returned, hard and heavy, stranding everyone for days, not that Snow minded. She spent time with her husband, time talking, time laughing, time making love, lots and lots of love and she smiled at the memories. What was even more wonderful was that shapes were beginning to take form and while they had first vanished as fast as she had seen them, they were beginning to last longer and longer.

Snow found herself able to maneuver around the keep more easily, and she let everyone believe it was because she had grown familiar with the area. She had to be sure that what she was seeing wasn't something temporary. That her vision was improving, if only a little, and would remain so, or dare she hope continue to improve.

"I don't think Lord Tarass is going to be pleased with you venturing out of the keep," Nettle said, handing Snow gloves. "It still snows, though not as heavily and while some paths have been cleared, it is still not easy to walk through the village."

Thaw barked and Snow smiled able to make out a shape, part of it wagging like crazy, near the door.

"He's eager to play in the snow and I'm eager to visit with Twilla," Snow said. "And isn't Rannock seeing to the repair of a roof that got damaged. I'm sure he wouldn't mind seeing you, since you two have been talking quite a lot lately."

Nettle laughed. "We went from arguing to talking, which I must admit is nice. I don't know what happened to change it in the last few days, maybe a week now, but it's been enjoyable."

"Then take Thaw and let him enjoy himself in the snow while you talk with Rannock," Snow said. "I'll be fine with Twilla until you return for me and if you see Lord Tarass before that, let him know where I am."

"As you wish, m'lady," Nettle said and took Snow's arm, Thaw leading the way out of the keep.

It was a bit more of a trek along the snow-covered ground than Snow had expected and she was relieved to park herself in a chair at Twilla's table, a hot brew in hand.

"My old bones ache with the winter cold," Twilla said, hugging her tankard. "This is the time I miss my husband the most. We kept each other warm in the winter. I won't be surprised if late summer or early fall brings a harvest of bairns."

Snow's hand went to her stomach, hoping she'd be one of them. "That would be nice."

"Tarass's da was beside himself when Haldana carried Tarass. She had miscarried two previous bairns and he feared they'd lose another, though he feared more that he'd lose her. It was a joyous occasion when Tarass was born and with more ease than expected. She miscarried twice after Tarass, then no more. They both had hoped for many bairns but fate thought differently."

Snow couldn't imagine the pain of losing a bairn before it even had a chance to be born. How difficult it must have been for Tarass's mum.

"How did Tarass's da meet Haldana?"

"At the market on a trading trip far north," Twilla said. "Her people had come to trade as well and from what I've heard they fell in love at first sight. When you saw them together, you could see how much they loved each other. His da had been furious when he brought her home and announced he'd wed her, but she won the old lord over and even more so when she had Tarass. It meant the Clan MacFiere would live on, as it will in you and Tarass."

"I pray for many bairns. I want our life filled with lots of love, laughter, and wonderful memories," Snow said, keeping the thought strong in her heart.

"I have no doubt your prayers will be answered. You and Tarass will have what his parents had so hoped for and they will live in both of you and your children," Twilla assured her as if she knew it was so.

Thaw's bark outside the door brought a smile to Snow. "He's come to fetch me home."

"Aye, and home is where you are," Twilla said and reached out to give Snow's hand a squeeze.

Twilla opened the door as Snow stood and Thaw ran in, shook the snow off himself, and ran to plop down in front of the hearth.

"He looks to be alone," Twilla said, taking a quick glance outside before shutting the door against the wind and light snow.

"I guess he wandered away from Nettle," Snow said, knowing Thaw would be urging her to follow him if anything had happened to the young woman. "Nettle probably got lost in conversation with Rannock and doesn't even know Thaw has deserted her."

"The two are warming to each other. It won't be long before they realize they were made for each other," Twilla said.

Snow stood. "I have heard the yawns you've tried to hide. It is time for me to take my leave."

"I'm old. I yawn all the time, and you can't think to leave without Nettle," Twilla said.

"Thaw will guide me home," Snow said confidently and Thaw barked as if agreeing.

"You should wait," Twilla urged.

"Thaw and I will do well. Worry not," Snow said and after slipping on her cloak and gloves, gave Twilla a hug and stepped outside. "Take us to the keep, Thaw."

The wind had grown stronger, whippingwiping at her face as she tried to make out shapes, but the wind and swirling snow made it difficult.

Snow kept her hood pulled low and her face averted from the wind as best she could and followed slowly as Thaw tugged her along. She stopped suddenly when she thought she heard someone cry out and when Thaw pressed against her leg and barked, she knew he had heard it as well.

The cry came again and it sounded like someone in distress. What if someone was hurt?

Snow looked around trying to make out any moving shape, but all was still, the snowstorm keeping most indoors.

The cries of distress continued and Thaw whined. He was impatient to hurry off and see what was wrong, but he would not leave her side without permission.

Snow made a hasty and she hoped not unwise decision. "Someone needs help, Thaw, take me to the person."

Thaw barked, grabbed the hem of her garment in his mouth and took off at a pace that had Snow slipping and sliding through the snow.

She listened as the moans grew closer and called out, "Who's there? Are you hurt?"

"Help," could be heard in the lingering moan.

When Thaw suddenly stopped and growled, fear nipped at Snow. Someone was there. Someone Thaw didn't like.

"It's Fasta, I need help."

Snow hesitated. A sudden thought that this could be a trap grew her fear. "Are you injured?"

"I'm in terrible pain. It's what made me collapse."

Snow heard her fear and her trembling voice betrayed her tears.

"I'm going to die," Fasta cried.

"No, I'll get help," Snow said.

"I prayed for help and what was sent me? A blind, useless woman," Fasta said bitterly.

Snow ignored her disparaging remark. "Thaw, we need help. Go get Tarass."

Thaw barked and didn't move.

"He's as useless as you," Fasta said.

Snow patted her upper thigh and Thaw jumped up, resting his front paws there. "I know you don't like

Fasta, but you must do as I say. Go and hurry. Get Tarass."

He barked at the strong command in her voice and took off running.

"We need to get you out of the snow and someplace warm," Snow said, leaning down, her hand stretched out searching for the woman, though worried she might refuse her offer of help. She was surprised when Fasta grabbed onto her hand, squeezing it tight as though she feared letting go.

Snow realized she was laying prone in the snow, which meant she was growing colder by the minute.

"Can you sit up?" Snow asked and with her other hand followed along Fasta's arm to her shoulder to slip beneath it. "You can't stay here in the cold."

"You are too small and fragile to be of any help to me," she complained through more tears.

Snow heard the disappointment and the tremble of fear that worsened in Fasta's voice. "I am stronger than you think." She lifted her back to help her sit up.

An anguished moan fell from Fasta's lips as her head dropped forward. "Oh my God! Oh my God! I'm bleeding. The dwarfs, they've come for me."

Snow was about to soothe her worries when she caught a blur rushing toward them and heard a cackle of laughter.

"We've come for you. We've come for you," a high-pitched, cackling voice called out.

A blur circled them so fast or it was the swirling snow that made it seem that way and made it impossible for Snow to tell if one or more were present.

"Don't let him get me, m'lady, please don't let him get me," Fasta begged, gripping Snow's arm. "He's ugly so ugly." Fasta cried and pressed her face against Snow's arm.

Snow responded out of instinct, yelling in a commanding tone, "Be gone with you. Your tricks will not work here."

A face popped in front of hers and Snow startled more from the fact that she could make out a long, hooked nose and that her own nose wrinkled at the horrid scent when the creature spoke in a whispery cackle.

"We're coming for you."

Thaw's distant bark could be heard and the creature vanished from in front of Snow's face and she watched, scrunching her eyes, to see a blur scurry off in the snow.

Thaw was suddenly at her side and she heard him sniffing the air, catching the awful scent. Fearing he would give chase, she gave a sharp command, "Stay, Thaw!"

"What goes on here?" Tarass demanded, coming upon Fasta buried tight in his wife's arms.

"Fasta is hurt. She needs help," Snow said.

Tarass stopped abruptly when he saw the blood.

Nettle and Rannock followed close behind him and one look had Nettle crying out, "Good Lord, you're soaked in blood."

Fasta let loose with a howling weep, still clinging to Snow. "It was one of the dwarfs. He came for my blood."

***

"Bless you, Lady Snow, bless you for defending one of us."

"You are a brave soul, m'lady. Proud we are to have you."

"You are a blessing to the clan."

Tarass sat in complete silence as clan member after clan member approached his wife after supper in the Great Hall to heap praises on her valiant act of courage for chasing off the dwarfs and saving Fasta. Not that Fasta had heaped praises on Snow, but the telling of the tell had been enough for others to see the truth.

He had hastily gotten Fasta to Runa's cottage. The healer was able to stop the bleeding and Fasta now rested comfortably. Tarass had warriors posted throughout the night outside Runa's cottage since she had insisted Fasta remain the night there.

He'd been annoyed at his wife for refusing to obey him and return to the keep. She had insisted on going with him and he had little to argue against since Nettle had taken Snow's arm to help guide her.

"You are a good soul, m'lady, for protecting one who was unkind to you."

"Fasta owes you much, Lady Snow. You are a blessing to us all."

Tarass watched his wife handle each compliment with grace and appreciation and saw how the clan admired her even more for it. He, however, had not had a chance to speak alone with her since the incident and he was eager to do so since he had much to say.

It took only two yawns for him to bring the evening to an end.

He stood. "Time to retire." He took his wife's hand for her to stand.

"Thank you all," Snow called out and more blessings were shouted out to her.

Thaw led her up the stairs by her hem, Tarass following behind them. The pup waited for his usual hug and kiss from Snow before going to the hearth and curling up to sleep.

Tarass had gotten into the habit of helping his wife undress at night. Nettle had first seen to it, but he found he preferred to help her out of her garments. It was purely selfish on his part since he loved seeing his wife naked and loved the feel of her soft skin. He had admitted it to Snow and she had admitted that she much preferred him helping her than Nettle.

It was a nightly ritual he intended to never see end, but then there was another reason for that. It always ended in them making love, slow and easy or fast and quick. It didn't matter as long as he could slip inside her, he was content.

Tonight, however, undressing his wife would have to wait. He needed to talk with her and if he helped her undress, there would be no talking.

"You frightened me," he said, going to her and taking her hand.

"I didn't mean to," she said.

"You should have never left Twilla's alone and don't tell me that you had Thaw. Did you forget how easily it is to get lost in a snowstorm even with Thaw at your side?"

293

Snow rested her head on her husband's chest. "I believe I had more confidence in making it to the keep since I was here at home."

Her words pleased him, which annoyed him since she had been wrong to go off on her own and yet to hear her acknowledge that this was her home warmed his heart.

She raised her head. "I probably should have been a bit wiser in seeking out the cry for help myself, but I am glad Fasta is doing well and that I got a chance to come face to face with the creature."

"You came face to face with it?" Tarass asked, thinking how close his wife had come to being harmed.

"I did. The creature placed its face almost on top of mine." She scrunched her nose. "It had a horrible odor, but then what better way to hide your identity than to smell so badly one would turn her head away and not look closely."

"You don't believe in the dwarfs?"

"My mum taught me to respect the myths of our people and your people do the same. What is true and what are tales I cannot say, though I have my doubts."

"I've thought the same. Someone wants to stir fear in the clan, but for what reason?" Tarass asked more of himself than Snow.

"There is one other thing I should tell you," Snow said somewhat reluctantly.

Tarass got the feeling he wasn't going to like what she was about to tell him. "What is it?"

Her reluctance remained as she drew out her words. "The creature said 'we're coming for you'."

Anger and a bit of fear gripped Tarass as he rested his brow to hers. "I'd never let that happen, *ást*."

"I know that. I know you'd always rescue me. You and Thaw."

"Thaw and I work well together and we both will always keep you safe."

Snow smiled. "And I will keep the both of you safe."

Tarass chuckled purposely, since she couldn't see his smile. "How will you do that?"

Snow brushed her lips over his. "I will shield you with my never-ending love."

"Then I will feel safer than I ever have," Tarass said and kissed her, his hands going to her tunic to tug it up, not wanting to wait any longer to make love to his wife. He moved his lips off hers long enough to pull the tunic over her head and toss it aside.

He worked her shift up, his hands going to caress her backside, giving it a playful squeeze. He was surprised when she pulled away from him.

"It's my turn," she said in a soft whisper and reached out, her hands feeling along his plaid until connecting with his belt and releasing it, then working to unravel the cloth that wound around him.

Tarass stood still, only moving his arms when necessary and keeping his lips locked to prevent the enjoyable moans from escaping when her hands lingered in intimate places. What proved the most difficult for him was when his plaid dropped to the floor and her hand found his manhood and her fingers closed around it.

"There's still my shirt," he reminded, fearful if she continued to stroke and tug his already stiff manhood that he'd come right there in her hand.

"I'll get to that," she said softly as her hand slid along his manhood to slip underneath and cup his sac gently. "It's so pleasing to know that this all belongs to me."

"Every bit of it, wife," Tarass agreed.

Her hand returned to his engorged manhood, to tease it senseless, and he had difficulty keeping from dropping his head back and moaning in endless pleasure. Her touch had gone from innocent to experienced more quickly than he imagined, but then she enjoyed exploring him, finding out what pleased him and herself. And he had encouraged her every touch, exploring her with equal enthusiasm and pleasure.

He gasped when she hunched down and took him in her mouth. He was too close to the edge, too close to falling off into the abyss of pleasure, but she had tasted him once before and enjoyed it, and he didn't want to spoil her fun or his.

He dropped his head back and groaned as she hungrily feasted on him. He silently warned himself not to let it go on too long. To stop her. Stop her before it was too late. Her mouth suddenly left him as if she heard his silent warnings.

"I'm going to come. I need you inside me. Your seed must be inside me," she cried out anxiously.

Tarass whipped off his shirt, then her shift, lifted her, dropped her on the bed, spread her legs and entered her with such a hard thrust that she cried out.

"Tarass!" she screamed, her fingers gripping the blanket beneath her as she felt herself explode with pleasure.

A few good, hard thrusts and he exploded himself and made sure she came a second time as they spiraled and spun in a whirlwind of pleasure that left them completely breathless and satiated.

Tarass dropped down over her. "Good God, wife, I never expected you to be so generous in bed."

"I am too demanding for you?" she asked with worry.

Tarass rolled off her, snagging her around the waist to pull her to rest against his side. "Look at me, wife," he demanded softly when she kept her face averted from his.

"It doesn't matter. I can't see you."

He gently took hold of her chin and turned her head to face him. "It does matter. You matter and I love that you are generous when it comes to making love and I love that you're demanding when it comes to making love. Mostly, I love that you enjoy making love with me as much as I do with you."

"Always, husband. Always," she said a soft smile surfacing.

He kissed her and they lay there content until he felt her skin begin to cool, then he pulled the blanket out from under them and tucked it around them.

"Tarass," Snow said after a few minutes of silence.

"Aye, wife?"

"You know what this incidence with the dwarf means, don't you?" she asked.

"Aye. You think the same?" he asked, tucking her tighter against him as though he suddenly needed to shield her.

"I do. The dwarf is someone in the clan."

Chapter Twenty-five

It took more than a week before paths were cleared through the village, making it maneuverable, and Snow was eager to take advantage of it.

"You are to remain with Nettle at all times," Tarass ordered, adjusting his wife's fur-lined cloak on her shoulders.

Snow rolled her eyes, having heard it several times all morning. "How many times must you remind me of that?"

"How many times will it take for you to obey me?" Tarass countered.

Snow laughed.

"That's what I thought, hence the constant reminders, which do no good anyway, and yet I keep trying."

Snow bounced up on her toes to give him a quick kiss. "Because you love me and want to keep me safe."

His arm snagged her waist and lifted her to press his nose to hers. "Then take pity on your husband, for he loves you beyond measure and couldn't live without you."

She kissed him again, more slowly this time and he responded, demanding a bit more from her, which she eagerly gave.

Donna Fletcher

Snow rested her nose to his, this time, after the kiss ended. "My word that I will do as you say, husband, while I wait impatiently for you to join me."

"Then I rest easy and will hurry to join you," he said, reluctantly placing her on her feet and letting go of her. "I have a few things to discuss with Rannock. I won't be long."

Snow watched him leave the Great Hall, her heart pounding in her chest, not just from the kiss. She could see a distinct shape to him, but what had gotten her heart pounding madly had been the shock of seeing a hint of the bold blue color of his eyes.

It had been her second sight of color, though still blurred some, since the accident, and she was ever so grateful it was the blue of her husband's eyes that she saw. Still, though, she had to be sure this was permanent before she told anyone. She didn't want to get anyone's hopes up, least of all her own hopes.

"Are you all right, m'lady?" Nettle asked. "Your eyes pool with tears."

Snow smiled and wiped at her eyes before any tears could fall and spoke the truth. "A joyful thought."

"That is good to know, m'lady, since many in the keep are joyful themselves with Fasta not here since the incident. None look forward to her return."

"I noticed a lightheartedness in the keep myself," Snow admitted. "Perhaps it is time to make the change permanent."

"Maude has done wonderful in Fasta's absence," Nettle said excited, "and everyone here does their tasks with little prodding, since Maude speaks kindly to them and treats them well. Though, it has helped that you ordered extra food to be given to them."

Snow had taken advantage of the days the snowstorm had forced her to remain in the keep. While she loved spending time with her husband, he had matters to see to and she did as well. She had talked with Maude after appointing her to Fasta's position while Fasta recovered, and she had discovered several things she didn't like about the running of the keep. The way servants were fed had been one. If Fasta returned to her position, she would return to a much different keep, and Snow didn't think it would work well for anyone.

"You will not scrub down the tables after every meal. It is a waste of time."

"Speak of the devil," Nettle mumbled and watched as Fasta entered the Great Hall with Maude following behind her.

"I am in charge here and you will follow my orders or else," Fasta threatened.

Nettle cringed, seeing Maude do the same, and she kept her voice low as she said, "There is fear on Maude's face, m'lady."

Snow was glad Nettle made her aware of that, though she sensed it herself, Fasta's tone far too threatening.

"You have not been given orders to return here yet, Fasta," Snow called out.

Fasta approached Snow. "I am well, my lady, and will see to my duties."

"Your duties have changed, Fasta," Snow said. "You will no longer be working in the keep."

301

"You can't do that. Only Lord Tarass can order me gone from the keep," Fasta said, her chin going up.

"You question my authority?" Snow snapped.

"Who dares to do that?" Tarass shouted, standing in the doorway.

Snow made out her husband's shape and that of Thaw's. The pup had gone and fetched him of his own accord. Thaw definitely didn't like Fasta.

"Lady Snow has informed me that I am no longer in charge of the keep's servants, nor am I to work in the keep, my lord," Fasta said with a tearful sniffle. "I did nothing to deserve this dismissal."

"Lady Snow owes you no explanation for her decision. You will do whatever chore she appoints you without comment," Tarass ordered.

Fasta's eyes shot wide and she appeared ready to protest, though thought better of it and bowed her head. "Aye, my lord."

Tarass turned and left the room, Thaw plopping himself down to lean against Snow's leg.

"You will return to your cottage and rest, Fasta," Snow ordered. "I will advise you of your new position in due time."

"Aye, m'lady," Fasta said and turned and walked off mumbling beneath her breath.

After informing a thrilled Maude that she now had Fasta's position permanently, Snow finally got outside to walk through the village. Those out and about called out greetings and blessings to her. The dwarf had yet to return and many gave credit to Lady Snow for it.

"Take me to Runa's cottage, Nettle," Snow said. "I wish to talk to her about Fasta."

"There is talk that Fasta bled as she did because she lost a bairn," Nettle whispered as she led Snow along a cleared path. "Many also believe she took something to bring on the loss of the bairn."

"A good question to ask Runa," Snow said, but she was unable to since the healer was busy delivering a bairn.

She stopped and talked and laughed with several people and was walking around the corner of a cottage toward Twilla's place when she was struck in a chest with a snowball.

"I'm sorry, m'lady, so sorry. I didn't see you," said the small lad. "Please, please forgive me."

"He's a young one," Nettle whispered as Snow dusted the snow off herself.

"There's only one way I'll forgive you, lad," Snow warned.

"What is that, m'lady?" the young lad asked, his limbs quaking.

Snow smiled. "I get to join in the snowball fight."

***

Tarass sat by the hearth in his solar talking with Rannock. They had daily matters to go over and some issues that had yet to be resolved.

"You've found no source of the last pool of blood?" Tarass asked after they had finished discussing the daily dealings.

Rannock shook his head. "Nothing. It's frustrating and confounding. No animals were slaughtered around that time and no one is missing from the clan, a blessing for sure."

"Cleric Norman?"

"There was little time to see if he made it back to the monastery unharmed before the storm hit, but from what area we were able to cover we found no sign of him. I assume his faith saw him home safely."

Tarass hoped it was so, since he didn't need any more issues the Abbot could fault him with and strengthen his claim that his barbarian ancestry voided his marriage to Snow.

"No word yet from the warriors you sent on that mission? Though, no doubt the snowstorm has delayed any response. I wonder if they will be able to find out what Finn had learned. He was trusted among the many friends he had and people talked easily to him. Our warriors won't be as trusted as Finn had been."

"Coins encourage the most unwilling man to speak," Tarass said. "Though Finn was well liked, he was also liked for the generous coins he offered in exchange for information. I am more than curious to find out what news he had discovered. It had to have been of great value to me for him to want to meet me while he was escorting Snow home, and even of greater importance if he braved the snow to do so. All Highlanders know that a few snowflakes can turn into a blizzard in little time. So why did he take the chance?"

"The news was worth the chance or the coins the news would bring him," Rannock surmised.

"How is it not one soul knows anything about my parents' departure from my da's ancestral home. And how is it that not a single tribe has heard a word on those responsible for the attack on the Sandrik tribe where my mum and da lost their lives. It was a small, inconsequential tribe slaughtered for no reason."

Rannock nodded. "You're right. If another tribe wanted to conquer it, they wouldn't have slaughtered everyone."

"If my parents were the target, why kill the whole tribe? That has baffled me the most."

"Maybe it wasn't your parents the person was after."

"I considered that, but the tribe had no enemies. They traded with all the other tribes and battled no one. The only thing different the day of the attack was my parents' presence in the tribe." Tarass stood. "Enough with thoughts that go nowhere. It's time I joined my wife."

Rannock also stood. "And time I see to the change in sentinels, that comes when least expected and leaves even the warriors wondering of their duties."

***

"Lady Snow can join us," a lad called out.

Snow recognized Roy's voice, the lad she had helped with a snowball fight her last time here.

"No, we want her," another lad shouted and it took a few minutes and an argument before it was decided which team got Lady Snow, memories of her last successful snowball fight having her in demand.

Nettle stepped back to keep a good watch on Lady Snow, but Thaw joined in, running and barking and letting Snow know where to aim snowballs. Complaints from the opposing team of the pup's help got ignored by the winning team.

Snow laughed every time a snowball struck her and was thrilled when she heard someone yell, "She got me!"

Snowballs flew, Thaw continued barking, lads and lassies laughed and cried out with joy as snowballs flew, until...

Tarass suddenly appeared and snowballs were already in flight. They hit him in the chest and back one right after the other. He stood, not moving, the scowl on his face deepening.

Silence reigned, not even a breath was heard, and Thaw crept over to Snow to hide under her cloak.

Snow could see her husband's outline, having grown familiar with it lately. She scooped up a handful of snow. "Be ready to protect me," she said and ran toward her husband, Thaw reluctantly following and stopping with her when she was a short distance from Tarass. She didn't hesitate, she threw the snowball, aiming for his chest.

It struck him directly in the face and gasps rang out in the cold air.

Tarass wiped the snow from his face slowly. "Now you're going to get it," he warned and ran straight at his wife.

Snow turned, Thaw turning with her and barking all the way as she ran and yelled out, "Get him! Get him!" When she caught no movement, she yelled. "Protect me! Protect me!"

Snowballs flew and Tarass swatted several away while his body took several hits, not that it stopped him.

306

He kept going, picking up speed, and reached out to grab his wife.

They tumbled down on the snow together, Tarass protecting her from the fall as best he could and Snow laughing as she came to a rest on top of him.

Snow raised her hand and yelled, "We won! We got him!"

Her victory shout was met with dead silence, the lads and lassies realizing what they had done.

Tarass heard the silence and saw the fright on the lad and lassies' faces. He got himself and Snow to their feet.

"Who is responsible for this?" Tarass demanded and all the children stared at him, though one lone lad stepped forward.

Snow saw the outline of the lad and spoke up before he could, keeping a smile on her face as she did. "It's my fault. I insisted on joining them and encouraged them to protect me against you."

Tarass's voice carried out for all the children and the villagers who had begun to gather around to hear.

"I didn't counter-command Lady Snow's command since I wanted to see what you would do. You made me proud when you followed Lady Snow's order to protect her. You all are brave warriors."

"Yeah, we won!" Snow yelled, raising her arm in the air, and shouts and cheers joined her this time.

Tarass took his wife in his arms and hugged her. "You win their hearts from the youngest to the oldest."

"I am glad since the clan finally feels like family to me," she said and reached up to touch his face, the outline clear to her, and cringed when she felt it was wet. "I'm sorry. I was aiming for your chest."

"I preferred you struck me higher than lower."

Snow chuckled. "So am I, but,"—her hand went to rest on his chest— "I think we should go to our bedchamber and let me make sure not a single part of you suffered an injury or if you did, I would just have to kiss it and make it better."

"I ache all over, wife," Tarass said quite seriously, though he smiled.

"Then I will see to kissing you and easing your pain," she whispered seductively.

Tarass scooped her up in his arms and whispered near her ear, "You'll not get very far, wife, since you turned me hard already."

Snow laughed softly and rested her head on his shoulder.

"You're free to do as you please, Nettle. Lady Snow and I will be busy for the next few hours," Tarass said as he walked past her.

Nettle smiled but had no chance to acknowledge him.

"Lord Tarass," Rannock called out.

Tarass cursed beneath his breath, knowing Rannock was about to disrupt his plans and turned to face his friend. "Who dares disturb me now?"

"Abbot Bennett and Lord Polwarth are a short distance away."

Chapter Twenty-six

Snow stood beside her husband on the keep's steps waiting for the Abbot and Lord Polwarth. Her heart pounded madly in her chest and her stomach roiled with fear. She told herself not to ask the question she already had the answer to, but she desperately needed her husband to confirm it.

"You won't let them take me, will you, Tarass?"

Tarass's hand left hers to snag her tightly around the waist and yank her against him to rest his brow against hers. "You know the answer to that, wife, though I understand your need to hear it from me. I will let no one, not a single soul, take you from me. You belong to me as I belong to you. We are one and will always remain so."

She sighed. "I do so love you, husband."

"And I you, Snow, for now and all time."

He kissed her, wanting to feel the tingle of pleasure he always got when his lips touched hers, whether the kiss was gentle or demanding, and feel the slight shiver in her body as passion flared in her, and know that she responded to his slightest intimate provocation so easily.

A bark from Thaw had them breaking apart.

"They approach," Tarass said, taking hold of his wife's hand snugly in his, letting her know he'd never let her go.

Tarass had never met Abbot Bennett and wondered if his wife was familiar with him. "Have you ever met Abbot Bennett?"

"I have, twice, when he came to visit my da. From what I recall he was a short man, thick in the stomach with a pudgy face, dark eyes that always seemed to judge, and no hair on top of his head."

"I would say he hasn't changed much," Tarass said, watching the Abbot approach on a horse, Lord Polwarth riding beside him.

Abbot Bennett spoke as soon as he brought his horse to a stop. "I will speak with Cleric Norman before speaking with both of you."

Abbot Bennett confirmed what Tarass had feared. Cleric Norman never made it back to the monastery.

"Cleric Norman left here in the snowstorm shortly after arriving here and against my warning," Tarass said.

"It must have been of the utmost importance for Cleric Norman to take his leave in a snowstorm. What happened here that forced him to take such a dangerous chance?" Abbot Bennett demanded.

"What makes you think you can come to my home and make demands of me?" Tarass's hand snapped up when Abbot Bennett went to respond. "This is my land, my clan, and I rule here. You have no authority here so I warn you... guard well what you say to me."

"I care not for your heathen soul, but I do care for Snow Macardle's soul and I have come here to save her. Your marriage is invalid and Lord Polwarth has been generous enough to agree to honor the valid arrangement that had been made between him and

310

James Macardle. Snow is fortunate that Lord Polwarth would do such an honorable thing under the circumstances."

"Snow is where she belongs… by her husband's side. She stays with me."

"Perhaps it would be best if we discussed this inside," Lord Polwarth said, glancing around at the crowd that was gathering.

"Nettle, direct our two guests to my solar," Tarass said as he turned and, continuing to hold his wife's hand, entered the keep.

Snow remained silent, her shoulders slumping in relief when her husband seated her in a chair in his solar and took her cloak to drape across her lap.

He bent down and kissed her softly. "You didn't actually think I wouldn't allow you to be part of this meeting, did you?"

"I should have known better." With a smile, she kissed his cheek and feeling the chill there placed her cheek against his and whispered, "I'll warm you later."

"You warm me now," he whispered in her ear and smiled when he felt a shiver run over her.

"Snow, you will leave us so we may discuss this matter," Abbot Bennett ordered upon entering the room and seeing her there.

"Do I need to remind you again that you don't dictate in my home?" Tarass's hand went up once more to silence the Abbot before he could speak, letting him know he didn't expect a response. "Speak your piece and be done with it."

Lord Polwarth spoke up. "You force Snow to live in sin."

"Tarass doesn't force anything upon me," Snow said, not able to hold her tongue. "I love my husband and I will stay his wife no matter what either of you say."

Abbot Bennett shook his head. "This is why things are decided for women. You are too foolish to make proper and wise decisions. This has nothing to do with love. It has to do with saving your soul. Stay and continue to couple with this heathen and your soul will be lost, and you'll suffer the eternal damnation of hell."

"Hell would be living without my husband," Snow said.

Her words struck Tarass's heart, understanding at that very moment just how much his wife did love him.

Snow's brow creased as she asked, "My sister Sorrell is wed to a man who is part barbarian and I don't see you disavowing her marriage. Why do you claim to invalidate mine?" Her brow went up as though she realized the answer herself. "Or is it that Lord Ruddock is a generous donor to your monastery?"

"I owe you no answer," Abbot Bennett said defensively.

"You owe me an answer, therefore, you owe my wife one as well," Tarass commanded, making it clear Abbot Bennett dare not refuse him.

The Abbot wrinkled his nose in distaste as he spoke. "Lord Ruddock's situation is far different from yours. Your father wed your mother knowing full well she was of barbarian descent. Lord Ruddock's father knew nothing of his wife's true heritage when they wed." He waved his hand in the air, annoyed. "None of this matters. I am officially annulling your marriage."

"Then I'll wed her according to my mother's peoples' custom," Tarass said.

Abbot Bennett's cheeks bloomed a bright red and his anger looked about to burst.

Lord Polwarth quickly spoke up. "If you truly love Snow, you would see the wisdom of what Abbot Bennett has said and see done what is best for her."

"Don't dare question my love for my wife and as far as what is best for Snow? I'm best for Snow and no one will take her from me. Now since there is nothing further to be discussed, I suggest you take your leave."

"This has not been settled," Abbot Bennett insisted.

"It has been settled and I'll hear no more about it," Tarass said.

Snow didn't need to see her husband's face, or even hear the powerful command in his voice to know he had frightened Abbot Bennett. She heard it in the way the man took several unsteady steps away from her husband.

A knock sounded at the door before any more could be said and Rannock entered along with one of the clerics that had accompanied the Abbot.

The short, wiry cleric spoke before Rannock could. "Cleric Norman has been found. He's dead," —he paused his eyes turning round with fear— "the clan's people want to know if his body was drained of blood like the others."

Tarass looked to Rannock and caught the slight shrug to his large shoulders. Rannock had no answer for him.

"What others?" Lord Polwarth asked. "Have you had other deaths where the bodies have been drained of blood?"

"That is the whispers I hear. I also heard them say it is dwarfs seeking knowledge," —the cleric shook his head— "but it is not so. It is the work of heathens with heathen beliefs."

A chill ran a shiver through Snow. This had to stop. They had to find out the truth to these killings. Or unrest would continue to mount in the clan and spread beyond, and that would bring bigger problems.

"What heathen practices do you bring here?" Abbot Bennett demanded his eyes suddenly going as wide as the cleric's had. "Is this what Cleric Norman had discovered and bravely left here in a snowstorm to warn me about?" He didn't wait for an answer, he turned to Lord Polwarth. "We cannot leave this poor soul here to suffer at his hands. She must come with us until this can be settled."

"I warned you far too many times about making demands in my home.," Tarass said, his voice rising in anger. "You will leave *now*!"

"Not without Snow," Lord Polwarth said.

Fear rippled through Snow at the tenacity in Lord Polwarth's response.

Not so Tarass, he walked over to the man, stopping right in front of him. "My wife stays here with me. You will leave now!" He looked to Rannock. "See them all escorted off my land."

Rannock gave a nod and turned to carry out his orders, the cleric following after a shooing wave from Abbot Bennett.

"Let us at least take Snow to stay with her brother James until this matter can be settled properly," Abbot Bennett said.

His attempt at a conciliatory tone sounded only half-hearted to Snow's ears and she was glad to hear her husband's voice sound more tenacious than Polwarth's had.

"You try my patience, Abbot, and I warn you that is something you will live to regret. I will repeat yet again what I have repeatedly told you only because you're such an idiot that you can't understand it."

Snow heard the Abbot and Polwarth gasp at the insult.

"Snow is my wife and will stay my wife. There is nothing in this world and beyond that will change that. This is her home, here with me, her husband, and this is where she will stay."

"I possess information that just might have you change your mind," Abbot Bennett said.

"No, Abbot Bennett, we agreed," Lord Polwarth said.

"We agreed not to use it unless necessary. While I would not think to divulge something confessed to me, it is obviously necessary," Abbot Bennett reminded. "It is the one thing that will make him see that they are not destined to be husband and wife."

Snow immediately got to her feet and reached her hand out to her husband, eager to see his familiar outline and was relieved she was still able to see it.

Tarass went to his wife, seeing the worry brighten the green of her eyes and took her hand, while slipping

315

his arm around her waist to tuck her close against his side.

He turned his glance on the Abbot. "I love my wife and there is nothing you can say that will change that."

Abbot Bennett smiled. "Not even finding out that it was Angus Macardle, Snow's father, who had your parents killed?"

Snow may have been shocked at the Abbot's remark, but not shocked enough to stop her from yelling, "Liar! My da was friends with Tarass's parents. He would have never hurt them."

"At one time perhaps, but not after the argument they had the very last time they saw each other. An argument that Tarass can attest to, his father having sent him from the room when it began." Polwarth looked to Tarass. "Isn't that right, Lord Tarass?"

Tarass didn't answer, though he responded, "What proof do you have that my wife's father killed my parents?"

"Lord Angus himself confessed it to me before he died, afraid he would burn in hell for all eternity for what he had done," Abbot Bennett said.

"So much for the sanctity of the confessional," Tarass said.

Abbot Bennett was quick to defend himself. "Her father wanted his daughters kept safe. Lord Angus would be pleased that his own words saved his daughter."

"Lies. You tell lies," Snow accused, her voice quivering with anger.

"Are they, Snow?' Lord Polwarth asked calmly. "Your father certainly wasn't of right mind having Lord

Cree's wife abducted, setting fire to his own keep that caused your blindness and eventually your mother's death. In his sane moments he knew what he had done, which is why he couldn't live with it and took his own life."

"A riding accident took my da's life," Snow said, protecting his honor, though had thought the same herself.

"If you need to believe that, my dear, then do, but you can't deny there were many times your father wasn't of sound mind," Lord Polwarth said.

"And what of Lord Tarass?" Abbot Bennett asked. "He has a right to know the truth and lay his pain to rest."

Snow turned quiet, thinking on their remarks. Could it be possible? Had her da done this horrible thing? He often had made no sense when his mind went bad. She couldn't ignore the possibility, but she couldn't believe it either.

Stunned by the news, similar questions haunted Tarass. Could it be the truth? Could Lord Angus have ordered his parents killed? His next thought he spoke out loud.

"What reason would Lord Angus have to kill my parents?"

"Who can say what goes on in the mind of a madman?" Abbot Bennett said. "At least your father, in a lucid moment, was wise enough to confess to me before he died and now his soul rests in peace. I would think his daughter would be as brave as her father and face her sins and make amends for them. Do what is

right, Snow. Do what would make your father proud.
Save your soul as he did his."

Snow waited for her husband's arm to wrap tighter
around her waist, or his hand to give it a squeeze,
anything that would remind her that she was not going
anywhere. She was where she belonged, beside him.
But it never came.

Did he believe the Abbot? Did he actually believe
her da had had his parents killed? Did this news make a
difference.? Did he want her to leave?

A sudden bout of nausea hit her and her sight
began to fade. She couldn't lose what sight she had
gained, she couldn't. Then darkness began to creep over
the gray and she realized, to her great surprise, she was
about to faint.

Chapter Twenty-seven

Tarass scooped his wife up in his arms when he felt her slump against him, his stomach plummeting when he realized she had fainted.

"Nettle!" he roared with such power that it echoed through the keep.

A moment later, Nettle burst through the door, sending it banging against the wall. "Fetch, Runa, and bring her to my bedchamber."

Nettle nodded and turned pale at the sight of Snow lifeless in Lord Tarass's arms and didn't hesitate to follow his command.

"Get out!" Tarass yelled, shooting a murderous glance at the Abbot, then Lord Polwarth.

The Abbot went to speak.

"One word, Abbot Bennett, and you lose your tongue," Tarass threatened and was glad to see Rannock rush into the room. He was relieved Nettle had alerted Rannock to the situation. He was also glad he didn't need to give Rannock any orders. He knew what to do.

"I'll see both men escorted off your land, my lord," Rannock said.

"We'll take Cleric Norman with us," Abbot Bennett said.

"He'll be sent to you when I allow it," Tarass said and hurried out of the room.

319

Tarass rushed through the Great Hall with his wife in his arms, worried that she had yet to stir. As soon as Thaw caught sight of Tarass and Snow, he barked and ran after them, running up the stairs before Tarass.

Thaw jumped up on the bed as soon as Tarass placed Snow down upon it and started licking her pale face. Tarass didn't stop him, hoping it would help bring her around. He joined the pup, sitting beside his wife, and took her hand.

"Snow! Snow, wake up," Tarass urged, patting her hand when he wanted to shake her awake. It didn't help that Thaw whined when Snow failed to respond to either of them, though neither of them gave up.

Tarass was surprised to see Nettle arrive with Twilla instead of Runa. Maude followed them in, a bucket in hand.

"Move," Twilla ordered Tarass as she approached the bed.

Tarass didn't argue, and Thaw followed Tarass's lead and jumped off the bed as well.

Nettle was quick to explain why she hadn't brought Runa as requested. "I'm sorry, my lord, but Runa was in the middle of a difficult birth and I thought Twilla could be of some help. Runa did tell me to let Lady Snow be, if it was a faint she would wake from it herself."

"Some snow will help with that," Twilla said and scooped a handful out of the bucket and placed it on Snow's forehead and cheeks.

To Tarass's great relief, and Thaw's too, Snow began to stir and her eyes began to flutter.

Twilla placed more snow on Snow's cheeks, patting them.

Snow's eyes burst open and catching the outline of a hand at her cheeks, reached out to shove it away, and screamed, "Tarass!"

He shot across the bed to take her in his arms. "You're safe. You fainted. Twilla helps you."

Snow slumped against him in relief. "I've never fainted."

"You have now," Twilla said. "Could you be with child?"

The whole room turned silent.

Twilla answered her own question. "It could be too soon to tell. Seek advice from your sister Willow. She is a far better healer than Runa." She turned and shooed at Nettle and Maude. "Out the lot of you." She followed behind the two women, though called out, "I'll see a hot brew sent to you, Lady Snow."

Tarass was grateful to the old woman for her help, advice, and chasing everyone out. He wanted to be alone with his wife. There was much for them to discuss.

"Let me get you comfortable," Tarass said and left her side.

Snow wasn't happy that his arms left her or that he removed her boots, a silent way of letting her know she wouldn't be going anywhere. That thought was confirmed again when he hooked his arm around her waist to pull her up and place a couple of pillows behind her and rest her back against them, then he tugged the blanket up to her waist.

Her stomach churned as it did earlier, though she felt no faint returning. It was worry that roiled her stomach. Had her husband believed the word of the Abbot? Or was it doubt, being unsure of what he'd been told that had him leave her side?

She never felt more relieved than when her husband removed his boots and got in bed with her and not just to take her in his arms once again, but to pull her onto his lap and adjust himself against the pillows, then he tucked the blanket around both of them.

Snow kissed his cheek. "I'm glad you stayed with me."

"My heart stopped beating when I felt you go weak against me." He shook his head recalling the frightening moment. "You scared me senseless."

"I never faint," she said again as if trying to make sense of it.

Tarass rested his hand on her stomach. "Is it too soon to tell?"

Snow placed a gentle hand over his. "About a week will at least give us a clue and after a month I should know for sure. I hope it is so. I want to make many bairns with you and have them fill our home with love and laughter, but…"

Tarass watched the joy fade from his wife's face and knew her thought. "Your da."

She nodded. "I want to tell you without any doubt that my da had nothing to do with your parents' death, and I can say without a doubt that the da I knew well would never have done that…"

Tarass heard another *but* without her saying it. He also heard the conflict in her voice, and he remained silent knowing it was difficult for her to continue.

"My da changed when his mind illness grew worse and he did things—" she paused, biting her lower lip to stop it from trembling. It didn't help. "He did things I never expected him to do. So while I can say with certainty that when he was lucid he would never have done something so horrific, but when he was someone I don't think even he, himself, knew,"—she shook her head—"I can't be sure and that breaks my heart." She buried her face against Tarass's chest and let her tears fall.

It broke Tarass's heart to see his wife cry and continue to suffer over her da's illness that had left her with a father that had been barely recognizable to her.

He held her and spoke gently, though his words held weight. "Angus Macardle was a good, fair man. That was what my da had said often about your father. My da was good at determining a man's nature and from what I recall about your da, I believe my father was right about him."

Snow sniffled as her tears subsided. "Do you recall what my da and your da argued about?"

"I only recall that your da was agitated about something when he arrived and he demanded my da not do something. Before your da said anymore, my da sent me from the room and I hoped to listen from outside the door but my mum was there and she chased me away."

"Maybe Willow would know something about it. She and my da talked often, and he relied on her after our mum died. Maybe we could visit them once the snow permits it."

"We'll see," he said, concerned with all that was going on that it might not be wise to travel just yet.

A rap at the door had Tarass bidding Nettle to enter. He didn't, however, expect Rannock to follow her in.

"What now, Rannock?" Tarass asked, annoyed at being disturbed.

"Abbot Bennett claims he's isn't feeling well enough to travel," Rannock said. "He insists on shelter for the night."

"That is not going to happen," Tarass said and with a finger to his wife's chin, gently turned her head to face him. "I will get rid of them and return here before you finish your brew."

"Please be sure to make them leave. I fear their presence will only bring more problems," Snow said, then kissed her husband's lips lightly. An excited ripple raced through her when his lips suddenly were partially visible to her, fuzzy, but visible.

Once her husband was gone, Snow turned and was pleased to see Nettle had a more defined shape to her gray blur. Could her sight actually be improving? She felt such joy at the possibility, especially now with a chance of her being with child. She would be so grateful to be able to look upon her bairn's face when he or she was born.

Nausea rose up to roil her stomach once again. Not as bad as before when she fainted, but enough to make her feel unwell.

"You pale, m'lady. Do you not feel well?" Nettle asked, concerned.

"My stomach churns again."

"Perhaps it's a bit of food you need."

Snow's stomach didn't recoil at the thought of food. "It's worth a try, Nettle."

Nettle was barely out the door when Snow got out of bed. Thaw was quick to rush to her side, letting her know he was there to help.

She slipped on her shoes, she kept by the bed, and made her way to the chair near the hearth. She had no intention of staying in bed. She felt much too vulnerable there and she already felt vulnerable enough with the Abbot and Lord Polwarth still in the keep.

Thaw's paws were suddenly on her thighs and she leaned over and gave him a kiss and a rub. She startled when his dark eyes came into focus.

Please. Please let it be so that my sight is returning.

She didn't dare say it aloud for fear of somehow chasing it away. Instead, she gave Thaw another kiss and looked more closely at his face, blurry but visible to her.

"You're a handsome one and you're getting so big." She smiled.

After she lavished him with kisses, rubs, and praise, Thaw curled up by her feet for a nap.

Snow hugged herself, not for warmth but out of sheer happiness. She never thought she'd be as happy as she was now. Even with all the problems facing her and Tarass, she still felt a sense of joy and most of all hope.

Thaw jumped up suddenly and started growling.

Snow followed suit, standing and listening. Thaw's growl meant one thing.

Someone approached he didn't like or he felt was a threat to Snow.

***

"You cannot expect me to leave when I'm not feeling well," Abbot Bennett said, sitting at a table in the Great Hall with a tankard of ale in hand.

"I don't care how you feel, Abbot Bennett, you're not welcome in my home. You will take your leave with Lord Polwarth and never return here," Tarass ordered, the strength of his command leaving no doubt he meant it.

"Your father would have never been so rude," Abbot Bennett sneered.

Tarass slapped his hands down on the table right in front of Abbot Bennett. "My father wasn't a heathen… I am. And I'll show you just how much of a heathen I am if you don't get your arse off that bench and leave."

Abbot Bennett's eyes grew as round as full moons and he drew his head back, his mouth falling open and his lips moving, though failing to find words.

"If you make me repeat myself, I'm going to reach across this table, drag you over it, and toss you out on your arse," Tarass warned.

Abbot Bennett stood and raised his hand, pointing a finger at Tarass.

Tarass straightened to his full height and glared at the Abbot. "Shake that finger at me and you'll be leaving here with nine fingers, maybe less if you continue to annoy me."

Abbot Bennett immediately dropped his hand to his side. "You'll rue the day you disrespected me."

Tarass walked around the table, Abbot Bennett backing up as he did, but not fast enough. Tarass reached out and grabbed him, the Abbot wincing as his hand closed like a shackle around his upper arm.

"Listen well, Abbot," Tarass said, forcing the man to keep step with him as he rushed him toward the door. "Threaten me or dare to bring harm to my clan and you will know a wrath like nothing you have ever seen. Try to take my wife from me—" Tarass stopped abruptly, the Abbot cringing as Tarass's hand squeezed his arm so hard the pain brought tears to the Abbot's eyes. "And I will see you die a slow, agonizing death. On that you have my word."

The Abbot paled and Tarass's abrupt steps had the Abbot stumbling alongside him to keep up.

Tarass didn't bother to ask Rannock if the horses waited outside for the Abbot and his entourage, he knew they would be there. He all but dragged the Abbot down the steps to the shock of the clerics waiting by their horses.

One wide glance had Tarass turning to Rannock. "Where's Lord Polwarth?"

"He was here a short time ago," Rannock said, looking around as well.

The Abbot cringed in terror when Tarass grabbed him by the throat. "Where is he?"

"I-I-I don't kn-know," Abbot Bennett struggled to say.

"Liar!" Tarass screamed and tightened his grip on the Abbot's neck. "Rannock, alert the warriors."

Rannock let out a vicious roar that sounded as if it echoed through the village, when actually his roar was echoed by others and suddenly men and women poured out of their homes weapons in hand, ready to battle.

"Tell me where Lord Polwarth has gone?" Tarass demanded again as the Abbot began to turn red and struggle for breath. Tarass loosened his grip when he saw that the man fought to speak.

In between gasps, the Abbot said, "He only wants to save her soul."

Tarass let out a roar that sounded as if it came from the depths of hell itself and shoved the Abbot so hard that he tumbled to the ground.

"Let no one leave the village," Rannock yelled out and rushed up the stairs behind Tarass.

***

"Is someone there?" Snow called out when Thaw's growls grew stronger.

"It's only me, Snow," Lord Polwarth said, entering through the open door.

Fear sent gooseflesh rushing over Snow, even more so when she caught more than one shape enter the room.

"You have no right to be here in my private chambers," she scolded, keeping her voice strong, though she trembled inside.

Thaw keep guard in front of Snow, his snarl warning not to approach.

328

"Your father would not want this for you, Snow," Lord Polwarth said and took a step toward her.

Thaw jumped forward snapping and growling, warning him to stay away.

"I don't want to harm your dog but if I must—"

"Harm Thaw, Lord Polwarth, and I will see you dead," Snow threatened with a snarl that matched Thaw's.

"I'm only trying to help you. Do what's best for you as your father would want."

Snow caught the anger in his voice even though he managed to keep his tone calm. She also realized he referred constantly to her da and what he believed her da would think best for her.

"I don't believe you knew my da as well as you claim to," she said.

"Of course, I did. We were good friends," Lord Polwarth insisted.

"If what you claim is true, then you would know my da would be happy that I found love."

"There is no time to discuss this now. Later, when you're safe at my home, we can talk about it," Lord Polwarth said.

"I'm not going anywhere with you," Snow said, fighting the fear that was growing ever stronger in her.

Thaw's growls and snarls increased, sensing her distress.

"If you don't want any harm to come to your pup, I'd advise you to come with me," Lord Polwarth warned.

Snow was shocked that he threatened to harm Thaw when he knew how much she loved the pup. He was nothing like the man she thought he was, which meant she had to be careful and do whatever she needed to keep Thaw safe.

"It's all right, Thaw. All is good," she said, keeping her voice light.

Thaw stopped snarling, but his growl remained low as he sat, leaning against her leg.

"You'll come with me quietly and all will be well," Lord Polwarth instructed.

Snow had little choice, if she didn't want Thaw harmed.

"I have your cloak," Lord Polwarth said and approached her.

Thaw jumped at the man, his teeth bared and snarling viciously.

Snow was quick to scoop the pup up, worried he sensed her fear, and soothed him as best she could. "It's all right, Thaw."

Thaw calmed some, but growled as Lord Polwarth placed the cloak over Snow's shoulders.

Snow startled when Lord Polwarth took her by the arm and Thaw snapped at him. She warned Thaw again. "No, Thaw. It's all right. I'm all right."

When they reached the door Polwarth stopped. "Leave Thaw here. When all is settled, I'll send for him."

Snow knew he lied to her and she knew Tarass would come for her. So it was easy for her to comply, though it did nothing to alleviate her fright.

"Once you all leave the room, I'll put him down and shut the door," Snow said and heard one of the other men urging Lord Polwarth to hurry. Taking no chances Thaw would be hurt, she hurried to set Thaw down and whispered as she did, "Find me when free."

Thaw's barking started as soon as she shut the door on him.

Lord Polwarth took her arm again, and she was surprised when he took her to the room she had claimed as her solar.

"We need to hurry," someone said.

Snow was suddenly tugged forward and surprised to see an outline of a narrow opening in the wall. She was shoved through it, a musty odor assaulting her, and with someone close in front of her and someone close behind her, she was led precariously down the narrow stairs.

She thought of one thing with each step she took.

Tarass would rescue her.

Chapter Twenty-eight

Tarass sped up the stairs, his heart pounding madly in his chest. When he heard Thaw's frantic barks, he took the steps three at a time. It was Thaw's soulful howl that made Tarass realize that Snow was gone before he reached the bedchamber door and threw it open.

"Find Snow, Thaw!" Tarass commanded as soon as he and the dog's eyes met.

Thaw took off and Tarass raced after him, Rannock keeping pace behind them both.

Both men were puzzled when Thaw brought them to Snow's solar and went to a section of one of the walls and began barking.

"The secret passage," Tarass said, shocked and wondered how Polwarth would know about it. "I know where it comes out. Let's go get Snow, Thaw."

The pup didn't hesitate; he followed after Tarass. Once outside, Tarass bolted for the back of the keep, Thaw staying right beside him, and as he rounded the one corner he saw the hidden door open. A man hurried out, tossing a torch to a pile of snow, the fizzled flame sending black smoke wafting into the air. His wife tumbled out behind the man, and Lord Polwarth grabbed her arm to stop her from landing face first in the snow.

Tarass let out a terrifying roar that his mum's people would use when going into battle and that never failed to have the bravest of men cowering. It didn't fail this time either. The two men with Lord Polwarth ran like the devil was after them, but Polwarth kept hold of Snow.

Thaw bolted past Tarass and launched himself at Polwarth.

Tarass didn't stop him.

Snow's eyes had difficulty adjusting to the change in light. She thought she saw Tarass running toward her, but there were so many gray blurs behind the larger one she couldn't be sure. However, she was sure of the small gray blur that headed straight for her. It was Thaw.

Thaw might have grown some, but he was still a pup and when Snow felt Polwarth lift his leg to give Thaw a harsh kick and stop him from attacking, instinct had Snow reacting.

She swerved around and his leg caught her in the knee and sent her tumbling to the ground with such force that her arm was ripped out of his hand.

Thaw immediately dropped down beside her, trying to get his nose under her face that was buried in the snow.

Fury and fear gripped Tarass and while he wanted to go after a fleeing Lord Polwarth, he was more desperate to see to his wife.

"Get him!" Tarass yelled, knowing Rannock and his warriors were coming up behind him.

They rushed past him as he dropped to the ground beside his wife and gently turned her over to lift in his arms. He was surprised and relieved when she started brushing away the snow that had stuck to her face, Thaw's tongue helping her.

"I'm good, go after Polwarth," she urged.

"No need, Rannock and my warriors will get him and the other two," Tarass said. "Besides, if I leave you, you'll just get yourself into more trouble."

"If I did, you would rescue me like you always do," Snow said with a tender hand to her husband's cheek.

"Aye, wife, always," Tarass said and turned so that his lips kissed the palm of her hand and Snow shivered.

"Let's get you into the keep and get you warm," Tarass said, standing and carrying her around to the front of the keep and groaned when he saw Abbot Bennett and his clerics shivering in the cold as six of his warriors stood guard over them. "Inside, you have much to explain. Your men as well, before they freeze to death," Tarass said as he walked past them.

"Thank the Lord your unharmed, m'lady," Nettle said when the couple entered the Great Hall.

"I suffered a bit of fright but no harm, Nettle," Snow acknowledged, hearing the worry in her voice.

Tarass's anger surged, learning she had been frightened and he hadn't been there to prevent her terrifying ordeal.

Nettle looked to Lord Tarass as she spoke to Snow. "Has this ordeal worsened your churning stomach, m'lady?"

Tarass was pleased that Nettle alerted him to the matter and acknowledged her with a nod.

"I had no time to think about it, but now that you asked, it seems to have settled," Snow said.

"Perhaps some food and a hot brew will keep it that way," Nettle suggested.

"A good idea, Nettle, and tell Maude there are guests to be fed," Tarass said and placed his wife on her feet.

"And please take Thaw with you and get him a treat," Snow said and went to bend down to give Thaw a hug and kiss and let him know how brave he'd been. As soon as she moved, a pain shot through her knee and if Tarass hadn't snatched her up in his arms, she would have tumbled to the floor.

Thaw whined and followed Tarass and waited while he lowered Snow to a bench at one of the tables in front of the fireplace, then the pup sat beside her and whined as if he shared Snow's pain.

Nettle hurried around the table to the bench to see if she could help and gasped when Tarass lifted Snow's tunic and shift and she saw the deep bruise covering her knee.

"That bad?" Snow asked.

"I'm going to kill him," Tarass mumbled.

A cacophony of raised voices had Tarass and Snow's heads turning as the door opened.

"We got them," Rannock called out, escorting Lord Polwarth in with a firm hand to his arm.

"Shackle Lord Polwarth and the two men that helped him and have the warriors keep watch over Abbot Bennett and his men. I'll let you know when I wish to speak with them," Tarass said and once again lifted his wife in his arms.

335

"Nettle, fetch Runa and bring her to my solar. Thaw, follow me," Tarass ordered.

Snow sighed with relief after her husband settled her in a chair near the hearth and placed her foot on a small stool to ease the pain in her knee. She wrapped the shawl around her, Tarass had ordered a servant to bring her, tucking it high around her neck.

"You're chilled," Tarass said, hunching down in front of her and draping a blanket over her legs and pushing it snug at her waist.

"A deep chill, I fear," she admitted.

"I'll warm you properly later, after this is all settled," he said and kissed her softly, though ached for more than a tender kiss. He dropped his brow gently against hers. "I want to feel you naked against me and bury my manhood deep inside you right now and know that nothing or no one will ever tear us apart and that nothing or no one can ever stop us from loving each other."

"Why do you wait," she whispered. "Take me, for I want to feel you inside me and know I'm safe."

"Your knee," he reminded and shook his head. "And Nettle returns soon with Runa."

"It's no more than a bruise and you can make it quick," Snow urged and slipped her hand beneath his plaid and smiled, feeling the strength and swell of him. "After almost having been taken from you, I need this. I need to feel we are one, and feeling how hard you I would say you feel the same." She took his hand to tuck beneath her garments and brought it to rest between her legs. "I'm more than ready."

Tarass grew harder when his fingers brushed her wetness. He could slip inside her with ease and make her come easily, himself as well, since he was just as ready as he was.

"Thaw!" Tarass called out and the pup got up from where he parked himself by the hearth and trotted over to him. "Come with me." Thaw followed obediently and Tarass opened the door. "Guard Snow and let no one in."

Thaw barked, turned, and sat, ready to do as ordered.

Tarass grabbed a stool by the fireplace and placed it in front of Snow's chair, right between her legs, making sure not to disturb her injured leg, then pulled off the blanket he had tucked around her. He settled his hands on either side of her backside and gave her a quick kiss.

"I'm near ready to come, husband," she whispered so excited she could hardly contain herself as he eased her forward in the chair.

"You fire my passion with words alone," he said and brought her backside to rest on the very edge of the chair.

"And touch," she whispered ever so softly as her hand found his manhood and guided it between her legs, brushing the tip over that tender spot her husband loved to tease.

She groaned softly.

Tarass wished they could linger in play longer, but they had no time. He brushed her hand off him and eased himself into her.

Between the strength of his hands and body, Snow didn't have to do anything but enjoy every thrust of his manhood penetrating her deeper and harder, over and over and over… until,

"Tarass," she whimpered in need.

"Let go," he ordered and she did, and he joined her.

Their low groans mingled as ripples of sheer pleasure raced through them, and they both shuddered simultaneously when the last ripple faded away.

"I want to stay inside you, grow hard again, and bring us both to pleasure again," he whispered.

"Later. Promise me you'll do that later," she said and kissed him gently.

"You have my word," he said and sealed his promise with a strong kiss.

Tarass barely had her settled in the chair, the blanket once again wrapped around her when Thaw started barking. He reluctantly went to the door, silently cursing, intending to see this done and finished once and for all.

Nettle entered with Thaw.

The pup rushed to Snow's side and after receiving his usual attention settled by her feet to sleep.

Nettle, seeing Snow's flushed cheeks, smiled, though made no mention of what she realized had gone on in her absence.

"I have a nice hot brew for you and some bread and cheese," Nettle said, placing it on the small chest next to the chair where Snow sat. "Runa will be here soon."

It was only a few minutes later that Runa arrived and looked over Snow's injury.

"A bruise that will heal well enough with a royal fern poultice and not staying long on your feet for a day or two," Runa said. "Come with me, Nettle, and I'll show you how to prepare one."

Nettle looked to Tarass for permission and he gave it with a nod. "Send Rannock to me, Nettle."

"Eat," he ordered his wife when he saw she hadn't touched the food Nettle had brought her.

"I'm not feeling hungry," Snow said, too anxious to hear what Lord Polwarth had to say.

Rannock entered the room before Tarass could cajole her into eating something.

"Bring Lord Polwarth to me," Tarass said.

"Abbot Bennett is demanding to see you," Rannock said.

"Ignore him," Tarass ordered.

Rannock nodded and returned moments later with a shackled Lord Polwarth.

"Must I remind you that I am a man of great influence and important friends?" Polwarth warned when made to stand in front of Tarass.

"Must I remind you that I am a man who has family and friends who don't live by Scottish beliefs or rule and can make you disappear never to be found again?"

"You wouldn't dare," Polwarth challenged.

"I dare anything when a man thinks he can take my wife from me," Tarass said anger sparking his every word.

"You're like your father, a shameful man," Polwarth spat. "Snow is a good woman and deserves better."

"How dare you claim my father dishonorable when you come into my home and try to abduct my wife," Tarass said, his hands fisted at his sides and fighting to keep them there.

"To save her," Polwarth said, his face blotched red with anger.

Snow could see the outline of the two men, but it was their mounting anger in their warring voices that she feared would cause far worse problems.

She spoke up, hoping to make Lord Polwarth understand. "I have explained over and over that I have no wont to leave Tarass. I love him and he loves me."

"So he says now, but he will discard you when he is done using you and cast you out as his father did to my sister?" Polwarth said, an ugly sneer spreading across his face.

Tarass shook his head, scrunching his brow. "What are you talking about?"

"Your father didn't have the decency or perhaps he had been far too ashamed of what he had done to my sister, Fay, to speak a word about it."

Snow caught the turn of his head toward her.

"I never meant you harm, my dear. My sole purpose of marrying you was to protect you. After hearing that you had been forced to stay with Lord Tarass for a few days, I feared he would destroy your honor as his father did to my sister. When I met with your da last, he was lucid, of sound mind, and he told me he didn't believe he'd live much longer. I asked if there was anything I could do to help and he told me that he worried the most about you. Sorrell and Willow, he believed would do well, but you being blind and it

340

being his fault, he feared what would become of you and asked me to be there to help you if ever needed. I was not only pleased to keep my word to him, but thought to redeem myself and save you when I couldn't save my sister."

"What is it you think my da did to your sister?" Tarass asked, unable to believe a word of Polwarth's tale, his da having been the most honorable man he had ever known, far more honorable than he was himself.

"Marriage arrangements were being discussed between your grandfather and my parents for Fay and your da to wed. Fay visited here often and when she returned home,"—Polwarth shook his head—"I had never seen her so happy. My parents believed they were making a perfect match for her. Then your da returned from that trip with your mum, his new wife, and my sister was utterly stunned and heartbroken. She took to her bedchamber and wouldn't leave it." His eyes flared with anger. "She grew ill and my family was shocked to learn that she suffered a miscarriage. She had been carrying your father's bairn. She begged for confession so her soul wouldn't suffer endless damnation, and I brought Abbot Bennett to her to absolve her from sin. She confessed all to him. How she would sneak into the keep through the secret passage and meet with him, fornicate with him, and how they planned to wed and have a life together. Worse, she told Abbot Bennett that she didn't want to live. She was glad she was dying."

"My father would have never done that to your sister," Tarass said.

"Ask Abbot Bennett. He heard the confession and told me about the secret passage."

Snow's heart broke for the young lass, she had never met. Loving Tarass as she did, she couldn't imagine the pain the woman must have suffered being betrayed. Yet just as she couldn't believe her da would ever hurt Tarass's parents, Tarass believed his da couldn't be so heartless and shameful. Were they both blind when it came to their fathers or was there something else to both tales?

Tarass sent for Abbot Bennett and he didn't waste time in ordering the man to tell him everything that Polwarth's sister had confessed to him.

His tale was the same as Polwarth's and he seemed to enjoy telling it.

"My da would have never been so ignoble. I don't believe you," Tarass said, defending his da as strongly as Snow had defended her da.

"And well you shouldn't, since it's a lie."

All eyes turned to see Twilla standing in the open doorway.

She shuffled in, closing the door behind her, and made her way to Tarass and laid her aged hand on his arm. "It's a secret your da swore me to keep, but with what went on here today, it's time the secret was revealed, at least to those in this room." She turned an accusing glance on the Abbot. "Though Abbot Bennett already knows it." She turned to Polwarth. "And it's time you knew it as well."

Tarass's silence gave Twilla permission to speak.

"Fay and Winton, Tarass's da, were good friends, but it wasn't Winton she loved. It was another man and Winton helped her hide it, since the man was one of

Winton's warriors, certainly not an appropriate husband for the daughter of a noble."

"Fay would never—"

"Love doesn't distinguish between nobles and peasants," Twilla snapped at Polwarth. "Fay didn't plan on falling in love with this warrior. It caught them both off guard and both tried to deny it, but love is impossible to ignore."

"Abbot Bennett told me it was Winton my sister snuck off to meet," Polwarth said, looking perplexed.

Twilla looked to the Abbot. "He lied."

"Fay never mentioned a name," Abbot Bennett said in defense of himself.

"Another lie," Twilla accused.

"You dare call me a liar," Abbot Bennett snapped.

"I think Fay's own words prove it since she begged to confess her sins. Isn't that right, Lord Polwarth?"

"Aye, she did, begged me with tears in her eyes to save her soul," Polwarth confirmed.

"Fay feared dying with a sin on her soul, never allowing her to join the warrior she loved when she died."

"The warrior's dead?" Snow asked, her heart aching for the poor lass.

"Fay came here as soon as Winton had arrived with his new wife along with his warriors who had accompanied him. While it was a joyous occasion for him, it was also a heartbreaking one. He had to tell Fay that the warrior she loved had died in an accident. Fay returned home distraught not over Winton's new wife, but over losing the man she loved. She kept the bairn a secret until it was a secret no more. Losing the bairn he had left her with was like losing her love all over again and she gave up. Fay wanted to die. She felt there was nothing left in this life for her."

"That is a ridiculous tale you concocted," Abbot Bennett accused. "You have no way of knowing the truth."

Twilla wiped at the tear that hung at the corner of her eye. "But I do know. I know because the warrior Fay loved was my son."

Chapter Twenty-nine

Lord Polwarth stood speechless, tears glistening in his eyes. No one else spoke either, Twilla having stunned them all silent.

"Your parents, Lord Polwarth, knew the truth, since your father came here demanding Winton's marriage be absolved and that he marry Fay. Winton refused, allowing your father to think him a dishonorable man rather than think less of his daughter. It was one of the reasons Winton's father disliked Haldana when she first arrived," Twilla explained. "Then one day your father arrived here with Fay. She had convinced your father that she would speak with Winton and he would change his mind and wed her. What she did next shocked all. She confessed the truth to your father and Winton's da, so that her friend Winton would be blamed no more. Fay was a good woman and I loved her like a daughter. I urged her to come live with me and we'd raise my grandchild together. I believe she was considering it when she lost the bairn."

"At least now she rests in peace, free of sin," Abbot Bennett said.

"You lied to me. I came to you for guidance, distraught over what my sister had endured, and you lied to me," Lord Polwarth said, turning angry eyes on Abbot Bennett. "You let me believe, even encouraged me to believe that Tarass was worse than his father when his father was a good friend to my sister and did what he could to protect her."

"A marriage to Snow was what you needed and would prove beneficial. Snow could give you what you've yearned for… children to carry on your name," Abbot Bennett said.

"Children that would continue to generously support the monastery after I was gone is what you truly mean," Lord Polwarth said with such a malicious tone that it had Abbot Bennett taking a step back.

"I did what was best for—"

"Yourself," Tarass accused.

"And in the process had me break my word to my friend to see Snow kept safe," Lord Polwarth said and shook his head. "Tell me, did you also lie about Snow's da being responsible for Tarass's parents' deaths in hopes he would walk away from her?"

"I do what is best for the people I serve," Abbot Bennett said.

"Another lie to add to your many others," Polwarth said and turned away from the Abbot to face Tarass and Snow. "An apology isn't adequate for the distress I've caused you, but I offer it with a penitent heart and ask for your forgiveness. I will also see the wrong done to your father made right."

"We forgive you, Lord Polwarth," Snow said her gentle heart going out to the man for speaking up for her da and for the suffering the secret and lies had caused him and so many others.

"Not quite," Tarass corrected quickly. "I hold no grudge against you for what transpired in the past, and my da made a choice to protect a friend and I will not see that taken from him now. What disturbs me is that you caused my wife unnecessary worry and an unnecessary injury."

"He didn't mean to," Snow said in Polwarth's defense.

"You forgive too easily, wife," Tarass said and reached down to run his finger gently along her cheek.

Snow looked up at him and smiled pleased that he was more than a gray blur standing there. He was still fuzzy, but she could almost see the color of his plaid and the impressive size of him. "You taught me that, since if I had held a grudge against you, rather than forgive you for all the times you were mean to me and made me apologize, ours would be far from a loving marriage. Lord Polwarth meant well and my leg was nothing more than an accident."

"That should have never happened," Tarass argued. "And wouldn't have happened if he hadn't tried to abduct you."

"Your husband is right, Snow," Lord Polwarth said. "I stand ready for punishment."

"Nonsense," Snow protested.

"It's not your decision. It's your husband's," Abbot Bennett snapped.

"You're right, Abbot Bennett, it is my decision as is the punishment. I deem this whole matter your fault," Tarass said. "And I will see you appropriately punished. Actually, I have the perfect punishment for you both." He turned to Lord Polwarth. "Your punishment is that you are to send a missive to whoever is in charge of Abbot Bennett and explain that you will no longer provide the monastery with a generous yearly stipend unless..." Tarass turned to the Abbot. "Abbot Bennett is removed from his position for failing to provide adequate and accurate counsel."

Abbot Bennett glared at Tarass. "You don't seriously think that Lord Polwarth would do such—"

"I agree," Lord Polwarth said, the strength in his voice leaving no doubt he meant it.

"You can't be serious," Abbot Bennett said.

"I am, and I will see it done," Polwarth confirmed and turned a slight smile on him. "And remember who also benefits from my generosity."

Abbot Bennett paled, his fate sealed as he barely got his words out. "The Bishop."

Tarass walked over to Abbot Bennett. "You leave here alive and well because of my wife's good and forgiving heart. Otherwise, I would have seen you suffer horrendously for your deceit, and the danger it brought to my wife." He looked to Rannock. "Take both men and remove their shackles. Return Lord Polwarth here to me and take Abbot Bennett and his men and see them escorted off my land."

"I'm not leaving. I will hear what you have to say to Lord Polwarth," Snow said as soon as the door closed.

"You need to rest that leg and have Nettle apply the poultice," Tarass said, returning to his wife's side.

"I'm staying here," Snow said, striking a stubborn pose by folding her arms across her chest.

"You're not going to win this one, *ást*," Tarass said.

348

"I'm not going anywhere," she said, sounding even more stubborn.

Tarass chuckled and scooped her up in his arms so fast she yelped in shock, her arms going quick around his neck.

"You're safe in my arms," he reminded and kissed her softly, then walked to the door. "You know I'll tell you everything."

"Depending on what he says, I may have questions for him," she argued though less stubbornly.

"We think the same, wife. I'm sure our questions would be the same," Tarass assured her.

Snow grew quiet, surprising Tarass. He thought for sure she'd bombard him with questions until they reached their bedchamber.

"What disturbs you, wife?" he asked, concerned.

"Thoughts of Fay and how terrible and frightening it must have been for her. And how horrible for Twilla to lose her son. Was he her only child?"

"I don't know. I didn't even know she had a son. I never heard anyone mention him, not even Twilla. I understand why that might be. Losing an only child must have been beyond heartbreaking. She is the only one left here of the original Clan MacFiere. My da did tell me to trust her beyond all others, that she knew all the clan secrets. Though, I'm grateful she didn't keep this secret."

Tarass entered their bedchamber. "Thaw must be worn out. He's already asleep by the hearth, and Nettle waits with a pleasant smile."

Snow had noticed that her husband painted pictures with words for her lately, just as Nettle did. And she

349

loved him all the more for taking the time and being patient so she could see through his eyes. She hoped and prayed with all her heart that her sight would continue to improve so that she could one day see him clearly and also be able to see the many bairns they would have together.

He placed her on the bed, kissed her, and ordered, "Stay put and be good."

She smiled. "I'll try."

Tarass turned to Nettle. "If my wife attempts to leave this room before I return, send Thaw to fetch me."

"Aye, my lord," Nettle said with a smile and got to work on Lady Snow's knee as soon as Lord Tarass left the room.

***

Lord Polwarth was waiting along with Rannock when Tarass entered his solar. With a nod from Tarass, Rannock left.

"Sit," Tarass offered and filled two tankards with ale that waited on a sideboard along with a full pitcher. He handed one to Lord Polwarth and took a seat in a chair opposite the man.

"Is Snow all right? I feel horrible that I hurt her. She's such a wee bit of a thing, though she has the strength and courage of a mighty warrior," Polwarth said, his worry evident in his aged eyes that looked anxiously to Tarass.

He was glad to see the man contrite, or he'd be tempted to land a blow or two on him. "That she does. I couldn't believe how many times she dared to challenge me as she did. I admire her for her courage."

"I am relieved to know that you both love each other. I loved both my wives, but my first wife was my one true love. My heart broke when she died and I don't believe it ever healed." Polwarth turned his head, to hide the tear that caught in the corner of his eye.

Tarass understood. His heart would shatter completely if he ever lost Snow. "Then you know how I felt when you took my wife from me."

"I do now," Polwarth admitted. "And I fear no apology will ever be enough for the harm I've caused you and Snow. I only hope someday you both will forgive me."

"Snow already has. My forgiveness doesn't come so easily. I'd rather beat you senseless."

"I don't blame you. I'd feel the same way if I were in your position."

"I do appreciate you confronting the Abbot about Angus Macardle. It will ease the burden it brought on my wife. Her da was a good friend to my da and had no reason to harm him or my mum."

"I agree. It made no sense when Abbot Bennett told me. I should have realized then the man was a liar and couldn't be trusted."

"What I can't understand is why you left the pools of blood. Was it to make me look worse in Abbot Bennett's eyes? Or did you wish to put fear in my clan? And how did you even know about the myth?"

Polwarth's brow wrinkled. "I don't know anything about the pools of blood. Learning about them was a complete shock to me."

"I believe you are contrite for what you have done, so why deny the rest?" Tarass asked.

"I have confessed the whole truth to you and believe me when I tell you how difficult that was to admit, especially to myself and at my age. And to realize what a fool I've been. My father had told me to let it go. Even when Fay died, he warned me again that it would do no good to continue to carry her pain and that my sister would never want me to. He should have confessed the truth to me, though he probably was too shamed by Fay's actions to do so." He shook his head. "Snow was right about grudges. They do more harm than good, especially when lies hide the truth."

Tarass thought of his parents. "Do you know if this matter with your sister had anything to do with my parents leaving Scotland?"

"I don't see how since the whole ordeal was kept between your family and my father and mother. And it wasn't until years later that your family left."

"Abbot Bennett knew and he knew more than you did," Tarass said.

"True, but only because he heard my sister's confession. He wouldn't have dared said anything to anyone for fear of losing support for his monastery. Many clans in the area had been surprised when your parents fled and that was how it seemed. That they fled as if fearful and running from something. And your father was too much of a fierce warrior to flee from anything."

Tarass had heard that about his da and had seen it for himself in battle. He had been a fierce and skilled warrior, taking men down with little effort. Tarass didn't think he'd ever come close to the powerful warrior his da had been. So why would a fierce warrior flee? And whatever could his parents have done that got them killed?

"Snow is like your da. She's kind and caring, but wrong her and she turns into a ferocious warrior. Did you know when no one would go into the burning room in the keep where her da had set a fire to rescue him, she ran in not even pausing to think about it? It was what caused her blindness. The funny thing was that her father often said to me, when in his right mind, 'Winton's son Tarass would be perfect for my Snow'. I thought him mad, but I now wonder if he saw something that I had failed to see."

Tarass was pleased to know that Snow's da would have approved of their marriage.

"You and your men are welcome to stay the night. While Abbot Bennett and his crew will make it to the monastery shortly after darkness falls, night would descend on you well before you reach home," Tarass said.

"And the long, tumultuous day has proven too much for these old bones," Polwarth said.

"A room will be prepared for you," Tarass said.

"You are too generous, Lord Tarass. I should at least be in the stocks for what I did."

"I agree and would oblige you, but my wife would come to your rescue and free you even if she had to sneak out of the keep in the middle of the night, paying no heed to her blindness, to do so. On that, I am certain."

Polwarth smiled. "I can see Snow doing that and succeeding."

Fear poked at Tarass at the thought of his wife doing such a dangerous thing.

"There is food and drink in the Great Hall for you and your men."

"My two men who followed my orders. What will happen to them?" Polwarth asked.

"While again, I would see them at least suffer the stocks for a few days, they brought no harm to my wife so I will let them go unpunished, not something I would usually do. Though, know this, Lord Polwarth. You owe me and some day you will repay me."

"On that you have my word," Lord Polwarth said.

***

Tarass ordered the evening meal brought to his bedchamber. It arrived well before he did, a few matters delaying his return to his wife. However, he was glad to see Snow sitting at the small table, big enough for him and her alone, and piled with food that Snow was enjoying.

"You're hungry tonight," he said and chuckled, since she couldn't see him smile.

"Very hungry," she admitted, her cheeks turning pink at how much food she had put in her bowl.

"I'm pleased to hear that, since I'm feeling the same and look forward to stuffing myself," he said and leaned over her to kiss her lips. He came away, licking them. "Meat pie, a favorite of mine."

"Hurry. Sit and tell me all," Snow urged impatient to hear what had been discussed.

"First you will tell me how your knee does," he said.

"It feels much better, and the pain is not as bad when I stand, and the swelling has gone down quite a bit."

Tarass lifted her and the chair with ease, turning it away from the table. "I'll see for myself."

Snow lifted her nightdress, Nettle had helped her into, exposing her knee.

Tarass flinched, seeing the bruise that had deepened considerably, though she'd been right about the swelling. It had gone down. It made him want to go and beat Polwarth senseless.

"His kick wasn't meant for me, and I would suffer anything to protect Thaw," she said, able to see, fuzzy though it was, his brow narrow in anger since he was so close to her.

"Thaw is there to protect you," Tarass scolded.

"He's only a pup," she reminded.

"And he will never grow into a warrior if you don't let him," Tarass said and kissed her before she could respond, then lifted her and the chair to settle her at the table.

Snow gave thought to the wisdom of his words.

Once Tarass sat, he didn't waste any time. He told her everything Polwarth and he had discussed in between enjoying the delicious fare.

"I didn't think he had anything to do with the pools of blood. The myth belongs to your mum's people so it would make sense the person responsible is of that origin," Snow said.

"I doubted it as well, but I needed to ask. The puzzle goes unsolved," Tarass said, frustrated that even the smallest clue eluded him.

"This snow doesn't help. It limits travel and discussion with others who may be of help," Snow said, enjoying the tasty heather ale. "I can't help but wonder if that man with the many markings had news for you."

"What makes you think that?" Tarass asked.

"He and Finn suffered the same fate and Finn had news for you, so it makes one wonder if the man with the markings also had news for you."

Tarass enjoyed talking with his wife. She had a sharp mind, sometimes seeing things he didn't.

Snow scratched her head and narrowed her eyes in thought. "I wish we could make sense of the pools of blood. Are they a message of some sort? Or are they meant to instill fear and weaken your leadership? It would help to know the why since it could lead us to the who."

They continued talking, conversation eventually turning to things they did when young and more laughter than talk followed.

Snow yawned once or twice, but when her yawns grew Tarass took note and saw what he hadn't noticed before, how tired she was. And why wouldn't she be with the day she had.

"You need to sleep," he said.

"First, I need you," she said with a smile that tempted.

Tarass stretched out of his chair and went to her, scooping her up in his arms. "That's not going to happen tonight, wife. You need to rest."

Snow laughed softly and nibbled at his neck before whispering playfully, "You're not going to win this one, husband."

And he didn't.

Chapter Thirty

Snow woke and smiled, seeing the wood ceiling overhead. It was a bit blurry but she could make it out just as she could her surroundings, and it all was in color. Her gray, drab world was gone. Now she saw colors, wonderful, beautiful colors.

Her sight had continued to improve in the last three weeks, though she had continued to keep the news to herself. She worried it wouldn't last and her sight would be lost to her again. Instead, her sight had continued to improve and if it improved no more than it had to this point, she'd still be grateful.

Her hand went to her queasy stomach and her smile grew. More time would confirm it, but she was pretty sure she was with child. She had thought it too early for any signs that she carried a bairn to show, then she recalled what her mum had told her one day.

I remember I knew right away you were growing inside me. I got a queasy stomach every morning as soon as my monthly bleeding was late. Then I would get hungry and want to eat and then the queasiness would return again.

Snow was glad her mum had spoken to her about it. She didn't want her daughters to be ignorant about the way of things for women.

Their mum had taught them well.

Snow turned and snuggled her face against her husband's pillow. He was usually there when she woke and the one who woke first usually stirred the other awake in an intimately, delightful fashion. This morning, however, Rannock had come for Tarass with an important message he'd been waiting for, and he had left.

All had been quiet since the incident with Lord Polwarth and Abbot Bennett. No other pools of blood had shown up or dead bodies. Runa had examined Cleric Norman's body and there had been no signs of any injury. The assumption was that the snowstorm had caused him to wander off course and he froze to death. Tarass had a troop of his warriors return the body to the monastery.

While Snow was pleased the problems that had plagued them seemed to have settled, she continued to be concerned over the threat from the supposed creature. Was this lull on purpose? Did someone want Tarass to let his guard down?

Snow sat up and glanced around the room. She was completely alone, Thaw having gone with Tarass and it too early for Nettle to arrive. She recalled how Lord Polwarth had almost whisked her away so easily, but she needn't worry about that happening again. Tarass had seen that the secret passage was made impassable. He'd also posted sentinels in the area where it was located in case there were others who knew of it.

She was safe in her home, safe with her husband around. She also felt safer with her sight having been almost fully restored. At least, she could see if any danger lurked nearby.

With her stomach settling, she knew what to expect next. She got hungry and couldn't wait to eat, since she knew the queasiness could return at any time. She got out of bed with a spring to her step, her knee having healed nicely, and began to dress, her stomach grumbling.

***

Tarass sat with Rannock in his solar. The warriors he had sent to find out what news Finn had learned had finally returned. It hadn't been easy but they had been successful in their mission, and the news had left him troubled.

Tarass had listened intently to the two warriors tell him what they had learned. It was a brief message.

A man with markings is on his way to you. He knows the truth about your parents' deaths and he knows the one responsible. There is also one in your clan who knows the truth.

"Someone in the clan knows the truth," Rannock said, repeating part of the news. "If only the man with the markings had made it here alive. This all would be solved." Rannock shook his head. "How do you find out now about your parents' deaths?"

"I find the one in the clan who knows the truth," Tarass said. "The traitor among us. The one who poses as a dwarf and brings fright to the clan. Though, I doubt this person works alone."

"How do we find this person? It's not like anyone is going to step forward and admit it."

"Unless forced to," Tarass said.

Rannock went to question again, but stopped a moment his brow shooting up. "Well-placed rumors certainly can have people speaking up."

"Precisely, and you can get that rumor started now," Tarass said, standing. "Go find Nettle and tell her to make sure she starts it as a whisper, as if no one is to know about it. That will spread it faster. Tell her that I search for someone who harbors information vital to the clan's safety. That should get people questioning things they see or hear."

Rannock's smile spread wide. "Nettle will have the rumor spread in no time with her never-ending chatter."

"That's what I'm counting on," Tarass said. standing. "I'm going to wake my wife, so make certain to keep Nettle occupied and away from my bedchamber for a while."

***

Snow was slipping her shift over her head when she heard the door open. She turned hastily, suddenly fearful from her experience with Lord Polwarth of who it might be, and got her face tangled in the shift.

Tarass smiled at his wife's predicament, though was glad for it, his hands eager to roam her naked body.

"You'll not be needing that, wife, at least not yet," Tarass said as he approached her.

Snow sighed with relief and smiled, and she stopped fighting the garment. She wasn't surprised when it was yanked off her.

Her husband's face was still fuzzy, though not the blue of his eyes, so bright and bold. They were clear when he was this close to her, and seeing them always sent a tingle through her.

Tarass settled his hands on her waist and was about to kiss her when her hand suddenly went to her stomach and she paled. He lifted her gently in his arms and went to the bed to sit with her on his lap.

"Not feeling well?" he asked, concerned since this had been happening each morning when she woke.

"It will pass," she said and laid her head on his shoulder.

"There's no denying it. You're with child," Tarass said with a smile. It waned when he saw her grow paler.

"I believe so," she said, her smile wide.

He rested his hand to her stomach. "I am thrilled beyond belief that our child grows inside you, but I hate seeing you suffer like this."

"My mum suffered the same carrying me, but it passed after a while," she assured him.

He grabbed the blanket and wrapped it around her. "Let's get you into bed."

"No, I want to stay in your arms," she insisted. "Tell me what took you from our bed so early this morning."

He knew she wanted her mind taken off her roiling stomach and he obliged her. Besides, he didn't want to let her go. He wanted to hold her close and do whatever he could to help her feel better.

Tarass explained everything to her along with his plan to find the one in the clan who betrayed him.

He was met with silence when he finished, something he wasn't expecting. She always voiced her opinion or gave advice, which he often found helpful. So why the silence?

"What's wrong?" he asked.

"You once mentioned that the whole tribe where your parents were staying when they were killed was massacred, except for one woman who managed to hide. Why would the whole tribe be massacred if it were only your parents this person wanted dead?"

"I and others have asked that over and over and can find no answer."

"Maybe you didn't ask the right question."

"I've asked every possible question," he assured her, though he wondered if it was himself he was reassuring, since he continued to feel he had failed his parents. Their deaths should have been avenged by now.

"Why massacre a whole tribe?" Snow asked.

"Pure anger and hate."

"For the tribe or what they didn't find?"

"What do you mean?" Tarass asked.

"Were you supposed to be there with your parents?" she asked and didn't know if her stomach roiled due to the bairn or the thought of what could have happened to her husband if he had been there.

"No," he said, shaking his head, then stopped abruptly. "I'd forgotten. My mum told everyone I was going to meet them there in hopes that I would." He shook his head annoyed for not realizing that, but then he'd never planned on joining his parents so it had never been a thought. Now, however, he looked at his parents' deaths differently. "You're saying that it wasn't only my parents this person wanted dead but my whole family."

"It's a possibility," Snow said.

"But why wait? My parents have been dead months now. Why not strike again and see me dead?"

"There was no opportunity to see it done before you came here to Scotland," Snow suggested. "And once here, it would take planning and travel, getting to know the area. Or sending someone with you to grow familiar with the area."

"Hence, the one among us who knows the truth," Tarass said. "That would mean I could eliminate those who joined me once I arrived here."

Snow poked him in the chest. "That would mean you're in danger and need to take precautions."

"As do you, since your family now as well," he said, angry that he had placed her in danger by marrying her.

"I don't believe so," Snow said. "This person wanted your family dead before I came along."

"Which would have basically ended the MacFiere lineage, not so now that we're wed and you carry my child." The realization flared his anger.

Snow couldn't argue with that premise. "Then we both need to be cautious and see that the culprit among us is caught soon." Her stomach grumbled.

"You need to eat," Tarass said, another grumble from her stomach confirming it for him.

"I would prefer to slip under the blankets with you and have you slip inside me, but I'm famished... for food this time," Snow admitted with some disappointment.

Tarass chuckled. "It's cold and gray outside. We can return here later and spend time warming each other."

"I can't wait," she said.

***

Mid-day found Snow walking through the village with Nettle and Thaw, her husband busy talking with Rannock in regard to the sentinels that patrolled the village. They came upon Runa leaving Helga's cottage.

"How does Helga's new bairn do, Runa?" Nettle asked, letting Snow know who she spoke to.

Snow looked at the woman, fuzzy, but at least not a blur. Her face wasn't clear, but her blonde hair was bright enough to see the color.

"The little lassie does well and Helga's thrilled she has a daughter after having two lads," Runa said and looked to Snow. "And how are you feeling, Lady Snow? Rumors say you're with child."

"Time will tell," Snow said, not ready to confirm anything yet.

"Nettle!"

The three women turned at Nettle's name being called out.

"It's Helga's husband, John," Nettle said to let Snow know who approached.

"I know who you should be talking to about bringing harm to our clan," John said, stopping by Nettle. "Fasta, that's who. She's a liar and cares not who she harms with her lies."

365

"What has she lied about?" Snow asked well aware the woman had a penchant for lying.

"Lady Snow," John said with a respectful bob of his head. "I'm sorry to intrude, but if someone is bringing harm to this clan it most certainly has to be Fasta. Her lies have hurt my marriage. She claims to have miscarried my bairn when that's impossible. I've never cheated on Helga. I have no reason to. She is a good wife to me and a wonderful mum to our bairns. I would never chance losing what we have together. Besides, I've loved my wife since we were young. There's no other woman for me."

"We both know that, John, and that's all that matters, so stop bothering Lady Snow," Helga said from the open doorway.

"No, it's not all that matters," John insisted. "I'll not have my good name sullied. Fasta is a menace to this clan. Besides, if she lied about me what else has she lied about."

"I will speak to my husband about this, John, and see what can be done," Snow said.

"I would be most grateful, m'lady," John said and hurried into the cottage.

"If John wasn't the father of the miscarried bairn, who was?" Nettle asked.

"I found it difficult to believe that John was the father of Fasta's bairn," Runa said. "He and Helga seemed so much in love and though she delivered their bairns easily, he still worried over her. He begged me to make sure nothing happened to her. He told me that he couldn't live without her."

"Why would Fasta lie about him?" Snow asked.

"Because that's what Fasta does, at least since I've known her," Nettle said and looked to Runa. "You have known her longer. Has she a fondness for lying?"

"I can't say I know Fasta well. She only joined the tribe—clan—a short time before we all arrived here."

That caught Snow's attention and she planned to discuss it with Tarass as soon as possible.

Snow continued walking with Nettle, Thaw exploring anything that caught his interest as they went along when he stopped suddenly and started barking, then took off.

"Thaw's tail wags as he runs," Nettle said.

"Someone is nearby that he knows and likes," Snow said. "Let's hurry and see who it is."

Snow wasn't far from the keep when her name was shouted with delight.

"Snow!"

Snow squealed with joy at the sound of Willow's voice and when she caught partial sight of her sister's form, she ran to her.

Chapter Thirty-one

Tarass watched from the top of the keep steps as his wife and her sister squealed like young lassies and hugged each other tight. Thaw even jumped up at Willow, his tail wagging madly as he vied for attention. Willow and her husband, Slatter's visit was unexpected, but he was pleased they were here. Snow had missed her sister and with her possibly being with child, it would help her to talk with Willow, who was beginning to round with child herself.

He walked down the steps to Slatter while the two women continued to hug and laugh and wipe tears away from each other's faces.

"I couldn't keep her away, not after Lord Polwarth stopped at our home and told us what happened. I seriously thought my wife was going to strike him, she got so mad. I was grateful the old fool redeemed himself by the tale's end."

"She would have done me a favor by striking him," Tarass admitted.

Slatter laughed. "Snow forgave him easily, didn't she?"

Tarass nodded. "She did."

"Polwarth also mentioned something about pools of blood and dwarfs?" Slatter said with a scrunched brow as if it made no sense.

"Let's get our wives inside where it's warm and I'll explain, since I'm sure Willow is looking for a reasonable explanation," Tarass said, aware she was the most practical of the three Macardle sisters.

"She can't wait to hear what you have to say about it," Slatter said with a laugh.

Both men went and collected their wives.

Slatter kept a firm arm around Willow's waist, not wanting her to slip on the icy steps and harm herself or the bairn growing inside her.

Tarass did the same, though it proved more dangerous for Snow, since she couldn't see the steps for herself, or so he thought.

The two couples settled at a table close to the hearth. After Thaw made his rounds to each one of them, getting a pet from the men and hugs from the women, he went and laid on the warm hearth stones until he couldn't keep his head up any longer, then he slept.

"I could not believe what Polwarth did to you," Willow said. "I wanted to thrash him senseless."

"I would have been ever grateful if you had," Tarass said and got a poke in the side from his wife.

"Has your leg healed?" Willow asked.

"It's fine," Snow said as if dismissing it as unimportant and not mentioning that she was probably with child. She would save that for when they were alone. "How are you? Are you feeling well?"

"I do well and so does the bairn, but we can talk about such things later when we get time alone," Willow said. "Right now I'm eager to hear about the pools of blood and the dwarfs that Polwarth mentioned. Whatever was he rambling about?"

"So he told you about them," Snow said, having wanted to do so herself and get her sister's perspective on the situation.

"You better tell your sister before she explodes with curiosity," Slatter warned with a smile.

Tarass detailed the myth and the pools of blood that had been found, starting with the first one they had come across when returning home after the wedding, to the last small one found as if cradled in a goblet.

"So you have no idea why these pools of blood have appeared?" Willow asked.

"It could be to cast doubt on Tarass as a leader and his ability to protect his clan," Slatter said.

Snow nodded. "We've thought of that."

"Or it could have more of a meaning," Willow said. "From what you've explained the first pool of blood was large, the second smaller than the first but not as small as the last one. Doesn't it strike you as odd that each one is a different size?" She didn't give anyone a chance to respond, she continued, "You say the pools of blood represent knowledge gained. If that is so then with such a large pool of blood how many would have died for the knowledge gained there? The second pool is not as large and could very well represent the knowledge gained from Finn and the marked man. The last pool of blood is a puzzle." Willow shook her head. "It would represent something small and since there are no deaths associated with it, it greatly puzzles me. But there is one more thing you should consider. Your people believe the myth is about the dwarfs gaining knowledge, but it's more about jealousy, about the knowledge the man has that the dwarfs don't have. So you might want to ask yourself, what do you have that this person is jealous of or thinks he deserves to have more than you?"

***

Snow and Willow sat in Snow's solar, blankets tucked around them and their feet stretched out to the heat of the hearth. Thaw had gone with Tarass and Slatter for a walk through the village, Slatter interested in seeing the improvements made since Tarass's return home.

"I believe I'm with child," Snow said, unable to hold it in any longer.

Willow jumped out of her chair and hugged her sister. "That's wonderful. We will have our bairns close together. They will grow to be like sisters and brothers."

Tears threatened Snow's eyes. "You don't know how happy that makes me."

"How are you feeling?" Willow asked, returning to her seat and tucking the blanket around her.

"Like Mum did when she carried me, queasy and hungry."

"It will pass as it did with Mum," Willow assured her. "I so look forward to delivering my niece or nephew. If you're like Mum when she delivered you, you'll spit the bairn out with ease."

"That would please me, and I will help you when you deliver," Snow said, hoping her vision would be clear enough by then. "Have you heard anything from Sorrell? She wouldn't want to be left out in sharing the birth of our first bairns."

"I've heard nothing since I last saw her, though a couple of messages have been sent. I fear the snow has prevented any responses. However, she did tell me that nothing would keep her from coming here in the spring, not even her husband."

Snow laughed. "Sorrell is a wee bit of a thing and Ruddock so large. I don't know how she commands that man."

"He lets her, until he doesn't," Willow said with a chuckle. "I am pleased to see how happy you are with Tarass and how much you love each other."

"It's that obvious?" Snow asked, glad her love for her husband was visible to all.

"It's undeniable, but tell me more of what goes on here, Snow," Willow said. "I feel that you haven't told me everything."

"I always thought that your practical nature allows you to be more perceptive than others," Snow said and obliged her sister, telling her about how Fasta suffered a miscarriage and how it led to her confrontation with the dwarf. She debated, only briefly, whether to tell her sister about what the dwarf had said to her.

We're coming for you.

Her sister might get upset, but she would examine it for what it was worth.

Willow remained quiet when Snow finished telling her everything and didn't disturb her, knowing her sister was giving thought to all she had told her.

"We're coming for *you*. Why you? Why didn't this creature,"—she shook her head—"this person, since I don't believe in the tale, mention Tarass? I would worry over you if I didn't know Tarass would protect you with his life and with the amount of sentinels I saw when we arrived, your husband has taken precautions. What makes no sense to me is the convenience of the incident and it makes me wonder if it could have been contrived?"

"How?" Snow asked, finding her sister's suggestion perplexing. "How would they know I would be there at that time and with only Thaw? And how could Fasta plan a miscarriage?"

"Someone could be watching your every move, lying in wait for the right moment. And the snowstorm that comes and goes provides perfect cover. Also did you consider that Fasta might not have had a miscarriage? Did your healer confirm it?"

"Why though?"

"Take your pick. To give more credence to the myth. To set a plan in action. To give Fasta time away from her duties at the keep," Willow said with a shrug. "There are endless reasons. I recall you telling me you didn't care for her upon first meeting her. Has she been as abrupt with you as she was the first time you were here?"

"She's been the same and I've caught her in lies. She was upset when I removed her from her duties at the keep," Snow said.

"A place where she could learn much. She could very well be the person who knows the truth behind

373

everything that goes on here. But tell me, do you believe in this myth and the dwarfs?" Willow asked.

Snow shook her head. "No, I believe someone is out to harm my husband, and I believe whoever was responsible for his parents' deaths intended for Tarass to die with them."

"That sounds like revenge and revenge can be a powerful weapon, often wielded without thought or reason. Can Tarass think of anyone who holds such a deep grudge against his father?"

"We haven't gotten a chance to discuss that and I've also just learned of another lie Fasta told that Tarass needs to know about," Snow said and told her about what John had to say.

"I would say this Fasta has a lot of explaining to do, but also think about what I said earlier concerning the true meaning of the myth… jealousy and revenge often go hand in hand."

***

"A moment of your time, my lord," Nettle said, approaching Lord Tarass as he neared the keep with Slatter.

Tarass stopped as did Slatter.

Nettle looked to Slatter, then to Tarass. "There's something I thought I should tell you."

"You can speak in front of Slatter," Tarass said.

Nettle did so without hesitation. "Lady Snow plans to tell you all about John's dilemma with Fasta so I don't wish to interfere with that. But I believe what I saw might be helpful in putting pieces of the puzzling matter together," Nettle said and continued. "The nights I walk the village when I cannot sleep, I sometimes see Fasta. Whether she is coming or going, I cannot say, though her steps are cautious in their gait, and she disappears before I see her reach any particular destination."

"I appreciate the information, Nettle," Tarass said.

Nettle bobbed her head and hurried up the keep stairs.

"It is good to have trusted eyes and ears in the clan," Slatter said. "I have the same myself."

"My da taught me the importance of it," Tarass said, his brow narrowing at a sudden thought. "I need to see to something. Would you take Thaw to Snow? I won't be long."

"Of course, but take what time you need," Slatter said and looked to the pup standing next to Tarass's leg. "Come on, Thaw. Come with me."

Thaw looked up at Tarass.

"Go with Slatter, Thaw. He'll take you to Snow," Tarass ordered and hearing Snow's name the pup ran up the keep steps, Slatter following several steps behind him.

Tarass made his way to Twilla's place and knocked on the door.

The door opened slowly, Twilla resting her hand on her lower back. "This cold has these old bones aching." She stepped back, making room for Tarass to enter.

Tarass cast an annoyed glance at the hearth where small flames barley flickered. He went straight to it and got more annoyed when he found no firewood in her basket. He went outside and grabbed wood from the pile several of the cottages shared and brought them inside. In no time, he had a fire blazing.

"Sit by the heat," he ordered, placing a chair in front of the hearth and once Twilla sat, he wrapped a blanket around her. "I will have someone see that your fire remains strong. You should have told me how difficult it has been for you."

"I don't like to be a burden," Twilla said, tears threatening her eyes.

"You're not a burden and it is my duty to see everyone in my clan kept safe. After all, we are family."

"You're much like your father," she said with a smile, keeping her unfallen tears at bay.

Tarass grabbed the other chair and placed it near Twilla and sat. "Da told me that I could always trust you. You know more about the clan and my family than anyone. If my da was an honorable man, why would someone want revenge against him?"

"Revenge?" Twilla asked, shaking her head slowly. "I know no one who would want revenge against your da, except, of course, Lord Polwarth, but that is settled. Your da was respected here in his homeland."

"Then why leave here?" Tarass asked the question he had asked repeatedly and never gotten an answer to.

"I have no answer for you," Twilla said sadly.

"I think you do and I hope someday you will trust me with it."

***

Snow tried not to yawn, but she had already managed to keep her husband from seeing a few yawns and this one she just couldn't hide. If he thought her tired, he wouldn't make love with her tonight and she so wanted to make love with him. She loved her husband like mad, but when they made love she felt as if they truly became one, that there was no separating them, that their love had become whole. It was like nothing she had ever felt before and she knew she'd only ever feel it with Tarass.

"You're tired," Tarass said, leaning down from where he sat in the chair beside her on the dais to plant his face close to hers.

"A little," she said, trying to make light of it.

"I'm tired," Willow said, a huge yawn confirming it. "It's been a good day and since we'll be staying for at least three days, there's plenty of time for us to spend together."

"Your sister is not only reasonable but wise as well," Tarass said.

"Actually, she's not being completely truthful," Slatter whispered not that softly and with a wicked smile. "She really can't wait to get me in bed and ravish me."

"Slatter!" Willow said, her cheeks burning red as she jabbed him in the arm.

Snow chuckled along with her husband.

Slatter wrapped his arms around his wife, hugging her as he laughed. "Deny it, wife, go ahead, and deny it if you can."

"You're incorrigible," she chastised.

Slatter snuggled his cheek against hers. "I'm not incorrigible, I'm loveable and that's why you can't keep your hands off me."

"Slatter, so help me!" Willow scolded, her cheeks flaming.

"Aye, wife, I'll help you straight to bed where you can have your way with me," he teased and stood, then scooped his wife out of her seat into his arms. "A pleasant night to you all!"

Snow laughed, hearing her sister scold Slatter as he carried her off. She turned to her husband and placed her hand on his chest, about to be as honest with him as Slatter had been with Willow.

"It's been a busy day, you're tired, and lovemaking can wait," Tarass said before she could get a word out. When she turned a wicked little smile on him, he knew he was in trouble, but he intended to be obeyed on this. "You will do as I say, Snow."

"Of course I will," she agreed her eyes wide with feigned innocence. "Though, I must admit that I'm pleased to know I'm right."

Tarass eyed her skeptically. "What are you right about?"

"That I would be too much of a demanding wife when it came to coupling and you wouldn't be able to keep up with my passion."

Tarass stood so abruptly that his chair almost toppled over and just as suddenly he snatched Snow up into his arms. "You shouldn't challenge me, wife."

He took the stairs two at a time, Thaw following behind him, and once in their bedchamber placed his wife on her feet, stripped her naked, and carried her to bed. After laying her on the bed, he stripped off his garments and got in bed with her, pulling the blanket over them.

Thaw was already curled in a ball by the hearth, his eyes closed.

He slipped his arm around her and tucked her against his side, his hand drifting down along her hip to her backside to give it a squeeze.

"First, I need to ask you something," Tarass said.

"Later," she said, her hand going to stroke his aroused manhood.

Tarass grabbed her hand, locking it in his, and brought it to rest on his chest. "No, now."

She looked at him, but with only the light from the hearth she couldn't see his face clearly. "I know what you're doing, trying to delay, and get me to fall asleep while we talk." She smiled. "It won't work."

"Then you need not be concerned about answering my question, since you obviously felt for yourself that I have a need for you," he challenged.

Snow smiled. "You're right. Ask what you will."

"Do you think Fasta could be the person who knows the truth of what goes on?"

"Odd you should ask that, since my sister asked the same as well. She also questioned if Fasta actually suffered a miscarriage. And today John, Helga's husband, claimed that Fasta wants to bring harm to the clan with her lies. He insists she lied about coupling with him. He says he loves his wife and would never turn to another woman."

"Nettle told me that when on her night walks through the village, she's seen Fasta, though couldn't tell if she was coming from someplace or going someplace. It's time I have a talk with Fasta."

"And Runa too," Snow was quick to add. "So we know for sure if Fasta had a miscarriage or not, though Willow suggests there could be a number of reasons for her to have done so."

"Willow's right and I intend to find out. You and Willow can see to Runa if you would?" Tarass said, knowing both women would learn much more from Runa than he would.

"Of course,"—a yawn interrupted Snow's words— "but I want to be there when you talk with Fasta."

"I couldn't keep you away if I wanted to, and I don't. You have a good mind for puzzles and offer sound advice."

"It's not me. It's us. We work well together."

"You're right. We do. We're a perfect fit."

"We are, so slip into me and show me just how perfectly we fit," she urged.

"You're tired," he said not with as much resolve as he had before.

"It can be quick," she whispered and began to nibble at his neck.

Tarass turned her on her back. "A quick one, then it is sleep for you."

"As you say, husband, though please take the time to satisfy my nipples that ache terribly for your skilled mouth."

A groan rumbled in Tarass's chest and he eagerly dropped his head to her breasts, his tongue licking the tight buds before his mouth settled over one to generously suckle.

After that, Tarass gave no thought to going quickly. He took his time, enjoying every inch of his wife, stroking, tasting, teasing until she begged him to slip inside her.

He dropped his head back and moaned when he felt her clench him after he settled inside her. He had little control after that, passion flaring far too hot and heavy in them both.

Snow climaxed fast, crying out, "Don't stop! Please don't stop!"

And he didn't, knowing another climax was building in her.

She screamed out when the second one hit her, feeling as if she was being devoured in the most delicious way.

A rumbling groan of pleasure shot out of Tarass as he climaxed with her. A slight smile burst from him as well, glad his wife had failed to obey him this time.

Chapter Thirty-two

Snow walked arm and arm with her sister to Runa's cottage, Thaw trotting alongside them.

Willow adjusted her hood against the cold and light snow. "It appears Fasta might be guilty after all since she can't be located."

"Her absence doesn't bode well for her. Tarass hasn't been able to find her and no one has seen her since yesterday." Snow lowered her voice. "Nettle told me that some think the dwarfs got her and others believe she ran off because she knew everyone believed she was a liar and was bringing harm to the clan."

"Tongues do spread news fast and one can only hope the clucking tongues are not doing more harm than good," Willow said.

"There's always that chance, but Tarass would never let an innocent suffer. If Fasta had nothing to hide, Tarass would have seen her vindicated."

"Let's take a brief reprieve from worrisome thoughts, tell me about Nettle and Rannock," Willow said, squeezing her sister's arm. "Nettle's eyes lit and went straight to Rannock when you told her you wouldn't be needing her for a while." She chuckled. "Then Rannock's cheeks heated when Nettle turned a generous smile on him, and I think I caught a wink as well."

Snow laughed along with her sister. "Rannock doesn't find it easy talking with women he's interested in and being he wasn't interested in Nettle, he talked easily with her."

"And found love where he least expected," Willow said. "Just like Slatter and me."

"I wouldn't say being lowered down into a pit where a naked man waited was conducive to finding love," Snow said with a grin.

Willow hugged her sister's arm and laughed. "No, it was terrifying, but I'm sure glad it was Slatter I found down there."

"Lady Snow, how nice to see you and this must be your sister Willow who I've been so eager to meet," Runa said, standing in her open doorway. "I was so pleased to receive word that you and your sister were coming to visit. Please come in. I have a hot brew ready for us."

Willow guided her sister into the cottage and settled her at the table before she took a seat herself and dropped her cloak off her shoulders to rest on the back of her chair as Snow had done.

"I have sweet cakes as well, sent from the keep," Runa said, filling the tankards on the table with a hot brew from the pitcher that sat near the hearth. "Would it be all right to give Thaw one?"

"I'm sure he'd enjoy it," Snow said, giving her permission.

Runa gave the pup one of the small cakes and turned to Willow as Thaw eagerly accepted the treat. "I have so much to ask you, Willow."

383

"I look forward to talking with you, but first Snow and I have some questions."

"Aye, of course, how can I be of help?" Runa asked eagerly, joining them at the table.

Snow saw clear enough to see Willow reach out for her hand to give the sweet cake to her and she almost reached for it, but stopped herself. She let Willow take her hand and place the sweet cake in it. She didn't like keeping the news about her sight from her sister, but she had to tell her husband first. And she planned to do that before the end of Willow's visit.

"Do you know for sure if Fasta suffered a miscarriage?" Willow asked, breaking a small piece of cake off to taste, not feeling hungry.

"I feared that might be so since she asked if there was something a woman could take to rid herself of an unwanted bairn. I told her there was but it was very dangerous, too little would do nothing and too much the woman could bleed to death. It was why I was so concerned with the amount of blood loss she suffered. I feared she had taken too much rue and would bleed to death. I never expected her to recover as quickly as she did."

"You gave her the rue?" Willow asked.

Runa shook her head vigorously. "No, I didn't, but I feared she may have stolen some and when I checked I realized some was missing."

"Why didn't you say something?" Snow asked and raised her hand to cover her yawn before finishing a second sweet cake.

"What was there to say. The deed was done," Runa said.

Willow was glad to see Snow eating since she had had little breakfast this morning. "How would she know which of your plant leaves was the rue?"

"I wondered the same," Runa said.

Snow shook her head, a fogginess taking hold.

"Something wrong?" Willow asked.

"I don't know," Snow said, and shook her head again and as she did, she saw Thaw laying on his side as if lifeless.

She turned to her sister. "Something is wrong. My head grows foggy and…" she couldn't get the words out and her head had grown too heavy to hold up so she laid it on the table.

"Snow!" Willow hurried to her feet to see to her sister when the door burst open.

***

Tarass and Slatter entered the Great Hall and sat at a table by the hearth to enjoy some ale.

"Fasta couldn't have gotten far. The ground is too heavily covered with snow," Slatter said. "It took double the time it would normally take for Willow and me to get here. And now that you've picked up her tracks, it won't be long before you find her and have your answers."

"Unless she's already met up with her cohorts," Tarass said. "She couldn't possibly have done this on her own. There has to be others."

"True, though the tracks were fresh which means she hadn't left too long ago and you could reach her before she reaches the other culprits," Slatter said.

Both men turned when Rannock and Nettle entered the Great Hall, their cheeks flushed from the cold or at least that's what Tarass surmised, not so Slatter.

"I'd say they got to know each other much better," Slatter said with a chuckle.

"Nettle, where is Lady Snow?" Tarass called out, concerned he hadn't seen his wife since this morning when she went with Willow to talk with Runa, and it was now mid-day.

"She hasn't returned from her visit with Runa yet?' Nettle asked with concern.

"That seems long for the two to be gone," Slatter said, getting to his feet.

Tarass stood as well.

Rannock and Nettle turned and headed for the door when it burst opened and the young lad, Roy, rushed in.

"Hurry! Hurry, my lord, there's something wrong at the healer's cottage!"

***

"She's coming around. Force her to take it now, before she has the strength to fight you."

Snow heard the man's voice, but her head was too fuzzy to understand until someone pressed down on her shoulders, keeping her from moving, and hands were at her mouth, forcing it open, then something was poured down her throat. She tried to spit it out but more of the liquid was forced down her throat. When they finally released her, she turned on her side on the snow-covered ground and pretended to cry in between

386

sticking her finger in her mouth to rid herself of whatever they had forced on her.

"How long?" the man with the commanding voice asked.

"Not too long after his arrival. Keep him talking, but then there is much you have to say to him. I will let you know when the time is right."

Snow recognized that voice. It was Fasta.

She quickly covered what had come out of her stomach with snow so that no one could see what she had done. She knew she hadn't gotten all of it. But she prayed she had gotten enough so that it wouldn't do her or the bairn harm.

She rolled on her other side, whimpering so that they thought her weak, and scooped up some snow to rub on her face and to help clear the sleep that lingered in her.

Not too long after his arrival.

They had to have been talking about her husband.

Tarass would come for her. He would rescue her like he always did.

Snow only hoped that if what they had forced down her throat was meant to kill her, that she wouldn't die before she had a chance to tell her husband she loved him one last time.

***

Tarass sped through the village, Slatter following not far behind.

Tarass was the first to enter the cottage. Helga was there, her eyes filled with fright.

"I found them like this," Helga said, a tremble in her voice.

Both Willow and Runa lay on the earth-floor, but Snow was nowhere to be seen.

"Willow!" Slatter called out when he saw his wife crumpled on the floor. He lifted her gently and sat on one of the chairs to cradle her in his arms. Fury raced through him when he saw the lump on the side of her head. Someone had hit her, knocking her out.

Fear at not seeing his wife had Tarass wanted to run out and search for her, but that wouldn't be wise. He needed to keep his head about him no matter how much fear threatened him.

He turned to see Rannock standing at the open door. "Send the trackers and a group of warriors to follow them, and find where the tracks lead."

Rannock nodded and hurried out, Helga following after him.

Tarass quickly looked around and saw Thaw laying on his side by the hearth. He went to the pup and shook him. He didn't move but was grateful the pup was still breathing.

He turned to Slatter. "Willow still breathes?"

"Aye, she does," Slatter said, relieved and began to tap gently at his wife's face. "Wake up, Willow. I need you to wake up. You must wake up."

Tarass went to Runa and gently turned her on her back to see that the side of her head was bleeding. He lifted her and he was relieved to hear her moan. He needed one of them to wake and tell him what happened and who had taken his wife. He laid her on the bed and turned to see Nettle enter the cottage, look

388

about, then grab a bucket and run out to return moments later with the bucket filled with snow.

She took it to Slatter. "This should help wake her."

Slatter scooped up a handful of snow and laid it against his wife's face and on the bump that was beginning to bruise.

Nettle went to the bed and began cleaning Runa's wound, talking to her the whole time.

Tarass almost hugged Nettle when Runa started talking before her eyes were even open.

"I tried to stop him."

"Who?" Tarass demanded.

"A stranger," she said, her eyes fighting to open.

The first words out of Willow's mouth as she came to and before she opened her eyes were, "He took Snow?"

"Easy," Slatter cautioned, relieved to hear his wife speak. "You have a good-size bump to your head." Concern for the bairn had his hand going to rest on her stomach.

"No worries there," Willow assured him.

A weak bark alerted all that Thaw was waking.

"Do you know who took her, Willow?" Tarass asked, his anger taking rein.

"No one familiar to me. He was a big man, older, gray hair. He hit me with the hilt of his dagger before I could do anything." Tears threatened Willow's eyes. "The sweet cakes. Someone put something in the sweetcakes that put Snow to sleep. She'll wake and not know where she is."

Tarass turned to Runa, and she responded before his question left his lips.

"Someone from the kitchen brought the sweet cakes."

A commotion outside the door had Tarass headed for it when the door opened and Fasta came stumbling in, Rannock having given her a rough shove.

"We found her a short distance in the woods. She was waiting for us," Rannock said.

It wasn't lost to anyone there that Fasta wore the garments of her people, rough cloth, fur and animal hides. She held herself tall, her shoulders drawn back, her chin raised more than a notch, her regal stance letting them know she thought herself above them.

"Where's my wife?" Tarass demanded.

"I'm here to take you to her. You and you alone," Fasta emphasized. "Unless, of course, you want her dead, which will happen if you don't come with me… alone… and without a weapon."

Willow gripped her husband's hand, fear for her sister and Tarass trembling it.

"Lead the way," Tarass said and when Fasta turned, he sent a look to Rannock. He would know what to do.

Fasta stopped at the door and turned, a command in her voice that left no doubt she was to be obeyed. "If any of you should think to follow, know that we have warriors watching. Any of them spot anyone following, and Snow dies."

This time when Fasta turned, Tarass looked to Slatter and he gave a barely noticeable nod.

Slatter had a way of not being seen and Tarass was counting on that.

When the door closed behind Tarass, Willow pressed her brow to her husband's and whispered, "Please, please don't let my sister and her husband die."

"You have my word, but promise me you will do nothing to jeopardize yourself and the bairn."

"I promise. Worry not, be safe, and know I love you. Now go," she said softly and kissed him quick.

Slatter didn't hesitate and Rannock hurried out the door after him.

No one saw Thaw sneak out behind them.

Chapter Thirty-three

Tarass didn't give Fasta the satisfaction of asking her any questions as they walked through the woods. He didn't think she'd tell him anything anyway. She enjoyed keeping him in suspense, believing it added to his suffering. He realized with each step he took, that it was what the person responsible for this whole horrific ordeal wanted. He wanted to cause Tarass pain, cause him to suffer the worst way possible, and he had done that by taking Snow.

A shudder of fear chilled him at the thought of what might have been done to her. As long as she was alive, as long as he could hold her in his arms again, nothing else mattered.

"It was so easy to become part of your clan and have you trust me," Fasta said.

He'd wondered when she wouldn't be able to take the silence any longer. Or not talk about what she perceived as a victory for herself.

He struck her with words he knew would hurt the most. "You were nothing more than an insignificant servant. I barely knew you were there."

She stopped abruptly and turned, her eyes round with fury. "We'll see how insignificant I am." She turned back around, her gait full of anger as she left deep tracks in the snow.

It didn't take as long to reach their destination as Tarass feared it might. He wanted to get to his wife, hopefully find her unharmed, and see her safe as quickly as possible. Then he'd deal with the man who had dared to take Snow from him.

Fasta stopped at the edge of a clearing in the woods. "Wait here," she ordered and walked to the other end and disappeared into the woods.

It wasn't a far distance away, but far enough that he wouldn't be able to reach Snow quickly if need be and that troubled him.

A man emerged a few moments later. A man Tarass didn't recognize.

He was a big man, though not as tall as Tarass, his body thick. His hair was gray and he wore it in a braid. He wore the cloth, furs, and hides of the Norsemen. His face was like a leathery mask wrinkled from the harsh winters of the far north. Looking past it, Tarass could see that he once had fine features, but he didn't recall ever meeting the older man.

"You wonder who I am," the man said, his voice strong enough to be heard between the distance that separated the two men.

"Where's my wife?" Tarass called out.

"In time," the man shouted.

Tarass feared the delay was for a reason that could have this meeting end far differently than he'd hoped.

"What do you want? Why does a man I don't know want to harm me and my family?" Tarass asked with a strength that could be easily heard.

"It would be over and done if you had been with your parents at the Sandrik village." The man shook his head. "It took me a while to realize it was better that you weren't there. That my revenge would be much more satisfying with you alive. That I could take from you what was taken from me and leave you to suffer as I have done all these years."

Fear twisted Tarass's stomach and he roared out, "Where's my wife?"

"Not yet," the man returned with his own roar.

Tarass never prayed, but he did now, silently, for his wife's life. If for some reason his father had taken the life of the man's wife, it meant sure death for Snow.

"What was taken from you that left you filled with such vengeance?" Tarass asked, a dread falling over him.

"Everything!" the man roared once again.

"Not everything," Tarass called out. "You're still alive."

"Would you feel that way if I took everything from you? Your wife and the bairn growing inside her? Your whole future?"

The dread that had fallen over him felt as if it choked Tarass, it squeezed at him so tightly.

"You would hate, feel jealous, and want revenge as well," the man called out, anger exploding from his every word.

"My father never would have killed a woman and child," Tarass argued, fear for his wife's life growing his muscles taut.

The man laughed, though it wasn't with joy. "It wasn't your father who took everything from me. It was your *mother*."

Tarass was shocked speechless. He was aware that his mum had been a skilled warrior, but he had never expected his parents' deaths was because of something his mum had done.

"Anora was the daughter of a powerful Norse chieftain, a skilled warrior in her own right, her tribe far superior to your mum's tribe. Anora became furious when she discovered that your father had told all in his clan that I was dead. It was my punishment for keeping my plans from him and hurting his friend Fay. I didn't care. I had no wont to return home, but it was an insult to Anora that I was banished from my homeland soil for what she believed was punishment for marrying her."

Tarass realized who he was then. "You're Conall, Twilla's son, and the father of Fay's bairn."

"I am," he cried out with pride. "I so regret ever poking that whimpering fool, Fay, not that Anora would have cared. However, she wouldn't have liked that Fay carried my child when she was carrying my child as well."

"You knew Fay was with child?" Tarass asked, thinking of the devastation secrets could cause.

"Aye, and I wanted no part of her. I was about to wed Anora and become husband to the daughter and only child of a powerful Norse chieftain who respected me. I wasn't going to throw that away for a weak woman whose family would never accept me."

"So you never told Anora the truth?"

"No, and she decided to seek revenge for the insult when she found out your mum was visiting with her people, though she kept it a secret from me."

Tarass had engaged in too many battles and confrontations not to know the man was borrowing time, and his concern grew for his wife's safety.

"Where's my wife? I want to see her now!" he roared.

Conall returned his roar. "Soon!"

Tarass wanted this done now. He wanted to see that his wife was unharmed. "From what you say Anora attacked my mum's village and my mum defended herself."

"If only that were true, I wouldn't have lost everything," the man bellowed, pounding his chest. "Your mum told her the truth. Told her about Fay. Told her that was the reason your father banished me from my homeland. Told Anora I cared for no one or nothing but the power of being wed to a powerful chieftain's daughter." The man's dark eyes turned round with rage. "You know what Anora did? She demanded the truth from me, threatening to go to my homeland and find out for herself. I had no choice but to tell her. She refused to listen to any excuse or apology I offered. She adamantly refused to wed me and refused to give birth to a coward's child. She rid herself of my bairn growing inside her and her father banned me from his tribe.

"With your father having banished me from ever returning home, I was forced to take shelter with a weak, menial tribe. I was treated like a slave. It wasn't until the tribe was set upon by renegade warriors that I finally got a chance to seek my revenge by joining that renegade troop, pulling the bunch together, and leading them. Then once again I lost what I had built. Ruddock, husband to Snow's sister, Sorrell, killed every warrior that had attacked the Sandrik village, leaving me with only two people I could truly trust."

"Fasta," Tarass said.

"My daughter. She is much like me, a fine warrior and an excellent marksman. She is more patient then I am. I wanted to see you dead sooner, but she convinced me it would be a weak revenge. She suggested she join your tribe and return to your homeland with you and when the time was right, we'd strike. She knew the time was right when she saw how much you loved your wife. Still though, she urged patience, telling me your thirst for coupling would see your wife with child soon, and she was right. It was also her idea to use the myth of your mum's people, leaving fear and disruption in its wake. Though, each pool of blood told a story."

Tarass didn't care. He only wanted to have his wife safe in his arms, but he had no choice but to listen.

"The first one represented the revenge I got from the massacre on the Sandrik village, the arrow Fasta shot at you and purposely missed was to let you know I was coming for you. The second pool of blood was the knowledge I stole when I killed Finn and the painted man. The latter knowing that Fasta was among your clan." He grinned. "The third and small pool of blood will bring me the most satisfaction. Do you know what it represents?"

Tarass knew. He knew as soon as Conall had said he wanted to take everything from him and he'd start with Tarass's unborn bairn.

Conall went to speak when he suddenly turned toward the woods, as if someone had called out to him, and when he turned back again his grin had widened. "It's time."

Tarass went to step forward.

Conall raised his hand and shouted, "Stay where you are."

Tarass wanted to race at him but that wouldn't help his wife, so he halted his anxious steps. He had to fight from running to his wife when Fasta appeared, gripping Snow's arm and giving her a shove toward Conall. He watched her stumble and fall to the ground, grabbing her stomach, and his heart nearly shattered and his fury soared.

"I've taken from you what you took from me—everything that means something to you—unless you can get your wife home fast enough to at least save her." He laughed. "But then she has to reach you first… on her own without help from you."

Tarass went to call out to her when Fasta grabbed Snow's arm and yanked her to her feet.

"Not a word," Conall warned and took Snow from Fasta, his thick fingers closing around her upper arm.

A short man appeared out of the woods and handed Fasta a bow and a cache of arrows and Tarass felt more helpless than he ever did, though his mind raced with possible ways to save his wife.

"Call out to your wife, make any sound or move at all, and my daughter will set an arrow on her, and she won't miss."

Tarass bit his tongue, fearful he'd not be able to hold it. And how could he not run to Snow? If only the distance between them was shorter, he'd have a chance of reaching her before the arrow did. But he'd never make it at this distance.

"Go to your husband, Snow," Conall said with a laugh and shoved her toward the woods to his right.

Tarass silently cursed the man when he watched his wife take a few stumbling steps, collapse in a mound of snow, and glance around confused. The trees would appear as gray blurs to her and she wouldn't know if he was among them. And if he dared call or move to alert her, an arrow would pierce her back. But if he didn't do something, they both would die here. He was no fool. Conall didn't intend to let them live.

Snow pressed her hand to her stomach, the cramps having grown dreadfully painful. She was losing the bairn. There was no denying it. And if she had swallowed too much of the liquid that had been forced on her, she would lose her life. She had to get to her husband, if it was only to have him hold her one last time.

She looked around and almost cried with joy at how clear everything appeared to her. The fuzziness that had been there was gone and while her vision blurred now and again, she still could see things almost as clearly as when she had full sight.

Relief filled her heart when she turned her head and spotted Tarass. He was a distance away and she worried she didn't have the strength to reach him.

"*You can do this, Snow. You can do this*," she heard her mum's voice encourage in her head.

She struggled to her feet and felt a warm liquid run down her leg. She didn't want to think about what it meant. She had to get to Tarass as fast as possible.

Donna Fletcher

Her first step brought such bad cramps that she had to force herself to push through the pain to take another step, then another, thinking only of one thing, reaching her husband.

Tarass watched puzzled as his wife headed toward him. She approached him without the slightest hesitation that she was going in the wrong direction. It took a few moments watching her, seeing that she didn't deviate her course, and there'd be only one reason for that.

She could see. Snow could see.

He was overjoyed at the thought, but his heart broke and his anger flared when he saw the trail of blood that followed behind her. She was losing the bairn and possibly her life. He had to get her home to Willow.

Snow kept silent, fearful if she said a word, she'd feel an arrow strike her back and never make it to her husband. She kept going and as she got closer, she saw her husband's whole face for the first time and a spark of joy filled her heart. At least if she died, it would be her husband's face she last looked upon.

Tarass kept his eyes on her and smiled, and he was pleased to see her return his smile. It confirmed that she could see him.

I love you, she mouthed.

Her words struck him like a sharp arrow to his heart. She was telling him she loved him because she thought she was dying. He wouldn't let her die. They might lose the bairn, but he damn well wouldn't lose her.

400

She was only halfway to him, but he couldn't wait any longer. He sped toward her, yelling, "Get down."

He was on top of her, covering her with his body right after she hit the ground, and an arrow narrowly missed his head. "Stay down," he ordered and turned to see Conall charging him, his sword raised and Fasta ready with another arrow to shoot at Snow as soon as he stood to battle Conall. But how did he battle the man without a weapon and protect this wife at the same time?

He stood, ready to do whatever he could to protect his wife and bairn, die for her or die with her.

Thaw came from out of nowhere behind Fasta, sailing through the air, launching himself at her and catching her by the throat. She barely got out a yell before the pup's sharp teeth sank into her flesh and blood squirted everywhere.

Conall ran at the pup.

"Tarass!" He turned and saw Slatter running toward him, raising the sword in his hand to toss to Tarass.

Tarass ran and grabbed it, and before turning to face Conall, yelled, "Get Snow to Willow! She's bleeding!"

Slatter didn't hesitate, he scooped Snow up, held her close to his chest, and took off running.

Thaw didn't stop tearing at Fasta until Conall was almost on top of him. His mouth was covered with blood as he ran away, leaving Fasta lying lifeless, the blood continuing to drain in a pool around her.

Conall let out a roar and seeing his daughter dead, turned, and charged at Tarass. He took only a few steps when a sharp bite to his calf had him tumbling down on the snow.

Tarass blessed the pup. It gave him enough time to reach Conall before he could stand, he having only made it to his one knee. Their swords clashed and Thaw went in for a quick bite, his teeth sinking into Conall's backside.

Conall screamed and fell to his side, moving, though not fast enough, as Tarass's sword came down and sliced part of his arm. He let out another scream as he scrambled to his feet, but Tarass was on him before he could steady himself, his sword catching his arm again, rendering it useless.

It wasn't Conall's sword arm that was damaged, and he didn't hesitate to swing his sword, though not with his usual strength. Tarass deflected it easily. Conall stumbled, losing his footing and Tarass didn't wait, he drove his sword through the man's stomach.

Conall glared at him in disbelief and when Tarass pulled his sword out, Conall fell backward to the snow-covered ground. Blood began to stain the snow around him and began to gather around his mouth.

He coughed and gurgled, and to Tarass's surprise smiled.

He choked out his last few words. "I won. She'll die. I made sure of it."

Anger had Tarass driving the sword through him again, then he took off with Thaw fast on his heels as he left a pool of blood gathering around Conall.

Tarass sped through the woods without worry anyone would attack him. Slatter would have seen to whoever lurked about. He had to get to Snow. He had to see her, had to hold her in his arms, had to keep her safe.

I won. She'll die. I made sure of it. Only two people I can truly trust.

The words tore at Tarass. Conall had made sure if he should fail that someone else wouldn't. Tarass ran harder, thinking of the one person who Conall could trust to finish this for him... his mum.

Chapter Thirty-four

Tarass and Thaw ran through the village as though the devil was after them. They stopped at Twilla's cottage and not finding her there, rushed to the keep. Tarass stopped when he reached the Great Hall, seeing Slatter talking with Rannock.

"Is Twilla here?" Tarass shouted.

"She's with the other women who tend your wife," Rannock said.

Curses flew from his mouth as he ran up the stairs, Slatter and Rannock hurrying after him, and Thaw rushed ahead of them all.

Screams and shouts were coming from the room when Tarass entered. He was shocked to see that Thaw had Runa on the ground, tearing at her arm, and dodging any attempts by her to stop him.

One command from Tarass and Thaw let go of her, but kept an attack stance, his teeth bared, growling at Runa.

Runa lay on the floor, holding her bleeding arm and crying.

"I don't know what happened," Willow said. "Thaw entered the room, sniffed the air, and charged at Runa."

Tarass sniffed the air himself near Runa and cringed at a horrid stench.

"The putrid odor is from a salve Runa wanted to use on Snow and I refused to let her," Willow said. "A stench as bad as that can't be good."

Tarass silently blessed Willow as he looked to his wife in bed. Her eyes were closed and her face so pale that she looked lifeless.

"Take her," Tarass ordered and Rannock reached down and yanked Runa up by the arm.

"Let me tend her," Willow said, stepping forward.

"No," Slatter said, his arm shooting out to stop his wife from going to the woman. "She meant Snow harm."

Nettle and Twilla gasped as Rannock all but dragged Runa out of the room.

Tarass walked around the bed to sit beside his wife and take her limp hand in his. He didn't chase Thaw when he jumped on the bed and licked her face. He hoped she'd respond, but she didn't, and he felt his heart shatter once again this day.

"You need to go, Tarass, I'm not done tending her," Willow said gently.

He nodded but didn't move. He brought his cheek to rest against hers and whispered near her ear. "I forbid you to leave me, *ást*, and this is one time you will obey me without question." He kissed her cheek, reached for Thaw and scooped him up, and turned to Willow, standing beside him. "I know you will do all you can to save her."

"I couldn't save the bairn, but I won't lose my sister," Willow said, tears in her eyes.

Tarass hoped that would prove true and reluctantly stepped out of the room, Thaw tucked under his arm.

405

As the door closed on him and the pup, his heart sank and Thaw whined.

He sunk to the floor, bracing his back against the wall to the right of the door. The pup lay curled up against him, whining as if understanding the severity of the situation.

He dropped his head back against the wall, hugging the pup. "It's all right, Thaw. I ordered her not to leave us. She'll obey me this time, since she loves us too much to leave us."

He sat, hoping, praying, and thinking that he didn't know how he'd live without his wife. She had become such a vital part of it. How would he ever get into bed at night without her there to take in his arms or wake in the morning without her curled around him? He shook his head. And how unfair that now with her sight restored, she would never get to see the love and passion he has for her in his eyes.

Thaw whined and whimpered and Tarass did his best to soothe him, but they both found it difficult. He didn't know when Slatter had appeared. He was suddenly there or perhaps he'd been there for a while and had said nothing.

"Tell me," Tarass said.

"I took care of the two that watched to see if anyone followed you. Rannock sent a troop of men to collect all the bodies and one was found alive, though not for long. The fool thought he'd run far enough."

"Don't return the bodies here. Have Rannock burn them all in the woods," Tarass ordered.

"Aye," Slatter said.

"You have something you don't want to tell me," Tarass said, hearing reluctance in his one word.

He nodded slowly. "Runa is dead... by her own hand. It took little persuading to get her to confess. She told Rannock and me that her father had paid three men to help them. They helped with the pools of blood. All the blood came from animals they killed in the woods, except for a small amount from Finn. She posed as the dwarf and helped fake Fasta's miscarriage, hoping it would put fear into Snow, and more fright into the clan, but she hadn't counted on Snow's courage that left the village praising her bravery. It also served another purpose. It gave Fasta an excuse to be absent from the keep so she could finalize plans with the culprits."

"Now I know how Thaw knew it was Runa... the smell. Snow had told me she had smelled a terrible odor when the dwarf was near her when Fasta had supposedly suffered a miscarriage. I wonder if it was something that caused Fasta to lose some blood, since Runa was about to do the same to my wife. Thaw had smelled the foul odor that night as well as just moments ago in my bedchamber."

"You were suspicious of someone when you rushed into the keep?" Slatter asked.

"Twilla."

Slatter thought a few moments. then nodded. "It all falls into place now. I would guess the man who caused all the harm was Twilla's son who wasn't dead after all, and you thought she had helped him."

"You're good at puzzles, but this is one puzzle that will remain a mystery to others. The only thing anyone needs to know is that it was a man from the far north looking for revenge against me for a previous battle fought."

"What about Twilla? Are you sure she doesn't know anything?"

"My da told me to trust her more than anyone, that she knew and kept family secrets. She kept the secret all these years about Fay and her son and she truly believed them in love. So, no, I don't believe she knew the truth about her son. I think if she had, it would have broken her heart."

The door to the bedchamber opened.

Willow stood in the doorway with tears in her eyes.

Slatter went to her and took her in his arms.

Tarass stood, placing Thaw on the floor beside him, and they both looked to Willow.

Willow choked back the tears. "Snow lost quite a bit of blood and if it wasn't for her quick actions of ridding herself of a good portion of the brew they forced down her throat, she would not be alive now."

Tarass went to enter the room.

"She sleeps and she needs rest," Willow said. "Nettle and I will keep watch over her throughout the night to make sure there is no more bleeding. If it remains that way, I believe she will do well along with rest and food to replenish her strength."

Twilla approached them. "There is little for me to do here. Snow is in excellent hands with Willow and Nettle." She placed a hand on Tarass's arm. "Snow is strong. I have no doubt she'll survive this and you will have many bairns in the years to come. Your father would be proud of the honorable man you've become."

Slatter sent a quick nod to Tarass as if acknowledging that he was right about Twilla. She didn't know anything.

"I will sit with my wife as well," Tarass said.

"There is nothing you can do for her," Willow said.

"There is," Tarass said. "I can be there with her."

***

It was morning when Snow woke to see her husband sleeping in a chair as well as Willow. Tears filled her eyes in relief and sorrow. The memory of losing the bairn tore at her heart until she feared it would rip her in two. Though, she knew there'd be other bairns, it didn't help ease her current heartache. The one thing that did soothe the hurt was to see her husband there, alive and well, and to feel Thaw cuddled against her side.

Thaw rose with a stretch, stuck his face in hers, and licked her cheek.

Snow smiled and hugged him to her, kissing his snout and the top of his head, and admired what a fine looking dog he was. Her sisters had done an excellent job in describing him to her. He looked just as they had said, brown with black paws, and an adorable face, though it was so nice seeing him for herself.

She hurried to turn her attention on Tarass, seeing him clearly, though her vision could turn fuzzy at times. The fine features he had as a young lad having matured him into a handsome man. One that women would take great pleasure in admiring, but he belonged to her and no other.

409

His eyes sprang open suddenly and the bold blue color startled her. They were so much bolder in color than she had remembered. They intimidated and appealed all at once, and she almost chuckled. If she hadn't been able to keep her hands off him when she was blind, how would she ever do so now that she could see how wickedly handsome and appealing he was?

"You're awake," he said and nudged Willow.

Her eyes popped wide and she smiled when she saw that a light pink color tinged Snow's pale cheeks. "You feel well? No pain? No bleeding?"

"I feel tired and weak, but no pain and no bleeding that I can feel."

"It will take time for you to heal fully. You need to stay off your feet for a few days, and then not attempt to do more than your body tells you it can," her sister advised.

"She'll do as you say," Tarass said.

"She certainly will since I'll be right here making sure she does," Willow said like a mum commanding her bairn.

"I have every intention of doing what I'm told," Snow said. "Besides, I just don't have the strength to argue with either of you."

Willow went to her sister and took her hand and gave it a squeeze. "You'll do well and you'll have lots of bairns. I'll go get you a light fare. Food will help you regain your strength."

Snow appreciated that Willow gave her time alone with her husband. She looked to him not sure what to say, then suddenly burst into tears.

410

Tarass went to her, slipping into bed beside her and took her into his arms, then gently eased her head to rest on his shoulder.

"You're safe now," he said, overwhelmed by the relief his own words brought him.

"I lost our bairn," she said and continued weeping.

He lifted her chin to look up at him. "No, you didn't. Our bairn was taken from you, and the ones responsible will never hurt you or any of our family ever again. It was senseless vengeance against my family that caused this and it is finally done. It will haunt us no more." He wouldn't tell her about Runa just now. Tomorrow or the next day would be time enough.

He pressed a gentle kiss on her lips. "I was so frightened I would lose you. My life, my arms, this bed would be empty without you. You've filled my life in ways I never imagined possible. I now understand why my mum cautioned me to settle for nothing less than love when I wed. She was so right. I love you, *ást*, more than you could possibly know."

Tears fell gently from Snow's eyes, rolling slowly down her cheeks. "After I went blind, I never imagined anyone falling in love with me, least of all you. And I do know how much you love me, for my love for you is just as impossible to comprehend, it goes so deep."

They kissed gently as if sealing their love.

Snow snuggled content in her husband's arms.

Tarass turned a smile on her. "So tell me, wife, when did your sight return?"

She smiled at him, her green eyes still wet with tears. "It was over time and it can still be fuzzy at times, but mostly it's been clear for a while now."

411

"I know why you didn't tell me sooner," Tarass said, his grin incredibly wicked.

"And why is that?"

"You could admire me naked as often as you wanted without me seeing how much you love my body."

Snow laughed in spite of the sorrow that lingered in her. "You caught me, husband, I just can't keep my eyes or hands off you."

"Then I suppose I have no choice. Whenever we're alone, I'll have to stay naked around you."

"You'll get no argument with me on that," Snow said and yawned.

"You're tired. You need to rest," Tarass said and went to ease away from her.

"No, stay a while longer with me," Snow pleaded, holding on to him and returning her head to rest on his shoulder.

"Did you hear all of what Conall had confessed?" he asked, ready to tell her if she hadn't.

"Aye, I did, and how sad that he didn't realize that he, not your da, was the one responsible for what happened to him. His lies and greed came before all else. He truly cared for no one but himself," she said. "Though, there's a piece to the puzzle I don't understand."

Tarass hugged her close, needing to feel her tight against him and know she was safe. "What is it?"

She looked up at him, seeing things about his face she had never gotten to see before now, a barely noticeable scar under his chin and fine lines at the corner of his blue eyes. It was almost like meeting him

412

for the first time and it filled her saddened heart with joy.

"I don't see a connection between what happened here and your parents' departure from your homeland. They would never take you back there if they believed it meant trouble for you."

"You're right. I've thought the same myself," he said with a bit of sadness. "Perhaps I'll never know the answer."

Snow turned quiet for a moment, then she whispered, "I do so love you, husband."

"And I you, *ást*," he murmured and kissed the top of her head.

Willow returned with Slatter carrying a tray of food and they both stopped at the open door when they saw Snow asleep, her head on her husband's shoulder and Tarass asleep, his head resting on the top of his wife's head, and them both wrapped snug around each other.

Slatter left the tray of food on the small table and with an arm around his wife, ushered her out the door, closing it behind him.

Chapter Thirty-five

A year later.

"I can't believe you got Ruddock to stay through the winter," Willow said, rocking her sleeping five-month-old son, Angus, in her arms.

"I didn't miss the birth of your son and you two were here for Tiernan's birth," Sorrell said, looking down at her three-month-old son sleeping peacefully in her arms. "I'm certainly not going to miss the birth of Snow's bairn. Besides, it's taken this long for her to tell me everything that has happened and I still have questions for her."

"You've asked me endless questions, no more," Snow demanded with a smile.

"She's gotten so commanding since she's gotten her sight back," Sorrell said with a grin. "And I'm still annoyed that I was the last one to know."

"Live closer and you would have known sooner," Snow said.

"See what I mean. She has an answer for everything now," Sorrell said.

"That's because she's married to a man who knows everything," Tarass said, entering Snow's solar.

Snow smiled and went to greet her husband with a kiss, but she had rounded greatly and getting up and out of chairs had grown burdensome.

"Stay," Tarass ordered and went to her, his arm disappearing low at her back to help her up. "Twilla is asking for you. She is not doing well."

"I should go to her," Willow said.

"No, she asked to speak with Snow alone," Tarass said.

Thaw stretched his big body after getting up from where he lay by the warm hearth and went to Snow, ready to follow along with her.

"I can't believe the size of him," Sorrell said. "And here I thought he'd be the runt of the litter."

Snow laughed and patted his head. "He's far from a runt."

Both bairns started stirring in their mum's arms.

"Feeding time," Willow said.

"We'll be here when you get back," Sorrell said.

"Which means she has more questions for you, Snow," Willow said with a chuckle.

Nettle was waiting in the Great Hall with their cloaks.

"How are you feeling?" Snow asked Nettle.

"After morning sickness leaves me, I feel wonderful," Nettle said while Tarass slipped his wife's cloak on her shoulders before taking his from Nettle.

"She needs to rest more," Rannock said, entering the Great Hall and frowning at her.

"My husband causes me more upset than his bairn I carry," Nettle said, sending Rannock a smile.

"I worry over you and the bairn," Rannock said, admitting guilt.

"There is no need. The bairn has seven months to go before he enters this world and by then you'll have driven me and him mad with your constant concern."

"It's my duty as your husband," Rannock said, planting his hands on his hips as he came to a stop in front of his wife.

With an arm around Snow, Tarass led her quietly away from the arguing couple.

Snow laughed as they stepped outside to a light falling snow. "I think Rannock likes arguing with his wife."

Tarass grinned. "He likes more when they make up."

Snow's smile faded. "You haven't touched me in—"

"You were far too uncomfortable the last time and too stubborn to admit it," he said gently, keeping a firm arm around her as they went down the steps.

Snow sighed heavily. "You're right. I was uncomfortable, though not so much stubborn as disappointed. I knew the wise decision would be to abstain these last couple of weeks until the bairn was born, but the thought of not feeling you inside me for that long was too much to accept."

"Believe me when I say I miss being inside you, hearing you moan with pleasure and almost bring the roof down when you scream in climax." He laughed when she elbowed him in the side. He patted her rounded stomach when they reached the bottom of the steps. "Besides, I don't think the little lad likes when I come knocking."

"He or perhaps she does make a fuss when we couple," Snow admitted.

Tarass took her hand as they headed into the village. "It won't be long before I'm inside you all the time."

"I can't wait," Snow said on another sigh.

"Either can I," Tarass said, fighting the arousal that crept up on him.

"I'll be back for you," Tarass said when they reached Twilla's place and kissed his wife's cheek.

"Take Thaw with you. I can tell he's anxious to go and explore." Snow watched them walk off, Thaw jumping up and down excited to be out in the snow.

She entered the cottage to find Helga fussing over Twilla. Snow had been pleased that Helga had taken over the duties of the healer, having been the only one with some knowledge of healing thanks to her mum who had taught her. All in the clan had been pleased as well and with guidance from Willow throughout the year, she was doing well.

"She's been asking for you, Lady Snow," Helga said, tears in her eyes.

Snow approached, Helga having placed a chair next to the bed for her.

"You do well for all in the clan, Helga," Snow said as she slipped off her cloak.

Helga hurried to take it. "Thank you, m'lady. I enjoy the task. I'll take my leave, since Twilla told me she wanted to speak with you alone."

Snow took Twilla's hand as soon as she sat. "I'm here, Twilla."

417

The old woman's eyes fluttered open. "I don't have much time."

Tears sprang to Snow's eyes.

"Don't be sad. It's time for me to go. This old body of mine has had enough. I've lived longer than I should have and it's time for me to truly rest. But first…"

Snow gently squeezed Twilla's boney hand as her breath caught. She had lost much weight in the last month leaving her far too fragile.

"I need to tell you something, though I hate to burden you with it, but I feel it is necessary." Twilla fought for a breath before continuing, "I know the reason Tarass's parents' left here…"

Snow was shocked and curious but she hated to see Twilla struggle to breathe. "You should rest and—"

"No time," Twilla said and rested her breath a moment, then continued, "Tarass's father was called away on some matter that concerned his wife. When he discovered what it was, he ordered her and his son to leave here and go to her people where he would meet her. He had to make sure those who knew what he'd been told and those who planned to tell others never got the chance." She rested again for a few moments, then resumed talking, getting straight to the point. "Tarass's mum, Haldana, was a direct descendant of the first Pict king. It was ruled years ago that in order to sit on the Scottish throne, the one claiming the throne had to be wed to a descendant of the Pict. If she was a direct descendant of a Pict king, then no one could deny her child's claim to the throne. Once Haldana married Tarass's father any child they had would be the true heir to the Scottish throne."

Snow didn't quite believe her words. Could they be nothing more than the ramblings of an old, ill woman? "Are you saying that Tarass is the true heir to the throne? And how was it that Haldana didn't know of her heritage?"

"He is the true heir, and it was kept from Haldana to protect her against those trying to claim the throne. I don't know how it was found out, but Haldana's people are the ones who alerted Winton to the information."

Snow was trying to understand it all, but it seemed an unbelievable tale. "Who told you?"

"No one. I overheard Tarass's da talking with who I assumed later was someone from Haldana's tribe. He had stopped here briefly before joining his wife and son. They discussed the whole ordeal and Winton was pleased with the news the man had brought him. All were dead who posed any threat to his wife and son, though the man urged Winton to keep his wife and son away from his homeland, at least until Tarass was a skilled warrior." Twilla paused for a much needed breath. "When news reached me of his parents' deaths, I thought it was what had gotten them killed and worried Tarass would face the same fate. I also worried that someone had found out about Tarass's heritage and wanted him dead. I was relieved along with everyone else to learn that the problems that had plagued the clan had been caused by a renegade band of barbarians who sought revenge against Tarass for a battle once fought."

Snow had strongly agreed with Tarass when he had told her that Twilla needn't know the truth about her son. That Conall was better off left dead years ago.

419

However, there was something she didn't understand. "Why not let the secret die with you? Wouldn't that best protect Tarass?"

"A secret is no secret when more than one person knows about it, and there may come a time when ignorance would do more harm than good for your husband or first born son. So the secret is yours to carry now and do with it what you will."

Twilla struggled to breathe, the effort it had taken to talk having stolen her limited breath, leaving her weak.

"You must rest," Snow said, her thoughts heavy with what Twilla had told her.

"I can now," Twilla barely whispered, her burden lifted. "Stay with me."

"I will," Snow said, knowing it was Twilla's way of saying she didn't want to die alone.

Twilla's eyes closed and she struggled to say, "Tell me about when you first met Tarass, though I was there, I love hearing you tell it."

Snow chuckled while her tears fell. "Now that's a story." And she proceeded to tell it.

It wasn't long before Twilla's breathing grew shallow and her hand went limp in Snow's hand, and she took her last breath.

Snow sat with Twilla, her heart saddened. She would miss visiting with Twilla and talking, having learned much about the clan from her. She also couldn't stop thinking on what Twilla had confided in her. Tarass's mum and da didn't tell him. They knew the danger of anyone knowing. He would be killed so he could never depose the King. Not that Tarass would want to, but others would believe him a threat. Did she tell her husband? Or keep the secret as Twilla had so faithfully done?

A sudden sharp pain had her bending over. She barely had time to sit up straight when another pain ripped through her stomach. She waited until the pain subsided and struggled to her feet. Another pain grabbed her when she neared the door and she braced her hand against the wall.

This wasn't what happened with Willow and Sorrell when their bairns made it known they were ready to be born. Then she remembered Willow telling her that their mum had spit Snow out easily when born. Was this bairn getting ready to do the same?

She made it to the door when she felt a gush of liquid spill between her legs.

She had to get help. She had to get to the keep.

She stepped outside. The snow was falling heavier than before, but not so heavy she couldn't see anything. She looked around for anyone who could get Tarass for her and spotted Roy, the young lad she had more than a couple of snowball fights with.

"Roy!" she shouted and the lad turned and hurried to her. "Hurry and get Lord Tarass."

The lad took off.

Another pain hit Snow, grabbing her so suddenly and so hard that her legs turned weak and the next thing she knew, she was on her knees on the ground. She shook her head, worried she'd never get to her feet on her own.

She blessed the heavens when she heard Thaw's barks and soon felt his licks on her face.

"Snow!" Tarass shouted when he saw his wife had collapsed, Thaw whining beside her, and he rushed to her, Slatter and Ruddock close behind him.

"The bairn," Snow said, reaching out to him as he got to her side.

Tarass scooped her up and ran.

***

"Put her on the bed and get out," Sorrell ordered.

Tarass sent her a scathing look and kept his wife in his arms. His biting look quickly turned to a cringe as Snow curled against him in pain.

"The bed," Willow urged, entering the bedchamber and Tarass was quick to comply.

"Get out," Sorrell ordered again.

"I'm not leaving her," Tarass said and took hold of his wife's hand even more determined to stay with her when her hand grasped his tightly.

Willow placed a gentle hand on his arm. "Your presence here will not help her. Leave this to the women."

"It's all right, Tarass," Snow said, relieved the pain had passed.

Tarass hunched down beside the bed and kissed his wife's cheek. "You might need me."

Snow smiled. "I always need you, husband."

Her playful manner made him smile until she began to cringe in pain again.

"Do something for her," Tarass demanded, turning to Willow.

"Snow will do what's needed just as you will leave us to help her," Willow said.

"My sister is right," Snow said through the pain. "It's time for you to go."

Tarass brought his face close to hers. "I will take my leave only if you promise me that you will shiver the rafters with my name if you should need me. Something I know you're capable of since you do it quite often." He grinned.

Snow chuckled and cringed at the same time and Tarass cringed along with her.

"Go. Now," Willow ordered, pointing to the door and was surprised to see Ruddock, Sorrell's husband standing there. Sorrell stood beside him with her arms folded across her chest.

Ruddock walked over to Tarass. "Time to go and leave your wife to the women and join the men for some ale."

"You know I'd kick your arse if you tried to take me from her," Tarass challenged, getting to his feet, though not letting go of his wife's hand.

"I have no doubt of it, but I doubt you'd survive an attack from Sorrell, so I'm actually here to save your arse."

"He's right," Snow and Willow said in unison and with a laugh.

"Go," Snow urged her husband. "My sisters will take good care of me."

Tarass kissed her cheek once more and whispered, "I love you always."

"And I you, husband," Snow said and felt him reluctantly let go of her hand.

"Come on, Thaw. You're coming with me."

The pup looked from Tarass to Snow from where he sat on the floor with his chin resting on the bed on the opposite side from Tarass, reluctant to leave Snow.

"Go with Tarass, Thaw," Snow said. "You will return soon."

The pup followed Tarass and Ruddock to the door.

Ruddock slapped Tarass on the back after leaving the room. "All will go well."

"I don't recall you wanting to leave Sorrell's side when her birthing time came," Tarass said as they descended the stairs.

"And who helped remove me from the room?"

"Me and Slatter," Tarass said, recalling how he thought he and Slatter would have to drag Ruddock away from Sorrell.

"How was it that Slatter left his wife's birthing room with no help from us?" Ruddock asked as they entered the Great Hall.

"I have a more charming tongue than the both of you do." Slatter laughed and handed tankards of ale to the two men. "Talk and drink will get you through the birth."

Tarass took the tankard, turning his head to glance toward the stairs, while Slatter and Ruddock talked, his thoughts and heart with his wife. The memory of almost losing her when she had suffered the miscarriage still plagued him and there was that small stab of fear that he could lose her to childbirth. His worry would not end until this birthing ordeal was done.

***

"I can't believe it. You're so fortunate. Why couldn't I be that fortunate and deliver my son so easily?" Sorrell complained, hugging her newly born nephew to her. "I labored for hours on end. I never thought the pain would end."

Willow laughed. "You did not labor long compared to most."

"But I struggled to get him out of me and she," — Sorrell nodded to Snow sitting up in bed— "spits out this one, a good-sized bairn, with ease. I tell you it's not fair."

Snow stretched her arms out to Sorrell and she reluctantly surrendered her nephew to his mum. She hugged him to her chest, looking down with delight, so grateful to see his face that so resembled his da's.

"He's a handsome one," Willow said.

"All the lads are," Snow said and laughed softly. "Though, I wonder how three sisters with no knowledge of brothers or the like will raise three sons."

"With lots of prayers and courage," Sorrell said seriously, then burst out laughing. "If we can handle our husbands, we certainly can handle wee lads. Though, I don't know about that husband of yours, Snow. He does like to dictate. It's like he thinks he's a King."

Snow almost laughed at the truth to her words, but then realized the danger of the thought, and understood why her husband's parents rushed him out of Scotland. But Tarass's da had seen to it that no one had lived to tell the tale. Or had he? It was a question she knew would forever haunt her.

425

"You pale. Are you not feeling well?" Willow asked, concerned.

"I've just delivered a bairn," Snow said with a smile, as if it explained all.

Sorrell pointed at Snow. "And color returns like magic to her cheeks. I was pale and tired for days after and here she is sitting up as if after a relaxing nap when she just spewed out a bairn."

"The details of your son's birth grows into a tall tale with each telling," Willow said, grinning.

"I think what matters the most about each of our sons' births is that the three of us were together, helping, encouraging, sharing, and loving as we always did. We've faced many things together and we'll face more through the years to come... together." Snow stretched her hand out and her sisters hurried to take hold of it.

"Always together," Willow said, sniffing back tears.

"No one will keep the courageous Macardle sisters from one another, not ever," Sorrell said.

Willow and Sorrell leaned down to Snow so the three of them could hug and when they parted, tears filled all their eyes.

"I believe we should let my husband know he has a son," Snow said, wiping at her eyes.

"I'll go tell him and bring him to you," Sorrell said, running her arm across her eyes.

"Maybe I should—"

"No," Sorrell said, not giving Willow a chance to finish. "I cherish the thought of—"

"Be nice, Sorrell," Willow and Snow said in unison.

"I'm always nice," Sorrell said and left the room mumbling.

***

Tarass paced the floor in the Great Hall, Thaw keeping stride with him.

"You'll both wear yourself out if you keep that up," Ruddock advised.

"It will be hours before the bairn arrives," Slatter said. "Don't you recall how Ruddock and I were so patient while our wives birthed our sons?"

Tarass paled, recalling both births and the hours he had spent with each man as they suffered impatiently through it. His worries started then for when Snow would birth their bairn and now here it was. "I can't do hours."

Ruddock and Slatter laughed.

"You're not the one doing the hours," Slatter said.

Ruddock offered his own advice. "They say it gets easier with each birth."

"Easier for the men, not the women who labor in endless pain to give you sons and daughters," Sorrell said, entering the Great Hall.

"You've got tears in your eyes," Tarass said, his heart suddenly pounding in his chest. "Something's happened. What's wrong? Snow? Is Snow all right?" He went to rush past Sorrell.

"You can run like a fool to find out for yourself or I can ease your pain and tell you. It's up to you," Sorrell said, folding her arms across her chest.

Tarass walked over to the petite woman and glared at her. "Ruddock should keep a firmer hand on you."

"Like you do with my sister?" Sorrell asked with a smug grin.

"Sorrell!" Ruddock snapped. "Don't torture the man."

"Whatever you say, husband," Sorrell said sweetly, and Ruddock shook his head.

"Snow delivered the bairn with ease. Spit him right out she did, and she's eager to introduce you to your son."

Tarass grabbed Sorrell and hugged her, then ran out of the Great Hall, Thaw rushing ahead of him.

Slatter followed behind him, his pace much slower.

Ruddock went to his wife, his big powerful arms closing around her to cradle her with love. "Cry as many happy tears as you want, wife."

And Sorrell laid her head against her husband's thick chest and did just that.

***

Tarass burst into the room and stopped when he saw his wife sitting up in bed, looking as beautiful as she always did and cradling his son in her arms as Thaw sniffed at the little bundle with curiosity.

He hurried to his family.

Willow turned to leave and saw Slatter enter. He spread his arms wide, and she eagerly went to him and stepped into his loving embrace, a few tears trickling down her cheeks.

They left the room together, Slatter keeping one arm around his wife as he closed the door behind them.

"Your son," Snow said proudly when Tarass stepped next to the bed and peered down at the bairn.

He stood speechless.

"He has his da's handsome features," Snow said.

Tarass touched his sleeping son as if he needed to see that he was real. "My son. My da would be proud knowing the Clan MacFiere lives on."

"Then it is only fitting that he has your da's name," Snow said.

Tarass once again found himself speechless, though not for long. "My da would burst with pride that a grandson carried his name."

"The first of many grandsons and granddaughters who will carry on the MacFiere name," Snow said with pride the thought brought her.

Tarass leaned down and kissed his wife's brow. "I'm relieved you delivered our son fast. I don't think I would have survived hours on end of you in pain."

Snow laughed. "Either would I."

Thaw got up on the bed, licked Snow's face, sniffed Winton, then went to the bottom of the bed and curled up as if the ordeal had exhausted him.

"I'm with you, Thaw," Tarass said and slipped off his boots before he got into bed beside Snow and slipped his arm around her, then reached down to gently touch his son's tiny fingers. He felt a tender warmth run through him, felt his heart fill with joy, and was reminded of what it was like when his mum and da had been alive. This was family. This was love, and he silently thanked the heavens for sending Snow to him.

He kissed the top of her head. "I love you, Snow, and that will never change."

"It better not, husband," she teased.

"I'm yours always," he assured her.

She looked up at him and frowned.

"What's wrong?" he asked anxiously, worried she wasn't feeling well.

"I don't know if that's long enough," she said, a soft smile spreading over her face.

"Can't do without me, can you, wife?" he teased, kissing her gently.

Her smile faded slowly and she shook her head just as slowly. "No, I can't do without you and I don't want to do without you."

"And I cannot do without you," he said and hooked her chin with his finger. "So, I guess that means we're stuck with each other for eternity."

A smile lit Snow's whole face. "That sounds about right to me, husband."

Tarass grinned and brought his lips to hers, sealing their words with a kiss.

Titles by Donna Fletcher

Macardle Sisters of Courage Trilogy
Highlander of My Heart
Desired by a Highlander
Highlander Lord of Fire

Macinnes Sisters Trilogy
The Highlander's Stolen Heart
Highlander's Rebellious Love
Highlander The Dark Dragon

Highland Warriors Trilogy
To Love A Highlander
Embraced By A Highlander
Highlander The Demon Lord

Cree & Dawn Series
Highlander Unchained/Forbidden Highlander
Highlander's Captive
My Highlander A Cree & Dawn Novel

The Pict King Series
The King's Executioner
The King's Warrior
The King & His Queen

For a full listing of all titles and to learn more
about Donna go to her website

www.donnafletcher.com

Made in United States
North Haven, CT
09 June 2024